Advance Praise for *Icefall*

"Newman and Land's thriller, *Icefall,* is a bombshell of a debut: scintillating and explosive action, characters that break new ground, a worldview that spans millennia, all wrapped up in a tour-de-force story that grabs from the first page to a climax that left me breathless. I loved getting lost in this world and can't wait to return to it. So, guys, get to writing!"

—James Rollins, #1 *New York Times* bestseller of *Arkangel*

"Wow, what an incredible novel! *Icefall* is a stunningly creative sci-fi thriller packed with mind-bending ideas, vivid characters, great settings, and a propulsive plot—an epic and original addition to the alien invasion genre. As I read this book, all I could think was that it would make an amazing television series. Outstanding!"

—Douglas Preston, #1 *New York Times*
bestselling author of *Extinction*

"Newman and Land tell an intense story that demands to be read in one sitting. With great characters and a fun take on an alien invasion theme, this is John Carpenter's *The Thing* meets *The Terminator,* with a dash of Michael Crichton if he didn't care about body count."

—*FirstClue*

"*Icefall* is a wild blend of horror, sci-fi, and superhero action! It's *Avengers* meets *The Thing,* but goes way beyond beyond! Thrilling from first page to last!"

—Jonathan Maberry, *New York Times* bestselling
author of *Red Empire* and *Ghosts of the Void*

"*Icefall* is a mind-blowing page-turner that blends an astonishing array of fascinating concepts into a unique, riveting, and propulsive sci-fi thriller."

—Jon McGoran, bestselling author of *The Price of Everything*

THE RISE OF THE NINE

ICEFALL

THE RISE OF THE NINE

ICEFALL

MICHAEL NEWMAN & JON LAND

A PERMUTED PRESS BOOK
ISBN: 979-8-89565-689-1
ISBN (eBook): 979-8-89565-690-7

Icefall:
The Rise of the Nine

Cover art by Cody Corcoran

Permuted Press
New York • Nashville
permutedpress.com

Published in the United States of America
1 2 3 4 5 6 7 8 9 10

For Rian, Jace, and Kai.
Because every world worth saving starts with family.

"We only have to look at ourselves to see how intelligent life might develop into something we wouldn't want to meet."

—Stephen Hawking

TABLE OF CONTENTS

PROLOGUE

Sentence

1,500 Years Ago

This place is called the Veyrion....

The boy had no conception of how he knew that. Nor did he understand how he knew that the shafts of white-blue lights in which each of the nine massive figures was contained were restraining shafts that functioned like individual cells of molten energy. Those figures were so tall and muscular they strained the limits of their electromagnetic bonds.

"Do any of you have anything to say before sentence is pronounced?" a disembodied voice demanded of the nine figures standing to his right, the words bouncing off unseen walls in a hollow, tinny echo.

The boy looked up and saw a ceiling of dull light in the shape of a convex cone. He knew he wasn't here physically. The experience felt like a dream of something that had happened in the past on another planet light-years from Earth, another lesson in the many teachings of Gaia he did not yet understand the significance of.

"I ask again," the disembodied voice boomed when the nine figures remained silent, each syllable seeming to hang suspended in the air, "do any of you have anything to say before sentence is pronounced?"

The demand was met by silence again. The boy also knew that in eras past, the Veyrion would have been overflowing with citizens packed in to watch these prisoners being sentenced and punished for their transgressions against the State. They would be made an example of for all this world to see, those not present to view in person required to watch over their personal screens. Now, the boy understood the unfolding scene would be beamed directly into the minds of the entire population, so they might experience what was to come instead of merely watching. No option to disregard it was provided, an example that functioned as a warning to anyone who dared to question or rise against a ruling body known as the Overseers.

Beyond the nine figures, the sprawling Veyrion was shrouded in darkness, as if a black curtain had been drawn over all that lay beyond the center of the floor that seemed to hover in the air, rolling slightly as if atop currents of water. The boy knew he was dreaming, so there was no reason to be scared. He was used to experiencing things in his dreams he was not meant to fully grasp yet.

"Do you renounce your belief in the old ways and a higher being who is no more than myth?"

Silence.

"Do you renounce your subversive actions against the Crown Arc and fellow citizens of this world?" the disembodied voice asked the nine figures restrained in their shafts of light.

Silence.

"Do you understand the sentence about to be dispensed as punishment for the offenses of treason and subversion against the greater good?"

Silence.

"Because you refuse to accept accountability for your crimes, you will surrender your very identities so you might be repurposed for a task determined by the Overseers. You will cease to exist as who you were. You will know only what is required and hold no memories of what came before. But first you must bear the loss of everything you hold dear, so your final experience will carry a pain you will carry forever in the black pits of your being."

In the dream, the boy watched the families of the nine figures materialize out of thin air, herded along within funnels of light, one for each of the groupings, that kept the family members squeezed against each other. He could hear the sobs and shrieks of the children and spouses, parents, and anyone else touched by the same blood as the prisoners. As punishment for the nine figures' crimes, their entire bloodlines, their very legacies, would be wiped out as the last sight their current memories would ever behold, to keep with them in blurred awareness for eternity.

"Now, bear witness to what you have reaped with your transgressions."

The boy met the terrified gazes of the families that would linger in agony forever in the deepest recesses of nine figures' minds, like an out-of-focus picture. In one of the funnels of light, he saw the tearstained face of a terrified boy about his age. In another, he watched a young girl squeezing a doll so tight her hands were pale from the blood being flushed out.

Wiping their memories clean would vanquish the experience from their consciousness, but not their souls, where the pain would carve its own dark void. They did not close their eyes because their doomed loved ones deserved to have them bear witness, to meet their pleading gazes this one last time, to take that final memory with them to whatever lay beyond, a gift these nine figures could not deliver onto themselves.

Five men and four women, the boy identified, noting that a man and a woman standing alongside each other in matching bright shafts pushed their hands as far as they could extend toward each other before those hands sparked against the borders of their electromagnetic confinements.

All at once, the nine funnels of light enclosing their families burned brighter and hotter until a single blinding flash seared the darkness in a white-hot fireball. The cries and calls for mercy were swept away in a single gush of silence, a sizzling followed by a crackling sound as embers cast by the remains of the nine families floated away to disappear into the ether. All that remained was the smell of burned skin and hair, accompanied by a corrosive, metallic stench hanging in the air that left the boy queasy. The funnels of white light were tinged by deep red slivers before they too were sucked up. He could see the nine figures struggling to remain stoic and still, but their expressions had twisted into inconsolable anguish mixed with suppressed rage and tortured resignation. The man and woman had stopped trying to stretch their hands toward each other, their expressions frozen in misery and shock.

The rank odor lingering in the air made the boy retch and, in that instant, one of the nine figures, their leader, he somehow knew, looked his way in a glimpse of acknowledgment.

He can see me! This isn't a dream! I'm really here!

Then the disembodied voice returned, the words launched in a rattling bellow as if the volume had been turned up too high.

"Hold this moment of grievous loss wrought by your own hands as your last remaining thought, a final reminder before everything you are and have been is stripped away to erase the black pit at the depths of your being so you may serve the State in a mission for the betterment of the encompassing all you sought to betray in your resistance and rebellion. May you find renewed purpose in that task and redemption in fulfilling it."

The boy heard a deep humming noise that made his ears bubble and filled his skull with air. He watched as the expressions of the nine huge figures seemed to lengthen, flattening out. Their eyes that just moments before had bulged with torment and anger had gone empty, no thought or emotion lurking behind them. Nothing to be kept hidden, because there was nothing at all.

"You are the Nine," the unseen voice boomed. "And your mission is to serve the interests of the Crown Arc on a distant planet we have been preparing for ten million of their years. Your time will be measured by theirs, as you await the occasion your service is required in a black void you have wrought for yourselves."

With that, the boy heard Gaia's voice in his head, soothing in its familiarity.

"And your service will be required too."

Part One
THE CHASM

"Across an immense ethereal gulf, minds that are to our minds as ours are to the beasts in the jungle—intellects vast, cool, and unsympathetic—regarded this Earth with envious eyes and slowly and surely drew their plans against us."

—Orson Welles, original *War of the Worlds* broadcast, October 30, 1938

CHAPTER 1

Missed Delivery

Juneau Icefield, Alaska

"So, is all I've heard about you true?" Alaska State Trooper Tom Dennehy asked his fellow trooper, who sat behind the wheel of their police-issued Ford Explorer.

"Probably not," Sakari Muhtuk told him, "if it's the same shit I've heard."

"That you kicked the asses of some Hells Angels in a bar fight."

"They kicked mine too."

Her name, translated from her native Inuit to English, meant *sweet.* But anyone who knew her would say there was nothing sweet about Sakari Muhtuk. Concerning the story her new and younger partner referenced, she had not bothered to tell him that the three bikers in question had beaten a fellow trooper she'd gone through the academy with into full disability upon learning he was an informant within their ranks. The trooper in question had stuck up for her through six months of rigorous training where she had proven herself the equal of any of the male trainees. She figured she owed him that much after a visit to the hospital revealed the extent of his injuries. He had given her the names, and she had taken it from there. She was tempted to shoot the bikers but figured going old school on them would leave more of an impression; being battered senseless by a woman would render them disgraces and lead to their banishment from the gang, something she took as much pleasure in as beating them senseless.

Muhtuk had also not told Dennehy that, although the incident had been kept under wraps outside the department, it had left a black mark on her record and explained why she was still just a senior trooper into her late thirties. And, in retrospect, she supposed she had known that would be her fate from the moment the first punch was thrown.

And it was still worth it.

"We've been riding together a month now, right?" Muhtuk asked her younger partner.

"Just about."

"So why did you wait that long to ask me what you've been itching to know?"

Dennehy gazed at her across the seat. "Because if it was true, I didn't want to piss you off."

"So now you know it's true."

"You pissed?"

"Haven't decided yet."

Dennehy's eyes fixed forward again, widening as he pointed out the windshield. "There he is, boss."

"I'm not your boss. We're the same rank."

Dennehy smiled thinly. "But you can kick my ass. That makes you my boss."

Behind the wheel, Trooper Sakari Muhtuk gently applied the brakes of their Ford Explorer to ease it to a halt alongside the Amazon delivery van, which had come to a stop amid snow cover that climbed to the top of its front tires. After the van had strayed off course into the middle of nowhere, an Amazon dispatcher had called Alaska State Police headquarters in Juneau with the GPS coordinates, but the dispatcher could not reach the driver via text or phone.

The Explorer slid to a stop atop the snowpack instead of grinding to one, thanks to the Track N Go snow tracks installed on all four wheels. Those tracks effectively turned the five-thousand-pound vehicle into a snowmobile capable of handling the hundred-plus feet of snow that fell in the southeastern rim of Alaska every winter. Muhtuk doubted they would have gotten here on regular snow treads and had no idea how the Amazon van had made it so far along the icefield riding on an ordinary set of tires.

She plucked the mic from its stand atop the Explorer's police radio. "Dispatch, this is Unit Fifteen. Please inform Amazon that we've found their wayward delivery van."

"Roger that, Fifteen. Approach with caution."

"Will do," Muhtuk responded.

"Drunk, you figure?" Dennehy said as he opened the door to a frigid blast of biting wind, the windswept snow dotting the black interior white.

"Or plum crazy, a real cheechako," she noted, joining him outside their vehicle.

Muhtuk noted Dennehy unsnapping his pistol restraint before he approached the van's passenger side through the blowing snow. Muhtuk took the driver's side, moving through what many would call a storm but Alaskans called business as usual.

Dennehy lifted his gaze briefly from the transit van. "Cheechako…that's someone new to the area, right?"

"More someone who's never experienced winter up here before."

Dennehy cracked a slight smile, hand on his pistol now. "Like I said: drunk."

Probably a good idea, Muhtuk thought, given what long snow-swept Alaskan winters could do to a man's mind. Having grown up here as a native Inuit, she'd seen the effects of those long dreary stretches on display more times than she could count, especially for non-Natives who often never adjusted to the monthslong plunge into the cold and ice. She didn't know how long the Amazon driver they'd located had lived in these parts. Knew only that his name was Daniel Riggs. According to a screenshot of the driver's license the Amazon dispatcher had forwarded, Riggs was thirty-five years old, stood five foot ten, and weighed 195 pounds. His license listed a Juneau address, and Muhtuk figured him for a recent transplant, likely experiencing his first Alaskan winter because he needed the work.

The lack of exhaust from the tailpipe told her the engine had either been turned off or the gas tank had run dry. The windows on both sides were closed and fogged up, along with the windshield. Muhtuk could hear soft music emanating from inside the cab—Frank Sinatra, she thought, flying his way to the moon.

She drew her pistol an instant ahead of Dennehy. Muhtuk eased her gloved free hand toward the driver's side latch, nodding toward Dennehy to signal her next move. The younger trooper nodded back and steadied his gun on the fogged-up window on his side of the van.

Muhtuk lifted the latch and yanked hard, free hand ready on her pistol by the time it drew open all the way, revealing Daniel Riggs shaking in the driver's seat. His bare hands clutched the steering wheel so hard he'd forced the blood from them. His eyes were glassy, and he was trembling horribly.

Muhtuk watched Dennehy jerk the passenger side door open, flooding the cabin with more frigid air. "He's freezing to death, boss."

Muhtuk leaned inside the van's cab and switched off the music before Frank had a chance to sing the next line. Then she checked Riggs's vitals, trailed by wind-blown snow that dappled Riggs's face and clothes.

"No," Muhtuk said, holstering her gun, "he's in shock."

Muhtuk checked the van's interior, focusing on the cargo Riggs was out delivering packed into the rear. On one side of the hatch, black, green, yellow, and blue tote bags were lined up. Across from them stood adjustable shelving units stacked full of packages of varying sizes. She knew there must be an operational reason for the arrangement but didn't consider it further.

"His pulse is racing," Muhtuk reported, prying Riggs's hands from the steering wheel.

The man's gaze never moved, no recognition flashing in his eyes of either trooper's presence.

Muhtuk gently turned the man's head so they were face-to-face. "We're Alaska state troopers, Mr. Riggs, and we're here to help you. Can you tell me what happened? What brought you out here?"

Riggs's expression acknowledged neither Muhtuk's presence nor her words. His gaze remained vacant, staring forward at nothing and barely blinking.

"Where the hell you think he came from?" Dennehy wondered.

"Let's find out," Muhtuk answered, easing across Daniel Riggs's frame further into the cab.

She smelled urine and realized the man must have wet himself. The key was still in the on position, accounting for the soft music and the heater fan blowing only cold air. Since the van's interior had been warm when she first drew open the door, the vehicle must have run out of gas only recently. Muhtuk switched the heater off and studied the van's high-tech navigation screen with a flashing dot indicating its current position and a zig-zagging line indicating its last location.

"Chichagof Springs," Muhtuk recognized. "Twelve miles from here, according to the map."

"Town's only got, what, a hundred residents?"

"Less in winter. Maybe half that."

"And Amazon delivers there?"

"Amazon delivers everywhere," Muhtuk told the younger trooper. "Let's get him settled in the back of our ride."

It took both of them to manage that task. Initially, they had to drag him until Riggs fell into an awkward rhythm in their trudge through the snow. The troopers also had to bend him at the waist to push him into their police utility vehicle, at which point he plopped down across the length of the seat behind the metal mesh transport enclosure. He was moaning softly when Muhtuk and Dennehy climbed back into the front.

"Dispatch, this is Unit Fifteen," Muhtuk said into the mic held close to her lips.

"Read you, Fifteen."

"We've recovered the subject from the stalled van approximately twelve miles across the icefield, alive but in shock."

"Does the subject require medevac, Fifteen?"

"It would take too long to get here." Muhtuk looked out at the winds whipping the snow into a tornado-like vortex. "And this storm's not letting up anytime soon. We can handle transport from here."

"Roger that, Fifteen."

"See if any units in the area are available to meet us in Chichagof Springs, Dispatch," Muhtuk resumed as she locked gazes with Dennehy. "That was the subject's last known location and where we're headed from here. It's on the way to the nearest treatment center."

"Roger, Fifteen. Will have units meet you there."

"Roger and out, Dispatch."

Muhtuk returned the mic to its stand, glimpsing Dennehy swallowing hard.

"You sure about this, boss?"

Muhtuk cocked her gaze out the rear window in the general direction of Chichagof Springs. "I'm sure that's where our friend Mr. Riggs was last, which means that's where we'll find whatever spooked him half to death."

CHAPTER 2

Awakening

Mohenjo-daro, Pakistan

Chronar waited.

The artificial entity had been waiting for a thousand years, the passage of time irrelevant to its operating system and mission. It did not measure time in minutes and hours, but in the intervals between the tasks it was charged with performing to ensure the nine life pods were functional and that the world it had been created to protect remained intact and secure. In fact, in the native language of the nine beings in its charge, Chronar meant Pulse of Eternal Time.

Chronar monitored atmospheric levels and the bioreadouts of the occupants of the nine pods without pause, its reactive systems triggered in the event of the slightest change or deviation. The occupants of the pods were to be awakened only once a precise set of parameters and indications were met. Toward that end, another of Chronar's tasks was to monitor the world beyond for any sign that its waiting had come to an end.

Chronar maintained detailed records from past potential alerts for comparison purposes to arrive at an accurate threat assessment. Its instructions were specific in that regard: The occupants of the nine pods were not to be awakened due to a naturally occurring phenomenon in the world above or the human race making war upon itself, as the species was so prone to do throughout its evolution.

Only in the event of a threat from, another world, were the Nine to be awakened. A threat man would be ill-prepared to handle and would thus imperil the civilization that dwelled in the world above. Chronar knew all there was to know about the nine beings in its charge. It knew the backgrounds, specialties, and personal histories that had brought them to this place millennia ago. Its constant observation and nonstop monitoring of the Nine meant they would emerge at peak physical and mental condition, if the need ever arose to awaken them.

Suddenly, Chonar's sensors were triggered. In the flash of an instant, it evaluated the data and measured it against the criteria that called for the Nine to be awakened. Intercepted communications were analyzed and weighed to ascertain the threat level.

Through all the centuries, Chronar had never encountered a threat of this magnitude. A low tremor rolled through the chamber. Then came the light, cold and blinding, pouring from nowhere. Unseen machines whirred and hummed. The pods holding the Nine shifted from black to an incandescent light, peeling back the shadows to reveal the shapes of the beings housed within. The lids of all nine pods rose in perfect synchronicity, and breathing sounds split the lair's silence as the Nine began to stir.

Chronar's wait was over.

CHAPTER 3

Out the Road

Mendenhall Glacier, Alaska

"We're almost there," the soldier behind the wheel of the Bombardier snowcat told Kai and Jules Bevins, their eleven-year-old daughter Charlie nestled between them, entrenched in her handheld video game. "Less than a mile out now."

"Glad we didn't come here for our honeymoon," Jules said to her husband Kai.

"It's snowing!" a wide-eyed Charlie exclaimed, looking up from her PSP game console with the enthusiasm of a kid certain school would be canceled for tomorrow.

"Been like this for two days straight," the driver said. "Been keeping us from getting a clear look at it."

"Clear look at what?" Kai asked, prodding him for information he had yet to give up.

"I'm not at liberty to say, sir."

"Like you're not at liberty to tell us your name, right?"

"I'm sorry, sir."

"It's not 'sir,' it's 'Professor.' Professor of astrobiology," Kai added, referring to a field centered around the search for, and eventual study of, extraterrestrial life.

"As a matter of fact, you've got two for the price of one," Jules added.

"We're almost to base camp," the driver said, flipping the snowcat's windshield wipers up a notch to clear the glass of the strengthening storm. "All of your questions will be answered then." His eyes fixed on Charlie. "Not the greatest place in the world to bring a kid."

"We didn't have much choice," Jules told him.

"It's not like your people gave us time to find a babysitter," Kai added.

Kai and Jules had been awakened the night before in their home near the campus of the California Institute of Technology in Pasadena, where both were tenured faculty members in the astrobiology department they had founded after Charlie had celebrated her first birthday ten-and-a-half years ago. Two men in dress army uniforms were waiting outside with explicit orders when they answered the door, giving them twenty minutes to pack what they needed, just the essentials. With no time to find someone to watch her, they had no choice but to bring Charlie along.

No, the soldiers couldn't tell them what this was about.

No, the soldiers couldn't tell them what they were needed for.

No, the soldiers couldn't tell them where they were going.

That didn't become obvious until the private, unmarked jet waiting for them at Hollywood Burbank Airport landed in Juneau. From there, they were driven to the leading edge of the Juneau Icefield, where they climbed into the waiting snowcat and headed northwest.

"Cool," Charlie said, as she slid across the seat, pushing past the heavy parkas that were waiting for them in the cab.

Most kids resembled one parent or the other. But Jules and Kai looked so uncannily alike as husband and wife that their daughter might have been more their clone than their offspring. She boasted the same brown wavy hair—her father's trimmed short and her mother's holding at her shoulders—and identical emerald green eyes often described as piercing. Kai stood a bit under five foot ten, exactly four inches taller than his wife. The most distinguishing feature between them was the beard stubble that rode Kai's face, the result of laziness as opposed to style. He had never forgotten the old story about Einstein having multiple duplicates of the same outfit in his closet to avoid wasting time deciding what to wear. Kai felt the same way about shaving.

"Maybe I'll stop shaving my legs," Jules had quipped once. "What would you think of that?"

"I'd shave them myself as soon as you fell asleep."

She'd patted his stubble-laced chin. "Good idea. I'll get the razor ready for tonight."

He had attended Harvard while she earned her degree a short distance away at MIT. Despite that, they hadn't met until both interned as juniors at NASA's Ames Research Center in their Space Science and Astrobiology Division, forty miles south of San Francisco in California's Silicon Valley. They celebrated being hired full-time upon graduation by getting engaged and were married just after they earned their first promotions on the same day a year later.

"Are the two of you twins?" their new supervisor had asked them at the time.

Kai was roused from his flashback when the snowcat crested over a jarring rise in the landscape, an apt metaphor for the past few years of Jules and Kai's lives. He saw they were still trudging through the snow, which thickened the further northwest they drew. The vehicle's heaters, blowing on high, made little dent in the cold that permeated the cab from outside.

"We're headed to the Mendenhall Glacier, aren't we?" Kai asked their driver. "You want to give us a hint about what's waiting for us there?"

This time, he drew a finger across his lips. "Sorry, sir. Orders."

"The answer's obvious," Jules told him. "There's nothing else out here."

"Yes, there is, ma'am," the officer said, cocking his gaze back briefly toward both of them as the snowcat crested over another natural rise in the tundra and settled back down with a thump.

Kai looked over and saw Jules squeeze her eyes closed, settling herself with a series of deep breaths. "How are you holding up?" he asked her.

He watched her open her eyes and force a smile, tilting her gaze toward their daughter in an unspoken message. "Just a little motion sickness. Nothing the Dramamine I should have taken couldn't have solved. Bumpy ride," she added as an afterthought.

Kai held his gaze on her. "I guess you could say that."

The Mendenhall Glacier, Kai knew, was thirteen and a half miles long and occupied nearly six thousand acres. It was officially part of the Tongass National

Forest, though nothing green could be spotted anywhere through the long winter months. Kai and Jules didn't have to be geologists to know the glacier's retreat, since its formation around four thousand years ago during the Little Ice Age, was increasing yearly due to climate change. Both were aware of significant cave-in activity as of late, including a rumored large crack that had appeared on the ice as a harbinger of a much larger collapse. For that reason, the Mendenhall Glacier recreation area had been closed to all visitors and tourists several days back.

Kai looked toward Jules and could tell from her gaze that they were thinking along the same lines. That wasn't unusual, given they maintained a virtual psychic connection to accompany their physical resemblance, often knowing what the other was thinking. In this case, that was to wonder if the area had been closed off for another reason entirely, the same reason that accounted for why they had been brought here.

Sure enough, Kai spotted several more snowcats, painted white to blend into the scenery, stationed strategically about the ice shelf. Their driver cast the soldiers inside each a wave they returned with a tilt of their assault rifle barrels. They surged past the perimeter defense line, their snowcat's windshield wipers fighting a losing battle against the elements. Each time the glass was briefly cleared, Jules and Kai spotted surveillance drones patrolling assigned grids in what looked to be a circular pattern.

Signs of life appeared first as mere specks against the stark white landscape. Drawing closer, Kai could see the base camp their driver had mentioned was composed of as many as a dozen mobile trailers, army vehicles, small Quonset huts, and large tents flapping in the stiff wind, testing the posts drilled into the ice. The camp looked like it could accommodate around fifty to as many as a hundred personnel, quite a feat to set up out here in the height of winter amid a storm raging for two days straight.

The snowcat lurched down a makeshift road carved between taller piles of snow, straight into the center of camp in front of a trio of the mobile trailers colored white that blended seamlessly into the scenery. A man stood waiting before another pair of snowcats flanked by two other vehicles that looked like armored, heavily armed personnel carriers that made Kai think of Humvees shot up with a heavy dose of steroids. Whatever had been uncovered here on the glacier must have required the attention of more than just scientists, as evidenced by the squat, stocky figure standing with hands clasped behind his back as if he were impervious to the storm.

"He looks like a snowman," Charlie said.

The figure stood stark still in foot-deep snow, wearing an army-green uniform powdered with white. Behind him, Kai could see the makeshift command post formed by the trio of what looked like high-tech motorhomes, with two bracketing a third in an upside-down U shape. Beyond the assemblage of structures was a makeshift fence line, steel rods drilled into the ice with twin rows of steel cable looped through them. Though the storm kept Kai from seeing how far the fence line extended, what he was able to discern fit the pattern of a semicircle enclosing a vast space that included a portion of the Mendenhall Glacier itself. And whatever was contained within the space must have been the source of their being roused from bed the night before to be whisked here.

They climbed down to the ground, Jules helping Charlie out last. Kai could see that the male figure was no more than average height, with a barrel-shaped chest and shoulders that stretched the bonds of his uniform. He wore no overcoat, just an army snow cap, and gloves revealed when he eased his hands out from behind him. It looked as if he was tempting the wind-whipped snow of the storm, appearing impervious to it.

"Thank you for coming, Professors Bevins," he greeted, saluting both of them before noticing Charlie and saluting her as well. "I'm General Avery Timur. I won't bother telling you what division I'm with because you've never heard of it."

"We also haven't heard why we've been brought here," Jules said tersely, the stress of the long hours of travel catching up to her.

"That task falls upon me, ma'am. Let's head inside and get you warmed up. How's a cup of hot chocolate sound?" he added toward Charlie.

"Yum!"

As soon as they entered what must have been the command trailer, the other personnel gathered behind the array of advanced computers and other machinery saluted General Timur and abruptly left, except for a single man who approached them stiffly.

"Professors Bevins, I'd like you to meet Major Smith from the scientific arm of the Defense Intelligence Agency," Timur said by way of introduction.

"I'm no scientist," Smith told them as he shook their hands. "Just regular DIA attached to the department that oversees a particular kind of research and development."

"Nice to meet you, Major *Smith*," Kai said, enunciating the man's clearly fake last name.

"How much do you know about the Mendenhall Glacier, Professors?" Timur resumed.

"That the large crack reportedly found was just a ruse to give the army an excuse to close the area down," advanced Kai.

"Unfortunately, the crack was real. So was a truly epic collapse that ranks with the largest ever, resulting in a chasm that extends down the length of two football fields."

"The wonders of climate change," Jules muttered, then spoke louder. "The bedrock layers become compromised and the surrounding permafrost gives way, and you've got your chasm. But you didn't need to bring a pair of astrobiologists here to tell you that."

"No," Timur told them both while Charlie worked an automated hot chocolate and coffee dispenser. "I brought you here because of what we found inside."

CHAPTER 4

Nobody Home

Chichagof Springs, Alaska

"Too bad there's no sheriff or LE officer we can dial up, right?" Dennehy posed.

"Just us," Muhtuk confirmed, firing up the Explorer's big powerful engine. "Alaska State Police jurisdiction."

"How many residents are we talking again?"

"Fifty, give or take a few."

The Track N Go snow tracks riding beneath the tires meant she'd have to keep the speed slow and steady instead of pushing eight cylinders for all they could give her. It took thirty minutes to reach the outskirts of Chichagof Springs, at which point Muhtuk eased their PUV to a halt to assess the situation with no backup in view.

Dennehy cocked his gaze back toward Daniel Riggs, who, stirred from his stupor, had suddenly sat up. "You okay back there, sir?"

Recognition flashed in Riggs's gaze and he dropped back down across the seat, curling up into a fetal position.

The first thing Muhtuk noticed was the desolation before her. As her eyes adjusted to the glare of the white-on-white landscape, she could see several vehicles sitting still and snow covered in the middle of a street lined on both sides with small commercial buildings. Modest homes rimmed the town in a neat circle around the main drag. Somewhere beyond lay the continuation of this two-lane artery that connected Chichagof Springs to the outside world via the Dalton Highway, stretching over four hundred miles from Livengood to Deadhorse.

As Muhtuk's vision sharpened, she realized that two of the abandoned vehicles were parked diagonally across the road, nearly blocking it.

"Those vehicles up there," Dennehy said, stopping there.

"Yeah," Muhtuk said, not sure until that moment that their placement wasn't a trick played by the windswept snow unleashed by the storm. "I see them too."

She unclasped the microphone from its stand. "Dispatch, this is Fifteen."

"Go ahead, Fifteen."

"Have reached the outskirts of Chichagof Springs. Checking on the status of backup."

"One vehicle responding to an emergency and the other stuck in traffic thanks to the storm. You're on your own out there for now, Fifteen."

"We'll take that under advisement, Dispatch. Roger and out."

Muhtuk clipped the mic back on its stand to find the younger trooper in the passenger seat staring at her.

"We're not going to wait, are we, boss?"

"Think that story you heard about me knocking the shit out of three Hells Angels in a bar fight was true?"

Dennehy nodded. "No doubt in my mind."

"Then you don't need to ask me if we're going to wait for backup, do you?"

Muhtuk saw a shadow rise behind her and realized that Amazon delivery driver Daniel Riggs had sat up again, his face pressed against the cage.

"No," he said softly, fingers looping through the steel mesh. "No." Louder. "No!" Louder still. *"No! No! No! No! No! No! No!"*

Then Riggs tugged at the cage, intent on pulling it down. When that failed, he tried the latch on the driver's and passenger side doors, only to find both locked.

"Out! Out! Out! Out! Out!" he screeched this time, pounding on the shatterproof windows.

"Easy there, pal," said Dennehy, trying to calm him down.

"What did you see here, Daniel?" Muhtuk asked, holding the man's stare. "What scared you so bad?"

Riggs sank back against the seat, shock claiming his features once more. His flesh tone seemed to pale as Muhtuk watched. Then he squeezed his eyes shut.

"Daniel? Can you hear me, Daniel?" Muhtuk tried. "I know you can hear me, friend. We want to help you, but we need your help first. What did you see? What's waiting for us here?"

But Riggs's eyes remained sealed.

* * *

"Oh, Great Spirit, as I venture into the harsh landscape, watch over me and guide my steps," Muhtuk muttered, reciting words from an old Inuit prayer as she aimed the Alaska State Police Explorer down Chichagof Springs's central artery, called Piedmont Street according to a mounted aluminum sign that mainly had stayed clear of snow. *"Keep me safe from the perils of the wild, the cold, and the unseen dangers, and grant me strength and wisdom to navigate this journey."*

Four times in her fifteen-year, perpetually stalled career, Sakari Muhtuk had found a dead body. The feeling she had when first regarding all four was the same one conjured by the sight of the town before her as she edged the Explorer down Piedmont Street, according to a sign peeking out through the curtain of snow.

Nothing moved, except when caught by the whims of the swirling wind. Muhtuk could see few lights shining in the ice-crusted windows, and not a single person was in evidence anywhere, no one peering out from behind cracked curtains at the arrival of the Alaska State Police. There were only those abandoned vehicles she had to ease around cautiously, noting the driver's door of one was open, the front seat caked with snow.

Muhtuk reached the middle of Piedmont Street, between a small market on one side and a tiny post office on the other, and slid the Explorer to a halt. Daniel Riggs was shivering in the backseat, alternating between moans, sobs, and something in between. Whistling, howling winds continued to whip the snow about, making it impossible to tell what was falling from what was being lifted from the already accumulated piles. Through the gaps in the wind, she saw higher mounds that reminded her of a dirt pile next to a freshly dug grave and ground their vehicle to a halt.

"You see those?" she asked Dennehy.

"What? I can't see shit."

Muhtuk pointed through the windshield as the wipers continued to keep the world before them clear. "Three snow piles. There, there, and there."

"You're seeing things, boss."

"Yeah?" She looked across the seat and held the younger trooper's eyes. "Let's see about that."

"We got backup coming."

"Not soon enough," Muhtuk said, pushing open her door against the wind.

She heard Dennehy's door slam, the younger trooper meeting her at the back of the Explorer as Muhtuk hoisted the rear gate to grab the twelve-gauge pump-action shotgun from its rack. Then she led the way forward, chambering a shell and poking at the ice-frosted air with the shotgun's barrel.

Dennehy grasped Muhtuk's shoulder. "Hold on a sec, boss." He pointed straight ahead. "Over there—what does that look like to you?"

Muhtuk squinted through the storm. "Let's find out."

"Because it looks like—"

"I know what it looks like, Trooper, but let's see for sure."

Moving closer, Muhtuk spotted a rifle stock sticking out of the snowpack.

"Winchester Model '94 lever-action rifle," Dennehy said, plucking what was left of the rifle up in a gloved hand. "Old-school weapon but plenty of—"

He stopped when only half the gun emerged from the snow. It looked as if it had snapped apart just past the loading chamber. All that was left beyond the stock was a jagged edge of wood and metal. Usually, Dennehy's encyclopedic knowledge of firearms annoyed Muhtuk, but this morning, she was grateful for it.

The younger trooper's gaze remained locked on what was left of the Winchester. Then he began kicking at the snow with a heavy boot, squatting to retrieve what he had exposed.

Dennehy rose and held the rifle's severed barrel for Muhtuk to see. Then he fit the two halves of the weapon together along the jagged edge, revealing a perfect fit before checking the chamber.

"It's been fired. Three shots, I think."

"Well, if those bullets hit anything, it didn't stop whoever or whatever was coming."

Muhtuk muttered some Inuit words under her breath, a simpler prayer her mother had taught her as a little girl when she was too frightened to sleep at night. She was always scared of something until she took up martial arts and football. Then, people were scared of her.

"Boss?" Dennehy said, when Muhtuk started toward the stalled vehicle abandoned diagonally across Piedmont Street with her shotgun leading.

The driver's door of this car was cracked open, and Muhtuk used her free hand to open it all the way. The driver's seat was empty, but the lap belt and shoulder harness had been torn from their fittings.

"What the hell?" she heard Dennehy mutter from just behind her. "We gotta call this in, but what the hell do we say?"

"Let's take a look at that first," Muhtuk said, gesturing toward the nearest of the three snow piles ten feet straight ahead.

Dennehy fell in step alongside her, still clinging to her side when she poked at whatever the snow was blanketing with the barrel of her twelve gauge. It felt soft, spongy, almost like pliable rubber, but not quite.

Behind them, the troopers heard Daniel Riggs pounding on the window, shouting something neither of them could distinguish through the wind.

"Hold this," Muhtuk said, handing Dennehy the shotgun.

Then she crouched gingerly over the mound, feeling every bit of the damage playing high-school football had done to her knees. There were two other girls on the team, but Muhtuk was the only starter and the only one to be invited to play in the Indigenous Bowl for Native American high-school football players.

She brushed the accumulated snow aside, careful not to disturb whatever lay beneath it. Finally, a plaid shape was revealed. At first glance, it looked like the fabric of a Mackinaw jacket, making Muhtuk think she had poked nothing more than a pile of clothes that somehow got dumped in the middle of Piedmont Street. She felt relieved and allowed herself a deep breath as she continued wiping the snow away with a gloved hand.

Muhtuk's relief fled with her breath. It was a Mackinaw jacket all right, wrapped around the remnants of what had been a human being.

"Jesus," she heard Dennehy rasp, "is that a *man*?"

"What's left of him," Muhtuk said, unsure what to make of the flattened body before her.

She pressed down lightly with a gloved hand and felt the torso contained in plaid wool compress. This sensation reminded her of pressing down on sliced elk or caribou meat to tenderize it, as her mother had taught her.

Riggs's pounding on the Explorer's window had intensified, his screeching from the backseat slicing through a break in the wind.

"Get out! Get out! Get out!"

Muhtuk's knees were on fire now, but she crouched to smooth away the snow from the Mackinaw-garbed figure's face. She first saw the matching plaid cap clinging to a head that looked like a balloon with the air let out. A pair of frozen-over, gaping eyes the size of big marbles stared back at her, absurdly large when set against flattened features that didn't resemble a man at all.

Muhtuk wobbled to her feet, ignoring the fiery pain in her knees, as Dennehy staggered backward at the sight revealed.

"What the fuck, boss, what the fuck?"

"Get out! Get out! Get out!" Riggs continued, still pounding on the glass.

Too late, Muhtuk thought.

CHAPTER 5

The Ship

Mendenhall Glacier, Alaska

General Timur directed Kai and Jules's attention to a wall-mounted flat-screen television, holding the remote like a pistol as he turned the monitor on. For his part, Major Smith from the Defense Intelligence Agency hung back, hands clasped behind his back, content to yield the floor to the general.

"This is courtesy of a drone we're currently holding stationary over the find," Timur explained. "I'm the only one authorized to share information with anyone lacking a proper security clearance."

"Ours is pretty high," Jules reminded.

"It's not high enough for what you are about to see," the general said, freezing the drone in place so the picture on the monitor stabilized.

"Oh my God," Jules said, speaking for both her and Kai before her hand moved involuntarily toward her face.

The dull ache in the back of her head that had started inside the snowcat had grown to a steady throb. She tried to tell herself it was the altitude, the fatigue, or the drastic change in climate from what they had left in Pasadena, but she knew that wasn't the case. She caught General Timur's glance flashing with momentary concern and made herself hold his gaze.

"Not quite," he said, "but close enough."

The hovering drone was perched high enough within the chasm carved beneath the Mendenhall Glacier to capture an alien ship's entire sprawl through the blankets of wind-tossed snow. A white, frosty mist was left as residue in its wake, allowing view of the ship when the snow gave way to clear air. At first glance, it looked circular, like a classic flying saucer from science fiction–film lore. But further scrutiny revealed it to be more oblong, with ridged extensions that looked fastened into place.

Timur noted Kai's interest in those and worked the drone's controls on a separate remote to lower it to provide a better view.

"Care to hazard a guess at what we're looking at here, Professor?"

"I'd say those extensions serve the same purpose as flaps on a commercial jet, likely used to slow the craft down upon entering a planet's atmosphere."

"But they're locked in the open position," Jules noted.

"And what does that tell you, Professor?" Timur asked her.

"This ship didn't land; it crashed, making a desperate attempt to slow its rate of acceleration, which didn't stop it from crashing deep into the ice beneath what would eventually become the Mendenhall Glacier around four thousand years ago."

"I assume you've taken measurements," said Kai.

"The ice volume indicates it's been here for between a hundred and fifty and two hundred thousand years. We have the ice thaw and cave-in to thank for the collapse that suddenly made its presence known."

Behind them, Charlie had found a seat at a narrow table, alternating sips from her hot chocolate with smashing aliens to smithereens on her handheld video game. Her earbuds kept her from hearing anything but the sounds of the game.

"My drone operator will bring it down as far as he can," the general told her. "The ship has some kind of magnetic field around it that sucks in anything metallic."

"By sucks in, you mean...."

"Absorbs, like a sponge soaking up water."

On the monitor, the drone lowered, and almost instantly, the ship's surface enlarged as the camera drew closer.

"Completely seamless," Kai said.

"But it doesn't look metallic, more like pressed leather. Slightly ridged instead of a smooth, flat surface," Jules added.

The image captured by the drone flickered on the screen, battling the mist and snow that cast the ice in an incandescent blue hue, creating the illusion that the ice was blue. Kai regarded the obsidian-hulled ship as a dormant titan, a silent testament to some distant civilization's artistry and engineering.

Suddenly, the picture started wobbling, then shaking.

"It's the magnetic field," Timur explained. "The drone's been snared. Watch what happens next."

Timur switched to the picture provided by a drone perched higher up, safe from the field. The lower drone plummeted, spinning wildly. Jules and Kai awaited the expected crash, but instead, the leathery surface of the hull receded slightly on impact, with no trace of the drone left to the eye.

"Thoughts, Professors?" Timur prodded.

Jules and Kai looked at each other as they spoke.

"The ship must be constructed of organic materials," Kai proposed.

"You already know our next question."

"Have we found any signs of life on board? The magnetic field only extends around the ship's immediate perimeter. Smaller drones we were able to get inside have managed a pretty thorough mapping of the ship's interior. I've got the recorded footage keyed up for you to view next. But the answer to your question is no, not yet. But there are areas of the ship the drones can't penetrate, so we waited until the two of you got here to get an up-close-and-personal look."

"You're talking about venturing on board," Kai realized.

"It's the only way to see what's inside, Professor."

Jules took a step closer to him. "Which suggests you've managed to locate an entrance, first for the drone and now for us. Some kind of doorway."

"Not a doorway, Professor, a breach. The hull must have ruptured in the crash, exposing whatever was inside to our atmosphere and the glacial environment. Our working theory is that any living organisms that made the journey here perished. As a result, their remains are likely long lost to the ages, unless they're confined to one of those other areas of the ship we haven't explored yet."

"Can we see this breach?" Jules asked.

"We've got a battery of still shots," Timur said, working his remote to bring up a series of those frames taken by drones from different angles. "Our artificial intelligence software took in all the pictures and extrapolated a three-dimensional rendering of the breach."

Another flick of the remote brought that rendering to the screen, rotating about so its entire shape and contours could be viewed. It looked lifelike, more like a recording, even though it was a computer-generated collation of all the data the AI program had observed.

"Measurements," prodded Kai.

Numbers appeared on the screen, either thanks to Timur's remote or the AI program responding to his prompt. Whatever the case, the breach measured twelve feet at its highest point and nearly ten feet at its widest.

Jules moved closer to the screen as if about to extend her hand through the simulated breach. The steady throb in her head was gone, the dull ache back in its place. "If the collated depiction is correct, this breach wasn't the result of the original crash, General."

Timur's gaze narrowed on her.

"You can see from the angle of the ruptured substance," Jules continued, "whatever its composition, that the edges are pushed outward, not inward as the effects of a violent crash would cause."

"If you're right," Kai said, moving to his wife's side to better regard the breach. "If you're right...."

"If I'm right, something got off that ship," Jules said to Timur and Major Smith. "The only question is when."

CHAPTER 6

The Nine

Mohenjo-daro, Pakistan

"Faster! Faster!" Usman urged his Marwari horse as the animal's hooves pounded the sands of the Thar Desert.

He was racing his older brother Ayan, whose name meant "gift of God," while his translated as "baby bird." Two years his brother's junior at twelve years old, Usman had never once bested Ayan in a race across the desert. Marwaris were known for their stamina, speed, and ability to adapt to harsh desert climates.

They were racing toward Mohenjo-daro, an archaeological dig that had unearthed one of the largest settlements of the Indus Valley. Some believed it was the most ancient of the world's cities. It had been abandoned around 1700 BCE for reasons long lost to history. If nothing else, Usman possessed a keener intellect than his brother, excelling in his studies that included a fascination, obsession even, over what led to the residents of Mohenjo-daro fleeing their homes and never returning. Its abandonment remained an unsolved historical mystery since the archaeological dig had unearthed ruins of a city extremely advanced and meticulously constructed for its time, the kind of place people would flock to and not flee.

No archaeologists had been on-site to dig further in months. Since the boys' father relied on his income as a guide to put food on the table, Usman and Ayan were well aware of the tension the lack of dig teams coming to Mohenjo-daro was causing at home. There had been rumors of unauthorized teams working the site without a guide or the necessary permits, and the boys thought they might catch one doing just that this afternoon.

Usman was two hundred feet behind his brother when the ruins came into view, a blotch of life upon the stark desert landscape.

"Ayan!" he called from atop his Marwari. "Ayan, slow down! I'm coming!"

Ayan glanced behind him, then picked up his pace even more. Usman kicked at his horse to do the same but fell further back.

"Ullu ka patha!" he cried out. "Stupid loser!"

Then, the ground began to quake. Usman had felt tremors before in this area but never anything this strong that lasted for more than a moment. His brother had just reached the outskirts of Mohenjo-daro when a fissure opened at Usman's feet, the world seeming to crack down its center.

"Ayan!" Usman screamed.

He could see his brother had drawn his horse to a complete stop. Beyond Ayan, the dome atop the unearthed ruins of Mohenjo-daro seemed to be shaking, plumes of its hardened, sand-shrouded shape coughed into the air. Then it collapsed, sinking into the desert sands right before his eyes.

Usman's first thought was that it must be a trick of the sun, a product of his overactive imagination, or a combination of the two. Then he watched in terror as all of Mohenjo-daro sank into the ground, dragging Ayan and his horse with it.

"Jee nahin!" Usman cried out in Urdu as his Marwari reared up and threw him.

Usman hit the still-quaking ground hard as his horse tore away back toward town. The boy lurched to his feet and took off in a dead sprint across the desert to find his brother.

"Ayan! I'm coming, Ayan, I'm coming!"

He could only hope his brother could still hear him.

Reaching the edge of where Mohenjo-daro had stood, he could see nothing but the thick cloud of dust rising from the abyss into which the ruins and Ayan had disappeared. He realized one of his ankles was throbbing horribly and sank to his knees, too shocked to cry, unsure of whether this was really happening or the product of a dream he'd soon awaken from.

"*Please be a dream, please be a dream,*" Usman prayed with his eyes closed, feeling a fresh quake shake the earth.

A gush of hot air struck him from the pit that had swallowed Mohenjo-daro. A cloud of blanket-thick dust appeared where the surface had been just minutes before. He heard the whir of a machine, first distant, then humming.

Usman jumped to his feet and stumbled backward. Then the humming stopped, and he thought he glimpsed shapes emerging from the dust. He tried to reel further backward, but his leg gave out, and he hit the scorched desert sand hard.

Looking up, the boy saw shapes emerging from the cloud, having risen from the pit Mohenjo-daro had vanished into. Their dust-shrouded frames were garbed in black; they couldn't be men because they were all giant in size, a foot or more taller than any person Usman had ever seen. The figures were broad too and thick with muscle. Even the four women who stood among the nine figures would have towered over his father. One of those, who looked younger than the others, had an x that looked tattooed onto the back of her hand, a black sheen in the blistering sun. The biggest of the male figures had what looked like a crease running across his skull that ended at the start of his forehead.

The nine dust-shrouded shapes approached him in a tight cluster that made them appear to be living, walking parts of the desert. The giant in the front, with black eyes and thick hair unruffled by the wind, had something tucked under his right arm that looked like a twisted sack of laundry. Usman watched him drop whatever it was at his feet, then continue on without breaking stride.

"Ayan!" he realized, as his brother stirred before him. *"Ayan!"*

Usman swung toward the nine figures that had strode past him after emerging from the pit with his brother in tow.

"*Shukriya*!" he cried out to thank them.

But they were gone.

CHAPTER 7

Crime Scene

Chichagof Springs, Alaska

The Explorer's warmth did little to diminish the chill that left Sakari Muhtuk trembling slightly as she closed the driver's door behind her. She had just taken the mic from its stand when the passenger door rattled shut behind Tom Dennehy, startling her enough to lose grasp of it.

"You okay, boss?" he asked.

"What do you think?"

Muhtuk had left the Explorer's engine on to keep their passenger warm. For his part, Daniel Riggs sat stiff and still in the backseat, breathing rapidly and staring blankly straight ahead.

"What did we just see out there?" Dennehy wondered, sounding as dazed as he must have felt too.

Muhtuk was having trouble processing the fact that it had been a body.

Before returning to the vehicle, they had checked the other two mounds in the snow to find another pair of remains in the very same condition. There had been no need to perform a detailed inspection to confirm that; pressing down with the shotgun's tip and then brushing the snow away to confirm their findings was more than enough. Two men and one woman, if Muhtuk's initial assessment was correct.

"No bones," she muttered.

"What was that?"

Muhtuk retrieved the microphone and cleared her throat. "I said no bones. That's what we just uncovered, bodies that had no bones."

"So, so is this a crime scene, boss?"

"I don't know what it is, Trooper."

Muhtuk pressed the call button on her radio.

"Dispatch, this is Fifteen."

"Go ahead, Fifteen."

"We have a Code Orange in Chichagof Springs. Repeat, we are reporting a Code Orange," Muhtuk said, using the call signal for a mass casualty event.

A pause followed.

"Say again, Fifteen."

"I repeat, we are looking at a Code Orange here with special circumstances," she added this time. "Request status on backup."

"The ice storm in your area has grounded all vehicles, including air support. Are there survivors?"

Muhtuk looked through the windshield at the assemblage of structures barely visible in the blowing snow and ice. "Unknown at this time."

"Observe and report, Fifteen. Use caution."

Muhtuk glanced at Riggs in the rearview mirror. "Our Amazon driver is unstable and likely in need of medical treatment stat. Please advise."

"After recon, you are to remain on-site and secure from a safe distance until backup arrives."

Muhtuk almost reminded the dispatcher that there was no backup. Instead, she said, "I will observe and report back, Dispatch. "

"Roger, Fifteen. Over and out."

Muhtuk snapped the mic back onto its stand.

"Are we really going to do that?" Dennehy asked her.

Muhtuk was already reaching for the door latch. "We need to check for survivors."

Dennehy didn't budge in the passenger seat. "Whatever did that to those people might still be out there. What if it's a disease or some biowarfare shit that blew in from Russia?"

"You think somebody fired three shots from that Winchester at a germ?"

Dennehy shrugged.

"You were in the army, right?"

"Reserves, yeah."

"Means you know your way around the AR-15 we've got in the back."

Trembling anew from the cold that had permeated the cab, Muhtuk turned to Daniel Riggs in the backseat. His angular face was a patchwork of segments through the iron mesh grid.

"What did you see before you hightailed it out of this town, Mr. Riggs?" she asked him. "Is there anything out there waiting for us?"

"Waiting," he intoned.

"That's what I'm asking you."

"Waiting," he repeated. "DSP."

"What does that mean, Mr. Riggs?"

"Amazon delivery service partner. Me. That's what I am. DSP. My job. Mentor app."

Muhtuk glanced across the seat at Dennehy. They both waited for the man to continue.

"ABCDS," Riggs said when he finally did. "Acceleration, braking, cornering, distraction, and speeding. Everything monitored. Everything recorded."

"When you were here earlier," Dennehy started, "was that recorded?"

Muhtuk watched Riggs nod a single time and got back on the radio.

"Dispatch, this is Fifteen."

"Go ahead, Fifteen."

"Please contact Amazon headquarters to see if they can access the camera footage from the van we located earlier. If affirmative, please advise and send it to my phone for inspection."

"Roger, Fifteen."

"Over and out, Dispatch." Muhtuk looked toward Dennehy. "Let's get you that AR-15."

* * *

The storm abated slightly, and snow fell instead of pellets of ice. However, the swirling wind continued to whip about, confusing Muhtuk's vision by conjuring shifting shapes that vanished as quickly as they appeared.

"Are we treating this as a crime scene now, boss?" Dennehy repeated.

"Only because I don't know what else to call it. Whatever did that to those bodies...." Muhtuk let her remark drift off, unable to conjure the rest of her thought.

She and Dennehy walked down Piedmont Street side by side, a yard or so between them, rotating their weapons and gazes about, Muhtuk with her twelve gauge and the younger trooper wielding the AR-15 that looked comfortable in his gloved hands.

"That thing gonna freeze up on you?" she asked him.

"So long as we avoid a full-fledged ice storm, it'll work just fine."

"Not your first rodeo up here, then."

"My Army Reserve unit out of Anchorage trained for cold weather ops. That's how I got assigned to this posting straight out of the academy."

"Lucky you." Muhtuk had meant her remark to sound funny, but the words didn't emerge that way. Having covered another third of Piedmont Street, they hadn't come upon any more bodies yet or glimpsed any sign of life or motion except for the swirling snow.

Dennehy squinted into the storm. "Fifty people here in the winter, you said."

"Give or take."

"No sign of any of them in the windows looking out onto the street."

"We'll check the buildings on our way back."

Suddenly, Dennehy ground his boots to a halt in the piled snow and raised his AR-15 to firing position, steadying it.

"Trooper?"

"Straight ahead, boss. Something's coming."

Muhtuk squinted into the storm. "I can't see shit."

But then she did: a shape visible only as motion through the snow. It was tall and bird-like, with extremities flapping on its sides that looked like wings.

"What is that?" Dennehy gasped, finger pawing the trigger of his assault rifle. "What the fuck is that?"

He edged forward, then burst into a sprint that cut a tunnel through the falling snow.

"Trooper, no!" Muhtuk shouted against the wind, thinking of the Winchester that had been broken in two. "Stop!"

But Dennehy had disappeared into the storm.

A scream rang out, followed by a burst of fire, muzzle flashes looking like pinpricks of light through the curtain of white as Dennehy's gunshots echoed through the air.

Then nothing.

CHAPTER 8

The Breach

Mendenhall Glacier, Alaska

Jules had never known a dark like that which enveloped the alien ship's interior. She could feel her heart thudding inside her chest, not from fear but excitement and apprehension over the greatest experience of her life's work. What good was being an astrobiologist if there was no astrobiology to study?

She knew she shouldn't be here right now, shouldn't have come. Daily activities had become a challenge for her these past few months, much less dealing with the rigors of a mission like this. But this opportunity had proved to be a great blessing for her, something to take her mind from the reality of what she was facing and provide the purpose she had longed for since she developed a fascination with life beyond our planet when she was around Charlie's age.

Charlie....

She didn't know. They hadn't told her.

Jules suppressed those thoughts and focused on this ship that had brought the first known alien life forms to Earth somewhere between a hundred and fifty and two hundred thousand years ago. Over the years, Jules and Kai had heard increasing rumors about a so-called alien division taking hold at the Defense

Intelligence Agency, or DIA. Its existence and purpose were shrouded in secrecy, but the presence on this team of the so-called Major Smith went a long way toward confirming the rumors were true and that, like Kai and Jules, such a division would now be able to use their expertise at long last.

Toward what purpose, though?

From the moment Timur had revealed the breach in the alien ship's hull to them, both Kai and Jules knew they could not venture into the ship together. The risk was great enough for one, much less both, if a worst-case scenario befell them, rendering Charlie an orphan.

With that, Kai produced the quarter he always carried for situations like this from his pocket.

"Call it, Jules."

"Heads."

"You always call heads."

"And I always win."

Kai tossed the coin into the air, and Jules caught it on the way down and laid it on top of the nearest counter.

"I win," she said, pulling her hand away to reveal it was heads.

"Do you?" Kai posed dryly and eased her aside. "You can't do this," he said, his voice lowered.

"I can, and I have to."

"We have no idea of the effects the atmosphere and pressure on that ship might have on you."

"The same goes for both of us, Kai."

He held her by both arms, squeezing tenderly. "We don't know what's waiting for us on that ship, Jules."

She managed a smile. No one had ever called her that until Kai came along. It was always Julia. He said she was too pretty for that name and proclaimed her Jules the first time they met.

"All the more reason why it has to be me who goes on board," she told him, then bent his head toward her to kiss him lightly on the forehead.

"And if something goes wrong?"

"The drones have been all over that ship and found nothing. I'll be fine," Jules insisted, not realizing the irony of her statement.

"You mean every inch of the ship they could access."

"I need this, Kai."

"And I need you, for as long as I can possibly have you. Charlie, too." He tried to smile. "If I didn't know better, I'd say you fixed the coin toss."

Jules winked at him. "I'll never tell."

Jules knew Kai's point about her being the one to enter the ship was well taken, but if one of them was lost down there in the chasm, it had to be her. They were about to encounter a technology entirely unknown to man. Jules was also aware that the spatial rules applied to our world might be entirely different for an alien race capable of traversing the universe to reach Earth. So, while the drones had charted and recorded as much of the ship as they could find, there could be levels upon levels yet to be explored.

"Your husband and I will be able to monitor everything you do and say through the cameras and mics built into the helmets of all your team members. Major Smith will be accompanying you along with three of my men," General Timur told her, adding, "just in case. We'll also, of course, be recording everything from the perspectives of all five of you to study in case you overlook something in your visual inspection."

"Meaning what we record is just as important as what we see."

Timur nodded. "It'll be easy to miss something vital in all that darkness. Our tech-enhancement software can correct that."

"Good to know, General."

Though the drones had found the air inside the alien craft to be breathable, Jules and her team would be wearing full space suits equipped with self-replenishing oxygen units. Neither she nor Kai bothered to ask General Timur how such a technology had been developed, because they knew no answer would be forthcoming. Nor did they ask the general about the drones Jules and her team were strapped to by harness to be lowered over five hundred feet into the permafrost where the long-buried ship had been found. The glacier's collapse had left plenty of ice to land on outside the breach, confirmed to be thick enough to support their collective weight.

After witnessing what happened to a drone that had strayed too close to the alien ship's magnetic field, Jules was more worried about the operation's lowering phase than anything else. But Timur assured her that the drones would be remote piloted by seasoned professionals in another trailer who would steer them clear of the now-mapped magnetic field.

The descent felt more like floating than dropping, nothing like the rides at Disneyland and Disney World that Charlie and Kai loved but Jules avoided at all costs. Her booted feet touched down gently atop the ice, and she was aware immediately of the sounds of her breathing inside her helmet. All the helmets were equipped with a powerful LED light that automatically followed the direction of the wearer's eyes and supplemented handheld flashlights that were even more powerful.

Before entering the ship, Jules performed a detailed study of the breach itself to confirm her initial conclusions from the footage recorded by drones. The fact that the color of the twisted and jagged edges matched the shading of the rest of the ship indicated it had happened recently, not two hundred thousand years ago. There was no scoring or scorching on what felt and looked like metal. She pressed a gloved hand against it and thought she felt the metallic substance recede, almost like thick, pliable leather, but visual inspection revealed it hadn't compressed at all.

Jules took a deep breath and let it out slowly as she led the way through the breach inside the ship, holding the moment in her mind the way Neil Armstrong must have when he was the first man to set foot on the moon. She was certain she was looking at an array of machines that were long powered down before her, but they didn't resemble anything like a machine by Earth's standards. The sheer bulk of rectangular flat masses, circular platforms, and spherical extensions rising out of the floor could only house the technology that enabled a distant race to come all this way from their home planet.

Toward what purpose, though?

The walls, slick and cold to the touch even beneath her layered but flexible gloves, gave nothing back of the light shined against them. The beam from her helmet skimmed the surface, which was not reflective. Instead, it seemed to absorb the light like the ship's surface had absorbed the drone. Jules knew that the ship's construction offered the clearest clues to how the race that had traveled within it functioned. Still, she had no idea what to make of walls that swallowed light instead of reflecting it and wondered if the ship was designed to somehow absorb energy from space to replenish its power banks.

Major Smith spotted something on one of the large rectangular structures set into the center of the floor. It appeared to be formed from the same metallic substance as the walls, the seams between them invisible, as if the entire ship had been molded from a single piece of this organic metal-like compound.

"Shine your flashlight here," he told her. "Match it to my beam."

The two beams together revealed a series of nearly invisible symbols, rows and rows of what must be the alien language imprinted on a wall centered on the floor it looked like an extension of. The drones too had missed that, but that didn't excuse her oversight.

I wouldn't have missed this a few years ago, but a few years ago, I hadn't been....

"Operating instructions, you think?" Jules asked Smith, stopping herself from completing her thought.

"Your guess is as good as mine, Professor, and at this point, all we're doing is guessing."

"Einstein was the best guesser of all time, and Isaac Newton was the second best. Enough said on that note, Major."

The next revelation came from her.

"Notice something we're not seeing anywhere at all?" Jules asked him.

"I'm listening," Smith said.

The steady throb had returned, and the confines of her helmet seemed to worsen it. Jules felt her head expand with each pound, as if someone was pumping air into it. She wondered if her features looked bloated through the faceplate of her helmet.

"Light patterns, banks, or fixtures of any kind," she told Smith. "I think this ship might have been operated completely in the dark."

"Something else potentially revealing of whoever flew it here. Let's continue our sweep, Professor."

* * *

Jules knew the chamber they had entered made up only a portion of the overall size of the alien ship. Because of its seamless nature, any doors would be indistinguishable from the walls that held them. That made uncovering the outer chambers beyond this primary one a formidable challenge that resisted the meager light at their disposal. Their sweeps up, down, and along the walls revealed nothing even suggesting a possible hatch or doorway.

"Maybe we're looking in the wrong place," she suggested, looking up through her helmet.

The chamber's ceiling was nearly thirty feet in height. Given the measurements the drones had taken of the ship's entire exterior, there was definitely enough space to accommodate multiple levels. However, there was no way to access anything of the kind in evidence, at least not in any form Jules recognized. Among the most challenging aspects of astrobiology was the need to unlearn everything you had studied and learn it all from scratch.

Major Smith reported their progress, or lack thereof, back to base camp on the surface, sparing Jules that task while the trio of soldiers hovered behind them. After he had checked in, the two of them swept their flashlight beams across the completely black ceiling, having no more luck than they'd encountered with the walls, until something caught Jules's eyes.

"The spot you just passed," she told Smith. "Run your beam over it again."

He nodded his helmet and did his best to comply.

"Stop!" Jules ordered. Then, after Smith had frozen his beam on her command, "See?"

"No."

"Move the beam a few feet to the side. See how it just sits flat on the metal?"

"Yes."

"Now move it back to where I told you to freeze it."

Smith shifted his flashlight just enough.

"There! The beam doesn't sit; it disappears."

Jules could see Smith's eyes widen through his faceplate. "Looks like we've found a passage to the next level."

"Let's confirm that."

Jules unclasped another device from her belt that could trace a red design that stuck briefly to the air to capture scale. The device was no bigger than a cell phone, with only a single beam and switch visible. She shined it upward, tracing the contours of the opening they'd found in the ceiling. The laser left a red impression in the air where the beam disappeared above instead of sitting on the metallic surface. The process was deliberate and painstaking, ultimately revealing what neither had expected.

“That’s no entryway,” Smith said, following the jagged, shapeless impression left by the laser in the air.

“No,” Jules agreed, noting that the impression had already begun to dissipate. “It’s another breach.”

Part Two
THE SPRINGS

"Nowhere in space will we rest our eyes upon the familiar shapes of trees and plants, or any of the animals that share our world. Whatsoever life we meet will be as strange and alien as the nightmare creatures of the ocean abyss, or of the insect empire whose horrors are normally hidden from us by their microscopic scale."

—Arthur C. Clarke

CHAPTER 9

Transport

Mohenjo-daro, Pakistan.

The Nine had run through the desert, their leader Jace setting a twenty-mile-per-hour pace. Although they greatly resembled the beings of this world, their metabolic rate and cellular regeneration were that of another species entirely. That explained why they were so much bigger, stronger, and cognitively superior to humans.

Jace and the rest of the Nine felt no strain of exertion and no rise in bodily temperature. There was no need for them to flush excess heat through perspiration and no strain placed on their respiratory systems by the length of their run or their pace. They never broke stride, and there was no need for them to rest. Their metabolisms didn't shed water, so they required no hydration.

Jace knew that to someone observing their sprint across the Thar Desert, they would appear to be running in perfect synchronicity as if a single mind was driving their bodies. That wasn't far from the truth. The Nine were a team in every sense of the word. They thought as one, acted as one, reacted as one—even dressed as one today in black tactical gear Chronar had selected for them, after matching the clothes to the time period and manufacturing them in a heavily advanced version of a 3D printer to fit each of the Nine's precise measurements.

And, short of the specialties that differentiated them, their skills and capabilities were equal, though Jace was their designated leader. Their brain capacity had been augmented by organic microchips to enable them to absorb information from Chronar the way a computer would. They had a vast wealth of knowledge about everything, except their own beings. All of them retained a keen awareness of their world's history but not their own.

And yet as he ran through the Thar Desert, Jace was struck by a wave of uneasiness. The mere consideration of the past he had left behind what felt like yesterday left him unsettled. Almost like every time a memory started to surface, something yanked it back down to the deepest recesses of his mind.

So Jace turned his attention to the threat they had been awoken to confront. Whatever had escaped the ship that had thawed out in the ice of Alaska might have been unknown, but the threat it posed had the potential to eradicate all life on Earth. That was all Jace knew about the enemy they would be facing and all he needed to know at this point.

The Nine found transportation in a town at the edge of the Thar Desert: a bus that would normally ferry tourists back and forth to the archaeological site at Mohenjo-daro. Another member of the Nine, a female named Xan, was an expert in managing all means of travel and propulsion. She climbed behind the wheel while Jace and the others took their seats. Their destination was the Mohenjo Daro Airport, where Chronar had located a Dassault Falcon 7X capable of accommodating the seven of them who'd be heading straight to Alaska and could manage a range of six thousand nautical miles without refueling, slightly more than the distance to the airport in Juneau, Alaska. The flight, accounting for all known variables, would take a full Earth day, approximately twenty-four of this world's hours at the jet's top speed. But if there was a way to coax more speed from the Falcon's engines, Xan would find it.

The keys to the blue tour bus were missing, but that proved only a minor impediment for Yusef, the Nine's expert on Earth's electronics, and resulted in only a slight delay before they were headed to the airport. Once there, Izumi and Brenn, the Nine's weapons specialists, would board a different jet headed instead to New South Wales, Australia, to retrieve the Nine's primary weapons, stored at the same time as their arrival on Earth within the Jenolan Caves, the oldest cave system in the world dating back 340 million years. Though inconvenient, this had been deemed a necessary precaution to guard against the potential of a catastrophic discharge of energy, in the event it grew unstable, over the untold number of years the Nine would be in stasis. They would rejoin the others in Alaska after a regrettable but necessary delay, during which Jace and the others would assess and evaluate the enemy they were facing.

Jace embraced the first signs he had ever glimpsed of civilization as it had developed on the planet it was the Nine's mission to protect. While they were in stasis, Chronar fed them data that covered the passage of time so they would have a historical perspective to weigh against the current context of their awakening, so the world they'd be entering would make sense to them. However, all those reams of data could not compare to the actual sights, sounds, and smells. Pictures and information, as accurate as they might be, could not conjure the presence of emotion and purpose.

Jace felt Xan grind the bus to a sudden halt that jolted him forward into the next seat. A young dark-haired Pakistani boy had rushed in front of the bus to chase down a wayward soccer ball spilled into the street from a makeshift game in a nearby lot overgrown with weeds. Jace's gaze fastened on the boy, feeling that familiar, unsettling tug whenever he searched his mind for missing memories. The boy retrieved the ball and looked toward the bus, waving. Suddenly though, he had longer lighter hair and was wearing a form-fitting suit that looked like a uniform.

I know this boy....

As soon as Jace formed that thought, the boy dashed back across the street to his game, dark hair lifted by the wind and clothed once more in shorts and a T-shirt. Jace followed him the whole way, fighting the tug inside his mind.

He heard horns honking, the bus still stalled in the street.

"Xan?" Jace raised, approaching her. "You can drive on."

"The animals," she muttered.

"What?"

"They were blocking the road. What happened to them?"

A stray goat had wandered across the road while the boy retrieved his soccer ball. Was that what Xan meant?

"The scar on the back of your hand," Jace said, watching her trace a finger along its x-shaped contours, "how did you get it?"

"It's not a scar," Xan told him, "it's a birthmark." She canted her gaze toward him. "How could I know that?"

"The road's clear," Jace told her, knowing she was feeling the same uneasy tug he was. "You can drive on."

She started the bus on again slowly, still fingering her birthmark that looked like an X. "It's why I'm named Xan, but I don't understand how I could I know that either."

Jace turned his gaze back out the window in time to see the boy slam the ball with a perfect kick into a goal drawn in chalk on the side of a building.

"Jeet gaye! Jeet gaye!" the boy exclaimed, hands thrust in celebratory fashion into the air as the other boys playfully mobbed him.

Before the bus passed out of sight, Jace counted them.

There were nine in all, something he took for a good omen.

"Thirteen minutes to the airport," Xan reported, shaking herself alert again. "We'll be airborne in thirty-three. Twenty-three hours fourteen minutes to reach our destination from there."

That long, Jace thought, before a war Earth didn't know was about to be fought began.

CHAPTER 10

Survivors

Chichagof Springs, Alaska

"*Dennehy!*" As she advanced into the snow-swept wind, Sakari Muhtuk could almost feel her cry blown back against her. *"Dennehy!"*

Her mind conjured the sight of a monster doing to him what it had done to the three clumps of flesh they'd found back up the street, and she imagined herself about to encounter it. Then she spotted a wizened, winged creature looming over the younger trooper, its taloned foot planted over the barrel of his AR-15.

Muhtuk steadied her shotgun with a pair of shaky hands, gloved finger feeling for the trigger when the creature looked at her and shook its cloaked head, beneath which strands of silvery thin branches scratched at the air.

"About the hell time you cops got here," a raspy female voice called out into the storm. "My fucking tax dollars at work."

* * *

"Name's Jane Piedmont," she said to the troopers once the three of them and Daniel Riggs were settled in the warmth of the local bar and grill that was deserted like the rest of the town.

"Piedmont," Muhtuk repeated. "Like this street."

"Because it's named for me, Trooper—well, my husband, on account of him keeping this town alive whatever it took. He had more money than God and left it all to me. Figured the least I could do was keep things going, and I was managing that just fine until last night."

"So you were in town last night," Dennehy said to her, "like everybody else?"

"Where else would I be, Trooper? I no longer know what the world beyond the Springs looks like. I'm older than old. That's me, the oldest person you'll find in town—well, right now, the only person you'll find in town. And if you wanna know what I saw, I didn't see anything. And if you wanna know why I'm still alive, you're asking the wrong person."

Muhtuk had packed wood into a stove that chewed at it with crackling, teeth-like flames, reflecting on how she'd come this close to shooting Chichagof Springs's oldest resident, who lived in the town's biggest home set against a sloping hillside. What she'd taken for wings were the sides of the old woman's saggy nightgown and thick bathrobe splayed to the sides by the wind. The talons were actually some kind of work boots she'd slipped into to emerge from her home after spotting the flashing lights. As for the branches, well, those were storm-matted bands of her silver-gray hair.

"You okay, kid?" the old woman asked Dennehy, who was already adding more wood to the stove.

"Just fine, ma'am."

Jane Piedmont moved her gaze toward Muhtuk. "Lucky for me, the kid slipped on the ice and went down before he could shoot me dead. Man, I must've have been a sight with his sore ass in the snow looking up at me, my foot clamped down on his rifle before he could find the trigger again."

Dennehy worked the wood around and then rejoined them at a table, with Muhtuk's chair positioned so she could watch Daniel Riggs, who was camped out near the woodstove. Riggs rocked back and forth, watching the black steel brighten from the heat bubbling within.

The old woman tilted her gaze toward him. "Who the fuck is he?"

"Amazon driver."

"That thing you wanted? It's right. In. Here," he said, reciting the motto printed on the side of his delivery van.

"Mr. Riggs showed up to make a delivery this morning. We found him out on the ice in shock." Muhtuk let that sink in for a moment. "What happened here, Ms. Piedmont?"

"It's *Mrs.* Piedmont, Trooper. My husband's dead more than a decade but I'm still a missus and always will be." Her eyes settled on the bar. "Hold on a sec."

Jane Piedmont lifted her crackling, creaky frame from the chair. As she brushed past Muhtuk, the trooper caught a spoiled odor rising off her she couldn't identify. The old woman shuffled to the bar, grabbing a bottle of Barrell bourbon and a single glass.

She sat back down at the table and filled her glass. "Didn't bother bringing you glasses since I know you troopers don't drink on duty. But they're behind the bar if I got that wrong." She took a hefty gulp. "And you already know what happened here, as plain as I do. Everybody else got themselves killed, as far as I know. I checked a few houses and saw bodies flat as pancakes. The first one was Bert Jones. Poor bastard has been trying to lose weight for as long as I've known him but to no avail. Well, guess he finally found a diet that worked."

"You found Bert Jones in his house?" Muhtuk asked her.

"I did indeed, and before you go thinking those kind of thoughts about us, he worked for my husband and I kept him on after a stroke put my dearly departed in the grave. Bert's a contractor—well, he used to be, anyway. I put him in charge of keeping the buildings from caving in—at least, I did."

"How close does he live to you?"

"Next house just down the hill."

Muhtuk weighed the implications of that. Whatever had killed those three people outside, now covered again by snow that had already reached the top of the evidence flags the troopers had planted, had also invaded houses to kill Bert Jones—and everyone else for that matter. That suggested the attack, or whatever it had been, had occurred last night when all but the three remains they'd found had been asleep in their beds.

"How long have there been lady troopers?" the old woman asked her.

"A while now."

Jane Piedmont chuckled. "First for me. Then again, I haven't been out of the Springs since my husband died, given moving around hurts like hell. Time tends to stand still here. And the life you can pretend to build behind a computer is amazing. I made my way into politics, supporting candidates all over the country, from members of Congress to presidents, to burn off some of that money. I tell you, you should see the names that come up in my caller ID. My husband never gave a shit about such things, so I suspect he rolls over in his grave every time I write a check. But, tell you the truth, I might have considered signing up if the troopers had uniforms made for women back in my day, and the hell with everything else."

"And you would have made a damn good one, Mrs. Piedmont."

She sat back in her chair, sipping the top-shelf Barrell bourbon instead of gulping it. "The answer is I don't know for sure when it happened because I passed out drunk around the same time I always do."

"What time would that be?" Dennehy asked, and for the first time, Muhtuk noticed the kid was taking notes on his memo pad with a department-issued pen.

"Don't know exactly. Around midnight maybe."

"And what was your last contact before that, ma'am?" Muhtuk asked her.

The old woman's eyes widened in realization. "Hold on a sec, you just jogged my memory. My husband and I never had kids, but I've got a niece in Los Angeles who likes to check in to see if I'm dead so she can go after my inheritance. She called last night at eleven o'clock, probably hoping to shock me awake and do me in that way. The call didn't last long, and right after, I rang Dave right here. He was closing up for the night but said he'd leave a bottle of this Barrell bourbon in my milk box on the front porch," Piedmont said, grasping the neck of the bottle before her. "I woke up, and it wasn't there. Neither was my newspaper, a day late this far into the middle of nowhere, but who gives a shit since the news is always so bad? The only thing there was an Amazon package."

"What time would that have been?"

"Oh, I don't know. Say, around eight o'clock."

Muhtuk glanced over at Dennehy doing his scribbling and did some figuring in her head. Whatever happened here had started sometime after eleven o'clock the night before. Then Daniel Riggs left Jane Piedmont's Amazon package on her porch sometime before eight in the morning. He must have come in from the west and started his deliveries at her big house at the base of the hill. At some point, he came upon the scene on Piedmont Street, a comparable one at another of the homes on his route, or both.

"Would you happen to know, Mrs. Piedmont," she resumed, "if Dave owned a Winchester rifle?"

"He sure did on account of I gave it to him. It was my late husband's, and he didn't have much use for it anymore. I gave it to Dave 'cause he was a cop for a while and fancied himself the unofficial law and order of the Springs. If there was any problem or dispute, Dave made sure it got handled right. Tough bastard, for sure. Whatever it was put him down, he didn't go without a fight, you can rest assured of that."

Muhtuk exchanged a glance with Dennehy, both thinking the same thing. Dave's remains must have been among the three they'd found on the main drag beyond. That meant the town's unofficial lawman had never made it home. He must have heard or seen something while closing up that led him to grab his rifle before going outside. Under that scenario, it was likely the other two victims had emerged from his establishment first. He must have rushed to their aid with his Winchester when they fell under attack. That tightened the timeline even further, right up to the point where they found Daniel Riggs in his idling van just before eleven o'clock this morning. That meant the fifty or so residents of the Springs, as Jane Piedmont called the town, had fallen under attack around eleven the night before, and it must have been over before 8 a.m. when the old woman retrieved her Amazon package from the porch. Until a broad canvass of the homes stacked along the perimeter was conducted, Muhtuk couldn't be sure everyone else was dead, though it seemed a pretty safe bet that was the case. And no such canvass could be performed until backup arrived once the storm abated. Until then, it was just her and Dennehy, and they might as well hold down the fort from right here.

"Saw you wrinkle your nose when I slid past you," Piedmont said to her suddenly. "What you smelled is the disease that's killing me, only God is taking His own sweet time."

"Looks like He spared you last night from where I'm sitting, ma'am," Muhtuk noted. "Lone survivor, as it goes."

She toasted the troopers. "Yeah, lucky me. I get to live long enough to plan a whole bunch of funerals. I paid to rehab the local cemetery, but who's going to dig all those graves in the frozen ground?"

As Mrs. Piedmont gulped the rest of her drink and refilled her glass, Muhtuk heard a sudden, scratchy, high-pitched sound coming from somewhere inside the bar.

"You hear that?" she asked Dennehy, rising from her chair.

He listened momentarily, squinting as if that would help him hear. "Sure do. Know it all too well from home. That's the sound of a baby crying."

CHAPTER 11

Cells

Mendenhall Glacier, Alaska

The breach in the seamless ceiling looked virtually the same size as the breach in the hull, measuring twelve feet at its longest point and nearly ten at its widest. Twenty-eight feet separated the team from it, an impossible height to scale.

Unless they didn't have to....

"Can you hear me, General?" Jules said into her helmet's built-in microphone.

"Loud and clear."

She made sure she was looking up toward the breach in the ceiling. "Are you seeing this?"

"I am. Drones must have missed it."

"We almost did too. It looks to be of the same dimensions as the hull breach. That might be where whatever got off this ship spent the last hundred and fifty thousand years or so."

"We need eyes on it. Given that there's nothing to secure a rope to, we'll use a drone."

"Drones have already missed too much. We need to rely on our own eyes."

"You plan on jumping thirty feet, Professor?"

"No, General. That's where the drones that got us here come in."

* * *

The special operations soldiers lugged all five of the drones inside the ship, placing them directly beneath the breach in the ceiling. To save time and be more maneuverable, the team would forgo the harnesses required for both the initial descent and rise back to the surface in favor of handholds for the twenty-eight-foot climb through the jagged breach in the ceiling. Inside another of the operational trailers above, it fell on the drone operators to raise them into position so each team member could position themselves correctly and grab hold to be lifted upward.

On Timur's orders, one of the soldiers went first, and the others were waiting for his all-clear signal to follow him through the breach. Once it was given, Major Smith went next, followed by Jules and the two remaining special ops personnel. She had never seen the kind of assault rifles they were carrying and could only hope they wouldn't need them.

* * *

In the command center, Kai watched the team's reconnaissance of the second level on the monitor featuring Jules's point of view. Since the drones had not explored this area of the ship, he had no idea what to expect.

"Confirming this breach's specifications and contours to be identical to the breath in the hull," he reported.

"Roger that," Jules acknowledged.

Kai could see she had fallen back to let two of the soldiers lead the way, with the final one bringing up the rear. All three, he saw, had their weapons steadied and ready to fire.

"Those weapons they're carrying," he said to General Timur.

"The M7, a replacement for the M4 as part of the Army's NGSW program," Timur explained. "Next-Generation Squad Weapon. It fires a bigger bullet, a six point eight–millimeter shell, designed to penetrate body armor and armor in general with the load they're packing. Forty cartridges in the mag instead of thirty."

Kai nodded. He wished that made him feel better about Jules exploring this unknown level of the ship, but it didn't. On screen, the team continued its sweep, their lights cutting through a measure of the dark cavernous space. Kai studied the monitor dedicated to Jules, seeing everything she saw an instant later thanks to AI enhancing the feed. That allowed him to spot something odd in a spray of light coming from Jules's helmet beam.

"Hold up," he said into his headset. "What's that, straight ahead?"

"Looks like a doorway. Normal opening, not breached."

She shined her light ahead, joining those of the two soldiers she'd drawn even with. More open doorways were revealed. Kai couldn't be sure how many, but the lights had passed ten, maybe as many as twelve of what looked like chambers of some kind.

Whatever had been inside them had gotten off this ship, first through the breach in the floor on this level and then the breach they had somehow torn in the hull below. In all probability, the effects of the massive ice collapse that had revealed the ship's presence had stirred whatever had resided in those chambers and awakened them from some form of suspended animation after all those centuries buried beneath the glacier.

Jules and the others moved closer to the open doors, continuing to sweep their handheld lights, giving Kai a better view of the chambers themselves.

Wait, they weren't chambers at all, Kai realized, they were—

His thinking froze when Jules's flashlight caught a change in the refraction off the obsidian floor.

"Jules, everyone, stop!" he called into his headset. "Shine your lights downward. Follow Jules's beam."

Once they obliged, creating a crisscrossing assemblage of beams, hunks of twisted and torn metal, black like everything else aboard the ship, appeared in what looked like molten clumps.

"What the hell is all this?" Major Smith managed.

"Looks like whatever left those pods did some damage on the way out," the lead special ops soldier said.

They're not pods at all, Kai almost said, but he didn't want to distract Jules's team from their work.

Instead, he covered his mic and looked toward Timur. "Pull them out, General! Now!"

Before Timur could respond, they both heard a metallic clanking, slight at first but rapidly picking up to a steady crackle in Kai's headset.

Flashlight and helmet beams rotated over the mass of twisted metal to reveal motion. The fragments of whatever had been torn apart somehow clung to life and were now reactivated, likely by a proximity sensor built into their circuitry. The mangled remnants began to move as one, with one mind. Kai could glean what looked like extremities, but nothing like human ones.

"Holy shit!" the lead special operator cried out.

Then the shooting started.

CHAPTER 12

Sentinels

Mendenhall Glacier, Alaska

Jules felt the lead soldier shove her behind him as he opened up with his rifle. She'd never heard a sound like the one it made, spraying on full auto, muzzle flashes bursting from its bore to capture the scene in eerie, staccato motion. She felt the barrage inside her head, turning the throb into a rhythmic pounding that felt like her brain was ping-ponging back and forth against her skull. Her balance wavered, a queasiness seizing her with the first wave of the familiar pangs of nausea. She felt her knees start to buckle and steadied herself just in time.

The torn black remains of these machine sentinels, or whatever they were, intensified their attack, pieces of them seeming to converge. Some were no taller than a foot, others stretching up as high as her waist. It occurred to the astrobiologist in Jules that she might be looking at some of the ship's inhabitants—a race of advanced robots instead of fully living organisms.

Before she could consider the ramifications of that further, a creature leaped up with what looked like iron, spiky teeth going for her throat. One of the soldiers blew it out of the air before turning his attention to another grouping of the things speeding across the dark dull floor like angry drunken spiders.

"Pull back!" she heard the lead soldier scream in her headset. "Pull back! General, get the drones up!"

Jules had been so entrenched with her study of the unexplored level that she had no concept of how far they had strayed from the breach in the ceiling. She and Smith clustered tight against each other. The soldiers formed a human shield before them, desperately trying to keep up with the relentless onslaught launched by fragments of what must have been genuinely terrifying metallic monsters when whole. Jules saw one of the soldiers stop to reload, only to be set upon by the robotic shards in a flurry so fast he never even got the magazine jammed home. They engulfed him and took him to the floor, leaving only two soldiers to fend off the attack, as his awful screams and shrieks inside her helmet made Jules cringe.

Suddenly, she recognized the surroundings revealed by the sweep of her helmet beam. They were close to the breach and sure enough, she could hear the drones powering up not more than fifteen feet behind her.

A torso-size machine remnant leaped up and somehow held fast to another soldier's rifle at the bore. He opened fire on full auto, but the gun jammed. The soldier shed it from his grasp and yanked his sidearm free in its place an instant before another wave of the mismatched things was upon him.

"Go! Now!"

She recognized the lead soldier's voice as he jammed a fresh magazine home and aimed his next barrage at the newly converging husks of churning metal. A black horde rattling, humming, and moving in a single deadly mass. She and Smith swung toward the waiting drones together and, a lunge later, reached up to take the handholds. Their gloves wrapped tightly around the rubber just as the horde swallowed the lead soldier, taking his shape briefly before he crumpled under their collective weight.

Jules had never wanted to live more than she did at that moment. She thought she had lost her fear of death, at least gotten used to the notion, but faced with it down here left her fighting back against it with everything she had.

Not here, not this way....

By then, the drones Jules and Smith clung to had risen, sliding over the breach and lowering them through it. She let herself think they were safe when pieces of the robotic sentinels dropped after them. Some bounced off the drones, while others tried to wrap makeshift appendages around the steel frames to hitch a ride. Enough piled on top to strip the drones of their maneuverability.

Jules watched Smith spin in the air and then tilt sideways before his drone crashed to the floor. Almost instantly, a blanket of dark liquidy metal converged upon him from everywhere, and he disappeared completely. His screams rang in her ears. She heard the faceplate of his helmet crack, followed by a horrible wheezing sound, and then nothing.

Jules's drone had managed to stay aloft, but just barely, speeding toward the hull breach a foot off the ship's dull obsidian floor. The sentinel remnants attached to the frame snapped and clawed at her with whatever was left of them, and she could offer no defense with both hands clutching the rubber holds. Then they were attacking her gloves, the thick material shredded down to the bare skin before she felt something like a dog bite to the back of her hand. The burst of pain made her reflexively let go ten feet short of the breach. She was still in motion when she landed, rolling across the floor fast enough to keep the scuttling metallic things off her.

The murky light beyond was welcome and reassuring after her desperate trek through the darkness. She pushed herself on, scrambling and pulling with her hands toward the ice upon which the alien craft rested. She felt the things closing on her boots, yanking as if to draw her back inside, away from the light.

The light! She had to reach the light!

That realization recharged her and gave her hope. She pictured Kai and Charlie as she kicked at the things snapping and clawing at her legs. Her torso crested over the sill of the jagged breach, and her legs fought for every inch they could manage. Suddenly, she felt her hands scraping against the ice, trying to find purchase on anything she could close her fingers around when she was tugged violently backward into the ship.

Jules continued to kick and twist, spotting a trio of soldiers land on matching drones one after another atop the ice. They steadied their M7s and moved to take hold of her instead. It took all three to fight back against the black, mangled, twisted mass's concerted effort to drag Jules back onto the ship, but the soldiers managed to yank her free of the breach with one final unified tug.

One soldier pulled Jules further away across the slick ice while the other two poured bullets toward the deadly assemblage that had piled up in the breach. It was as if these disembodied machine fragments couldn't venture beyond the ship to fight back, Jules thought, watching the powerful 6.8mm bullets tearing them further apart to a sound like screeching that made her ears ring.

"Kai," she said, remembering her helmet mic, "can you hear me?"

* * *

"Loud and clear, Jules," Kai replied, his trembling starting to still. "Thank God you're okay."

"God and General Timur for sending reinforcements."

Kai felt Charlie tugging at him, forgetting that if it hadn't been for her earbuds and being enraptured in her video game, his eleven-year-old daughter might have witnessed everything that had just transpired. He looked down and saw the concern stretched across his daughter's face.

"Is Mom okay?"

Kai stroked Charlie's hair. "She's fine, Char," he said, using his pet nickname for her, pronounced like her real name, Charlotte. "On her way back right now."

"Thank you, General," said Jules over the radio built into her helmet.

"I only wish it hadn't been necessary, ma'am," Timur said from a few feet away. "The fault's mine for putting you and the others in danger. We lost four good men in there."

"Don't blame yourself," Kai told the general, drawing even with Charlie still pressed against him. "You couldn't have known."

"Known what, Professor?"

"I don't think those chambers Jules's team found were chambers at all," Kai said, knowing Jules could hear him too. "They were jail cells."

CHAPTER 13

Road Trip

Chichagof Springs, Alaska

"Only one infant in this whole town," Jane Piedmont told the troopers as they swept about the bar and grill called Dave's Place, trying to find the source of the sound. "We got four older kids who get bused to local schools. Guess I should say *got* now instead. Anyway, the family with the baby is the Bunkers. The father, Jim, makes me look like a social drinker."

Muhtuk focused on the baby crying, unsure whether she was getting closer to it or further away.

Suddenly, Dennehy crouched down and stretched his hand under one of the tables.

"Got it!"

He stood back up with an iPhone wrapped in an industrial-strength case. Sure enough, the crying got instantly louder.

Dennehy studied the screen. "This Jim Bunker must have a baby monitor app installed on his phone."

"Sure," nodded Jane Piedmont, "so he can make believe he's there while his wife does all the work."

"Where do the Bunkers live, Mrs. Piedmont?" Muhtuk asked her.

The old woman pointed to the northeast beyond the row of buildings Dave's Place was a part of. "That way. On the flat ground diagonally down from me."

"How far, ma'am?"

"A couple hundred feet, give or take, from Dave's back door."

Might as well have been a mile in these conditions, Muhtuk thought. When she looked toward Dennehy, he was already moving toward his AR-15.

"We better get going."

"No," Muhtuk said to the young trooper, "we can't risk both of us. I'm going for the baby while you stay here and guard the fort."

"With all due respect, I think I'm better cut out for this."

"Because you're a man?"

"Because I'm army. And a dad. Think about it."

Piedmont stepped in between them. "You just made yourself a case to do as the lady trooper here says, soldier boy. 'Cause if we don't come back, whatever gets us will and you got a better chance of making it regret that."

"We?" posed Muhtuk. "Us?"

"That's right, Annie Oakley. I pointed you toward the Bunkers' place, but you'll never be able to find it on your own out there in this muck, since all the houses look the same. You need me with you, leading the way."

Muhtuk hoisted her shotgun. "Okay," she said, "but not until we get you something warmer to wear. And I'll lead the way, Mrs. Piedmont."

* * *

Something warmer came courtesy of the combination storeroom and office in the rear of Dave's Place. A thick, padded jacket with an insulated hood and fur-lined collar hung from a hook.

"It's Dave's," Jane Piedmont noted, stopping short of donning the coat. "I'd recognize it anywhere." She started to slip it on. "Even smells like the old bastard."

The coat swam over Piedmont's thin bony frame. Muhtuk saw she was severely misshapen, as if her skeleton was pushing through her skin.

"Guess he didn't bother wearing it to have a go at whatever was out there." Piedmont lumbered for a door with a painted emergency exit sign hanging over it. "Right this way, Trooper."

Muhtuk looked toward Tom Dennehy before following her. "You good?"

"Good enough, boss."

She tried for a smile that didn't come, then just nodded. Leaving the warmth of Dave's Place for the storm felt like running into a wall, the wind slamming into them.

"You're Native, right?" Piedmont asked her, loud enough over the wind to be heard.

"Since birth, ma'am."

"I know your people got plenty of superstitions about this land. Any of them you can think of to explain what happened in my town?"

"A monster from myth or folklore didn't do this, Mrs. Piedmont."

"No? Then what kind of monster was it?"

It was a question Muhtuk hadn't had time to consider. Something that could break a Winchester in half and suck the bones out of its victims wasn't a thought she wanted to ponder further at this point. She kept her focus trained on finding the baby, a second survivor, well aware that whatever may have killed everyone else in the Springs might still be lurking about somewhere.

They came to the first house in a row of neatly arranged, small homes. At first, Muhtuk thought the front door was open, but then she realized it was gone.

"That handyman you found...was his door missing?"

"No, just busted open, hanging off its hinges." Jane Piedmont extended a finger forward, just the tip visible through the long sleeve of Dave's coat. "Straight this way, another hundred feet or so. Split-level house with a big welcome sign painted on the front door."

"Only if it's still there, Mrs. Piedmont," Muhtuk said, the shotgun feeling heavy in her gloved hands.

"Your people are trackers, right?" the old woman asked.

"Some of us."

"You find any tracks out there where you found what was left of the bodies?"

"If there were any, the storm buried them."

"So you looked."

Muhtuk nodded, not bothering to tell the old woman she was almost grateful for not having to conjure in her mind whatever had ravaged the Springs based on prints it left in the snow.

"We must be getting close," Piedmont said, stopping before an object lying across the narrow street that accessed these homes.

Muhtuk kicked enough of the snow from it with her boot to reveal a blue door and the letters W-E-L stenciled in red.

The old woman pointed to the right. “Next house down. Hear that? Baby’s still crying up a storm.”

Muhtuk willed herself to be calm, wondering again what might have become of whatever had set upon the Springs last night. Was it lying in wait, watching them even now? Would her shotgun have better luck against it than Dave’s Winchester?

“Coming?” Jane Piedmont asked her.

CHAPTER 14

Prisoners

Mendenhall Glacier, Alaska

As soon as Jules entered General Timur's command trailer, Kai threw himself on her, hugging his wife the tightest he ever had.

"Are you okay? Tell me you're okay."

He could see her eyes narrow, the way they did when the pain she struggled to keep down was at its worst.

"I'm okay," he heard her say softly. "I'm fine."

By then, Charlie had joined them, arms wrapped around both her parents, tall enough now to stretch past their chests.

When had she grown so much?

The answer eluded Kai, and then the question slipped from his mind as he clung to his wife and child.

"I'm here," Jules uttered louder before continuing, "it's over."

But Kai knew it wasn't over at all. It was just beginning, thanks to the prisoners that had fled the confines that had contained them for hundreds of thousands of years.

* * *

"Prisoners," Jules repeated after Kai had summed up the substance of his conclusions for her.

Charlie sat at an empty workstation nearby, only pretending to play her game. Kai knew his daughter was listening to everything now, her young mind finally processing the uncertainty and danger they were facing.

"That would make those things that attacked us their, what, *jailers*?" Jules continued.

Kai nodded as General Timur ended a call on a satellite phone so he could listen without distraction. "When they were whole, yes," he confirmed. "Your presence set off what's left of their motion sensors. Their circuity and memory banks must still be functioning. They attacked because that's the job they were programmed to do."

"Even torn apart like that?"

"Suggests they don't act as individual units, but as one, a central processor controlling all of their actions."

"Meaning they failed at their primary task and couldn't stop whatever got out of those cells."

Kai nodded. "I think a closer inspection of those chambers would reveal the inhabitants were kept in some kind of hibernation or suspended animation. The collapse and cave-in caused the chambers to malfunction and open. The robot sentries tried to do their job and follow their directive, but were clearly no match for whatever emerged."

"A fine working theory, Professor," interjected General Timur, "suggesting that ship was the equivalent of a nineteenth-century prison hulk."

"Prison hulks?" Kai raised.

"I see your expertise in astrobiology doesn't extend to world history," Timur resumed. "In colonial times," the general continued, "English prisons were overflowing with inmates. Back then, pretty much anything besides breathing was a crime, and the government needed to figure out what to do with all the excess prisoners they had no place to house. Initially, they were shipped across the Atlantic to serve as laborers on cotton plantations in the South and factories in the north. That practice, of course, ended with the American Revolution, so 1776 also marked the passage of a new act of Parliament to allow floating prisons to relieve the inmate problem. Instead of being packed into jails, they were herded onto ships that took the name prison hulks."

Kai listened, intrigued and captivated by the connection Timur was making. "You're saying that ship in the ice is an alien version of a prison hulk, sent out into space instead of sailing the sea?"

"Pretty much the same thing in a relative sense, isn't it? And it makes perfect sense, given the conclusions you've reached in the past few minutes."

"Twelve open cells," Jules noted, "one for each of the prisoners on that ship."

Kai added it all up in his mind. "So our working theory is that these twelve *prisoners* were sent off into space on a fully automated ship, guarded by the robot sentinels Jules found torn apart. That means those sentinels were completely overwhelmed once the occupants of those cells got out."

"So where did they go once they tore that breach in the hull and escaped?" Jules raised.

"I can tell you," Timur responded, "that we have scoured the ice and snow in every direction for tracks, heat signatures, dead animals—anything that might give us some indication of where whatever escaped that ship went after exiting, and we've found nothing. It's almost like those twelve prisoners stepped through that breach in the hull and disappeared."

Before Jules or Kai could respond, a soldier burst into the command trailer and exchanged quiet words with General Timur. Kai watched the general's expression tighten, his eyes growing uncertain, even fearful, for the first time.

"Correction, Professors," he said. "According to a report that just came in, whatever got off that ship didn't disappear at all. And I believe we know where our guests went from here."

CHAPTER 15

En Route

Airborne Aboard the Falcon

Jace joined Xan in the cockpit, still concerned over the animals she'd seen in the Mohenjo-daro street that weren't there. The autopilot had been engaged and she was fiddling with the ship's onboard computer system.

"Chronar's helping me trim hours off our flight," she reported without regarding him. "I've reprogrammed the course heading to increase lift and reduce drag and have increased this craft's expulsion of gases to increase thrust, cutting our time in the air in half."

"Won't that burn more fuel?"

"No, because of the decreased drag."

"Back in Mohenjo-daro," Jace started.

"You're wondering about the animals." She cocked her gaze toward them. "They were there…and then they weren't."

"Like the boy."

"The one who ran out before us?"

Jace nodded. "He seemed to change right in front of me. Then he changed back."

"So it wasn't just me. I saw more than just the animals, Jace. I saw some kind of farm, a man working the land. He looked at me and I saw an x on the back of his hand too."

"A birthmark, then, just like you said."

"But how could I know that too? And who was the man? My father, grandfather?"

Jace shrugged. "I don't know."

"What's happening, Jace?"

"I'm not sure," he told her, not bothering to mention the nagging sense of unease he continued to feel tugging at him. "I just wanted you to know I experienced it too. Keep me informed of our progress in the air."

"Will do."

When Jace was seated again, Chronar provided an update based on its analysis of the intercepted footage from the team that entered the alien ship. It had managed to provide a visual representation of the sentinels charged with guarding the life forms being transported on that ship from the remnants captured on the video feed. In his mind, Jace saw an almost reptilian-looking droid standing nine or so feet tall with nine appendages. Its multiple mechanical arms and legs were indistinguishable, except the legs were longer and thicker—three of them, which made for a secure base. He wondered how much that appearance might mirror that of the escaped creatures.

Jace knew reaching Alaska before the team heading to the Jenolan Cave system in New South Wales returned meant they'd have to confront the enemy without their primary weapons. But he didn't dare delay any longer than was necessary, which meant potentially taking on the enemy with only the individual handheld weapons each of them had mastered fifteen hundred years ago.

He was heading back down the aisle in the cabin when he noticed Zareb's gaze locked on Mazz, seeming to focus on the scar-like crease that ran along the center of his bald skull. Jace stopped even with his seat.

"I thought it was a scar," Zareb muttered, looking up at Jace through one brown eye and one blue one. "I was wondering how he got it when I had this vision of some kind of electromagnetic restraining helmet fastened to my head with a sharp ridge across its center. The pain was awful, more than I could bear. But then the vision passed and I thought it must have been a waking dream or something. Then I reached under my hair."

Zareb peeled back his thick black hair, only slightly darker than his coffee-colored skin, to reveal a crease identical to Mazz's riding his scalp. He was a Tal'nera, which in English roughly translated as "dark-skinned folk of the ground," because he came from a tribe of fierce warriors who lived on lands distant from concentrated areas of population where they kept almost entirely to themselves. Throughout their planet's history, the Tal'nera had been greatly sought by all combatants in any conflict to join their sides, but they almost invariably retained their independence.

"Let me see your scalp."

Jace touched his ear. "Chronar has an update. This will have to wait."

But on the way back to his seat, he ran a hand into his thick black hair, feeling for his scalp. He felt a crease there, just like Mazz and Zareb. Such a restraining helmet would be used to totally disable a prisoner or criminal, sending waves of indescribable pulsing pain through them if they tried to move or break free.

A prisoner or criminal....

Jace was spared further consideration of what made no sense when Chronar showed him the strung-together footage of what had unfolded inside the ship within the context of its actual time frame, along with details about the lone survivor, a female astrobiologist named Jules, short for Julia. He noted that she remained calm and composed throughout all of the footage, her reasoning and rational thought continuing to process information in spite of the stress of what she was enduring. She was a scientist, not a soldier, but she had survived the ordeal due to her lack of panic and level of determination, which Jace found impressive. He also believed both Jules and her husband, whose name was Kai, might become valuable resources for the Nine. If they were to emerge successful in the battle to come, they would need humans like this to join forces with them.

Unfortunately, Chronar was unable to glean anything further about the alien species from the ship itself. The ship resembled no alien craft in its vast data bank, and there was no way to determine its planet of origin or how long it had traveled before crashing into the ice beneath what was now the Mendenhall Glacier between a hundred and fifty and two hundred thousand years ago.

Chronar was, however, able to collate all communiqués coming from the settlement, a town called Chichagof Springs, where, by all indications, the enemy had struck first. The settlement was located across the Juneau Icefield, twelve miles, or 19.3 kilometers, from the ship's location.

In one of the communications, a female enforcement officer had labeled what she had found as "Code Orange," which meant "a mass casualty event" had transpired in the settlement. That was enough to tell Jace that all, or virtually all, the residents of the settlement had been extinguished. Unfortunately, none of the communications detailed the means by which this had transpired. There was also apparently no further indication of the invaders' presence in the form of tracks or any biological trace residue. It was clear to him that their destination after escaping the alien craft was purposeful and not random since the settlement in question held the closest concentration of human beings.

He was about to ask Chronar to project the next location their enemy might strike so Xan could set a course straight for that location when Chronar's voice chimed in his mind.

"Jace, the retrieval team has come within scanning range of the weapons cache. I'm afraid they are reporting a problem...."

CHAPTER 16

Babysitters

Chichagof Springs, Alaska

Muhtuk saw the old woman had slid ahead of her, waiting on the front porch before the missing front door. The trooper mounted the steps fast, snow boots slipping in the deep ice-crusted snow that had accumulated since the door went missing. She led the way inside the house and felt waves of electric heat against her, musing humorlessly that the Bunkers no longer had to worry about next month's bill. Muhtuk could hear the baby's cries clearly, coming from the second floor, as soon she reached the staircase.

Snow blown in from the storm had coated the first three steps with a shiny sheen of ice, and she chose her steps cautiously as Jane Piedmont clutched the railing for dear life.

"Careful," Muhtuk warned when her boot slid across a patch of snow that had melted and hardened into ice.

Piedmont slipped anyway, and Muhtuk caught the old woman with her free hand before she fell.

"Thanks," she said. "Yesterday I didn't give a shit whether I woke up alive or not. Funny how all of a sudden I care again."

Muhtuk advanced up the stairs slowly, twelve-gauge poking at the air to lead the way, the baby's cries growing closer with each step. She could make out three doorways, one for each bedroom on the second floor. The cries were coming from the middle one, closest to what must have been the master, where the door being torn off must have awoken Jim Bunker's wife while he was still drinking up a storm at Dave's Place.

At the top of the stairs, Muhtuk saw what looked to be a shed pair of flannel pajamas that matched like a workout suit. Except the remains of the baby's mother were raised three or four inches. This was the first clear look she got at a victim's remains uncovered by snow, and she could see it happening in her mind, the way her grandmother used to describe it as a vision.

The breaking sound of the door being ripped off roused Mrs. Bunker from her slumber, her first thought that it must be her drunken husband making a racket as he entered....

She moved to the top of the stairs, prepared to curse him out as the cries of their newly awoken infant rang out....

And that's when whatever these things were pounced....

The vision ended there, and Muhtuk could not conjure anything else besides the fact that there was no blood, no visible wounds through Mrs. Bunker's sleepwear, and no tears in the fabric.

"We going to get the kid, Trooper?" Jane Piedmont wondered, drawing even with her.

"Boy or a girl?"

"Boy, because he screeches so goddamn much, as you heard for yourself. Girl babies are quieter."

Muhtuk nodded and mounted the last stair, careful to skirt what was left of Mrs. Bunker's body on the way. Inside the nursery dominated by walls painted with Disney characters, a crib sat beneath a bird mobile suspended from the ceiling. The mobile churned slowly, splashing shadows against Mickey, Goofy, and Pluto.

"You better pick him up. I never held a baby before in my life."

Muhtuk moved to the crib and eased the baby into her arms. She'd changed her sister's kids enough to know this one desperately needed a diaper change, so she swept her eyes about for diapers.

"What's his name, Mrs. Piedmont?"

"Damned if I know, Trooper."

She found the changing table in the corner, out of reach of the little light the window yielded and the shadows splayed by the mobile. Her insides seized up, thinking that this had all happened last night, in the dark.

Muhtuk checked her watch. It was five fifteen, an hour short of sunset.

"We need to go," she told the old woman after stuffing her pockets full of what she needed to tend to Baby Bunker.

When they reached the top of the stairs, Muhtuk reflexively covered the infant's eyes so he wouldn't see what was left of his mother. After descending them carefully with the baby in tow, she handed him to Jane Piedmont.

"I told ya, I never held one of these before."

"First time for everything, ma'am. And I need both hands free for my shotgun," the trooper said, trading the twelve gauge in the old woman's grasp for the infant.

"Who's more likely to slip and drop the kid?" Piedmont challenged.

Muhtuk nodded, conceding her point, and extended the shotgun back her way.

"Ever use one of these before?"

"Sure, on my first husband. Don't worry, he had it coming to him. No need to investigate further." She somehow managed a smile and took the shotgun from the trooper's grasp. "Just kidding. A little levity never hurts. And everybody who lives somewhere like the Springs knows their way around firearms. I've fondled more shotguns than men, Trooper."

Muhtuk grinned and tucked the infant under her heavy coat to shield him from the pounding winds and snow. She stopped even with the empty snowswept doorway and gazed up at the gray sky spilling blankets of snow through the air. She thought she gleaned the first signs of it darkening.

"Let's get back to Dave's Place, Mrs. Piedmont, quick as we can."

The wind was at their backs for the trek back to Dave's Place, which was still a trudge but not nearly as blinding or challenging. They retraced their path through the back door, the old woman immediately shedding Dave's snow-encrusted coat to rid herself of a garment last worn by a dead man. Muhtuk left hers on, reluctant to turn the baby over to Piedmont's frail hands riddled with bulging veins.

Tom Dennehy appeared with the AR-15 in hand, drawn by the sounds of their entry and looking relieved when he saw it was them. They returned to the main room, Sakari Muhtuk rocking the baby in her arms the whole time.

The baby had stopped crying and seemed to have fallen off to sleep, which didn't stop Muhtuk from handing him over to the younger trooper after Dennehy shouldered his assault rifle.

"Since you're the expert."

Dennehy frowned but didn't argue. He took the baby in his grasp like someone who'd done it a million times, allowing Muhtuk to finally shed her coat and flap the snow from it.

"Anything to report?" she asked him.

Dennehy glanced toward Daniel Riggs, who had edged a bit closer to the woodstove. "Nothing further from our guest over there. I've got a feeling we've gotten everything out of him we're going to get. What about the Bunker home?"

"Baby's an orphan, Trooper."

"Shit."

"By all accounts, everybody except Mrs. Piedmont and that baby was dead by the time Riggs showed up on his route."

Dennehy glanced out the window. "Less than an hour before we lose the light."

"We need to secure this place as best we can," Muhtuk said, leaving it there.

That's when she heard a roaring sound like thunder cutting through the storm. She'd heard enough "thunder snow" to know it was a very real weather phenomenon in these parts, but this roaring kept getting louder, enough to trump the wind blasts that hammered the building.

Then Muhtuk saw the blinding lights coming down Piedmont Street, an array of them attached to machines that looked like nothing from this world.

Part Three
CONTACT

"Everything is theoretically impossible, until it is done."

—Robert A. Heinlein

CHAPTER 17

Piedmont Street

Chichagof Springs, Alaska

Sakari Muhtuk's first thought, born of instinct, was to keep clear of the windows and hope their weapons could hold off whatever was coming. Then the sight pushing through the swirling snows beyond left her breathing easier.

Through gaps in the storm, Muhtuk saw a pair of Bombardier snowcats that had been a fixture in these parts for as long as she could remember. They ground to a halt in the snow just short of the logjam caused by the stalled vehicles and the PUV she had left parked there.

Her next thought was that this must be the backup she had requested, finally responding to the urgency of her calls to headquarters. Only the Alaska State Police didn't own any snowcats, and she doubted the department could have rounded up two of them in these conditions.

Then Muhtuk spotted a third vehicle positioned further back, centered between the two snowcats. It looked like a tank at first glance and something else entirely when a crack in the storm revealed a quad-axel, eight-tire monster of a vehicle. A long-barreled artillery-style weapon extended from a gun turret, poking into the storm, with 7.62mm miniguns mounted on either side of it upon what looked like fully articulated platforms that would allow the modern Gatling guns to fire in any direction.

So who had responded to her desperate pleas for assistance?

Tom Dennehy drew up alongside her. "Looks like the cavalry has arrived. How about we go pay our respects?"

Muhtuk pressed a hand against his chest when he started to move. "I'll go. You stay here and keep guarding the fort."

Dennehy looked down at the hand restraining him. "All due respect, boss, I speak the language of our guests."

"Maybe, but let's find out who our guests are first."

The baby had started crying again, held in Jane Piedmont's arms so tightly that Muhtuk thought the old woman's feeble arms might break.

"In the meantime, see if you can do something about Baby Bunker," Muhtuk told Dennehy. "You'll need these," she added, as she pulled the supplies she'd brought along from her coat pockets.

* * *

Muhtuk approached the civilian who'd just emerged from the snowcat while more than a dozen soldiers spilling out from all three vehicles took up flanking positions along Piedmont Street, wielding next generation M7 assault rifles.

"Trooper Sakari Muhtuk, Alaska State Police, sir," Muhtuk greeted, extending an outstretched glove with her voice raised above the screams of the wind whipping the snow about the street.

The man grasped her gloved hand. "Kai Bevins, Trooper Muhtuk. And it's Professor, not sir."

* * *

An hour earlier, back at the command post erected over the chasm containing the alien ship, Timur had reported what he just learned.

"Approximately five hours ago, two Alaska state troopers called in a mass casualty event from a town twelve miles due west of here."

Kai and Jules looked at each other, each having come to the obvious conclusion the source of that event had originated here, with whatever had gotten off the alien ship.

"Did they provide any more details about these casualties?" Jules wondered.

"They did not. We've been able to ascertain this town, Chichagof Springs, maintained a winter population of somewhere around fifty people, all but two of which are presumed dead, according to the latest reports."

Kai and Jules exchanged another glance.

"Any further details there?" Kai asked this time.

"That's a negative too. Following protocol, the Alaska State Police has been told not to respond further, that the matter is now under military jurisdiction."

"Protocol," Kai repeated.

"Which also requires officials at the department to button up all communications that came in since the troopers located a missing Amazon driver whose last known location was the town in question."

Which meant he got out alive, Kai thought, assembling a mental picture and timeline in his head.

"When was the driver found?" Jules asked before he had a chance to.

She still looked shaken to Kai but seemed reinvigorated by the report indicating where the inhabitants of the alien ship had gone from here. He knew she was thinking the same thing he was, that this was confirmation of what both of them anticipated, given what the former alien prisoners had done to the robotic jailers programmed to hold them in place. In contemplating the possibility of engaging with an alien species over his career, he had tried not to consider the possibility, even the likelihood, that such visitors would be hostile as this species clearly was.

"Approximately one hour before the troopers arrived in Chichagof Springs with him in tow," Timur answered. "He was found dazed and incoherent ten miles along the Juneau Icefield. We need to get a team out there to ascertain more about this mass casualty event."

"I'm up this time," Kai said, gazing at Jules and continuing before she had a chance to argue. "You've been through enough for one day."

Jules nodded, and Kai watched her force a smile. "Then, by all means, saddle up, cowboy."

* * *

"What are you people doing here, Professor?" Muhtuk asked the civilian.

"We're the backup you called for," Professor Kai Bevins told her.

Muhtuk noticed none of the soldiers' uniforms bore nametags. She had worked with the FBI's Hostage and Rescue Team once on a kidnapping rescue, which was more than enough for her to know a special operations team when she saw one. HRT personnel trained at Fort Bragg with the elite commandos of Delta Force, and she had a pretty good idea that's what these soldiers called home.

Muhtuk nodded, realizing whatever had happened in Chichagof Springs had caught the attention of some very important people in the military and government, a blessing for the firepower they had brought with them that exceeded the entire Alaska State Police force.

"You reported a mass casualty event," said Bevins. "We're here to help."

"Glad to hear it," she told him. "Where would you like to start?"

"With the casualties, Trooper."

CHAPTER 18

Examination

Chichagof Springs, Alaska

"You seeing this clearly?" Jules heard Kai say through her earpiece.

"Wipe the snow from your camera," she told him.

Jules watched him pat the body armor he wore inside his unzipped jacket to feel for the small optical device rigged in place. While he followed the state trooper from the snowcat to the first body, his camera jumpily picked up the special ops team in position along the street, M7s aimed into the storm on the chance whatever had done this was still out there.

Kai found the lens, and she watched him brush the snow from it with a gloved hand. Then he returned his attention to what looked like a lumberjack outfit laid out on the snowpack next to a yellow flag revealed when Kai brushed the snow aside to expose the first body. Except it didn't look like any remains Jules had ever encountered before.

"Do we have an ID on the victim?" Jules asked, not sure whether the remains belonged to a man or a woman.

The painful pounding in her head that had followed her from the ship and the chasm had not abated at all. It had only gotten worse, and none of her coping mechanisms against the pain were working this time. That left her longing for the relief promised by one of her pills that would dull the pain, except it would leave her mind foggy.

Kai looked toward a female Alaska State Trooper. “Any idea of this man’s identity?”

“We believe it’s Dave Kemp,” the trooper said loud enough to reach Kai’s microphone, which was also clasped to his ballistic vest. “Owner of the town’s lone eating and drinking establishment. Also, the owner of a Winchester rifle we found broken in two, but not before he got off a few shots. If you’d like to see it, I bagged it as evidence.”

On the monitor inside the command trailer, Kai’s sightline lowered back to the remains. Jules watched one of his gloved fingers press down on the plaid Mackinaw jacket where the man’s chest should have been. The slight pressure compressed it.

“The ribs are missing,” Kai reported, pressing the same gloved finger down against one of Dave Kemp’s arms and then one of his legs. “All the bones are missing, either liquefied or removed. Organs appear to be intact, but have collapsed and degraded.”

“Any signs of wounds or punctures in the clothing?” Jules asked him.

Kai continued pressing. “You’re seeing the same thing I am. There’s no indication of any penetration and no blood anywhere in evidence.” On the monitor, he looked up at the Alaska State Trooper again. “How many other bodies have you found?”

“Two others here on the street and one inside a nearby home.”

“You inspect any of the other homes, Trooper?”

“No, sir. We only moved to that one after learning a baby was still alive there.”

“One of the survivors?”

“One of two, sir. The other is the old woman who’s been keeping this town alive.” The trooper looked down, seeming to realize the irony of her words. “At least until last night.”

“We need to get those bodies back here so we can perform a more detailed examination,” Jules told Kai, aware one of the snowcats came outfitted with a rear bed to handle that chore.

“You ever come across anything even remotely like this, Professor?” General Timur asked her.

"I've been an astrobiologist for fifteen years, General, and I've never encountered anything alien. You might say I've been waiting for this day my entire career."

"You and me both, Professor," Timur said. "Looks like we got what we wanted."

That made Jules wonder exactly what his role in the Army might be and how he had come to be the officer in command of man's first encounter with an alien craft and now, species. She had worked with military personnel on many occasions, especially in her years at NASA's Ames Research Center, where she began her career. Still, she had never encountered anything approaching a rapid reaction force like Timur's in any of those experiences.

"Brush the snow from your camera again," Jules told Kai over her headset. "Now, let's have a look at the victim's face."

She saw it tilted to the side and watched Kai turn it face up—at least what was left of the face, which looked more like a mask waiting to be fitted into place. The pale, flat skin was crusted with ice, and the eyes bulged sightlessly from the collapsed sockets.

"I'm going to peel back the lips," Kai said, elaborating no further on what he was trying to discern.

Kai fumbled the process at first with his bulky gloves but finally managed to part both the upper and lower lips to reveal a complete set of upper and lower teeth. Jules knew he was thinking the same thing she was, the two of them arriving at their first major finding about what had transpired in Chichagof Springs.

"What's the significance of that, Professor?" Timur asked her.

"Teeth are composed of minerals while bones are made of living tissue. That tells us our visitors were specifically feeding on that living tissue."

"For sustenance?"

"It's too early to tell," Jules told him, returning her attention to Kai. "Did you bring a knife?"

She watched Kai's camera turn from the body.

"I need a knife here," he called out.

"Will this do?" the state trooper asked, her arm entering the frame long enough to extend an ornate blade etched with carvings and a wooden handle. "It's a tribal blade. Inuit warriors never go anywhere without it."

Kai took it in his gloved hand. On the monitor, Jules watched him fold the victim's shirt up to expose what looked like a molten lump of flesh, almost as if the skin had melted and then froze out of its original shape. He eased the blade's tip into the camera's field and worked it through the rigid, frozen surface into the softer skin below. Then he withdrew the blade and held the knife before the camera so Jules could see precisely what he was seeing.

On the monitor, she studied a purplish glob stuck to the tip that didn't look like blood at all.

"I didn't know blood can freeze," General Timur said.

"It can in certain conditions when the water in the blood forms ice crystals. But that's not what happened here," Jules told him, leaving it there.

"What did happen here?"

"Removal of the bone marrow eliminated production of red and white blood cells and platelets."

On the monitor, she watched Kai hand the trooper back her knife, knowing there was no further need for it.

"We'll get the bodies bagged, load up, and head back to you," Kai said. "That will give me a few minutes to speak with the survivor who can talk."

CHAPTER 19

Setback

Airborne Aboard the Falcon

The problem Izumi and Brenn reported upon reaching the Jenolan Cave system was that the containers holding their weapons were missing. Somehow then, impossibly, the weapons they needed to defeat an enemy threatening the destruction of humanity had been located and removed.

Mazz was the Nine's master strategist when it came to battle, from laying traps to setting up impregnable perimeter defenses. He was seated forward of Jace aboard the Falcon, pressed against the window and appearing to be in deep thought. When Jace reached his seat, he saw Mazz had shredded a number of small pillows and was using the stuffing to mold something with tape he must have found somewhere on the jet.

Mazz turned and looked up at him. "I'm making a doll. Why am I making a doll?"

Jace thought of the boy back in the Mohenjo-daro street and of Xan spotting nonexistent animals blocking their bus's path en route to the airport. "I don't know. A side effect of being in stasis for so long. It's not just you. I thought I saw…something back in Mohenjo-daro."

"What?"

"It doesn't matter."

"But you're not making dolls."

Jace managed a smile. "Not yet." He regarded the crease that ran across Mazz's baldpate. "Any notion of how you got that?"

He shook his head. "Not a clue. Do you remember anything about your life before we entered stasis?"

"Not a thing," Jace told him.

"Another side effect you think?"

"More likely the result of us being fed so much information while in stasis. Could be our minds had to make room for all of it, which means dumping memories rendered irrelevant by the passage of so much time."

Mazz glanced down at the half-formed doll he was making, then back up again. "It feels like something more than that."

"We have something more important than dolls to discuss, Mazz," Jace said, suddenly eager to change the subject.

After conferring with Mazz about the ramifications of their missing weapons, Jace heard Haran call out to him in his mind and walked down the aisle to her seat in the very rear of the plane, away from the others. She had short blonde hair and was the smallest among them, with white eyes that identified her as a Serath, a rare, mystical seer on their home planet.

"I have something to show you," she said.

Haran had removed her boot to reveal of a small "G" on the back of her heel.

"Check your heel, Jace."

Jace took off his boot to reveal a matching tattoo in the identical spot.

"That G can only stand for one thing."

He met her gaze that was so piercing in its colorless intensity it was difficult to hold. "But why? She was no longer spoken of thousands of years before our time came. What could she possibly have to do with us?"

"I don't know, but I feel…I feel…."

"What?" Jace prompted.

Her gaze suddenly looked faraway. "Something, Jace, something…."

Jace thought of how they all seemed to be experiencing strange thoughts that felt like fragments of unexplained memories. "What is it?"

She found him again in a gaze that had gone suddenly empty. "We're not who we think we are…."

Jace replaced his boot and returned to his seat, doing his best to set aside his unsettling thoughts to focus on the task at hand.

"Chronar," he said in his mind instead, "is there any chance the containers have been opened?"

"No, Jace," the familiar calm voice responded. "I would have detected that while you were in stasis. The containers were equipped with a beacon. I'm scanning the entire planet to hone in but have been unable to get a fix on the signal."

"What's the status of the alien presence in Alaska?" he asked Chronar.

"According to the transmissions I've picked up, a scientist accompanied by a team of special operations soldiers has arrived at the settlement. They've just been ordered to return to base with the recovered remains of three victims of the initial alien attack."

"How long until we reach the area, given the modifications Xan made to generate more speed?"

"Based on current fuel consumption and, accounting for expected winds and atmospheric conditions, just over five hours from now."

"Have you found us a place to land?"

"There are no airstrips in the area, and the nearest airport would take you in the wrong direction," Chronar responded. "I'm working up alternative scenarios now, Jace."

"Are you able to scan this town, Chronar?"

"I have measured movement, heat signatures, and below-ground seismic disruptions. Enough to conclude the humans currently in Chichagof Springs are about to come under attack."

CHAPTER 20

Sunset

Chichagof Springs, Alaska

Kai left Trooper Muhtuk and the soldiers to handle the process of bagging the bodies in the spill of the LED headlights of all three vehicles which cut swaths through the wind-blown snow and descending darkness so he could make his way to the restaurant where the others were holed up. Trooper Muhtuk's partner yanked open the door when he got there, and Kai welcomed the blast of warmth that greeted him inside.

"Trooper Tom Dennehy, sir," the young man said.

Kai noticed the assault rifle slung from Dennehy's shoulder. "Professor Kai Bevins, Trooper."

Kai didn't bother extending a hand to shake this time but pulled his gloves off so the room's warmth could flush the life back into them. He spotted a man wearing a jacket emblazoned with the Amazon logo rubbing his hands in front of a woodstove, identifying him as the first person on scene of whatever had happened here last night.

Then he fixed his gaze on the old woman Muhtuk mentioned, awkwardly holding the infant who had also survived against her.

"Hey," she said to him, "you know your way around babies?" She held the snoozing infant in her arms like a fragile crystal bundle, extending her arms slightly toward him.

Kai thought of Charlie at that age, snuggled in Jules's arms in the delivery room before Jules had passed her up to him to hold for the first time in their life as a family. There would be no more kids unless they adopted, thanks to Jules's cranky uterus. Concerned doctors gave her only a 50 percent chance to survive the birth, but she had refused to sacrifice what would be her only chance at having a child, insisting that she stood just as good a chance to live. That was Jules, and Charlie had inherited all her fire and courage in stark contrast to her father's cautious nature and aversion to risk-taking.

"Name's Jane Piedmont," the old woman said, thrusting the infant into his grasp. "What's yours?"

"Kai Bevins."

He cradled the baby, wrapped in a blue blanket and cooing like Charlie did at that age. A smell rode Jane Piedmont that made him think of corroded engine oil.

"Paget's disease," she said, no doubt used to his reaction. "In healthy bones, old bone is replaced with new bone. With Paget's, the new bone is weak and misshapen. That's why people confuse me with the hunchback of Notre Dame. My bones are as brittle as toothpicks. Some are just as thin too, while others are the size of bones out of a dinosaur museum. The Paget's got started wasting me away a year or so back and brought with it that lovely smell that makes me stink like I haven't bathed in twice that long." She swept her gaze about the room. "How lucky I was to live to see all this shit."

"What about available treatments?"

The old woman sneered at his suggestion. "I used to have a calendar on my fridge marking all my appointments, infusions, drips, prescriptions, and whatnot. Then I dumped it and every other calendar in the house that reminded me how miserable I was. Last thing they tried was called photodynamic therapy. Cost me a hundred grand and I could've done the same thing with a flashlight."

Kai swallowed hard. Jules often said she thought she glowed after radiation treatments.

"You a doctor or something?"

"A professor."

"'Cause I get the impression you know your way around the stink that rides sick people like me."

Kai nodded.

"Somebody close to you?"

"My wife. Cancer."

"Shit."

"Yeah."

The old woman cleared her throat. "So what are you a professor of exactly?"

"Astrobiology."

"What the hell's that?"

"The study of life in the universe beyond humans."

"Well, I guess you haven't been too busy until now. I don't really give a shit, long as you help kill whatever it was killed my town. I never thought I gave a shit about anything until I didn't have anything to give a shit about it. Almost funny when you think about it that way."

* * *

Timur took off his headset and gestured for Jules to do the same.

"How long have you had it?" he asked her.

She was about to resort to denial mode, then just sighed. "Going on two years."

"What kind is it?"

"Brain. Glioblastoma."

"Prognosis?"

"Doctors say it's a miracle I've lasted this long. The miracle's coming to an end."

Timur's rigid face softened, the deep lines and furors seeming to smooth and stretch out. "I'm sorry. If I had known…."

Jules turned her gaze out the trailer's window toward where Charlie was engaged in a snowball fight with one of the general's men, watching her dart about the remaining vehicles for cover as she pelted the poor soldier again and again, laughing the whole time.

"If you had known, I wouldn't be here, General. But I'm right where I belong, where I'm supposed to be. This is my life's work, and now I have the chance to see it through."

* * *

Kai had managed to suppress the tears that normally came when he told someone about Jules's condition. Jane Piedmont must be in her mid-seventies, early eighties maybe, meaning she had forty years or so on Jules. What he wouldn't give to have his wife by his side for that many more years, but the harsh reality that he wouldn't struck him hard and fast.

"People survive cancer all the time these days, Professor," she told him.

"Not this one."

"That bad?"

Kai nodded.

"Baby looks right in your arms. How many you got of your own?"

"One."

"One more than me, then." Piedmont turned her gaze out Dave's Place's plate glass front window, even though there wasn't much to see through the storm and descending darkness. "I heard the woman trooper say they found Dave Kemp's body without any bones. This disease I've got has been messing my bones up big time, makes them break easier than chicken wings. I imagine that made me pretty unappetizing to these things. I'd probably give them alien indigestion."

Kai watched the old woman's eyes fasten on the baby in his arms.

"What about the little tyke, though? He seems healthy enough."

"Infant bones are primarily composed of cartilage," Kai explained, glad for the scholarly distraction, "which gradually hardens into bone as they grow, a process called ossification, while adult bones are fully ossified and have a higher density."

"So what you're saying is neither of us was worth the bother to whatever it was that filleted Dave Kemp and that baby's parents."

"That's a workable theory."

"So these things, whatever they are—we're food to them? Our bones, that is."

"More or less."

"Which is it, Professor? Don't play dodgy with me."

"I'm not, Mrs. Piedmont. I'm just not sure yet."

She fastened her gaze on the baby again. "Guess we've both got the luck of the Irish. Say, isn't St. Paddy's Day around this time?"

"Last week," Kai told her, unable to hide his surprise that she hadn't known that.

"I don't keep track of the days anymore, Professor. What's the point? Keep living the same day over and over again, and I figure it won't hurt as much when there are no more left, and I don't have to worry about breaking a bone from bending over the wrong way."

A rumble punctuated the end of her words. It seemed to be coming from underfoot, like an earthquake, measuring enough on a figurative Richter scale to shake the bottles on the shelves behind the bar and leave the glasses jingling.

"Uh-oh," said Jane Piedmont.

* * *

Out in the street, Sakari Muhtuk felt the rumbling, too. Living in Alaska, she had experienced her share of tremors, which inevitably left a hollow feeling in her gut. But this was different. It felt like the ground wasn't shaking so much as....

Moving.

The meager light was just about gone from the sky, leaving a dark shroud over the snow-swept scene broken only by the spray of LED headlight beams burning through the storm. She'd been helping pack the three bodies with the air let out of them into the bags that still looked flat when they were zipped up. It took three men to carry each to the cargo bed rigged to the back of one of the snowcats because when they tried just two, the bag sagged so much in the middle that it looked like the pliable contents were stretching out, even coming apart. So a third soldier was needed in the middle to complete the task. That drew all three drivers out of their vehicles to speed the process along and maintain an optimal security perimeter at the same time.

Muhtuk watched the Special Forces types, still arranged in a protective semicircle, exchange glances, and hand signals when the rumbling persisted, crouching low with M7s in the ready position as they swept the barrels back and forth across their assigned grids. Following their lead, she raised her pump-action twelve gauge and chambered a shell with a loud clack.

* * *

"Base, this is Ramrod," Jules heard in her headset.

Timur reflexively touched his mic. "Go ahead, Ramrod."

"We have activity at our twenty."

"Elaborate, please."

"Can't, Base. Feels like an earthquake. Any reports of seismic activity on your part?"

"None, Ramrod. Get your asses out of there, and I mean now. Clear?"

"Clear, Base. Moving now to—"

The voice stopped when Jules saw all monitors with camera angles of Piedmont Street show fissures of snow bursting from the ground, movement flashing amid the blanket of white.

* * *

Muhtuk saw something coming at her through the storm, almost like the rolling pockets of snow erupting from the ground had taken on their own life. Then she glimpsed dark splotches amid the white, growing as they seemed to congeal into a shifting shape lacking a cohesive form.

She fired her twelve gauge into that spreading swirl of darkness, heard a thud as the bullet struck something that kept coming, as the street erupted everywhere in gunfire.

CHAPTER 21

Siege

Chichagof Springs, Alaska

Pressed up against the plate glass window, Kai heard the clack of automatic fire echoing beyond, muzzle flashes looking like candles flickering in the dark. Screams, cries, and shouts resounded. The headlight beams caught flashes of dark shapes silhouetted against the pearl-white snow. Whatever was out there seemed to be moving above the ground, but he couldn't distinguish any clear shapes within the mass of movement.

"Astrobiologist, eh?" he heard Jane Piedmont say from alongside him. "So how's this rate for a field trip, Professor?"

"Back away from the window!" the younger trooper named Dennehy ordered them, his assault rifle stabbing at the air.

Kai pulled the old woman with him away from the glass in his free hand, realizing he was still clutching the infant in the other. Awakened by all the noise, he was crying up a storm. The trooper moved up to take their place with rifle raised and ready as if he intended to shoot straight through the glass.

"Can you shut that kid up?" Dennehy screeched, panic leaving his voice scratchy. "I can't see shit out there. What the hell's happening?"

"They're back, aren't they, Professor?" Piedmont asked Kai. "Whatever killed my town last night is back."

Kai placed the infant back in her grasp. "Take him, please."

"Kai, can you hear me?" Jules blared in his headset, her voice even more panicked than Dennehy's. "Kai, come in!"

"I'm here, Jules."

"Thank God! Where are you?"

"Inside a building overlooking the street. Safe for now."

The next moment brought more screams, horrible high-pitched ones, piercing the glass from beyond. And fewer muzzle flashes were coming now, which meant there were already fewer soldiers shooting out in the street.

"They must be nocturnal," Jules said over the cacophony of gunfire from the street. "The attack last night and now this," she added. "What are you seeing on your end?"

Kai moved closer to the glass. His eyes had adjusted to the ambient light beyond enough to recognize waves of dark shapes like shadows cast against the stark white of the blowing snow. He couldn't tell if they were flying or leaping or being blown apart by the soldiers' guns. From behind the plate glass, it looked like an unbroken wave of them converging on one soldier after another, engulfing and pitching them down into the snow. Portions of the wave fell, erupting in bursts of what looked like oil in the path of the remaining soldiers' fire. But it diminished quickly, replaced by horrible, high-pitched screaming that managed to penetrate the storm and thick plate glass.

"What are you seeing, Kai?" he heard Jules's voice crack.

Through the storm, Kai glimpsed four figures stumble and fall to the snow just short of the diner's door.

"Four people! They're down!" he blared. "I've got to help them!"

* * *

Trooper Sakari Muhtuk had emptied all seven shells from her twelve gauge in the moments between one breath and the next, tossing the shotgun aside in favor of her pistol. She had never served in the military or seen combat, but she understood now what an ambush must have felt like.

She emptied two of her Glock's magazines without being sure if her bullets did any damage to the things at all. A few she was sure she hit changed direction, maybe dropped, but she stayed on the move to avoid becoming a stationary target, trying to keep within the spray of the headlight beams knifing through the darkness and the storm.

Muhtuk froze when she neared three of the creatures she thought at first were burrowing into the frozen ground and then realized they were devouring a uniformed shape at the far edge of one of the headlights' reach. The things seemed to have no fixed form, just a mottled assemblage of tentacles attached to nothing she could see. Each tentacle looked to be finished in a mouth with rows and rows of needle-thin teeth pressed against the uniform of the soldier they had toppled.

No, Muhtuk corrected herself in the shadow of the next instant, *not against—through....*

Her last thought before she started firing her final magazine was that the soldier's body was deflating like he was some kind of man-shaped balloon, and these things were sucking the air out of him. But it wasn't air they were sucking out of him.

It was bone.

The soldier was long gone, so Muhtuk fired indiscriminately, her bullets coughing chunks of black muck into the air. The things smelled so bad she had to swallow down some bile that sped up her throat. What was left of them scurried away, tentacles curled around something that looked like a sack she hadn't noticed before.

She realized she was still pulling the trigger even though the slide had locked open. Her ammunition spent, she tossed the pistol aside and retrieved the M7 dead soldier had shed when the things took him. She'd fired an AR-15 on the range a few times, not well, but she knew her way around a trigger, and this one screamed on full auto when she pulled it back. The weapon felt light in her hands and didn't kick at all as she fired into the rolling dark blanket that raced through the storm with tentacles whipping and crisscrossing each other.

She felt a tightening on her leg, followed by a burst of pain, and looked down to see one of them wrapped around her calf, the stinging like that of liquid nitrogen sprayed over the skin. She didn't dare try to shoot the thing off, worked to pry it free with the tip of the barrel instead, but it only tightened its tentacles around her calf and ankle in response.

Then she remembered her knife.

Holding fast to the M7 with a single arm, Muhtuk yanked the blade once more from its sheath, about to stab at what looked like a spider's distended abdomen from which all the tentacles extended when three more of the things scampered into her field of vision, converging on her. She watched them stop and prop themselves up on their assemblage of tentacles as if preparing to leap. Before they could, Muhtuk emptied the rest of the assault rifle's magazine into them, painting the white air briefly with more of the black, gelatinous ooze. She thought she might have heard them utter a collective screech but couldn't be sure because of the soldiers' screams and shrieks still echoing in the dark snow-swept night.

Muhtuk tightened her grasp on her knife and jabbed at the thing fastened on her leg dead center. The blade sunk through a leather-like hide into something soft and fleshy. The tentacles spasmed reflexively and retracted into a protective ball as Muhtuk hoisted the thing and tossed it aside, blade and all.

Weaponless now, she slid sideways and managed to stand up, before crumpling to the snow when she tried to take a step. The lower part of her left leg was numb, her foot locked into place. Another pair of things scurried toward her from the thick blanket of the storm, and Muhtuk rolled away into the tight spill of a headlight's bright stream.

She watched the things freeze in place, stopping short of the light field.

As long as I stay in the light, I'm safe....

These things had struck late last night by all accounts and had risen from the ground as soon as darkness fell again. More muzzle flashes coughed orange bursts into the night. Muhtuk guessed maybe four or five of the soldiers were still offering resistance. They continued to scream out their positioning, trying to ascertain how many of their squad remained. A gust of wind blew the snow off the remains of a body the things were already finished with, lying prone on his stomach with his M7 partially pinned beneath him. Muhtuk shuffled sideways on her butt through the snow, prying the gun free and then rolling back into the safety of the light.

Kneeling on her leg that had gone numb, she propped the rifle butt against her shoulder and began firing short bursts toward the converging shapes of dark motion. Tentacles flailed through the air before going still under a fountain of more of the gray-black ooze that showered upward with each hit.

How many of these things were there?

Muhtuk didn't know any more than she could tell how many bullets remained in the magazine, so she kept her fire to single shots while clinging to the spray of the LED light. Once this magazine was drained, she would be defenseless, without even her knife. She figured her best chance lay in making her way back to Dave's Place and rose awkwardly from her kneeling position, careful to put no weight on her numb leg, and began dragging it along the tunnel of light up the street toward Dave's.

She was just ten feet away from the entrance when she banged into a trio of dark shapes that tumbled with her into the snow.

* * *

Kai burst through the door into the night, the storm battering him from all directions at once. For a moment, he lost track of the clump of figures that had seemed to collapse into the snow. Then he saw one of them rise, firing a nonstop barrage at an attacking horde of the creatures. They converged and seemed to engulf the soldier in a collective grasp. The storm winds swallowed most of the screaming that followed, but not the sight of what looked like a cloud of seeds extracting from the creatures as they dropped into the snow with what was left of the soldier.

Oh my God, Kai thought, realizing what he had just witnessed.

He pushed through the storm toward the others and recognized the Native state trooper, a soldier on either side of her. He spotted no further muzzle flares flashing in the street beyond, meaning this trio formed the last of the resistance that had been vastly overwhelmed by the creatures.

Kai hoisted the trooper to her feet, the two soldiers reclaiming theirs as well, clinging to each other. The group trudged toward the door with a wave of black slicing through the snow toward them.

CHAPTER 22

Dave's Place

Chichagof Springs, Alaska

"Come on!" Trooper Dennehy wailed, holding the door open for them.

Kai dragged the trooper through, the two soldiers right on their heels. Dennehy almost had the door sealed again when what Kai's mind first identified as a rubber hose before recognizing it as some kind of tentacle wedged itself in, preventing the latch from engaging.

Kai and Trooper Muhtuk put all their weight against it, while Dennehy unslung the AR-15 he had shouldered to hold open the door.

"Trooper!" Kai cried out.

The creature reminded Kai of Medusa, the mythological monster with snakes growing out of her head, only this thing had no head he could spot, just what looked like ten, maybe a dozen, snakelike tentacles attached to an overstuffed pouch from which they had sprouted. Kai knew he was getting the first close look at a life form from another world, having imagined this moment for his entire adult life, never picturing it would be anything like this.

Dennehy pressed the assault rifle's barrel flush against the base of the tentacle and fired a three-shot burst that launched plumes of a black oil-like ooze into the air as the severed thing dropped to the floor.

"Nice shooting, Trooper," Piedmont complimented, infant clutched in her arms as she kicked at the stilled tentacle with a booted right foot.

It sprang back to life, skittering toward Kai when Dennehy slammed the butt of his AR-15 against it and kept bashing until the tentacle had been flattened into a sludge-like pool of black ooze.

Kai realized his camera must still be broadcasting, but he'd lost his wireless headset at some point and spotted it on the floor between where he'd been standing by the window and the door. He stooped to retrieve it and fitted the device back in place.

"Jules, do you read me?"

"How many of you are left?" General Timur's voice chimed in instead.

"Me, the two survivors, the Amazon driver, two troopers, and two soldiers."

The two soldiers on either side of Trooper Muhtuk looked shaken and barely mobile from the wounds they'd suffered. The Amazon driver, meanwhile, was seated on the floor before the woodstove, rocking back and forth and whimpering softly.

Kai turned his gaze back toward the street when one of the creatures, swimming with matching tentacles, slammed against the glass and stuck there. A second followed, then a third.

"Light," Muhtuk muttered from the floor, with Dennehy stooped over her to check her injured leg. "They avoid the light."

"Dave's got emergency lanterns in the back," Piedmont recalled. "Bright as a bitch."

Needing no further coaxing, she headed that way with the infant clutched in her arms like an extra appendage.

That allowed Kai to slide over and check the wounds of Trooper Muhtuk and the downed soldiers seated on the floor on either side of her. One was badly scratched up and bleeding but otherwise appeared spared of any serious injuries, save for a wound in his leg he had tourniquetted himself outside. But he sat unblinking and still on the floor, catatonic. The other looked to be in shock as well, favoring his left arm, which Kai noted appeared to be folded up. On second glance, he realized the arm wasn't folded up. It had been flattened by one or more of the creatures having sucked out the bone the same way they did to the victims across the town last night.

Having one pressed against the glass allowed Kai to view it from a safe distance away. Thanks to the tentaclelike appendages, it most resembled a land-based squid or octopus. But he could see nothing resembling a mouth, eyes, teeth, or ears. More evidence to support the realization that had struck him in the street.

Another of the creatures hit the glass with a thud, followed by a fourth, then a fifth. He could feel the glass buckle with each strike, even from four feet away.

"Professor, this is General Timur. What's the status of my men?"

Kai looked out into the street as more creatures thudded against the glass, obscuring his vision. The lack of movement, muzzle flashes, or gunfire pretty much told him the fate of the remaining soldiers who hadn't made it to Dave's Place.

"Looks like the two that made it in here are all that's left."

A pause followed before Timur's voice returned. "Where are you with weapons?"

"One of the troopers has a sidearm and an assault rifle. That's it. No, wait," Kai corrected after gazing toward the downed soldiers again. "One of your men has a holstered sidearm."

"We've got no backup to send your way. You need to get to the Jaguar."

"The what?"

"The armored vehicle. Is either of my men in a condition to drive it?"

Kai looked over at them again. "No, General. And the vehicle's more than a hundred feet away. We'd never make it there."

"Well, goddamn shit."

"Look what I found," said Jane Piedmont, holding a pair of heavy-duty battery-operated lanterns by the handles. "Bright bitches, like I said." She looked down at the infant asleep again in her grasp. "Bet you dollars to donuts the first word out of this kid's mouth is *bitch*."

Kai heard Jules in his ear. "Any chance you can hold out until dawn?"

He almost wanted to say, *If you can live six months longer than the doctors said you would, we can hold out for ten more hours.* Instead, he said, "I don't know. Possibly."

"See how the creatures pressed against the window respond to light."

Kai grabbed one of the lanterns. He glimpsed Trooper Dennehy steadying his weapon as he approached the plate glass with a bright LED light leading.

The nearest creatures dropped to the snow and scurried off. Kai repeated the process up and down the window, shedding all the creatures from their perches.

"Good," Jules said, her voice starting to crack. "At least you've got—"

The rest of her words were drowned out by what appeared to be a concerted attack launched by the creatures against the glass, one after another, slamming against it in an endless wave.

"Jules," Kai said, backing away with a lantern.

"I see it."

Kai grabbed the second lantern, prepared to press both against the glass, when the first spiderweb crack appeared, widening even as others followed, one after another. Then the plate glass shattered inward in an ear-numbing, massive crack that showered the air with shards as chunks of the window crashed to the floor.

"Everybody to the storeroom!" Trooper Dennehy screeched, firing on the creatures as they tumbled inside and skittered across the floor.

"Take these!" Kai said, handing Jane Piedmont back the lanterns.

He needed free hands to help Trooper Muhtuk and the downed soldiers get to the back room. She had already struggled to her feet, one of her feet dangling uselessly, helping one soldier and leaving the other for Kai. He was dragging him across the floor under cover of Dennehy's fire when he remembered the Amazon driver by the woodstove and spun his way.

Too late. The first line of creatures descended on his dazed form, completely enveloping him and swallowing even his screams. Kai made it to the back room just behind Trooper Muhtuk and dragged Dennehy in with him just as the trooper's AR-15 clicked empty.

He got the door slammed just ahead of the next wave of creatures and could feel them slamming up against its steel face. A reinforced fire door, thankfully.

This storeroom had no window, a major plus. And as far as Kai could tell, none of the creatures were yet massing outside a rear door that formed the only other way out. He looked over at Jane Piedmont gently rocking the infant in her arms as if she'd raised a dozen kids of her own.

"Jules," he said into his headset, "do you have eyes on the main street through the vehicles' cameras?"

"Yes, but we can't see much through the storm."

"Can you see the creatures? Give us an idea of how many are out there?"

"They're everywhere, Kai."

"That's why you need to get to the Jaguar, Professor," Timur's voice blared through his headset. "We can set the weapons on full auto and blast these things to hell, but somebody has to activate the system."

"Reaching it means getting through them, General. Our best chance is to hunker down in this storeroom. Both the doors are reinforced steel, and the walls are solid maple. We might just—"

He stopped when the floor creaked, followed by a rumbling sensation like an old burner kicking on in the cellar.

"Mrs. Piedmont, does this building have a basement?"

"No sirree, it does not. None of the buildings in the Springs have one on account of the permafrost. We got crawl spaces under buildings elevated on posts or pilings to keep them clear of damage from the frozen ground."

Kai heard the scratching next, followed by more creaks, making it sound like the floor was whining.

"Jesus Christ, they're underneath us!" screamed Tom Dennehy, looking down.

"How much ammo you got left, Trooper?" Muhtuk asked him; Kai was glad she had finally found her voice.

"Last mag, boss. Thirty shots." He looked toward Kai, his voice pleading and panicked. "What now? What are we supposed to do now?"

Kai trained his eyes on a nearby storage shelf, forming a plan that would have been entirely absurd if it hadn't been their only chance.

"I've got an idea," he told them all.

CHAPTER 23

The Jaguar

Chichagof Springs, Alaska

"Squeaky wheels ain't exactly our problem," Jane Piedmont said, watching Kai pull twin cans of WD-40 from the storage shelf he'd been eyeing, "in case you haven't noticed."

"Did Dave smoke, Mrs. Piedmont?"

"Like a chimney. We were racing to see which of us could shave more years off our lives until I trumped him with the Paget's. What else you looking for?" she asked.

"Cigarette lighters," Kai said, rummaging around the shelves. "And rubber bands, strong ones."

After handing the sleeping infant to Trooper Muhtuk, the old woman started yanking open drawers in the desk Dave must have used for his paperwork. "Bingo," she said, standing over one of the drawers. "Found the mother lode of lighters here."

"Pick out two of the biggest, Mrs. Piedmont," Kai instructed. "Make sure they're full."

She started pawing through the drawer while Kai resumed his search of the shelves, looking for one thing in particular.

"What is this, some kind of half-assed science project or something?"

"Only if it works," Kai told the old woman, closing his hands on a tube of industrial-strength superglue.

"Got them…" With that, Piedmont produced two clear, oversized disposable cigarette lighters filled with fluid. "Will these do?" she asked him.

"For sure," Kai told her.

The activity beneath them had gotten louder, more of the creatures massing there to work the floorboards of the storage room free.

"So," Piedmont continued, "you plan on telling us what you're going to do with all this shit?"

"Watch."

Conscious the whole time of the floor seeming to shift beneath them, Kai laid the components of what he was building atop Dave's desk. The two cans of WD-40, each with an aerosol straw already inserted, were joined by the lighters, tube of superglue, and four rubber bands. First, he plucked a small screwdriver from a storage shelf to remove the flame regulator on each lighter. Then he attached each lighter to the WD-40 cans with generous globs of the glue affixed to their ridged bottoms so the lighters extended horizontally outward. The final touch was to stretch rubber bands from the rims below the nozzles to the spark wheel that normally ignited the flame once flicked. That would keep the spark wheels engaged so the hefty flames, minus the regulators, would shoot upward continuously.

He held the lighters tightly in place for a half minute to ensure the glue set.

"Ready to go," he pronounced.

"What exactly does that mean?" Jane Piedmont asked him.

Kai used a third lighter to ignite the flame on one of his jerry-rigged devices and then pressed down on that WD-40 can's nozzle to shoot out the oil-based lubricant. A flame between one and two feet long shot outward with a sucking sound.

"Miniature flamethrowers," Trooper Dennehy realized.

"Hope you don't think you can incinerate the whole lot of them with those."

"I won't have to," Kai told her. "I just need to clear a path."

* * *

With one of those miniature flamethrowers in each hand, Kai stood by the rear door, Jane Piedmont awaiting his signal to jerk it open. He cast his gaze toward Dennehy, who stood ready with his assault rifle in case any of the creatures lurked beyond.

"If this works, lead the others out when you hear the shooting start and loop around to the Jaguar. Use the lanterns to keep any strays off you," Kai finished.

Dennehy nodded and tightened his grip on the AR-15.

"I'm ready to move, General," he said into his headset.

"You can serve in my unit anytime, Professor," Timur told him.

"I'll pass if you don't mind. I don't want this hero thing going to my head."

"Roger that."

"Kai," he heard Jules's voice crack.

"What?"

"Nothing. Just, just get to that vehicle."

"I ever tell you I played football in high school?"

"No."

"Because I sucked, never saw the field. This is my chance to start."

Kai glanced one last time at Dennehy to make sure the young trooper was ready, then looked toward Piedmont and nodded. The old woman nodded back and yanked open the door, letting in a shivery blast of cold and thin spray of ice-laden snow. None of the creatures were in evidence, so Kai surged through the storeroom door into the night.

He trudged along the street through the thick snow, orienting himself to where he was in relation to the Jaguar. He reached a thin break, like a small alleyway, between two buildings, and glimpsed the snowcats parked on Piedmont Street beyond. The Jaguar was parked just behind them, so he started along the narrow route, pressing down on the twin nozzles in case any creatures were in his path, cloaked by the darkness.

Flames shot out in both directions to clear the path ahead, and Kai stepped up to a jogger's pace, emerging on the street to find an endless mass of the creatures shifting about, all seeming to acknowledge his presence at once. The rancid stench they gave off filled the air, thickening as he moved straight toward them, aglow in the light cast by the twin flames that cut through the wind and the night.

The snow-covered white ground had blackened under the creatures' shifting, writhing mass, one shape indistinguishable from the next, as if they formed a single, massive organism. Until the creatures scampered from his path of hot light and flames in both directions, leaving a tunnel that ran straight through them as Kai swept the cans about to showcase the threat they formed. He kept his gaze fixed ahead on the Jaguar, aware of the tentacles lashing at him from beyond the spray of his flame-splashed light.

"Can you hear me?" he heard Timur's voice in his ear.

"Clear but not loud, General," he said, thanks to the collective crackling noise the things made.

"Access the Jaguar through the rear door and slam it behind you."

Kai tightened his focus on his target. "I'm thirty feet away now. It's working."

"Hallelujah to that."

"What happens when I'm inside the vehicle, General?"

"You're going to bring the rain down on these things, son."

CHAPTER 24

Bringing the Rain

Chichagof Springs, Alaska

Kai had to release the pressure on one of the WD-40 cans to open the rear hatch. Immediately, creatures on that side seemed to swim through the snow toward him. He reignited the flame, and the creatures slithered away, looking like mobile oil slicks.

The makeshift flamethrower in his left hand faded out, and he discarded it, leaving him only the device clutched in his right. He held it at the ready to discourage any creatures' approach. He had just opened the hatch with his left hand when a trio of tentacles lashed down at him from the vehicle's roof. He lurched backward as more tentacles flapped in the air, groping for him. He saw the distended-looking abdomen from which the tentacles extended perched on the sill of the roof and aimed his remaining flamethrower straight for it, compressing the nozzle all the way.

The flame shot out, the creature shining in its spray. The abdomen erupted in flames, quickly spreading along the thing's tentacles, unleashing a scent that reminded him of spoiled meat. Kai thought he heard the thing hissing as it burned, its tentacles flailing wildly as the fireball flopped past him in the air just as his second jerry-rigged flamethrower went dark. The flaming creature landed in the snow, scattering creatures on both sides of Kai that had resumed their deadly advance.

Kai discarded his second jerry-rigged flamethrower and lunged inside the vehicle, as tentacles whipped about everywhere, a few trying to wrap around his legs. He resealed the hatch before the things could launch themselves toward it. The stench they carried followed him inside, swallowing even the harsh scent of the oily residue from the flames that had coated his jacket, hair, and face in a smooth layer.

He moved to the cab and found four chairs separated from the cramped seating in the rear that could accommodate around a dozen soldiers. Reflexively, he took the driver's chair. There was no windshield, just a glass plate no more than one-by-two feet that looked directly over the dark mass spread over the white blanket beyond, movement illuminated in splotches by the still-burning LED headlights.

Kai quickly reconnoitered the spaceship-like control array before him and touched his headset. "I'm in the pilot's seat, General. What now?"

"Move to the next seat over. That's where the weapons control systems are located."

Kai shifted seats. "Okay. Ready."

"Look directly in front of you at the screen slightly to the right. Touch the tab marked 'automated.' That leaves the firing mechanisms to the onboard computer, rigged to motion once activated. They'll fire at anything that moves. All we need to do is draw the creatures' attention, bring them toward you. But first, the start button's just to the right of the steering wheel. See it?"

"Yes."

"Then start her up."

Kai leaned over to press the button, and the powerful engine roared as loudly as a race car. He leaned sideways to check the view plate and saw a single shapeless mass moving toward the Jaguar, looking like black water flowing across the snow.

"They're coming, General," he said, knowing his body cam was mounted too low on his body armor to capture that perspective.

"Good. Now press activate on the touch screen and cover your ears."

* * *

Kai didn't cover his ears, not at first. The cab burst to life with sound and light as indicators flashed everywhere, including ammo counts for the twin long-barreled miniguns and the turret's 40mm cannon. The miniguns fired in a dual ear-wrenching whine that rumbled in the pit of his stomach, while the cannon fired shell after shell with loud thumps he felt as hollow pings inside his skull.

He realized the touchscreen controls had shrunk to make room for a frontal, enhanced view of the carnage the constant bursts of projectiles was leaving. He could feel the miniguns rotating above him to train their fire on fresh areas of motion. The ammo counters were speeding downward from one thousand as gray globs and ruptured pieces of the squid-like creatures were coughed into the air by the incessant fire. They seemed not to have the forethought for retreat, only the instinct to continue straight into the deadly spray tearing them apart. He could feel the turret rotating above slightly, enabling it to train its 40mm fire in the heaviest concentrations. On-screen, each hit from one of the shells sent a plume of flame-singed black leaping into the air, an untold number of the creatures perishing under each strike.

Kai pictured the others moving from the storeroom while the incessant fire continued to ratchet. It would be slow going, with an infant to carry and three wounded adults pulling themselves along. He pictured Dennehy in the lead, assault rifle in one hand and lantern in the other to clear a path and shoot anything that strayed into it.

Meanwhile, the mechanical whirring whine of the miniguns rotating above continued to pierce the frigid air, their 7.62mm shells pouring straight into the rolling mass of black shapes. The cannon kept pumping 40mm shell after shell toward the heaviest area of movement, each explosion showering the air with black viscous ooze that made Kai think of an oil-well strike.

The ammo counters continued to drop to the point he began to fear they'd hit zero with the black tentacled wave still coming. On the screen before him though, the scene had gone almost still, the black wave before him flashing less and less motion. Kai realized General Timur's voice was sounding in his ear.

"I need a report, son."

"The Jaguar's doing the job. Jules, can you hear me?"

"Loud and clear."

"Please tell me you and Charlie are okay."

"We're fine."

The cannon had gone quiet, and the miniguns were slowing with lengthening intervals between their fire and ammo counters both clicking under a hundred rounds. A few more sporadic bursts followed before the guns fell silent, leaving an awful ringing in Kai's ears.

"It worked," he said, hearing the words as if someone else had spoken them. "Oh God, it worked."

"You need to load up your survivors and get back here, soldier," General Timur told him.

Kai felt his heart reflexively skip a beat when the Jaguar's rear hatch was yanked open. He swung round to see the young trooper Dennehy standing there, supporting one of the wounded soldiers.

"I could use some help here."

Crouching, Kai retraced his path through the personnel hold and back into the night, the air laced with a stench so bad he covered his mouth with his sleeve. Kai steeled himself against it, and he and Dennehy helped load Trooper Muhtuk and the two wounded soldiers on board the Jaguar, leaving only Jane Piedmont with the infant cradled in her arms, wailing loud enough to pierce what felt like water filling his ears from exposure to the deafening percussions.

"Little bastard's hungry as shit. Anybody besides me got a tit handy?"

Kai took the baby so she could climb inside. The old woman looked about almost dreamily, regarding her town for the last time.

"Never thought I'd leave the Springs again. Looks like I was wrong."

The old woman took a seat and extended her arms back toward him for the child. He handed the infant over, and the baby stopped crying once resettled in Piedmont's arms. Kai realized his boots were sloshing around the muck left by the blown-apart creatures that had turned the snow black. The thought struck him that this might be his only opportunity to get a sample organism to study and analyze. He remembered a steel storage box bracketed into the Jaguar's wall in the back. Then he reached inside, flipped the restraining bolts, and lifted it out to place it down atop the ooze-stained snow.

Kai opened the top and quickly eased a whole dead sample from the snow. When he lifted it in his gloved hands, black ooze drained out of its oblong-shaped body. He then placed the sample inside the storage box. The thing felt almost weightless, which told him it was not supported by a skeletal structure. He shed his muck-riddled gloves, closed the top, and secured the box back into place. Then, he climbed back inside the Jaguar and sealed the hatch behind him.

"You expect us to ride back with that thing stinking so bad?" Jane Piedmont asked him, moving to the forward-most seat that remained empty.

Meanwhile, Dennehy took the rear-most seat to keep eyes on the storage box, his AR-15 ready.

"It's dead, Trooper."

"You sure about that?"

Kai didn't answer him and retook the seat behind the Jaguar's controls.

"General Timur, can you hear me?"

"Loud and clear, Professor. We'll send a team in to mop up the mess and make sure all of these things are dead. Case closed. Congratulations. Looks like you saved the world," he added lightly.

"Not yet," Kai told him, recalling the conclusion he'd reached out in the street. "Not even close. These weren't the creatures that escaped the ship, General. They were their offspring."

CHAPTER 25

Offspring

Mendenhall Glacier, Alaska

"Please tell me I heard you wrong, Professor," Timur said after a pause, the levity gone from his voice.

"I wish I could, General. But I believe these things are most like insects with some properties of plants. Insects, in general, require particular essential nutrients to reproduce. Female mosquitoes, for example, need to feed on blood to ingest the necessary protein and iron to lay eggs."

"Just like whatever escaped that ship needs human bone," Jules elaborated.

"Meaning the fact that they shed spores isn't surprising in itself, just the speed at which these spawned versions of what escaped the alien ship developed. In the street, I saw the creatures shed what looked like seeds or spores. That's when I realized we weren't fighting what we thought we were. They must have gestated underground until the sun set."

Every resident of the Springs one of the escaped creatures killed last night had spawned some incalculable number of offspring. There might have been a thousand of their infantile forms before him, or five thousand, or even more—it was impossible to say in the storm and the dark. The more bones they sucked out of their victims, the more progeny they spawned, which left him thinking this species behaved even more like a cancer on the land intent on reproducing itself until it kills its host.

In this case, Earth.

Kai tried not to consider the ramifications of these things reaching concentrated areas of population, like cities, from which millions, even billions, of them might be birthed.

"You're telling me the fully formed creatures that escaped those cells are still out there," Timur said, as if suddenly grasping what Kai had told him.

"Yes, and certain to feed again."

"It's been dark for two hours, Professor. We need to figure out where—"

The blare of a screeching alarm inside the command trailer drowned out the rest of his words, and Kai felt panic grip him anew.

"What's going on, General?"

"Perimeter defense warning system activated. Just a false alarm."

"An animal, maybe?" he heard Jules raise.

"Where's Charlie, Jules?"

"Right here, holding her ears. I'm looking out the window. Can't see anything through the storm."

"Like I said," Timur resumed, "just a false alarm. Happened yesterday, too, so I'm not—"

This time, it was the dim echo of gunfire coming from outside the command trailer that broke off his words.

"General?"

Nothing.

"Jules?"

Nothing, not even the shrill alarm sounding.

Communication had broken off.

Part Four
ARRIVAL

"Science never solves a problem without creating ten more."

—George Bernard Shaw

CHAPTER 26

Under Attack

Mendenhall Glacier, Alaska

"We've lost outside communication!" Jules heard a voice blare through General Timur's headset as he removed it in frustration. "The satellite relay was just cut!"

The shrill alarm continued to blare through the entire makeshift camp. On several screens, Jules glimpsed the shapes of soldiers rushing toward the chasm where perimeter sensors had picked up something. Another monitor picked up black shapes emerging from the chasm, shapes that could only be the mangled remains of the sentinels that attacked her party on board the alien ship.

She heard the converging soldiers open up with their weapons over the monitors, as well as through her naked ear, a strange stereophonic effect. Through the storm and chaos, it was impossible to tell whether the soldiers' gunfire was stopping the robotic creatures that had been reduced to little more than patchwork pieces.

"I should have anticipated this," General Timur said, his voice as stiff as his back and shoulders. "I should have sealed the breach."

"You couldn't have known, General. They didn't come after us down there after your men got me off that ship."

"In the light, but it's dark now. I should have anticipated that too."

Charlie was hugging Jules tightly, pressing against her with enough force to leave her unsteady on her feet. Jules felt her balance teetering for a moment and thought she might drop to the floor until she managed to steady herself at the last instant by placing a hand atop a nearby table. She focused on the monitor centered on the chasm where more of the mangled remains of the sentinels continued to pour over the crest, drawing the relentless onslaught of fire from Timur's troops. It stopped for a moment, Jules letting herself think hopefully that it was over, though she knew it wasn't, even before she saw the next series of creatures appear over the crest of the chasm.

Only these were different.

These were bigger than what she had encountered during her deadly foray on board the alien ship, the mismatched product of the sentinels reconstructing themselves as best they could from the available pieces and fragments that still functioned. The night and the storm cloaked much of their form, but Jules discerned sets of fully articulated mechanical leg extremities arranged in tripodal fashion, often mismatched in size but nonetheless functional. Their upper halves, above where their waists would be if they were humanoid, were dominated by multiple arm appendages, almost like the legs of a spider.

"Oh my God," Timur rasped, realizing the same thing she was about to. "The first wave was just a distraction meant to draw us out and use up our bullets."

The lights in the command trailer died with the power, then flickered back on dimly.

"I'm scared, Mom," Charlie muttered, hugging Jules tight.

Jules tried to find words of comfort, but the best she could come up with were, "It's all right; everything's all right," while stroking her daughter's hair.

But it wasn't. The screens were showing the larger reassembled robotic creatures emerging from the crater now, impervious to the soldiers' fire. Only Timur turning down the sound spared Charlie from hearing the awful screaming when liquid metal parts that looked stitched or soldered together converged on the soldiers, swallowing each of them in a blanket of black.

Jules moved her gaze from the monitors onto Timur, whose expression had lost all its certainty, looking tentative and fearful. He turned away to check the status of his remaining troops, calling out to them again and again, but received few responses. She heard it all over her headset, including one word from the other trailers forming a perimeter.

Attack....

Jules turned her gaze out the window through the storm, and spotted dark shapes converging upon them. Then she felt thuds against their trailer's exterior, some hard enough to shake it. The wave of the smaller robotic fragments was upon them, a corrosive scent like burned metal somehow penetrating the steel and glass. A realization that these mechanical monsters had also harvested pieces of the ship to reconstitute themselves struck her hard and fast, explaining how their numbers seemed to have multiplied since the deadly confrontation she had barely escaped.

She heard a creaking sound that she identified as the things using their spider-like arms to peel back the steel and forge a way inside. Others were slamming parts of themselves against the windows, spiderweb cracks appearing in the moments before the black metallic remnants of the ruined sentinels shattered the glass with violent thrusts, showering shards inside the trailer.

Jules felt the pieces sting her scalp and plucked a few shards from Charlie's hair while her daughter squeezed against her. She found General Timur in her gaze again, handling an M7 assault rifle, readying it to fire.

"Stay in the middle of the floor!" he shouted to her.

Timur let loose with a spray from his assault rifle every time one of the robotic things tried to push its way inside through one of the shattered windows. The deafening sound it made in such tight confines left Jules's ears on fire, but she covered her daughter's ears instead of her own with her hands.

"Rescue's coming!" Timur blared, firing another spray. "Five minutes!"

Rescue? Jules thought. *How is that possible with the storm still raging?*

She had no idea of the answer to that and didn't want to distract the general by posing the question. He looked firmly in his element with a deadly weapon in his hand, blasting away at the mechanical monsters one after the other while turning his aim from one window to the next, stopping only to eject the spent magazine and slam home a fresh one.

In between the general's shots, Jules could hear the distant clack of gunfire coming from the other trailers. That became her greatest source for hope, since it meant the already reduced sentinel forces weren't all concentrated here, likely the only thing that had prevented them from overrunning the command trailer.

"Four minutes!" Timur shouted at her.

A sudden quiet filled the trailer, Timur standing at the ready and rotating his gaze among the windows where the invasion had stopped, at least for now. Then a new sound overcame that of the wind blowing frigid air and the storm's icy snow through the ruptured windows.

Wop-wop-wop....

A helicopter!

Wop-wop-wop....

Louder this time.

Jules swung toward Timur.

"An Airbus H225," he said, needing no further prompting. "Capable of rescue operations in the harshest conditions the climate can produce. We've had it on station in a transportable structure ten miles away from here just in case."

"But how can it land?" she said, through a mouth caked dry.

"It can't," Timur told her.

He checked his watch, shouldered his weapon, and turned his gaze up toward the cutout of a hatchway in the ceiling.

"That's our route out, Professor."

CHAPTER 27

Next Stop

Chichagof Springs, Alaska

"Trooper," Kai called to Dennehy. "Do you have any experience driving a rig like this?"

His thought process had seized up after losing contact with Jules. He tried to tell himself it was a technological glitch caused by the storm, the simplest and most logical explanation. Though not very convincing, it provided enough reassurance to consider their next course of action.

"I've never even seen a rig like this."

But the young trooper shuffled forward anyway, sliding toward the cab on an angle that let him hold his gaze on the storage container now holding alien remains.

Kai saw Muhtuk extend her hands when Dennehy drew even with her. "Give me your gun. I'll keep an eye on it."

Dennehy held fast to his weapon. "You up to this, boss?"

"It's my leg I can't feel. My hands work fine. Now hand it over."

This time, the younger trooper complied and then slid into the cab. Kai had already taken the copilot's seat, leaving the controls to him.

"Okay," Dennehy said, "let's see what we've got here." He studied the controls and LED display gauges. "Same basic drive system as a Humvee," he said, mostly to himself. "And I can drive one of those in my sleep."

"We gonna get going here or wait for these stinking sons of bitches to mount another attack?" Jane Piedmont shot out from the rear.

As if on cue, the baby started wailing again.

"This is why I never had kids of my own," she said, rocking him gently while Dennehy continued familiarizing himself with the control panel. "Hey, any of you ever see the movie *Rosemary's Baby*?"

No one responded until Kai managed, "Not me."

"In the end, after she's given birth to the son of the devil, Rosemary tells this old bitch that she's rocking him too fast and takes over, caring for the devil's kid. Feels to me like it's the devil himself out there tonight."

Kai wanted to try hailing Jules in the command trailer again but didn't because he knew that her not responding would only make things worse. She'd be contacting him as soon as the communications there came back online. In the meantime, they couldn't stay here. Nor could they risk returning to the base camp without a clearer notion of what had cut off communications.

"Trooper Muhtuk," he said, cocking his gaze toward the Jaguar's rear compartment, "how far away are we from civilization?"

"There are two small villages, like the Springs, six miles due west and four miles due east."

"What about to the north or south?"

"Galena," she managed, through labored breathing and the pained grimace stretched across her features. "Inuit fishing village located on an inlet ten miles northwest of here."

"Then that's where we should head," Kai said, as Dennehy tested the vehicle's brake and accelerator pedals, then sought a comfortable grip on the steering wheel. The engine revved under pressure from his foot. Kai's hollowed-out hearing had kept him from realizing it was still on, even with so much horsepower at its command.

He retreated into the mind of a scientist. Since the creatures moved and fed at night, they likely burrowed into the blackness below ground while the sun was out. As soon as the sky darkened though, they would surface again in either of those villages nearest to the Springs.

"We're ready to set out, Professor," Dennehy said from behind the wheel, lifting Kai from his stupor. "Strap yourself in."

Kai held his gaze. "You know the way to Galena, Trooper?"

"There's only one road that leads from here to there, so, yeah, I do."

Kai twisted his gaze toward Muhtuk in the back. "Trooper Muhtuk, would you happen to know anyone in that village?"

"There's a tribal policeman I've worked cases with who lives there. He's responsible for policing several villages, but he calls Galena home."

"Do you have a cell phone that you can use to try to reach him?

He watched her ease one from her pocket. "Sure. He always answers, even when he's off duty."

Muhtuk hit the proper contact and pressed the phone to her ear. Kai watched her through the ringing, her pained expression tightening even more.

"He didn't pick up," she said finally, ending the call. "Storms like this can play hell with cell coverage though."

"That's one possibility," Kai told her.

CHAPTER 28

Fragments

Airborne Aboard the Falcon

"Have you located the weapons yet, Chronar?" Jace asked the disembodied voice in his head.

"I'm afraid not. I need to widen the parameters for my scan."

Chronar explained that the soldiers who'd accompanied the scientist to Chichagof Springs were not equipped with body cameras, and the batteries on the state troopers' cameras had died. With satellites unable to penetrate the storm cover, that meant the only footage of the battle came from an armored attack vehicle's onboard camera. Along with the poorly rendered view through the night and storm, Chronar was able to provide the communications between the scientist and the man in charge back at the site where the alien craft had been found. Those communications had allowed the scientist, not a soldier by any means, to activate what for humanity passed as an advanced weapons system. Both the visuals Jace could make out and subsequent communications indicated the scientist had succeeded in his mission. All communication from the military encampment had since ceased, and all Chronar had been able to pick up was a desperate call for some rescue helicopter.

There was so much the Nine didn't know. But one thing they did know was that they were awakened because this invasive species could eradicate all of humanity in remarkably short order. With their primary weapons missing, the Nine needed to stop them while they were still relatively contained.

"Is there any other conceivable landing point close to Chichagof Springs?"

"Negative, Jace. There are flat stretches of land, now iced over and covered in thick snow. Even with Xan piloting, the chances of survivability in such a landing are close to zero."

"Then we need an alternative."

"I have been able to come up with one, but it's extremely precarious with many variables to consider, including the fact that your survival cannot be guaranteed."

"We have no choice. Let's put your plan into action." Jace stopped, then started again. "Chronar…some of us have been experiencing strange flashes—fragments of thought that don't feel like ours but somehow are."

"There are known cognitive effects from prolonged stasis," Chronar replied, its tone as even as ever. "Temporal disorientation. Residual neural echoes. I believe you were briefed, though it appears that knowledge, too, has been lost."

Jace hesitated. "This isn't confusion. It's…familiar. Like a shadow of something just out of reach."

"That data falls outside mission-relevant parameters. I am not authorized to engage further on the subject."

Jace said nothing, but his jaw tightened. He rose and retraced his steps to the rear of the plane, where Haran sat with her eyes closed, apparently asleep.

"Chronar is holding something back," she said without opening her eyes.

Jace was grateful for not having their piercing luminance stare into him. "You heard?"

"I didn't need to hear. I felt it as you approached."

"A true Serath."

Haran opened her eyes. "You expected something different?"

Jace thought of what she had said earlier in the flight, how the Nine weren't who they thought they were. "What does that tell you?"

"Our experiential memories were erased purposefully, not as a result of ten-thousand-year stasis."

"Why?"

"That I haven't discerned yet. But I can tell you something else. As a Serath."

"What's that?"

"These memories we're recovering fragments of—we may be better off without them, Jace."

CHAPTER 29

The H225

Mendenhall Glacier, Alaska

"They're going to drop rescue ropes and hoist us up," General Timur told Jules as he positioned a step stool directly under the pull for the hatch built into the ceiling of the command trailer.

He climbed to the third step and stretched his hand for the latch but stopped short of grabbing it. Timur unslung the as M7 from his shoulder instead.

"Ever fire an assault rifle, Professor?"

"Never even held one."

"First time for everything. If anything tries to get in when I open the hatch, just pull the trigger and the gun will take care of the rest."

Jules eased Charlie behind her and took the M7 in her grasp. Watching Timur handle it so agilely made her think it was lighter. Maybe she was just worn out after such a long day on virtually no sleep the night before. She backed up to get a better firing angle, slowly since Charlie had clamped onto her from behind now.

Timur looked at her from the top of the stepladder. She nodded.

Then she watched him grab the latch and yank downward. The collected snow dropped upon him, and he shook it off to let it join the rest of the pile on the floor. The hatch flapped open on its hinges, revealing only darkness and the relentless storm.

Jules didn't know if the reconstituted remnants of the sentinels from the alien ship could set an ambush, so she held her breath the whole time Timur extended his arms through the open hatch, fastened his hands on the sill, and hoisted his frame through onto the trailer's roof. She extended the M7 up to him, only then breathing easier.

"Raise Charlie toward me," the general said, laying the rifle off to the side so he could extend both hands downward.

Jules could hear the sound of the approaching chopper clearly now, coming almost directly overhead. She crouched slightly so she was eye to eye with her daughter.

"You hear that? I'm going to lift you, and the general's going to take you."

"No," she muttered.

"We need to do this so we can get out of here and see your father."

Charlie lifted her arms, and Jules scooped her up. It was all she could do to manage her daughter's weight, and she still had to climb at least two of the stool's three steps to raise Charlie through the hatch.

She looked as weightless as a doll in Timur's strong grasp. He hoisted her through the hatch and looked back toward Jules after setting her down.

"Come on, Professor," Timur said, jarring her from whatever trance she was slipping into, "reach up and I'll grab you."

Looking up had left Jules dizzy, the world starting to spin. But Timur's powerful hands locked onto her forearms and hoisted her through the hatch as effortlessly as he had Charlie. Her feet grazed the roof, and she was immediately conscious of the snowpack that had accumulated there, her boots sinking into it until she found her footing. In the air, she could hear the H225's engine roaring now and saw the chopper's lights flickering through breaks in the storm. As if on cue, the first rescue rope, formed of tight cord over carbon filaments, lowered through the storm cover like a snake slithering along the air. A second quickly joined it, dangling over the trailer's roof.

Then Jules heard a screech of metal and spotted a trio of metallic arms peeling back a section of the steel roof, as the rebuilt sentinel attached to them pulled itself onto its slick surface.

"Go!" Timur ordered, positioning Jules on the rope and starting to lift.

"No, Charlie first!"

Both of them spotted two more of the reconstituted sentinels mounting the roof. One was no more than a torso, the others looking as if they had been put back together with mismatched pieces, including what appeared to be a grated section of metal-like flooring.

"Go!" Timur shouted again, thrusting Charlie into her grasp, then unslinging his M7 into position.

"Hold on to me!" Jules said to her daughter, "Close your eyes and hold on as tight as you can!"

Then she felt her mind seem to separate from her body, her thoughts unable to propel her actions. It had been one of the first symptoms of her cancer and had begun to occur with increasing frequency, especially in times of stress. The only thing that could keep it reasonably under control was the antiseizure medication that left her lethargic and loopy. She hadn't even thought of bringing the bottle of pills with her last night, and now she was paying the price.

"Jules!"

Timur shouting her name snapped her out of her trance. He held the rifle in his right hand, opening fire as he tugged on the rescue rope with his left.

"*Grab the rope!*" Timur shouted above the ratcheting of his gunfire, holding the reconstructed sentinels at bay.

Jules reached up and took hold of the rope in both hands, then felt a sudden jerk thrust her airborne as she was winched up from above. She released one hand from the rope to hold fast to Charlie. Her daughter was wrapped so firmly to her that it hurt, and she clung tighter to the rope with a single hand.

Timur shrank in shape below her, firing away at the trio of sentinels that had claimed the roof. His fire blasted the one lacking a lower half into the air, leaving the other two converging upon him. That was the last thing Jules glimpsed before the storm stole her vision. Timur's gunfire kept clacking, growing softer the further the rope was winched toward the waiting H225.

Then Jules's hand holding the rope spasmed, followed swiftly by the other one clutching Charlie for dear life.

Oh God, not now....

The spasms were another symptom that had begun to occur with increasing frequency, usually controllable with patience and breathing exercises. But she could afford neither of those now, not with her daughter's life at stake as well as her own. Jules tilted her glance upward and saw the flashing lights and angular shape of the helicopter growing through the storm.

"Don't let go! Hold on, don't let go!"

She thought it was Kai's voice urging her on, enough to quell the spasms and return control of her hands.

"You're almost there!"

She realized it was General Timur's screaming at her, a glance downward revealing him twenty or so feet beneath her being winched toward the H225 on his own rope. Jules felt buffeted by the winds, starting to twist in a spiral that left Charlie squeezing her so hard she felt her pelvis might crack. She clung to her daughter tightly with her left hand, even as she felt herself losing purchase on the rope with her right.

The rope stopped twisting, but above, the helicopter was starting to waver in the air, its nose lowering scarily before snapping up even again with the tail in the next instant. She was just ten feet away now and could see dark shapes extending their hands from the rear hold to grab hold of her and Charlie as soon as they were within range. Drawing closer, she discerned they were belted to the frame like rock climbers scaling a vertical peak.

Jules looked down and saw Timur just a few feet behind her now. She was close enough to the H225 to smell fuel fumes and feel the heat of the rotor cutting through the icy night. She felt hands grasping her and Charlie, raising them upward when she suddenly felt as if she was floating, the snowy sky around her like soft cotton, leaving her cushioned and safe.

Then the world went dark.

CHAPTER 30

Shadow People

Galena, Alaska

The storm had finally diminished somewhat, at least in terms of wind force, by the time Dennehy brought the Jaguar to a halt on the outskirts of Galena, a fishing village perched on an inlet fed by Mendenhall Lake along a seagoing route called the Inside Passage.

"Why are we stopping?" Kai asked, the hopeful sight of lights twinkling through the still-falling snow ahead.

Dennehy turned his gaze to the weapons counters. "Ammo's low in both the miniguns and the forty-millimeter cannon. I trained in a later version of the Bradley Fighting Vehicle. The Jaguar resembles that, which means I'm familiar with the reloading process. It's a simple matter of plugging in new ammo packs into the internal feeding system."

Kai and the others watched as he moved to the center of the rear compartment.

"Just be quiet," Jane Piedmont whispered. "I've finally got this damn baby to fall asleep. Could you have found any more bumps to travel over?"

Dennehy leaned over to grab and twist a square latch built into the floor. Once it was engaged, he lifted a section of the steel flooring to reveal a storage hold.

"Shit," he muttered.

"Watch your mouth in front of the fucking kid, Trooper," Piedmont snapped at him, covering the baby's ears.

"It's empty," Dennehy resumed, aiming his words toward Kai.

It was no wonder, Kai thought, recalling the team's rushed departure from base camp that must have left no time for anyone to check if extra ammunition had been loaded into place.

"Fuel's an issue for us too," the young trooper reported, as he settled back in the driver's seat. "We're not going to get much further than Galena with what's left in the tank."

"Hopefully, we won't have to," Kai noted, and looked back toward Trooper Muhtuk. "Still nothing from your friend?"

She flashed her phone and shook her head. "I don't like this; I don't like it at all."

"You'd rather we hold here for the backup that's not coming?"

"The motto of the Alaska State Troopers is Loyalty, Integrity, Courage. The first two aren't always applicable in our work, but out here, in the middle of nowhere, these people rely on us to protect them. That's where the courage part comes in. So just because I don't like this one bit, it doesn't mean I'm not all for doing my job."

"On one leg," Kai reminded.

"I don't shoot with my toes, Professor."

At that, Dennehy slid the Jaguar into motion again, having kept the vehicle's speed slow atop the stretch of road from the Springs, which lacked any visible markers and was essentially a bed of ice with snowpack on top.

"When I was a little girl," Muhtuk resumed, her tone quiet and reflective, "the oldest among my people would scare us with stories of the Qallupilluk, these scaly humanoid creatures that would steal children from their beds at night and take them into the sea. I was more scared by the Inupasugjuk, giants who caught humans and ate them. But what scared me the most were stories of Taqriaqsuit, known as 'Shadow People,' since no one could describe what they looked like. In drawings I have seen, some dating back so far that they're found on the walls of caves, they're portrayed as shapes with no real or definable form. I remember how impassioned my grandmother became whenever she spoke of the Shadow People." She stopped, Kai watching her swallow hard, before continuing in a dry cracking voice. "I think that's what we're facing here, our own Shadow People."

"Not our own," Kai corrected. "They came from another world."

"In her stories, my grandmother said the Shadow People came from the air. I think she was talking about space. I think maybe our shaman made prophecies of this."

Kai turned back to the front, eyes on the view screen before him. Galena was coming into clear view through the diminishing storm, the village's lights burning through the darkness, shining on an empty central street and square, with nothing but unplowed snowpack crunching under the Jaguar's massive tundra tires. Dennehy stopped the vehicle on the outskirts of the twinkling lights, providing Kai the opportunity to view the village they were about to enter.

Not surprisingly, given the storm, no one was in sight, but nor was anything suggesting an attack of the sort that had transpired last night in the Springs. Structures mostly uniform in design and similar in footprint lay on both sides of the street, layered with snow. They were designed to handle all the varied elements that nature could serve up. Kai noticed a central square where the road widened for a stretch, in the center of which a fifteen-foot-tall ceremonial totem pole had been wedged into a circular rock garden surrounded by ornate wooden framing that made it look as if the totem had grown into this perch from a seed. The buildings that looked out upon the makeshift rotary created by the totem appeared entirely commercial, with the residences climbing up a graded hillside shrouded in the snow still pasting the air. That snow all but swallowed even the thickest trees, a mixture of elm, spruce, and maple forming natural groves in which the majority of the homes for the nearly five hundred year-round residents, according to Trooper Muhtuk, were clustered.

Small groupings of homes nestled closer to the shoreline on either side of the snow-covered trees that cast shadows onto the waters beyond, with the homes to the east stretching farther along the water than those to the west. The newer commercial structures had been constructed of fresh logs, likely culled from the village's trees. The rest of both single- and two-story structures resembled clapboard, and Kai guessed that the bulk of those structures had been built long before, potentially by the government body responsible for the tribe at the time. They were small and tightly packed within shared spaces, instead of having individual yards.

A single sweep of his gaze along both sides was enough for Kai to spot a one-story building with a peaked roof and bold letters pronouncing it GALENA SCHOOL. A familiar red cross designated a nearby building as what must have been the village's medical center. Kai also spotted a combination hair and nail salon, a municipal building, and a smaller structure with a United States Post Office sign posted on its front, featuring "PRINTING AND FAXING SERVICES AVAILABLE" stenciled beneath it. He took the largest building as some village center that doubled as a meeting hall, a gray structure longer than it was wide but still the widest in sight. It bore paint color distinctions in patches, denoting several additions made over time that were all uniformly shrouded in a blanket of snow. Satellite dishes were affixed to a number of the buildings, a few having been blown off their mounts by the storm's powerful winds.

"Drive on," Kai told Dennehy.

The Jaguar crept down Galena's central street, the only sound that of its massive eight tires crunching through the snowpack, not about to be denied forward passage by anything.

"Stop in the middle," Kai resumed. "In front of the post office."

"Mail out in these parts is slower than shit," said Jane Piedmont. "Pony Express was a hell of a lot faster."

The baby in her arms cackled.

"Kid loves me. Proves there's no accounting for taste."

Kai looked back toward Trooper Muhtuk. "You want to try your friend again?"

"Just did."

"Anybody else you can try to raise?"

"Sorry, no."

Kai thought for a moment. They couldn't camp out here forever, but they needed a destination, somewhere to head.

"You know where this friend of yours lives?"

"I think I can guide you there."

The radio speaker crackled, went staticky, then fell silent again.

"Base camp, this is Kai Bevins. Can anybody read me?"

"Professor, this is General Timur," the familiar voice greeted through a loud humming sound.

"General! What's that sound in the—"

"Rotor wash. We're on board a rescue chopper."

Kai heard his following words as he spoke them. "My wife, my daughter. . . ."

"Safe. A little worse for wear, but safe. Your wife is unconscious, but there's a medic on board who says her vitals are fine. She's been through a lot, Professor," Timur said, leaving it there.

"I want to talk to my daughter. Put Charlie on."

"Not now. I need to know your current location and status."

"We just entered Galena, an Inuit fishing village that's the largest population center close to the Springs. There are two smaller villages closer the creatures are likely to target. I need to talk to Jules, General," Kai said, thinking of the conclusions he needed to share with her. "As soon as she wakes up. And, please, let me speak to my daughter."

"Stand by," Timur said, after a brief pause.

"Hi, Dad," a voice almost too soft to hear came over the radio.

"Hey, baby, how are you holding up?"

"We got lifted into a helicopter."

"How does Mom look?"

"Like she's sleeping."

Kai swallowed down the lump forming in his throat. "She'll wake up soon."

"Maybe she hit her head or something."

"That's possible."

He felt a wave of indescribable relief knowing that Jules and Charlie were safe, heading somewhere secure on board a helicopter that somehow managed to rescue them.

"You see that?" Dennehy posed from behind the wheel.

"What?" Kai said, looking at the screen, which provided an enhanced view ahead, widening out to a full ninety-degree perspective of the street ahead.

"Movement. I thought I saw something moving."

"Professor," Timur's voice returned over the speaker, "I'm dispatching a second rescue chopper to your beacon."

Kai thought of the wounded soldiers and Trooper Muhtuk. "We've got wounded here."

"There will be medical personnel on board, and they can be winched up once the chopper is on station."

That's when Kai saw the dark shapes flitting through the snow-swept landscape, black blotches set against the white world beyond. Growing in size as they drew closer, converging straight for the Jaguar.

"The rescue chopper won't get here in time, General," he told Timur. "We've got company."

CHAPTER 31

The Drop

Airborne Aboard the Falcon

"I've picked up a new communication, Jace," Chronar said. "The humans who fled the settlement in that vehicle are about to come under attack in the second settlement they've just entered. I'll display the feed from the vehicle's camera."

Jace saw enough of the projection in his mind to know he was looking at the blurred shapes of the creatures who had escaped the alien ship. What he could see of them was enough to confirm that Chronar's extrapolation of their physical forms from available data was remarkably on point. When moving, they used only two legs, with the rear-most extremity raised upward, almost like a tail. In the brief flickers when they stopped, he could discern the third leg lowering to establish a firmer base. He was unable to clearly discern the upper bodies due to both the diminished view and the swirling tentacles that obscured the rest of their physical features.

"Chronar, can you extrapolate a rendering based on visuals obtained?"

"Rendering depiction now, Jace. You'll note that visual and hearing apparatuses appear to be located in the upper extremity above the swirl of the tentacles. In contrast, the mouth, or respiratory intake apparatus, is located where the torso would be present for a humanoid form. I'm sorry I can't provide a clearer depiction. I will need to examine a specimen to analyze its full inner workings and bodily functions."

"What's our distance from the site?"

"Twenty-two miles. At our current speed, we will reach a drop point I have located in six minutes. I estimate six minutes more following evac from Falcon to reach the settlement."

"What's our altitude?"

"Five thousand feet, continuing slow descent. The lowest this craft can go is one hundred feet, but the survivability of a drop cannot be guaranteed above seventy-five. However, the snow cover provides a pliable cushion that is difficult to factor into my estimates."

Jace wasn't as concerned about the drop as he was about what awaited them within the settlement itself. With Xan piloting, and both Brenn and Izumi missing, there would be only six of the Nine to confront the twelve fully mature life forms that had decimated the previous settlement before venturing to this one. On top of that, they each carried only a single weapon on their person to confront their enemy. The fact that those weapons were formed by an infinite number of reconstituting nanobots programmed to take a specific, deadly form proved of little comfort against an enemy he knew so little about.

The Nine referred to these weapons as kaelens, which meant "tears of the maker." In their dormant form, they resembled truncheons, a term that originated in Victorian London, where police began the practice of carrying hard rounded wooden clubs measuring eighteen inches long by an inch-and-a-half in diameter and affixed with a fluted handle for easy gripping. The Nine's kaelens mirrored those dimensions and were similarly solid and smooth to the touch until they were activated by an energy source contained within the nanotechnological particles comprising each and controlled by the individual wielder's mind. No two nanotechnological weapons were the same, and all complemented one another. The Nine had practiced with them under Chronar's tutelage while in stasis to assure their mastery of the weapons was retained from their past lives.

The enemy's ability to procreate vast numbers, and their spawn to mature quickly, held the greatest threat to this planet. Chronar had compared this enemy to fungi, extrapolating that they actively ejected their spores using comparable mechanisms, such as surface tension catapults or utilizing hydrostatic pressure to spread those spores over a wider and less-concentrated area. This alien species did not resemble a single Earth-bred organism but rather combined the traits of many. Comparisons, in any case, provided only a frame of reference, a means to better understand an alien species that was incomprehensible on its face.

Suddenly, the Falcon began to shake from the pressure of flying through the storm below at an altitude that was unsafe under any circumstances. Xan, with Chronar's help, did her best from the pilot's seat to account for wind speed and shear. Pulling back on the jet's speed helped quell the shaking, and out the window, Jace could see the endless white landscape below, powdery snow lifted into blankets by the force of the jet soaring over its piles.

"Jace," Chronar said, "we are coming up on the drop point. It is time to assemble."

The five of the Nine who'd be making the drop with Jace were already poised before the door, prepared to do something they had neither practiced nor even contemplated. As he approached, Jace saw Valeria and Zareb holding hands, eyeing each other as if bonded by something beyond the mission.

Another inexplicable anomaly, on top of the others, including them all having a G tattoo on their heels, G for Gaia. And, as he moved toward the plane's door, he saw Mazz clutching the patchwork doll he had fashioned against him, squeezing it so hard the pillow stuffing had flattened out.

What was happening to them, all of them?

At two hundred feet, Jace yanked open the cabin door to a frigid burst of air that gushed in through the breach.

"Five seconds," he counted, "four, three, two, one…."

Jace flung himself through the breach, vaguely conscious of the others following in his wake after a moment's delay, enough to assure they didn't collide in the air or upon landing. The free fall from one hundred feet seemed to end a breath after it began, with the white blanket seeming to rise toward him. Instinct propelled him to tuck and roll, but the impact, even against the snowy cushion, was nonetheless jarring. The roll that would hopefully spare him any injury whisked him forward at a dizzying speed. Jace was holding his breath through the length of it that ended when he bounced back onto his feet, still in a gravity-defying motion. He turned his gaze about and found the five others drawing even with him, all with their kaelens already in hand.

No words needed to be exchanged, just a single gaze shared by all six of the Nine, before they burst into their charge toward the lights that looked like tiny stars flickering in the darkness of the night.

CHAPTER 32

Missing Monsters

Airborne over Alaska

Jules awoke to find her head in Charlie's lap. She was completely disoriented with no awareness of where she was until her mind settled and snapped back to being hoisted onto the rescue chopper. She smelled metal and perspiration and could feel the chill air of the cabin. The loud rumbling noise buffeted her ears and brought the familiar throb back to her skull. She wondered if the tumor itself was the source of it. Before long, it would take far less than what she'd been through today to anger it.

She had come to see the tumor that chemo could no longer stop or even slow as a monster living inside her head, soon to strip away the parts of her life she'd always taken for granted. Taste, smell, hearing, seeing, memories, basic bodily functions, and thought processes. All the things that formed life by any definition would be stripped from her one by one.

"Kai," she said suddenly, sitting up despite the burst of agony it sent through her skull.

Before her, Timur watched her wince and grimace, his eyes speaking for him. "Your husband and the others just spotted our missing monsters, Professor."

"Where?"

"An Inuit fishing village called Galena. Just about shut out from civilization and nearly self-sufficient. The nearest supermarket is forty miles away. Folks there are the hardiest of the hardy."

"I want to speak to Kai. I want to speak to my husband."

Timur handed her a wireless headset, which she struggled to fit into place in hands that wouldn't stop trembling. From fear or the tumor, she didn't know.

"Kai, it's me."

"Thank God."

"What's your status?"

"Can't get a clean count of the things through the storm, but they're out there. I think our arrival drew their attention from the villagers."

"Listen to me," Jules said, the dull throb in her head growing to a full pounding, "I think they function as a single organism with some instinctive telepathic recognition system. That means these creatures are aware of what that vehicle did in the Springs. That explains why they're massing. They see you as a threat. How long since the sun set?"

"Almost four hours now. General, do you have any aircraft in the area?"

"No. Why?"

"Because something that could only be a jet just flew over us, low enough to make my teeth rattle. I was hoping it was a fighter jet. Oh shit...."

"What, son? Report!"

"Something just slithered past the front of the Jaguar. They're here."

"Professor, what are the weapons counters reading?"

"One of the miniguns is at sixty-five, the other at eighty. The cannon's got six shells left. Not much."

"The weapons worked on the offspring. Maybe that's enough to take care of the parents. Get ready to press activate again, son."

"Finger already in place, General."

CHAPTER 33

Tulok

Galena, Alaska

Kai could see the huge oily shapes swimming with tentacles projected against the white backdrop of the snow. He heard those tentacles slapping against the reinforced armor, realizing the Jaguar's greatest vulnerability.

The hatch!

"Muhtuk!" Kai cried out, lurching from his chair.

Muhtuk had the AR-15 already aimed toward the hatch when Kai reached her. The sound of something like metal grating against the steel beyond scratched at his ear. The latch started to move, and he slid the locking mechanism into place just in time. It continued to jiggle, accompanied by more of the metallic scratching of the tentacles against steel. Then the hinges began to buckle. Kai imagined those tentacles had locked onto the exterior of the hatch somehow and were now pulling.

The strength it would take to make the reinforced hinges of armored steel bend....

"Of all the times to discover my maternal instincts," Jane Piedmont said, clutching the baby tight against her.

Kai realized the dazed special ops soldier, who hadn't uttered a word since he'd entered the diner with Muhtuk, was muttering something.

"What's he saying?" Kai asked the special ops soldier with the withered arm, who was leaning in close to him.

"Grenades. I used mine out there against those things, but he's got one left. It's clipped to a holster around his right ankle, just above the boot. I'd get it for you, but…."

The soldier cast a forlorn gaze toward his flattened arm, reduced to nothing but unsupported flesh.

Kai eased the grenade cautiously from the slot fitted for it and placed it in the soldier's remaining whole hand.

"They get the door open, maybe this will buy us some time."

But it wasn't just the door. He heard shrill, grating sounds across much of the Jaguar's frame and pictured tentacles with those razor-sharp teeth held in what looked like mouths at the tip of each working to tear back layers of the armor-plated steel. The Jaguar shook from side to side under the force of those tentacles trying to tear their way inside.

"Professor, you need to get your ass back up here," Dennehy called from the cab. "We've got more company."

* * *

The six of the Nine ran through the cold and the storm, neither feeling nor acknowledging the elements. They were closing on the outskirts of this settlement, the armored vehicle that had wiped out the spawn of the creatures in the first settlement growing in shape.

Along with something else, Jace saw.

The creatures had surrounded the vehicle, which seemed to be swimming in a sea of tentacles, and looked remarkably close to the likeness conjured by Chronar from extrapolated data that captured virtually all of their features, scale, and size. Judging from the scale provided by the vehicle, they stood between nine and ten feet tall when fully upright. The lashing about of their tentacles cloaked any clear sight of what lay above their three legs, but he trusted the image Chronar had conjured there as well.

And there was something else he detected, thanks to the Nine's advanced olfactory glands: variations of a rank corrosive stench intermingling in the air.

That must be how they communicate! he realized. There was ample precedent on this world for that, though. Jace knew that species ranging from ants to bees to dogs, cats, and snakes used their scent to convey messages about territory, mating, and threats. He doubted the sophistication level of their enemy was much beyond the insect world.

That enemy hadn't seemed to notice the six of the Nine yet, which made Jace ponder the comparable levels of their ability to hear and see. Given that they communicated via scent, he guessed that was their strongest sense. Their sense of sight would be trained mostly toward shapes and motion, likely limited given their clear antipathy toward light.

The wind was blowing in his face, meaning the scent of the six of the Nine was being pushed away from the creatures. He thought if they widened their perimeter, they might be able to close on the creatures and strike them down with their kaelens while the advantage was still theirs.

Then he glimpsed a new element being added to the scenario.

* * *

Kai could see on the display screen what Dennehy had glimpsed through the small windshield:

The Inuit people of the village poured into the street, bearing all manner of weapons. He noted a healthy assortment of firearms, along with several bows and arrows and, if he didn't know better, what looked like a portable harpoon launcher being wheeled out like a cannon.

Kai figured their arrival in Galena had interrupted the creatures' house-by-house devastation of the town. How many Natives might they have fed on before word spread, activating this response?

"Trooper, you need to see this," he called back to Muhtuk.

Kai watched her hobble into the cab, hardly surprised by what she saw.

"It is the way of my people, Professor. They are tuloc, warriors coming to confront the Shadow People."

Kai regarded the screen again. "They don't look like warriors to me, Trooper."

"Appearances can be deceiving."

Alerted by the cries and hoots of the onrushing mob, the creatures swung away from the Jaguar. In the next instant, the grating sounds of them trying to strip away the steel enclosure stopped. A moment later, they were in motion as black blurs, slinging themselves across the white landscape through the storm toward the massing villagers.

Kai followed the harpoon-like weapon speeding through the air, seeming to draw a line between the advancing forces. It struck one of the creatures just above its legs and passed straight through, drawing a river of black ooze that sprayed what looked like Ping-Pong balls in all directions across the snow. They could only be the gestating spores spawned by the monsters after consuming nutrients from human bone. That told him the creatures must have been feeding nonstop since entering the village.

The creature that the harpoon had passed through dropped to the snow. Almost instantly, the black ooze the harpoon had scattered was drawn back into the creature, as if by a magnet, leaving not a drop of it anywhere. And when the snow was all white again, the creature rose and joined the others in a blinding surge toward the tuloc making a final heroic stand.

The black blur of the creatures' motion seemed to smash into the first wave of Natives, at the far edge of the camera's effective range. Kai couldn't see much through the darkness and the storm, but it was enough—more than enough.

The initial wave of gunfire and arrows from the Inuit warriors held the black wave back for a few moments. Then the creatures resumed their surge forward, disappearing into the mass of Natives who had rushed from their homes to confront them.

Kai heard Muhtuk muttering a prayer in her native language as the screen broadcast a horrific scene that chilled his spine and turned his stomach. He saw creatures swallowing men in the wrap of their tentacles. To the eye, it seemed as if they were squeezing their prey, but Kai knew he was looking at the way these things sucked the bones out of their victims. He had imagined it to be a slow process, but mere seconds after the squeeze engaged, the body of each victim seemed to deflate, like the air draining out of a balloon.

The creatures discarded the flattened bodies and moved on to their next victims, even as the line of Natives continued firing bullets and arrows into them. Kai pictured more spores spawned from the feeding showering into the air, where they would sink into the ground to birth more of the offspring he had cut down in the Springs before they had a chance to become fully mature like these original twelve. The whole time the creatures' sweeping tentacles drew in more Inuit, more bullets and arrows sizzled through the air, producing no effect. The largest of the men, still dwarfed by the massive size of the creatures, went at them with axes and spears. Kai registered the night air being showered with pools of black ooze before the Inuit defenders fell victim to this impregnable force.

There was no retreat. These tuloc would fight until the last man. And when the creatures were done with them, they would come back to the Jaguar to finish the job of shredding its armor plating until their tentacles could sweep their way inside.

* * *

"Kai," Jules said into her headset, through the pounding in her head, "talk to me! Kai, are you there?"

"I'm here," Kai's voice finally came back.

"What's wrong? I can hardly hear you."

"Sorry," he said, louder. "I just witnessed a massacre. Villagers stormed the street, maybe a hundred of them. All gone."

Timur leaned in so Jules could see he wanted to say something. "Switch the targeting system to manual. Fire on them more selectively. Do you see the button on the touch screen?"

"Yes."

"Press it to engage the manual targeting system."

"Done."

"You up to the job of taking these things out with what shells you've got left?"

Kai looked toward Dennehy. "There's someone else on board who's a better shot, General."

* * *

Kai vacated his seat so the young trooper could take his place behind the weapons control systems. He watched as Dennehy engaged the miniguns first, working the targeting system. The last of the Natives had fallen by the time he circled a trio of the creatures in his digital crosshairs and opened fire with both roof-mounted miniguns.

The barrage took the legs out from under all three, spewing the now-familiar black oily substance into the air. Kai was beginning to think the 7.62mm fire had done the trick when all three seemed to pull themselves back together and rise back upon all three legs as if nothing had happened. This, while Dennehy turned the cannon on a pair of the creatures closing on the Jaguar. It boomed six times, exhausting the last of its ammo.

Kai watched the screen from over Dennehy's shoulder, the explosive shells blowing the two creatures apart, splashing blankets of black across the snowpack that looked to him like inkblots from a Rorschach test. Then, yet again, the loosened fragments congealed, retaking their original shape.

"You gotta be fucking kidding me," Kai heard Dennehy say under his breath.

The creatures were back in motion, moving slowly and almost lethargically at first. Their pace quickened rapidly, but still short of the speed they had originally displayed before reconstituting, at least for now.

Dennehy drained the rest of the miniguns on them and then retook his place in the driver's seat.

"I'm getting us out of here!"

However futile that sounded, Kai knew it was the only chance they had left to try. Dennehy had spun the vehicle all the way around to retrace their path out of Galena when the first thuds of creatures leaping atop its exterior sounded through the armored shell. Still, he pushed on through the storm-splattered night, dislodging the creatures from their holds on the Jaguar. Its bright headlight beams cut through the darkness to reveal the impossible sight of six spectral figures charging toward them.

Dennehy instinctively jammed on the vehicle's brakes, without consideration of the icy surface beneath all eight of its massive tires. The Jaguar spun around in a neat arc, the energy and heat generated by the spin tearing through the frozen ground. The tires dropped into the resulting gaps, leaving them facing back toward the center of the town.

"What the hell?" Dennehy managed. "What the fucking hell?"

Kai watched the six huge shapes drawing upon them, straight for the line of the creatures once again converging on the Jaguar.

"I was wrong," Trooper Muhtuk said. "Those are the Shadow People."

CHAPTER 34

Kaelens

Galena, Alaska

Jace activated his kaelen, feeling the other five of the Nine do the same. As he surged past the armored vehicle, his kaelen lengthened, thinned, and became a twelve-foot-long whip that he snapped in the air, drawing a spark. In the instant before the six of the Nine encountered the enemy converging upon them, Jace recorded the bright blue flame, tinged with white at the tip and down the sides, flaring at the end of Yusef's kaelen and the long black blade Mazz's had extended into. They took up his left flank, while the remaining three took up his right: Haran with her kaelen turned into something like a lasso, Zareb with his having extended to five feet in length with both ends finished in black blades, and Valeria's splitting apart to form two smaller versions connected by razor-sharp black wire formed of pure energy.

Throughout their millennia-long hibernation, they had fought countless battles together, simulations under Chronar's tutelage, in which they thought as one, acted as one.

Fought as one.

* * *

"Kai, come in!" Timur practically shouted into his headset. "Kai, give me your status!"

"There's something else here, General."

"What?" Timur managed, gaze locked with Jules's.

"I don't know what they are, but whatever they are, they've engaged the creatures. They're not your men?"

"Son, if I had any men at your twenty, I think I'd know it."

Kai regarded the viewing screen as the two lines were about to converge. "I'm not even sure they're men. Their size, the way they move…."

"Say again, please?"

"They're big and they're fast and don't look scared of these things at all. And they've got weapons like nothing I've ever seen before."

"Describe them."

"I can't. Our rescuers are too far away. All I can see are occasional bursts of light and sparks. It looks like they're wielding lightning. But whoever they are, whatever they are, they better kill these things," Kai said, as the battle began in a blur on his screen. "Because we're stuck here."

* * *

The six of the Nine worked together and alone at the same time. Jace lashed out with his whip, snapping it across the tentacles of an onrushing creature and slicing through four of them, which fell to the white ground in a thick pool of black ooze. This, as Haran spun her lasso through the air and closed it around the extremity above the tentacles, where the enemy's vision and hearing apparatuses were located. The lasso tightened organically, and Haran yanked back on it, severing what might have been the thing's head, which dropped to the white ground in its pocket of black ooze before the rest of the creature crumpled.

Jace's peripheral vision caught another of the creatures coming up on Haran from behind, when Mazz slashed his blade across the top of the torso from which its three legs extended. This creature spewed a fountain of black ooze into the night air before both halves of it spilled to the frozen ground.

Nearby, the first one Jace thought they had killed seemed to be pulling its severed pieces back together when Yusef shot a blinding white-tipped blue flame that burned at nearly five thousand degrees out from his kaelen and held it on the thing until the stench told him it was burning away. Two more of them were converging on Zareb from either side when he whirled his double-edged weapon into a blinding blur that left these two enemies standing still briefly before collapsing in twin piles of severed pieces.

As Yusef turned his flame on these remains next, another of the enemy lashed its tentacles for him, wrapping around his torso and tearing him off his feet. Valeria pounced with her twin kaelens connected by deadly wire from behind and pulled hard on the squarish head-like shape that rode above the sweep of the tentacles.

The severed shape dropped to the snow, black ooze pooling beneath it, the tentacles left flailing about blindly right into the path of Mazz's blade, which neatly severed the thing in two with a vertical cut that peeled the two halves off to crumple to the ground in twin pools of the now-familiar black ooze. Jace noted the tentacles kept whipping wildly about, reflexively, he thought at first. However, when they continued to grope the air blindly, he realized they were likely still functioning in some capacity.

Then he noticed Yusef standing motionless in the storm, the blue flame of his kaelen illuminating his frozen expression.

"Yusef!" Jace wailed, shaking him at the shoulder.

"That smell...."

Jace was aware of the corrosive, almost metallic stench of the burned remains of the creatures. The smell was familiar, as if he had come up against these things before. "What?"

"I know that scent. How do I know that—"

Before Yusef could complete his thought, a creature wheeled in toward him, tentacles flapping in the air. Jace snapped his whip out, slicing through the tentacles closest to Yusef and sending them plopping to the snow with black pools of ooze spreading beneath him. Yusef regained his senses and set the still squirming tentacles ablaze in a white-hot pool of fire.

For his part, Jace moved into the center of the remaining creatures, his strategy not planned but formed from instinct and in keeping with the shared thoughts harbored by the six of the Nine acting as one. He whirled about, flowing with the shrill wind blowing off the nearby inlet on which this settlement was perched. He lashed out with his whip in a constant blur, not so much to inflict maximum damage as to keep the enemy's still superior numbers from overwhelming his forces. Jace detected a change in the odor emanating from the things, which he took to mean they were communicating with each other about their plight. He had no idea if they were capable of strategizing or even retreating, doubting that either was the case, since everything Chronar had extrapolated about this enemy indicated that they were capable of only basic, instinctive actions that were genetically programmed into them.

"Yusef!" Jace formed that thought, alerting him to the severed and misshapen remnants of the fallen creatures, which appeared to be reconstituting themselves, a process that stopped under Yusef's blueish-white flame many times hotter and more destructive than what humanity could produce. By his count, four of the enemy were down, still leaving eight creatures for the six of the Nine to deal with.

"Yusef!" Jace called again in his mind, spotting Yusef rushing toward him with his blue-white flame cutting through the night.

* * *

"Who the hell are they?" Dennehy asked, watching the battle between the monsters and this newly arrived force.

"The better question, Trooper, is *what*?" Kai told him.

After what he'd seen over the past day, Kai wasn't ready to make any pronouncements about what he was witnessing before him. Whoever, or whatever, these beings were, they were gaining the upper hand thanks to weapons of a kind he had never seen or heard of.

Because they didn't exist. Not on Earth, anyway.

"What's happening, Professor?" Timur's voice blared over the speaker.

"Our new arrivals are taking these things on, and they're winning. As near as I can tell, they're winning."

"Could they be aliens too?" Kai heard him ask.

"They could be anything, General."

* * *

Yusef burned them with his fire.

Mazz cut them with his blade.

Haran tightened her tossed lasso around them from the rear so the others could have their way.

Valeria wielded what she called her nano-chucks in a blur, knocking the things off-kilter and seeming to short-circuit their tracking abilities. She seemed to be working in tandem with Zareb, who pounced on the suddenly easy targets for his dual spearheads, which he used to skewer and slice in a nonstop blur.

All this, while Jace snapped his whip out in repetitive blurs of motion, shredding whatever it struck and showering the white-frosted air with more of the black unctuous ooze. The enemy might have acted with one mind, but so did the six of the Nine.

None of the things stood whole at that point, and just as their enemy didn't tire or slow, neither did the six of the Nine. On a few occasions, the creatures managed to lash a tentacle to trip them up or reel them in, and it would be Mazz or Zareb who cut them free with a blade or Haran yanking the creature off its tripodal stance with her lasso for Yusef to light ablaze. Finally, after a stretch of time the six of the Nine did not bother to measure, the enemy lay vanquished, their remains smoldering in the last of Yusef's white-hot flames, their tentacles twitching until they melted to finally be absorbed into the air.

In that moment, Jace turned back to the armored vehicle and the humans who by all rights should never have survived the battle in the first settlement. The fact that they had gave him hope that the species the Nine were sworn to protect was worth saving and a potential ally in the fight yet to come. He did not think for a moment the war itself had been won here.

"How many dead in this settlement, Chronar?"

"Over four hundred, Jace, most in their homes. There are survivors as well, numbering fifty-seven, hidden in the structures."

Jace didn't bother to ask Chronar how many offspring that meant had been spawned from the enemy feeding on the nutrients of all those bones. This battle had been won, but the war, he knew, was still to come.

Chronar's voice sounded in his head, attuned to his thoughts as always. "You will have your weapons to help you, Jace. I've found their location."

* * *

On the viewing screen, their saviors were there…and then they weren't. To Kai, it was almost like they had melted away into the air.

Kai had been narrating the events as best he could to Timur and Jules, knowing how crazy it was to say that the last of all twelve of the creatures who had escaped the alien ship were dissolving in blueish-white pockets of flame.

"What now, General?" he asked when he provided a final update.

"We get your asses out of there in a chopper to rendezvous with us just outside of Anchorage."

"What's outside of Anchorage?"

"Mission control, Professor, headquartered inside a base that doesn't exist."

CHAPTER 35

Numb

Juneau International Airport, Alaska

Jules watched General Timur yank off his headset when the lights of Juneau International Airport flickered beneath the H225.

"The Ranger evacuating your husband and his team will be on station by the time we land," he told her. "We'll hold the jet until they arrive so they can join us for the flight."

"Flight where, General?"

"You've heard of Joint Base Elmendorf-Richardson outside of Anchorage, I assume."

"I've heard of Elmendorf Air Force Base," Jules told him, biting her lip when she felt it trembling to no avail.

"It's a joint base now, but we're headed to a second base constructed beneath it." He noticed her lip quivering. "Are you okay, Professor?"

"Just a little airsick, that's all."

Jules could tell Timur knew she was lying but nodded anyway in recognition of Charlie's head still cradled in her lap.

When they landed on the tarmac at Juneau International several minutes later, Jules spotted a sleek silver private jet completely devoid of markings parked nearby, guarded by six armed soldiers in black tactical gear. Three of them moved to take up positions as close as the slowing spin of the rotor would allow and then approached when it stopped. A crewmember lowered the manual set of stairs. They had barely touched the concrete when one of the soldiers garbed in black appeared in the Ranger's doorway and saluted Timur.

"Take Professor Bevins's daughter to the jet."

"No, Mom," Charlie whined, her face scrunched in protest, "I want to go with you."

"It's okay," Jules said, easing her daughter toward the waiting soldier. "I'll be right behind you."

Her daughter resisted briefly, then nodded, staring at Jules the whole time the soldier led her from the cabin onto the stairs.

"Thank you for that, General," she told Timur, sighing in relief.

"What's wrong, Professor?"

Jules tried to swallow, but failed. "I—I can't move my legs."

Part Five
DEEP BASE TITAN

"We live in a society exquisitely dependent
on science and technology,
in which hardly anyone knows anything about
science and technology."

—Carl Sagan

CHAPTER 36

The Boy

Deep Base Titan, Anchorage, Alaska

"Are you ready for today's lesson?"

The boy nodded. He sat cross-legged on the floor of the room that encompassed his world, facing the woman. She wore different clothes, themed by what feature of the world or the universe formed the basis of the day's lesson. Today, Gaia, as she was known to the boy, wore a shapeless, ice-gray dress with a matching top. That felt odd to the boy because he couldn't grasp what that color signified in relation to the topic for today.

"Today, we will discuss something entirely different from our norm. Time instead of place, the future instead of the past. Do you understand?"

The boy nodded again, his smile widening slightly. Various wooden and cord necklaces dangled from Gaia's neck, clacking together when she shifted her position before him. She sat cross-legged too, directly across from him, close enough for either to reach out and touch the other. Her black hair, which dangled past her shoulders, was streaked along both sides with a whitish-gray hue. Her eyes were the same shade of gray as her dress today, as opposed to the crystal blue, shimmering brown, or emerald green he had grown used to through the course of his many lessons over the years. Usually, they were radiant and full of life. But today the light had dimmed in them, and that made Gaia look sad.

Gaia was more than the boy's teacher. She was his guide to the world beyond these four walls, to things he had never seen. He closed his eyes as she spoke and could see and feel it all in his mind. The smells, sights, and sounds were so real that under Gaia's tutelage, he was able experience what she revealed to him in the reality she created. When they strolled down a foreign market along some far-off street, he could smell the grilling food and listen to the meat sizzle. When they walked on the beach, he could smell the salty air and feel the waves washing over his bare feet, his long brown hair blowing in the breeze lifted from the currents. When they took flight over cities and landscapes, he could measure the world by the stars and felt himself lost within the clouds as he floated in the air.

"You understand the principle of graduation," Gaia prompted, a statement instead of a question.

"I do," the boy nodded.

"Good. Because your lessons have ascended to the next level, and with this new level comes a new name to replace Taravúli. You recall the meaning of the name I gave you long, long ago."

"For the good of the Earth," the boy said, translating the ancient language that no one else in the world spoke anymore, except for him and Gaia.

"Now you will be Teraválar. From our lessons, can you tell me what that means?"

"Protector of the Earth."

"Very good," Gaia complimented, smiling.

It always made the boy, Teraválar now, feel especially happy when she smiled. Her praise filled him with warmth. They had spent hours every day together for as long as his mind could recall. His favorite lessons were those journeys in his mind, where Gaia whisked him beyond these four walls, where space and time bore no meaning and posed no restrictions.

"You wish to know how I can take you into the past and how we can cover thousands of miles in the time it takes to blink your eyes," Gaia said suddenly.

The boy nodded, aware as always that his thoughts were not secret to her.

"Spatial awareness and the passage of one moment to the next are how humanity resigns itself to the world around it and nothing more. I have taught you to go beyond such limitations inflicted by preconceived notions. Your mind suffers no such limitations, Teraválar. I have removed them so you may learn the secrets of the Earth and fulfill the purpose of the name you now bear."

"Because I am to be the Earth's protector."

A statement, not a question, that drew another smile to Gaia's lips. This one was different, seeming to emanate from deep, deep inside her. And it warmed the boy even more in a feeling of repose that lingered inside him. Through the twelve years of his life, the touch of others was not something he had known often and, for long stretches, at all. He longed for touch because it seemed to pass onto him a sensation of warmth he could not generate from any other source. But those he saw the most, his keepers who made up the only family he had ever known, were prone to keep their distance from him. And when he reached out to touch them, they would often shrink away, or even recoil, as if his touch would bring pain or discomfort.

"Have we ever discussed the word feylora?" Gaia asked the boy, in place of the touch he so craved.

"No, Gaia."

"In the ancient language that is ours alone, fey stems from a root word meaning 'course' or 'path.' And lora originates in 'unfolding' or 'unwritten.' Together, feylora means destiny. Everything we have done together, all the lessons you have learned and places I have taken you to teach you of this world have been about bringing you to the feylora that awaits."

"As protector of the Earth."

Gaia didn't smile this time, only nodded. The boy sensed a sadness that emanated from deep inside her. No, he corrected himself, it wasn't sadness so much as resignation born in the awareness that whatever all his lessons at her hand had been building toward was upon them. That so much she had shown him of the Earth would soon perish if he did not intervene.

"Teraválar," she resumed, "it has been thousands of Earth's years since I encountered someone worthy of that mantle and capable of taking it. I have longed for those times past and feared they were gone forever, until you arrived. Know that for you, time and space are merely tools. And, like any tool, they are fixed only by what the mind can conceive of them." She gazed to her left. "When you look toward that wall, what you can see of the world stops with it. But the world only stops from your perspective. To realize your feylora, you must see through that wall to what exists beyond what your vision permits. That is what makes you a válar, a protector or guardian, the first to emerge from times long past. It is a great responsibility I entrust upon you but one that we have been preparing for since our very first lesson."

In that moment, the boy looked into Gaia's eyes and saw the source of her sadness, her resignation. He sensed a looming separation between them, a time when his lessons would cease and be put into practice. He understood in that moment that she would not be able to join him in the great task that lay ahead, the very reason for his being, which defined his feylora. In that moment, he felt very much like the twelve-year-old boy he was. He saw his reflection in the wideness of her eyes, saw the sandy-brown hair that dangled past his shoulders and deep brown eyes that had seen so little beyond these walls, except for all that Gaia had shown him in their journeys.

"What is it you wish to ask me, Teraválar?"

He swallowed hard, sniffled, and choked back his tears. "Are there others like me?"

"There are no others exactly like you."

"So, I'm alone?"

"No," Gaia said.

And in that moment, she reached out and touched his forearm, then slid her hand down and took his in hers. The boy felt a rush of warmth surge through him. This was what the dreams he could remember felt like, capturing the contentment and serenity his conscious mind had never experienced before. In that moment, he felt whole, he felt secure, he felt....

Loved.

The boy completed his thought tentatively, afraid it weakened him. He had never known the love of another person, so what Gaia had just given him opened a door beyond which lay a great unknown.

"There are others," Gaia told him, squeezing his hand. "You are not alone."

I can feel them.

Had he said that or merely thought it? It didn't matter. Gaia could hear his thoughts as plainly as his words, and she smiled softly at him as if in acknowledgment.

"I have shown you how they came to be so that you may know them better. And soon they will know you, Teraválar."

"I don't want to wait."

"You're going to meet someone else sooner."

"Who?"

"A friend who will help you, as you must help her."

The boy wished Gaia could hold onto him forever. His long hair slipped past his eyes, and he flipped it aside with a quick jerk of his head, revealing the tears he couldn't choke back.

"Things have been as they must be," Gaia told him. "The truth of your reason for being will soon be revealed. Trust my word when I tell you none of this has been random. Your existence has been of my making through the flat plane of existence, where time holds no meaning. Now, take my other hand in yours and close your eyes."

The boy obliged, and a fresh wave of warmth flowed through him.

"Now, see the world with my eyes—the past, present, and future indistinguishable from each other. I want you to look forward into times that have not yet been and tell me what you see."

The boy tried, but only darkness greeted him. He squeezed his eyelids tighter and tried again, met by the same result.

"I'm sorry," he said, opening his eyes.

"Why?"

"I failed."

"You did not tell me what you saw."

"Because I saw nothing."

"No, you saw darkness, the absence of all that bears light, rendered from what once was. What you saw was the extinguishing of the Earth spirit. You saw one possible version of what is to come." She released his hands, and they plopped to the floor, the pulses of warmth that had surged through him fading with each breath. "Because soon you will leave this place to embark on the mission you were born to fulfill, the mission we have been preparing for."

The boy could not help but feel a tremor of fear. "Why did you show the darkness to me, Gaia?"

"Because you are the only one who can stop it."

CHAPTER 37

Test Tube

Deep Base Titan, Anchorage, Alaska

General Avery Timur turned his eyes from the monitor picturing the boy sitting cross-legged on the floor of the only home he had ever known.

"This is the matter of concern, what you rushed me here to see?" he said to Dr. Kevin Sharkey, whom he fondly referred to as the boy's keeper.

On the monitor before them, which was fed by a camera hidden within the boy's quarters, their subject sat cross-legged on the floor, continuing to speak to someone who wasn't there.

"These interludes are growing longer, General, and, yes, that is concerning indeed," Sharkey told him, pushing his glasses back up atop the bridge of his nose beneath his thinning hair.

A patch in the front kept dropping over his forehead, and Sharkey continued brushing it back to no avail. He always wore a white lab coat and carried the scent of stale sweat on his person, as if he were forever in need of a shower.

Sharkey had muted the sound, but Timur could still see the boy's lips moving from one of the angles the monitor afforded.

"He's a kid with an imaginary friend," Timur noted. "What's the big deal?"

"He calls her Gaia."

"He always has."

"But it's intensifying, General," Sharkey said, the concern evident in his voice. "I'm afraid for what this portends. I'm afraid he may be creating an entire alternative reality that he may eventually disappear into. I know it can be easy to treat him like a specimen trapped in a test tube, but we do so at the peril of all our work, our mission here, because it keeps us from viewing him as growing, changing, evolving."

"Evolving into what?"

Sharkey returned his gaze to the monitor. "That could well be what we are witnessing now."

Timur followed Sharkey's gaze. Since it was night, sections of the boy's enclosure shaped into windows showed a night scene beyond, complete with trees blowing softly in the breeze and the stars twinkling through the clouds rolling past in a constant loop. The practice had begun when the boy was much younger, aiming to produce the artificial effects of a natural environment, thereby providing the illusion of a world beyond his walls. The three-dimensional effects of the scenes that rotated across each twenty-four-hour period at staggered intervals were generated by artificial intelligence, rendering them incredibly lifelike. Even after the boy demonstrated a clear understanding that the world beyond his enclosure was nothing more than a projection, Dr. Sharkey had left the manufactured world in place because the illusion appeared to produce a calming effect on the boy, at least on a subconscious level.

Joint Base Elmendorf-Richardson itself was a massive facility, covering over sixty thousand acres outside Anchorage on coastal lowlands surrounded by high mountain ranges. More than thirty-two thousand service members and civilians, along with their respective families, lived and worked there. The air force and army bases were combined in 2005 by the Base Closure and Realignment Act, one of twelve joint bases to be merged.

Deep Base Titan had been initially constructed during the Cold War, underground on the outskirts of the base where the mothballed remains of a massive, but now decommissioned, AN/FLR-9 antenna stood to this day. The facility was envisioned as one of the locations selected for command-and-control operations to be utilized in the event of a nuclear war, long before Timur's time. He couldn't even imagine what the cost had been back then, or how the challenges of constructing such a facility deep beneath rock, ledge, shale, and frozen ground had been overcome. Back then, of course, the arms race meant no price tag was too large to assure superiority over the Soviet Union.

In later years, also before the general's time, the base had been retasked to replace Area 51 as not only the primary repository for alien artifacts and remnants but also as a base of operations to lead a response in the event visiting aliens turned out to be hostile. Timur imagined the funds required for the extensive renovation of the facility were even greater, likely far greater, to the budget for the original construction itself. In this case, Timur was well aware of the origin of that funding, belonging to a very select group that was part of a chain of command outside the military and government.

Because this group essentially *was* the military and government, at least behind the scenes, where the greatest power was inevitably wielded.

"Should we consider meds?" he asked Sharkey as the boy looked up toward the camera, seeming to regard Timur as the general regarded him.

"Only if you want to squash the development we've so painstakingly achieved."

Timur studied the boy for a few long moments, the shifting of emotions clear on his expression. Sharkey was right about him becoming more animated lately, and although that was cause for concern, there might well be a simple explanation for it.

"Maybe he's experiencing puberty, Doctor. Maybe that's the reason for this escalation or recalibration you're referring to."

Sharkey removed his glasses and closed his eyes, pinching his brow. "His latest physical exam did show signs of that, something else we should greet as a cause for concern."

"You haven't factored such an expected occurrence into your appraisal?"

"Because such a normally ordinary milestone introduces an unknown variable here. There is no precedent to go by, no research to consult or past case studies to rely on." Sharkey put his glasses back on. "In other words, as far as the boy's development goes, we are flying blind."

"We've been flying blind for twelve years, Doctor. You've been with him ever since his birth."

Sharkey chuckled.

"Is something funny?"

"Your use of the word *birth*, under the circumstances, I mean."

Timur brushed his comment off. "Let's focus on the present, shall we? Have you asked the boy about this imaginary friend he calls Gaia?"

"No. Because she is so real to him, I'm afraid any questions to that effect could potentially damage his psyche. And I don't want him to know that we're watching him always, especially now that he has reached a stage where he will begin to demand privacy."

"You don't think he already knows that, Doctor?" Timur scoffed. "Given his capabilities."

"My primary concern here rests with continuing their development, which could be hampered by this alternative reality he is in the process of constructing. Having imaginary friends is a natural and expected occurrence during a child's formative years. But I had expected that with maturation, these encounters would wane. Instead, they have only increased and intensified. Again, that leaves us in uncharted territory here. That's why I called you here to see for yourself."

Timur couldn't take his eyes off the boy on the monitor. He had watched him grow from an infant, watched him take his first steps and utter his first words, yet he felt no particular paternal instincts toward the boy they called Elias. He was a project, like any other weapons or intelligence system, to be honed, refined, and further developed.

Just like his own sons.

Timur had badly wanted to love his two boys. And when that failed to happen with the first one, he convinced himself things would be different two years later when the second arrived to the same result. Ultimately, the best he could do was mold them as he had molded Elias. Ironically, the twelve years he had been doing that was longer than the opportunity he had with his own sons. After his wife divorced him, she was granted full custody. Even more ironically, both his sons followed his footsteps into the army and combat, one being killed in Iraq and the other Afghanistan. Timur believed they wanted to die just to get back at him, which didn't stop him from crying at both their funerals.

The only times in his life he could remember doing that.

"Tell me of the boy's progress," he asked Dr. Kevin Sharkey, wishing he cared about his charge beyond the progression of his capabilities he was responsible for overseeing.

"His strength is that of someone twice his age, on par with one of those elite soldiers of yours. His intelligence would likely mark him as possessing an IQ approaching two hundred. He learns, he practices, and he masters any act he performs."

"That's very good to hear, Doctor."

"Would you like to hear what's not?" Sharkey continued before Timur could respond. "His emotional development. We've paid a significant price for the decision to isolate him this way."

"Made because no one outside of this facility can know he exists, Doctor."

"I'm well aware of that, General. But it likely explains the imaginary friend he calls Gaia and the increasing depth of the exchanges he's having with her and, thus, himself. We may be wise to consider introducing more human-type stimulation to replace his daily visits from Gaia."

"Does he ever speak of her to you?"

"He used to," Sharkey told him, "but not for several months now, since the onset of what we now believe was puberty. Their imagined conversations have become longer, with increasing vocal lapses during which the boy appears to be absorbing information from her. And not just that. Brain scans conducted in the midst of those intervals have revealed the kind of activity associated with movement, exercise, even training—always in the company of Gaia."

"You speak of her like she's real."

"Because she is to the boy."

He heard the phone in his pocket buzz. Traditional cell coverage didn't exist within Deep Base Titan, but the device he had been provided operated differently.

"I'm needed elsewhere, Doctor," he told Sharkey. "I'll be back to check in with the boy myself as soon as I attend to this other matter."

"I'll be here, General."

Timur waited until he was outside Sharkey's lab, located one level above the boy's enclosure, to ease the device from his pocket and read the text message, in all caps as always.

COME TO MY QUARTERS, GENERAL

CHAPTER 38

Treatment

Deep Base Titan, Anchorage, Alaska

Kai sat at Jules's bedside, Charlie nestled against her mother, sleeping in Deep Base Titan's expansive sickbay.

"We knew this was coming," Jules said softly, so as not to disturb their daughter.

"Not this soon."

"It should have been sooner. We both know that too."

"Is that supposed to make me feel better?" Kai asked her, fighting to keep his voice from cracking.

"You never wanted to face it. How many miracle cures did you chase, Kai?"

"As many as it takes to find one that works. I'm not giving up."

"Neither am I. But there comes a time...."

"What?" Kai prompted when her voice trailed off.

"We have to accept the things we cannot change."

"This is no time for the Serenity Prayer, Jules."

Kai heard footsteps shuffling and saw Jane Piedmont standing at the entrance to Jules's curtained cubicle. She was holding the infant against her with what passed for a baby bottle in her free hand, made from a laboratory beaker with a jerry-rigged rubber stopper serving as the nipple. Even though Deep Base Titan maintained this fully stocked infirmary that was more like a self-contained hospital, Kai had to figure that the formula must have been jerry-rigged too.

"This your wife, Professor?"

"Mrs. Piedmont, meet Jules. Jules, Mrs. Piedmont."

"Jane. You look about as bad as I do. Your hubby here recognized the stink from my bones from Paget's disease, so I pressed him as to how. Sorry, girl."

"Right back at ya, Jane."

The old woman scowled. "I'm nearly twice your age. No sympathy required, especially since I hear I have the two of you to blame for that bone biopsy they did on me. As if I've got any good bone left to spare…."

Jane Piedmont wore a shapeless hospital gown in place of her nightgown and slippers instead of her old boots. The gown made her frame look even more deformed, her bones jutting out at odd angles thanks to the disease that had so badly distorted them. Kai cringed at the thought of what she looked like beneath the smock. He watched the old woman's gaze slide to the snoozing Charlie.

"Pretty girl."

"Thanks," Kai and Jules said together.

"With the two of you as parents, she must be smart as a whip too." Piedmont's gaze tightened. "Look, I moseyed down here to ask you a couple of questions, Professor. Who the fuck were those men who saved us in Galena?"

"I don't know, Mrs. Piedmont, not who they were or where they came from."

"I was too busy taking care of the kid to see much on your screen, but they sure were big, weren't they? And those weapons…. You figure maybe they came from outer space too?"

"Everything we saw was recorded. Tech experts are reviewing the footage now."

"Tech experts…. Sounds like a job for a couple of astrobiologists, if you ask me. Not that anybody has."

Kai waited for her to continue.

"Anyway, I'm guessing it's not over. Far from it."

"They killed a lot of people in Galena, Mrs. Piedmont, a lot more than the Springs. Means more offspring, lots more in all probability."

"So tell this General Timer to nuke the place."

"I'm sure something like that is being discussed. And his name is Timur."

"Runs this place, does he?"

Kai nodded.

Piedmont shook her head. "I've seen places like this in the movies a hundred times. Always figured they might exist for real but never thought I'd see the inside of one."

"Have you seen the troopers?" Kai asked her, eager to change the subject.

"The young one, not the lady. He said they're operating on her leg."

And preserving the damaged tissue for closer examination, Kai knew, to gain a better understanding of how the creatures functioned. Understanding them was the best way, the only way, to determine their vulnerabilities and weaknesses.

"You ask me," the old woman resumed, "she'll be lucky to walk with a limp the way that thing clamped onto her. Meanwhile, I've outstayed my welcome. I'll leave you young folks to it." Her gaze fell on Charlie again as she continued to hold the makeshift baby bottle to the infant's lips. "Hope they find parents as good as you for this little tyke."

Then she drew the cubicle's curtain closed and was gone.

"You think she's right?" Jules wondered.

"About what?"

"Your saviors. That maybe they're aliens too."

"I don't know what they were, Jules. Only that the weapons they killed those things with don't exist in our world."

"We never thought a place like Deep Base Titan existed here either."

"I told Mrs. Piedmont the truth," Kai said. "I don't know who they were, what they were, or where they came from, besides that jet we saw pass just a few hundred feet off the ground."

"So, what, they parachuted out or something?"

Kai shrugged. "Maybe. One thing was clear: They knew exactly what they were after and what was waiting for them in Galena."

"Maybe that makes them some kind of intergalactic cops or bounty hunters, tracking down escaped prisoners like those things from the alien ship."

"They wouldn't have arrived in a jet if they came from outer space."

Jules dropped her gaze to Charlie and held it there when she responded, "Is this what we became astrobiologists for?"

Kai shook his head. "We became astrobiologists to encounter alien beings someday, to study them alive…or dead."

"The specimen you brought back," Jules realized, perking up.

"It's time for us to examine it."

CHAPTER 39

The World Consortium

Deep Base Titan, Anchorage, Alaska

The black metallic door slid open as Timur approached it, requiring no keycode, handprint, or scan. He entered, heard the door *whoooosh* closed behind him, and found himself within the spacious, elegantly furnished domain of William Franklin Takashi.

"Welcome, General," Takashi's soft, soothing voice greeted. "It's so good to see you. Having learned of the threat you were facing, I was worried our paths had crossed for the last time."

"I've been underestimated more than my share of times, sir."

On the verge of becoming the world's first trillionaire, Takashi had become the ultimate recluse, having withdrawn from the world he owned vast portions of in a manner not seen since the days of Howard Hughes. The son of a Japanese industrialist father and an American philanthropist mother, Takashi had bankrolled virtually all the funding required to update Deep Base Titan from a Cold War relic into the technological marvel it was today. His lifelike projection stood atop a platform in the sprawling quarters he had constructed for himself within the base, though he no longer frequented it in person. His hair never varied from its black shade, styled straight back with gel that shone in whatever lighting captured his image. Although he was half-Japanese, he looked far more American, only the slight bend of his eyes suggesting any hint of Asian heritage. But the most curious feature Takashi boasted was also the oddest: He never smiled.

Timur could not recall a single occasion where his expression had been anything but flat, either during their in-person meetings or the years since he had withdrawn from society. Anger and disappointment rode his face when he expressed either, but never joy, never happiness, never the kind of compassion that made him and Timur kindred spirits. To that point, one of the few things the general knew about Takashi's personal life was that all three of his children had perished tragically before the age of ten: one to cancer, one who drowned in the family's pool, and a third to a drunk driver that had ultimately claimed his wife's life too after she lay in a coma for six months. It was right after her death when Takashi had withdrawn from society. As far as Timur knew, no one had seen him in person since.

"Outline the next steps and tell me exactly when I'll have the results I need," Takashi ordered.

Thanks to having weathered the years so well, the sound state of the base's structural integrity made its drastic upgrade feasible, though only slightly less daunting. Underground roads needed to be built to allow passage for the construction vehicles required to remake the base to specifications that would securely house the finds yielded by deep space exploration. Whatever probes and space drones were able to bring back from distant stars, asteroids, and planets could now be examined and studied without fear of release or contamination. Dealing with such scientific unknowns required the utmost level of containment, not to mention the base's primary purpose of serving as command central for both the study of alien life forms and the headquarters for a potential war fought against alien invaders.

Because the base had been constructed to withstand a nuclear explosion, few modifications to the structure were required to make it as impregnable as possible from an alien attack as well. The US military and government were parties and partners in the rebuild, which had taken nearly a decade to complete due to the logistical challenges involved, even with unlimited funding available. What neither the military nor the government knew at the time was that Takashi's efforts were conducted on behalf of an even larger concern composed of other wealthy and powerful men, as well as women, who fancied themselves the owners of the world and, thus, its masters, known collectively by a term that aptly described them: the World Consortium.

Its members dwelled in the shadows, pulling the world's strings like master puppeteers working behind the curtain. Timur could not name a single member of the Consortium other than Takashi. When the military had placed him in charge of Deep Base Titan, no mention of the Consortium's existence had been raised. And to this day, Timur remained unsure whether his superiors knew anything of the base's true backers, or whether their ignorance was based on the plausible deniability of such a partnership, or why he had been personally chosen for this command.

The lighting in the quarters was soft and ambient, dominated by the flickering firelight from an old-fashioned hearth housing gas-fed flames. The walls were adorned with priceless artwork, and the floors were lined with custom-made furniture that Takashi had enjoyed before the leader and founder of the World Consortium vanished into isolation.

Proceeding further into the spacious windowless confines, Timur approached the platform upon which a life-size, perfectly rendered, three-dimensional hologram of William Franklin Takashi stood.

"I've reviewed all the footage you forwarded me, General, as well as the audio tapes. Quite a remarkable situation, I'd venture to say."

"I'm not sure if remarkable is the word I would use, sir."

"Remarkable can mean many things. Unprecedented might be a better way of putting it."

"I'd prefer dangerous and threatening, sir."

"Indeed, General. And what else can you report about the beings that laid waste to our visitors in Galena, Alaska?"

"No more than what my original report indicates."

"No notion, then, as to what became of them after they dispatched our visitors?"

"None with any certainty. But a private jet that turned out to be of false registry took off from Juneau International Airport two hours later with a flight plan filed for Seattle before it disappeared off radar."

"You believe these beings were on board?"

"It's an anomaly, just like they are. If I've learned anything in my career, it's that anomalies like that are normally connected."

"I find their involvement fascinating, General," the perfectly rendered, three-dimensional projection noted. "Apparently, by all accounts, they are neither alien nor human. Would that be your current assessment?"

"They were of humanoid form but capable of physical feats in terms of speed, strength, and reflex far beyond anything man is capable of. And nothing remotely approaching the weapons they wielded exists today."

"So, where, General, did they come from? I've viewed the enhanced versions of the recording made by the armored vehicle. It's not all clear, but the effects of those weapons were clear enough. They appeared to be self-generating and self-powering, which would suggest the weapons are based on principles of nanotechnology beyond anything we can conceive of or formulate today. I'd ask you to imagine what the Consortium could do with that technology."

Timur remained silent, waiting for Takashi to continue on his own.

"As for our alien visitors, we know they can be killed. A good thing. What we don't know is if they can be controlled. A better thing. Or if the specimen you have and the additional ones you will need to procure will yield something we can use to our advantage—the best thing of all. I assume you understand the point I'm making with this."

"I do, sir. You want to explore our capacity to weaponize them somehow."

"Along with the technology that powered those robotic sentinels that nearly took your life. Imagine an army of those things, General, virtually indestructible and self-repairing. The wielder of such an army would have the world at their feet, would they not?"

"Until someone else finds something better, yes."

Takashi's expression flirted with a smile that never quite broke. "That someone will be the Consortium, General. People elect politicians to secure their belief that they can control their leaders. But they don't even know of our existence, those of us who have blended government, technology, and the military into one. Our greatest weapon lies in the fact that we hide in plain sight, maneuvering and manipulating to suit our own ends. Toward that end, how are we assuring the threat faced in Chichagof Springs and Galena is contained?"

"We believe the threat within the former has been neutralized. As for the latter, we have set up a containment zone with strike aircraft and helicopter gunships on station to respond in the event more of the creatures surface after dark. If those efforts fail to subdue them, we have air force fighter jets prepped and ready. Several of those jets are equipped with missiles containing tactical nuclear weapons as a last resort."

Takashi weighed that possibility, appearing completely unmoved. "Now tell me of what might be our greatest weapon of all—our test subject."

The boy's existence, too, had been made possible by the Consortium.

"His development has progressed to another level, thanks, we believe, to puberty."

"A new set of tests to determine what this means for his capabilities should be ordered, General. This development could be the opportunity we have been awaiting his entire life."

"I've sent you the recordings of him addressing an imaginary friend."

"A minor source of concern. You feel otherwise?"

"The interactions are growing longer, hours and hours every day, when he is outside the company of those assigned to monitor and train him. My concern, sir, lies in the notion that he could vanish into this fantasy altogether, in which case he would be lost to us."

Takashi's projection seemed to be pondering the ramifications of that. "And what would you suggest to ameliorate the situation?"

"We may have to resort to radical, almost primitive techniques. Psychotropic medication, even electroshock therapy."

"We can't risk damage to his brain."

"We can't risk his consciousness slipping away either, sir."

Again, the projection pondered the prospects. "Do what you deem best but at the lowest possible dosage or charge."

"Thank you, sir. If there's nothing else," Timur added, starting to turn toward the door.

"Just one other thing: I understand why you brought our guests to this facility, and I understand how they may serve our purpose. But they can never be allowed to depart. I leave their fates to you, General. Is that clear?"

Timur nodded.

CHAPTER 40

Reconnaissance

Joint Base Elmendorf-Richardson, Anchorage, Alaska

"*You will have your weapons to help you, Jace. I've found their location.*"

With that, Chronar had directed the Nine to Joint Base Elmendorf-Richardson in Anchorage. Seven of them had assembled on a ridge overlooking the far edge of the military installation, where the secret facility housing their weapons lay beneath an ancient, no-longer-functional spy antenna.

Deep Base Titan, Chronar called it.

After destroying their enemy in the settlement of Galena, the six of the Nine had run through the hard-packed snow and the rest of the lingering storm to reach Juneau Airport, where Xan and their jet were waiting. Brenn and Izumi were en route back from their failed attempt to retrieve the weapons which had somehow been discovered and relocated here to this base.

Once Xan had parked on the tarmac in Anchorage, the seven of the Nine made off in a passenger shuttle bus, shut down for the night, that serviced the private air terminal to make the drive to the outskirts of Elmendorf. They had proceeded the rest of the way to this ridge on foot.

"The weapons are being stored on the lowest underground level of this facility," Chronar told Jace. "I have been able to identify several construction tunnels, sealed now, but still capable of providing your means of access."

"Can you send me the facility's schematics and detailed locations of these tunnels?"

"Of course, and I've already chosen the most direct route to penetrate the facility at its lowest level. You will find vehicles there on which to load the containers and machines to lift them."

"What of the enemy we were awoken to face, Chronar?"

"Your initial conclusions in the second settlement have been confirmed. We are looking at a potential worst-case scenario. Without your weapons, you stand no chance of defeating them, since the weapons of this world are woefully inadequate toward that end."

Jace didn't need Chronar to tell him that. It had taken everything the six of the Nine's handheld weapons could provide to defeat the original twelve of the enemy. The next confrontation would be with many times that number, thousands easily and even tens of thousands. And if the Nine failed there, the mission they had been awakened to fulfill would be lost, and this civilization would perish horribly.

"There's something else, Jace," he heard Chronar say in his mind. "A presence in the underground base I cannot identify."

"One of the enemy?"

"Undetermined at this time. But its energy is powerful enough to register on my scan. If it is hostile, your chances of success will be severely diminished."

CHAPTER 41

Specimen

Deep Base Titan, Anchorage, Alaska

"Why couldn't I stay with Mom?" Charlie asked.

Next to her, Kai adjusted the cameras over the vacuum-sealed plastic container in which the near-whole specimen he'd brought back from the Springs rested on a raised platform in the center. In years past, there would have been pliable slots in which to insert his hands so they wouldn't come into contact with the specimen under study. Today, the examination would be handled remotely thanks to robotic controls, and fortunately, he was well-versed in the operations of this particular model. He would view the results of what would essentially be an autopsy on a monitor identical to one placed near Jules's bed so she could follow along and offer input.

"She needs to rest," he told his daughter.

"Working with you isn't rest, Dad."

Touché, Kai thought.

"She couldn't walk when we landed in the helicopter," Charlie resumed.

Kai made sure not to look her way.

"I know she's sick." Charlie swallowed hard to steel herself before continuing. "I know it's bad. I can see that for myself, even though you haven't told me."

Kai couldn't avoid the issue any longer and couldn't bear to lie to his daughter. "Yes," he said, as if in answer to a question she hadn't posed.

"But she's going to get better, right? They can give her a shot or something, or pills maybe."

"They're trying, Char."

He met his daughter's stare and tried not to let his eyes reveal the truth. Children were so intuitive about such things. He forced a smile and reached over to stroke his daughter's hair.

"I don't like this place," she said. "I want to leave."

"We have this work to finish first."

"I want to leave *now*!" Charlie insisted, tears brimming in her eyes.

"Let Mom and I finish our work, and we'll talk about it."

"Promise?"

"Promise."

Charlie's eyes fell on the lab container. "That's one of them, isn't it? Did you kill it?"

"You bet. Just like in your video games."

"You suck at playing video games."

"Guess I'm getting better."

Charlie regarded the infantile creature again, wrinkling her nose. "You really killed it?"

Kai thought back to the miniguns and 40mm cannon firing in automated mode. "And a whole lot more," he said, omitting that detail.

She nodded and managed a smile. "You *are* getting better, Dad."

Kai steadied his hands on the controls rigged to the robotic extremities contained in the sealed plastic enclosure. "I'm going to start, Jules," he said toward the panel's hidden speaker.

"I'm with you, babe. Turn the monitor so I can see Charlie."

Kai angled it to his right and watched Jules cast a wave to her daughter, managing a smile.

"Hey, little girl."

"Hey, Mom. But, really, I'm not a little girl anymore. You always tell me that, even though you always treat me like one."

Kai could see how much Jules was struggling with this. Her cheeks were sunken, and her coloring was somewhere between pale and yellow. He hoped that was because of poor lighting in the base's hospital facility but suspected it wasn't.

"My bad."

"That's okay. You need to get better."

"I know," Jules said and swallowed hard. "But I need to work with Dad now."

Kai tilted the monitor back toward him, so only he could see Jules. The controls for the robotic dissection system he sat before made him feel like he was about to play one of his daughter's video games on the full-size game console attached to their flat-screen television back home. He wondered if Jules would ever see that home again.

"Where would you like me to start?" he asked her, a three-dimensional rendering of the creature projected on a twin screen before him, so he could properly manipulate the robotic fingers.

"Like any autopsy. With an incision down the center of the thorax, or what passes for one."

Kai cut straight along the center of the oblong dark shape from which the tentacles extended, stopping when he came to a cavity that looked like a perfectly round mouth, and then picking up again on the other side. The dozen attached tentacles spasmed in unison, a reflexive action that nonetheless cost him a breath and left his heart pounding. Then he peeled back the rubbery flesh on both sides to reveal the infantile creature's insides.

"It's nearly hollow," Kai narrated, even though Jules could see for herself.

"Unformed," she added, "little more than fetal. Bring the camera in closer to the interior walls."

Kai did and waited for Jules to continue. "Two cell layers with the outer epidermis and inner gastrodermis, separated by mesoglea," she said, referring to a gelatinous layer that functioned as a kind of fluid-based skeleton that held the creature together, forming its structural integrity. "The gastrovascular cavity that surrounds the mouth must house the undeveloped central digestive system."

"I left med school behind a long time ago, Jules. By gastrovascular, you mean...."

In spite of herself, she managed to chuckle. "A single cavity with one opening that both digests food and distributes nutrients to sustain metabolic function. Now, see those pustules attached to the inner shell of the gastrodermis?"

Anticipating Jules's next thought, Kai used a robotic scalpel to pierce the outer membrane of one of the tiny pimple-like shapes. Instantly, black viscous fluid leaked out.

"The pustules rupture," he started, voicing her thoughts, "spreading that black ooze to form more pustules. That's how these things grow. Any notion as to how quickly they might reach full maturity?"

Jules pondered that briefly. "I would postulate that their initial feeding cycles, like what you witnessed in that town, stimulate the division of the pustules. They utilize the nutrients from human bones to accelerate their cellular growth on a geometric level. It was impossible to notice under the circumstances, but I'm guessing the creatures who fed on those soldiers were already significantly bigger than this specimen."

"So they require sustenance to grow, like all creatures," Kai surmised.

"At this stage of development, they likely use the ingredients in the ground soil they were nesting in as nutrients. Remember, ground soil and human bones share a significant level of common elements, including oxygen, carbon, hydrogen, calcium, phosphorus, and sulfur."

"And given the crucial role soil plays in preserving vegetation and insect life, they must also have utilized it to fuel their growth in the Springs."

"Quite the perfect organism we've got here, isn't it, Professor Bevins?"

"Indeed, Professor Bevins," Kai said back to her.

Jules's voice had come to life again, her eyes as well. She was back in her element, alight in the expertise that defined her career as she found herself analyzing an alien species—a defining moment in her life's work.

"I would postulate we're looking at a very advanced version of the freshwater hydra," Jules proposed, referring to small carnivorous creatures that could also regenerate themselves and never aged. The freshwater hydra boasted up to a dozen tentacles, each outfitted with deadly stingers, attached to a narrow body that tapered to a hole-like mouth at the bottom. "Close in on the refuse from those ruptured pustules, particularly those white specks that look like pinpricks."

Kai did. Under the microscope, they looked like—

"Eggs," Jules said, completing his thought for him.

"I saw larger versions of them spewing from the creatures that killed the soldier out on the street in the Springs. Ingesting bone must fuel the development and expulsion of their spores." Kai took another look at the creature's entire exposed inner layers. "Notice what's missing in the projection of this creature's bodily mechanics?"

"A brain cavity."

"Exactly. When I got an up-close-and-personal look at the hatchlings in the Springs, I thought they bore some resemblance to cephalopods like squids or octopuses. But those creatures exhibit some degree of rudimentary thinking, especially octopuses, given their ability to consider complex scenarios. Lacking a brain cavity, though, means our alien creatures have no more capacity for thought than the plants and insects they most closely resemble. These creatures must rely entirely on primal instinct."

"Or," countered Jules, "their brain capacity is spread on the cellular level throughout the entire form. There may be no precedent for that here on Earth, but that's an entirely moot point, given they originated who knows how many millions, even hundreds of millions of miles away. They could have been traveling for thousands and thousands of years in that ship before it crashed into the ice."

Jules stopped, seeming to freeze up. Kai feared she was losing consciousness and he might be losing her. Then her gaze sharpened and the life returned to her voice when she resumed.

"I just thought of something, an experiment of sorts, to test a rather frightening hypothesis. Spray some water on the exposed cavity, focusing on those pustules."

Kai had one of the robotic hands lift a thin tube from a collection of available tools, position it over the creature's exposed insides, and gush a steady stream of water onto the pustules growing on the inner layer. Instantly, all of them ruptured to almost immediately form new ones.

He lurched back involuntarily. "It's still alive?"

"Not as a functioning organism, no. The individual parts are something else again. Can we have a look at one of those pustules under the electron microscope?"

Kai worked the robotic controls appropriately to slice off one of the pimple-like growths and move it onto a slide beneath the lens of the microscope connected to the vacuum-sealed chamber. Then, he sharpened the focus manually and brought up the sample resting beneath the lens.

"You're right," he said, studying the microscopic cells growing in number. "Exposure to water lifted these components of the organism from dormancy. Even though they can no longer fuel their growth as a fully functional organism, these cells can continue to divide under the right circumstances."

"Just as I thought," Jules said. "Human bone is primarily composed of hydroxyapatite, a mineral form of calcium phosphate. Calcium and phosphorus are also found in water. That's why spraying the interior wall of the cavity reactivated cellular division, which proves my hypothesis. You know what this means, Kai."

"These hatchlings can develop in the water as much as they can while nesting underground."

"Maybe even faster."

Kai thought of Galena, the anomaly that had plagued him as to why the creatures had bypassed two other towns closer to the Springs to target an Inuit fishing village next. Now that made perfect sense.

"If we're right about this, Jules...."

"I know, I know. But there's one more avenue to explore that's more in our favor," Jules said, her voice sounding even weaker and more strained. "Do you have the sample taken of Jane Piedmont's bone?"

Kai reached for a nearby syringe. "Mixed with normal saline, as we discussed."

"Have the robot spray the contents over the exposed interior wall so we can view how the pustules react."

Kai inserted the syringe into the slot, entered the proper coding to give the robotic controls their marching orders, and pressed enter. The robotic arm took the syringe in its grasp, positioned it over the creature's interior wall, and pressed the plunger, releasing the liquid compound. Instantly, the pulsing pustules regenerated by exposure to water closed up and shriveled, their black exterior layers hardening into gray-toned protective shells.

"We have confirmation that the scent of Jane Piedmont's bones does indeed act as a repellant to the creatures," Jules pronounced, sounding stronger in the moment.

"Congratulations, Professor Bevins," Kai followed, "we have our first measure of defense against these creatures. But given the reason why they struck Galena next, it may already be too fuck—"

He stopped himself too late, forgetting his daughter was only a few feet away. He started to turn toward her to apologize.

"Sorry about—"

He stopped again.

Because Charlie was gone.

CHAPTER 42

Lost

Deep Base Titan, Anchorage, Alaska

Charlie walked along the dark halls that smelled like nothing at all. She kept looking for something familiar, something that told her this big, giant place wasn't so dark and scary.

She thought she knew the way back to her mother in the hospital. Being away from her mother left her scared, because Charlie knew she was very sick. She'd known that for a while but didn't bother asking since her mother wouldn't tell her a terrible truth she didn't want to hear.

Charlie couldn't contemplate life without her mother, so until she came to this place, she kept herself from thinking about it. Something about being away from her though, even for just a few minutes, left her thinking about nothing else. She had to get back to her bedside because then she'd see her mother was still alive, and as long as she stayed right there and never left, her mother wouldn't die.

Except, Charlie realized, she was lost amid the sprawl of twisting turning hallways that made her think of a maze. She couldn't even remember if this was the right level. She remembered riding the elevator with her father, but had they gone up or down? And where was the elevator?

A dread fear seized her, twisting her insides into knots. She wanted to stop, sink to the floor, and cry, or scream loud enough for her dad to hear and come find her.

Then, suddenly, a wave of warmth washed through her, leaving Charlie calm and composed. It felt like somebody had put the directions to wherever she was going in her mind, almost like a GPS route she couldn't see but was following anyway. She was headed somewhere she was supposed to go, steered by a murmuring voice at the edge of her consciousness.

Is that you, Mom?

Her mother could always make her feel better about stuff, no matter what it might be. And, sometimes, when she had a problem in school, Charlie would hear her voice in her head, even if she wasn't there. But this felt different, and the voice she couldn't quite make out wasn't her mother's.

Time felt different too, like in a dream. She found herself in a different hall on what looked to be an entirely different level with no recollection of how she'd gotten there. Almost as if she'd gone to sleep and woken up where she was now.

Then she saw two of the black-clad soldiers slumped on the floor on either side of a door at the far end of the hall. She drew closer; it looked like they were sleeping, having slipped off the chairs each must have been occupying. She thought maybe one of the men had a phone she could use to call her father, so he could come and get her. Both had funny-looking devices clipped to their ears, but no cell phones were visible on their belts or bulging from their pockets. So she thought maybe there was a phone inside the room she could use. The knob turned in her hand, and she pushed the door open enough to slide through.

"I've been waiting for you," a boy's voice said.

CHAPTER 43

Friends

Deep Base Titan, Anchorage, Alaska

Startled, Charlie swung toward the voice.

"How'd you know I was coming?" she said, searching for the boy in the dim lighting. "You scared me."

"A friend told me."

"What friend? Do I know them?"

"Not yet."

The boy finally emerged from the shadows in the corner, as if he'd been hiding there. He held her gaze, almost like he was studying her, unsure of what she was exactly. He had the deepest brown eyes she had ever seen. It was hard to let go of them. Charlie didn't pay a lot of attention to boys in school, but she and her friends liked picking out the cute ones. This boy certainly would have qualified there, maybe the cutest. Everything about him seemed perfect, and she liked the way he flipped the long hair from his face with a quick snap of his head. He was wearing a gym suit that rode his shoulders too tightly, as if he had outgrown it and nobody had noticed.

"How old are you?" Charlie asked him.

"Twelve."

She narrowed her gaze. "I thought more like fifteen. You're big for your age."

"How old are you?"

"Eleven and a half."

"Maybe you're small for your age."

"I am. But don't let that fool you, because I'm tough."

The boy smiled and liked the feeling of it, liked being around Charlie. "She told me about you," he told her.

"Who?"

"Gaia."

"Who's Gaia?"

"My friend."

Charlie hesitated for a moment. "I'll be your friend."

"That's what she told me. I'm supposed to help you."

"Help me what?"

The boy shrugged. "And you're supposed to help me too."

"How?"

The boy shrugged again. "I've never had a friend before except Gaia."

"What do you do with Gaia?"

"Talk."

"That's all?"

"She shows me things, teaches me things."

"You play games with her?"

"Games? Not really. But I know how to play chess. I've been playing since I was really little."

"What's your name?"

"It's supposed to be Elias, because that's what they call me."

"I don't like that name."

"Me either. They call me that because it means something. Gaia gave me a new name."

"What?"

"Teravālar," the boy said after a pause, as if he had to remember it.

"I don't like that name either. It's too hard to say. I'll just call you Terry."

"Okay."

"Hi, Terry."

"What's your name?"

"Charlie."

"That's a boy's name."

"My real name is Charlotte."

Charlie studied the boy's room closely. It didn't look like a kid's room at all, at least not hers. She didn't spot a single toy, trophy, or wall poster of a band or sports team. Come to think of it, there were no pictures evident anywhere. The walls were stark, and because it was so big, the room looked somewhat desolate, with only the bare essentials of furnishings. And the windows looked like the world outside, except it couldn't be because they were underground. There was a big flat-screen television mounted on the wall, bigger than any one she'd ever seen before.

"Do you play video games?"

"What are those?"

"You don't know what a video game is?"

The boy shook his head, looking down at the floor shyly.

"Do your parents work at this place? Is that why you live here?"

"I don't have any parents," the boy said.

"I'm sorry."

"Why are you sorry?"

"Because I thought maybe something happened to them."

"Maybe," the boy echoed. "I don't know. I never met them."

Charlie wondered if there was something wrong with the boy, if he was nuts or crazy or something. Or maybe he was dangerous and had to be isolated, like this was some kind of prison. That would explain the guards at the door.

"Why are there guards outside your door? Are you important or something?"

"I don't know. I must be to somebody."

"They fell asleep or something. That's how I walked right past them. One was snoring. So, what did your friend Gaya tell you about me?"

"It's pronounced Guy-ah. And she just told me we were going to be friends and that I needed to help you."

"Help me what?"

The boy looked down shyly, the way he did when he couldn't answer her. "I don't know. Gaia hasn't told me yet. We're supposed to help each other."

"How can I help you?"

"I don't know that yet either."

"Is Gaia your age?"

"No, older."

"How old?"

"I don't know."

Charlie resumed her scan of the spacious room. There was a couch, a soft easy chair, and a table with four matching chairs set around it, all within clear view of the wall-mounted television. There were lots of books stuffed everywhere on the shelves too.

"What do you watch on TV?"

"They show me things."

"Like shows and movies."

The boy nodded. "About the world. Places and things, history and science. I like when they do that."

"What about shows and movies?" Charlie repeated. "Which ones are your favorite?"

"I like cartoons. I've been watching the same ones for a long time, but they still make me laugh." The boy cocked his head to the side, as he regarded her closer. "Why haven't I seen you before?"

"I just got here with my parents. We live in California, but these soldiers came and brought us to Alaska because my parents are scientists, and they needed their help." Charlie swallowed hard. "My mom's sick."

"What's wrong?"

"Cancer, I think," Charlie said, her words barely audible as if speaking them made her mother's fate real. "My parents pretend everything's okay, and I pretend I believe them, but I know she's really sick. She can't walk right now."

The boy, Terry, flipped the hair from his face again with an agile toss of his head. "What did the soldiers need your parents' help with?"

"Monsters. I saw them, not in real life, but on the TV screens. Then there were these machine monsters we got away from in a helicopter. I was so scared."

"I get scared sometimes."

"Of monsters?"

"No, because I'm alone mostly, except when Gaia visits."

Charlie frowned. "I don't like this place. I don't mean your room, I mean the whole place."

"It's not so bad."

"Where were you before you came here?"

"Nowhere," the boy told her. "I've always been here."

This was definitely weird, Charlie thought. "Did somebody kidnap you?" she asked, lowering her voice to a whisper. "I can take you to my dad. He'll help you."

"Nobody kidnapped me. But they're always watching." The boy pointed at three spots on the wall. "The cameras are hidden, but I know where they are."

"So, they're watching us now?"

"Not today," the boy said, flashing the kind of smirk that rode boys' faces like skin. "I took care of that just before you stepped through the door. I told you I knew you were coming."

Charlie wondered about the guards in the hallway. Had the boy somehow managed to put them to sleep too? She looked about the room again, hoping to spot something she had missed the first couple of times.

"They won't like that I'm visiting you. They're going to be really pissed."

"I'll protect you from them."

Charlie scoffed at him. "You're just a kid, like me."

"I guess," the boy shrugged.

"Can I meet Gaia?"

"I'll ask her next time she's here."

"Is she, like, your teacher?"

"I guess so, because I learn a lot from her."

"Like what?"

"Mostly about the Earth. How we're all a part of it, a part of something greater."

"I don't know what that means."

The boy took a step closer to her. "Close your eyes."

"Why?"

"Just do it."

"Is this a game?"

"Kind of."

"Okay."

Charlie closed her eyes. Suddenly, she saw dinosaurs in her mind. She felt like she was standing in their midst. They smelled awful and didn't acknowledge her presence, even when they lumbered or sped past her. Then one seemed to charge right at her, and Charlie opened her eyes to make it go away.

"That was cool! How'd you do it?"

"I thought of the image and sent it to you. Those were baby iguanodons, the first dinosaurs who could walk on both four legs and two."

The boy looked down, then up again. "What's it feel like, having a mom and a dad?"

"Good mostly, because they make you feel better about stuff. You don't have to worry because they're around."

"I guess Gaia is like my parent."

"She gave you a funny name."

The boy flashed a smile that seemed to surprise him. "Coming from a girl with a boy's name."

"I told you, my real name is Char—"

Before she could finish, the door burst open, and a man with stringy hair and glasses and wearing a white lab coat like a doctor stormed in, trailed by two different guards than the ones who'd been asleep in the hallway. And these guards had guns.

"Who are you?" the stringy-haired man demanded.

"I'm—"

"How did you get in here?"

"The door was open, so I—"

"You need to leave!" the man snapped at her. "Get out! Go!"

Then the soldiers were on either side of her.

"I was looking for my mother and got lost. She's in the hospital here."

The man in the doctor's coat looked toward the guards. "Take her up there." Then, to Charlie, "You don't belong here. You are not to come back. Never! Is that clear?"

"You don't have to yell at me," Charlie said, fighting back tears. "I was just looking for my mom."

The man took a step forward, but the boy, Terry, got in his way, and the man seemed to bounce off him.

"She's my friend," Terry said.

The doctor guy's eyes widened behind his glasses. His lips quivered, seemed to trap whatever he'd been about to say behind them.

"Well, she has to leave, Elias," he managed finally.

"That's not my name. Don't call me that."

Charlie thought the man dressed like a doctor suddenly looked scared. His lower lip was shaking, and his eyes had narrowed. She watched him take a step back from the boy and look toward her instead.

"You're a guest here, young lady. You should remember that."

"Just take me back to my mom."

The doctor nodded toward the guards. One reached out to grab Charlie, but she twisted from his grasp.

"Thank you," she said to the doctor. "And I won't come back anymore. I promise."

Then she cast the boy a wink.

Part Six
ENEMIES

"Nothing in life is to be feared, it is only to be understood. Now is the time to understand more, so that we may fear less."

—Marie Curie

CHAPTER 44

Trauma Center

Deep Base Titan, Anchorage, Alaska

Deep Base Titan reoriented its infirmary to allot two curtained cubicles to Jules instead of one, so cots for both Kai and Charlie could be set up near her. There were only twenty such cubicles in all, ten on each side, bathed in the harsh spray of fluorescent lighting pouring from fixtures built into the ceiling. Kai had a sense that most of them had gone unoccupied since the base was reconstituted in its current form. Charlie's cot turned out not to be needed, since she snuggled up with her father. She couldn't sleep at first, unable to stop talking about a boy who lived here within Deep Base Titan.

"Was he cute?" Kai tried to quip, believing initially he was no more than a creation spawned by her overactive imagination responding to all the stress she'd been exposed to over the course of two days now.

"Dad!" Charlie snapped at him, her expression wrinkling. "Really?"

"I was just curious."

"Well, yes, he was *really* cute." She looked away shyly, as if regretting she'd said that. "What do you think he's doing here?"

"Did you ask him that?"

"Sure, and he didn't seem to know himself. All he said was that he'd always been here, that this was home."

Kai stroked his daughter's hair, trying not to picture life without her mother.

"He said some funny things."

"Like what?"

"That I was in danger, and he was going to protect me. And he said he knew I was coming." Charlie twisted in the cot to face him. "How could he know I was coming?"

Kai wondered if she was exaggerating her encounter with this boy. Charlie had always been blessed with an overactive imagination that went into overdrive when she was under stress, and the past forty-eight hours certainly qualified there. Then there was Jules's deteriorating condition. No matter how hard they'd tried to hide the truth from Charlie, they were well aware she knew something was very wrong, shielded by a state of denial that was further fed by their stubborn reluctance to tell her the truth, unable to face it themselves.

Until recently, Kai and Jules had been holding out hope that one of the new treatments or clinical trials would buy them more time, maybe even lead to a miracle cure. But the cancer had progressed to a level that rendered Jules ineligible for any options beyond the treatments that had stopped working. There was no way to fully predict what came next because the effects of the cancer manifested differently in sufferers entering the disease's final stages.

"Dad?" Charlie prompted, lifting Kai from his thoughts.

He snapped alert again. "Sorry. Are you sure he knew you were coming?"

"He said he did. But that's not all. Did I tell you about the guards outside the door?"

"No."

"They were asleep on the floor. And he showed me where the cameras were in his room—he has his own bathroom, by the way. He told me he had taken care of them so that no one would know I was there. How could he do that?"

Kai found himself growing increasingly intrigued by his daughter's tale. It was far too explicit to be the product of her imagination. He had no doubt the boy was real and that she had seen him before being returned here by a pair of soldiers clad in their familiar black tactical gear all of General Timur's men wore.

So what was the boy doing here, living in apparent isolation?

"And he said he doesn't have any parents," Charlie resumed, seeming to have just remembered that. "How can that be?"

That led Kai to turn his attention to the Deep Base Titan itself. The price to build, or even retrofit, such an installation would easily have stretched into the billions. Not the kind of sum that could be justified by simply a center out of which to base all operations involving the investigation of extraterrestrial encounters. Beyond that, as seasoned astrobiologists at the forefront of the field, he and Jules should have been aware of the existence of Deep Base Titan. The fact that they weren't further suggested more was going on here than the technological purpose Titan had been chartered to fulfill. Something more had to be afoot here, which turned his thinking back to the boy.

"Do you remember where he lives here?"

Kai could see Charlie's forehead scrunch up the way it did when she was thinking. "I was trying to get to Mom, but I got lost and just kept walking. I don't know how I found the boy. It was like I was in a trance or something, drawn to him. It felt like someone was guiding me."

"Could you find him again?"

"I'm not sure, Dad. I can try." She stopped, then started again. "I think he's lonely, the boy, I mean. Can I tell you something crazy?"

"Sure."

"I don't think he'd ever seen another kid before. That's wild, right?"

Kai was glad to have this conversation about a mysterious boy because it distracted Charlie from fixating on her mother's condition or even, at long last, peppering him with questions in search of a truth she knew in her heart but didn't want to hear. He had rehearsed that conversation in his mind more times than he could count and was grateful for the fact that he could put it off a little longer.

Forty-eight hours ago, Jules's cancer dominated their lives, a vast black void they could not see beyond. Then soldiers showed up at their door and brought them to Alaska, where they became the first scientists to encounter an alien species. A life dream realized, which served only to magnify the fact that it would be Jules's final one. Kai wanted to believe that it had been a great gift bestowed upon them. How much, though, had her descent into the alien ship and the battle against the reconstituted robotic sentinels taken from her? How much of her little remaining time had it sapped? They could have told the soldiers no, could have told them the truth that she was in no condition to make this trip. And now Kai felt a vast emptiness and shame for letting the only woman he had ever loved take such a risk. He knew Jules would disagree with him on that, but he didn't care. Charlie deserved to have her mother around for as many days, hours, and minutes as possible. Now Jules's remaining time had dwindled to the point where Kai feared she would take her last breath in the cold sterility of Deep Base Titan instead of peacefully passing in the home she loved.

And, if the conclusions he and Jules had reached about the alien organism were correct, the world might not be far behind.

CHAPTER 45

The Vault

Deep Base Titan, Anchorage, Alaska

"How did this kid get in?" General Timur demanded, feeling his blood heating up and the sweat caking up beneath the stiff collar of his uniform shirt amid the cool darkness of "the Vault," as he had come to call it. "Can you just tell me that?"

"I was reviewing tapes at the time," Sharkey told him. "When I looked over at the monitor, the feed was all static. I couldn't reach the boy's guards, so I called for a backup team. We found the guards unconscious and the girl inside the boy's quarters."

"So she incapacitated the guards, is that what you're saying?"

"No, that would be impossible."

Timur cracked a slight smile laced with irony. "Look around you, Doctor. Do you really think *anything* is impossible?"

The Vault, located on the facility's lowest level, known as the Crypt, was Deep Base Titan's repository for alien artifacts, most of which had been brought here from Area 51 upon the base's opening fifteen years ago. It was reserved for artifacts undergoing active research, analysis, and testing toward potential weaponization. The challenge with all the objects under study, including those more recently brought back by probes from deep space, was that variances in technology provided no frame of reference off which to build. Analysis of any object required starting from scratch, turning the research into a long, arduous slog that had paid few dividends over the years. The origins of Deep Base Titan purportedly lay in the exclusive study of all vestiges of alien life forms and relics, like those collected over the years, in preparation for a confrontation with another species that humans would otherwise be ill-prepared and ill-supplied to fight. Only Timur and a select few others knew of the World Consortium's true, far more nefarious plans for the work product achieved here, though that product hadn't amounted to very much over the years.

Among the most promising finds were the remnants of an alien propulsion system that appeared to be capable of harnessing dark matter. But it was useless without the ability to generate the dark matter required, and it continued to languish while the most advanced particle accelerators under the Consortium's control still could generate dark matter for only a flicker of a second.

There was also a nearly intact alien exoskeleton, which Titan scientists theorized would allow its inhabitant to adapt to any living environment. The fact that the suit was formed of an impenetrable alloy made it incredibly attractive to the Consortium, especially for its ability to withstand the highest levels of radiation, except that the suit had resisted all efforts to even harvest a small sample for study.

And there was, by all accounts, an antigravity system that could greatly facilitate space travel, while if weaponized, might also render the battlefield obsolete due to its effects on massing soldiers. But so far, Titan's scientists had failed to even approach developing a manageable source capable of powering it. So far, they'd succeeded in reducing the size of that source from a city block to a large building, where they'd been stymied and no further progress had been made.

"Take these, for example," Timur said, standing with Sharkey before a trio of identical obsidian rectangular shapes, each six feet by ten feet and five feet in height, formed of a dull metallic alloy absent any seams that had proven impenetrable to all attempts to gauge their contents. "As you know, they were found deep within New South Wales's Jenolan Cave system more than a decade ago. And, as you also know, we remain unsure of whether they are some form of self-contained power source of unlimited capacity or containers holding something we've not been able to identify."

All the relics relocated here from Area 51 had come from alien craft that had either crash-landed on Earth or been shot down by fighter planes or other defensive measures. But this find, Timur knew, was considered to be the greatest of any in human history because it offered irrefutable proof that aliens had roamed Earth eons before man's inception. The best scientific minds had been unable to use carbon dating or any other method to estimate its age. However, geostratigraphy indicated that the cave system itself was at least ten million years old.

But an even more remarkable find had been uncovered in the Jenolan Cave system in the form of trace DNA from whatever had left the rectangular objects behind however many eons ago. The World Consortium had decided to use that trace DNA as the basis for cloning a being to learn more about man's forebears on Earth. Given the number of strands that needed to be filled in from ordinary human DNA, they couldn't be sure the match would be exact. Yet, the fact that the recovered DNA had spawned a humanoid child strongly suggested that those forebears from millions of years ago were the real fathers of humanity.

The more they followed Elias's development, the more all concerned realized the experiment had succeeded beyond their wildest expectations. The boy's anatomy was entirely human, although with more advanced respiratory and circulatory systems, as well as a larger brain capacity. Because he was truly a first of a kind though, no one had a clear idea of what to expect as his development continued, what he might be capable of outside the bounds of an ordinary human. Suddenly going through puberty seemed to have drastically altered not just his biomechanics but also his self-awareness. Timur had ordered exposure to people to be kept to a bare minimum to avoid any stimulus that could prove an unexpected reaction. Until today, Elias had never encountered another child, and now Timur feared the stimulus had provoked a belligerent response that was revealing new, previously unseen features of the boy's development. He hated the notion of controlling his behavior with drugs, even if those drugs could work on the boy's advanced metabolism, but was starting to think that might be the only means available to keep Elias under control.

"You were asking about the girl," Sharkey was saying, returning to the subject raised earlier. "It wasn't the girl. She didn't manage to make the two guards fall asleep or open a locked door. Nor was she responsible for us losing the monitor feed, for which our IT people have yet to provide any technological explanation."

Timur found himself intrigued by all this; he was also curious but a bit concerned. What could have caused the two guards to fall unconscious on their station at precisely the same time? Both men professed to have no recollection of anything unusual leading up to that, including unlocking the door to the boy's quarters. And the security feed confirmed that no one else was present in the hallway at the time. Timur could buy into one inexplicable occurrence taking place, but there were three here that defied any rational explanation.

"You think the boy was responsible for all of this, don't you, Doctor?"

"The boy or Gaia."

"Gaia's not real."

"She is to Elias, an entirely separate persona who shares his brain toward whom he channels whatever abilities he's developing outside of our control."

"Everything in Elias's life is within our control and has been since we created him."

"Is it, General, is it really? You can raise a tiger or lion cub for six months, maybe even a bit longer, but with maturity, it reverts to its primal instincts and turns into a different creature entirely."

"You're referencing the boy reaching puberty again."

Sharkey held Timur's stare with unprecedented temerity and resolve. "Perhaps he has reached the same stage that a lion or tiger cub does when, instead of you feeding it, you become the food. Unless...."

"Something on your mind, Doctor?"

"If the boy's development has reached the level I fear it has, we may soon be under *his* control."

"Need I remind that reaching that very level is exactly what we hoped for?"

"When man discovered fire, General, he got burned."

"Until he learned to control it." Timur thought for a moment. "I'm going to have a talk with the boy myself."

"Would you like me to join you?"

"No, Doctor, I think I'll accomplish more on my own."

CHAPTER 46

Infiltration

Joint Base Elmendorf-Richardson, Anchorage, Alaska

"Is the tunnel monitored?" Jace asked Yusef, the Nine's expert on Earth's electronics.

"No. It's equipped with a surveillance system that is no longer active. Saves me the bother of disabling it, which would have attracted attention and potentially compromised this route of entry."

The route of entry in question was a nearly mile-long access tunnel constructed underground below the coastal lowlands, backing up against the mountains of the Chugach range to the east and the Alaska Range to the north and west. The surrounding area featured glacial formations, lakes, and swamps, with Knik Arm, a northern extension of Cook Inlet, mere miles off and one of the routes of flight from the area the Nine had considered once they had retrieved their weapons.

The tunnel's construction required blasting through layers of shale and ledge. Anchorage's climate and landscape were entirely different from what they'd faced along the Juneau Icefield. It was still cold but far more temperate with no trace of ice and snow, save for the white-tipped tops of the mountains looking down upon them. The start of the tunnel had been dug a mile out to minimize the chances that the massive renovation Deep Base Titan had undergone would be spotted from orbiting satellites, adding substantially to the project's cost. A necessary expense, given the need to provide access for the construction vehicles required to rebuild pretty much the entire facility, as well as add another ultra-secure sublevel known as the Vault, according to the original plans Mazz had analyzed in determining their route of entry.

That was where the weapons the Nine would sorely need in the looming battle were being stored. This tunnel terminated on the same level as it was located, offering direct access and shielding the transport of artifacts and technology that man was incapable of understanding.

The entrance to this construction tunnel was cleverly concealed beneath thick fake brush and hard-packed steel-reinforced concrete disguised to blend in with the rest of the scenery. Once breached, the entry would reveal a ramp that sloped downward onto the tunnel itself, wide and high enough to accommodate large construction vehicles. From there, they would proceed to the Vault where their weapons were located and use one of the trucks utilized to ferry objects in to retrace their path out once the three containers were loaded on board. They would be able to handle any resistance they encountered with their kaelens. Jace hoped no human lives would be lost in the process.

Izumi and Brenn arrived right on schedule, and Jace pulled them aside.

"I need to ask you something that may sound crazy," he said. "Have either of you experienced something you can't explain, almost like a waking dream?"

Izumi and Brenn exchanged a nervous glance, enough to answer Jace's question for him.

"While I was flying here from Australia, the sky looked wrong," Izumi said finally.

"Wrong?"

"The constellations I was seeing were not the ones visible from this world. Then they were gone and there were no stars at all."

Jace waited for her to continue.

"I think I was seeing the stars from our world. But how can that be?"

Jace looked toward Brenn, who settled himself with a deep breath.

"I saw something too, but they weren't stars. I saw people, a woman and four children. Terrified, crying, reaching out to me. I tried to reach back and struck the plane's windshield."

"Almost broke the glass," Izumi added.

"What do you think it means, the stars and those people?" from Brenn.

Jace thought for a moment. "Can I check your scalps?"

Izumi and Brenn looked at each other, then nodded. Jace parted Izumi's thick nest of tangled brown hair and found the same crease the others had running down the center of her scalp. Same for Brenn through his tight mat of stubble. He didn't have to check their heels to be certain they too each had a "G" tattooed there.

"Memories," he told them. "I think we're all starting to remember our pasts. Who we were before we were chosen for this mission."

Jace didn't bother adding that those memories included all of the Nine being fitted with electromagnetic restraining helmets at some point.

How the weapons of the Nine had been recovered on the other side of the world would remain a mystery, irrelevant to their retrieval of them. Jace had selected this early hour of the morning to launch their incursion into the base due to lower levels of active security and the natural malaise that time of day brings with it. He found Mazz standing apart from the others, waiting to access the tunnels.

"We'll have our weapons in hand before you know it," Mazz said confidently.

Jace reached into a side pocket of his tactical pants and came out with the doll Mazz had painstakingly taped together on the flight from Pakistan. "This must have fallen out of your pocket during the air drop outside of Galena," he said, handing it to him.

Mazz took it gratefully in both hands. "Thank you." He looked down at the doll and back up again. "It's not just me, is it?"

Jace shook his head. "It's all of us, old friend, a mystery to be solved after we've saved this world."

Mazz nodded and stuffed the doll into one of his pockets.

Yusef had already located the keypad control panel that activated the camouflaged entry to the tunnel, and Jace watched him switch on a handheld wireless device that broadcast all conceivable six-digit codes in under seventeen seconds.

At eleven seconds, the keypad flashed green, and the hidden entryway slid open to reveal the steel ramp. Valeria entered first, wielding a handheld proximity-sensing device already set to its maximum range.

"We're clear," she called up from the darkness below.

The other members of the Nine descended in her wake.

CHAPTER 47

Elias

Deep Base Titan, Anchorage, Alaska

"Why don't I have video games to play?" the boy demanded almost as soon as General Timur was through the door to his quarters.

As a precaution, there were now four guards on duty in the hallway beyond. And, as a further precaution, all of them were armed with weapons loaded with tranquilizer darts.

"Well?" the boy prompted.

He was sitting cross-legged on the floor, staring up at the blank television screen as if willing it to come to life.

"Because they don't suit you," Timur told him. "You're too advanced for them."

"Well, I want them. I want to play them."

"Did your visitor tell you about video games, Elias?"

"That's not my name. E-L-I-A-S—that's an acronym for something, isn't it? Don't lie to me, General."

Timur held the boy's stare, trying not to show how unsettled he was by the boy's sudden display of obstinance and even belligerence. "Elias—"

"Don't call me that. It's not my name. My name is…Terry."

"Your visitor called you that, didn't she?"

"She's not my visitor; she's my friend. Her name is Charlie, short for Charlotte. And she called me Terry because she thought my full name, Teraválar, was hard to pronounce. Gaia named me that."

"I'd like to meet Gaia, Elias."

"You can't."

"Why?"

"She doesn't like you."

For some reason, that unsettled Timur. "Why?"

"I don't know. I can just tell. Maybe because you don't believe she's real."

"That's why I'd like to meet her."

"I already said you can't."

"Give me a chance."

"You don't understand. You can't meet Gaia because you can't see Gaia. Her energy vibrates too fast. She could be standing here right now, and you wouldn't be able to see her."

"Is she here now, Elias?"

This time, the boy didn't recoil at being called that. "No."

"You can't see this girl again."

"I know."

"Do you?" Timur took a step closer, close enough to enforce the dominance he always exerted. "Are you telling me the truth?"

This time, unlike all the others, the boy didn't back down or shrink away. "Yes. But if I'm lying, General, then maybe that's a lie too."

"We're your friends too, son."

"I'm nobody's son—both of us know that. And you're not my friends; you're my keepers. Both of us know that too."

Something changed in the boy's expression. His eyes gaped as if just struck by a realization.

"E-L-I-A-S stands for Experimental Lifeform Integrated Assault System. Is that what I am to you, General?"

Had the boy just read his mind? "Elias is just a name."

"You are lying to me. Gaia says I exist toward a greater purpose, but it's not your purpose; it's the one she's giving me. I don't belong here."

The assurance with which the boy spoke those words made Timur's heart seem to skip a beat. He had to remind himself to breathe. "This is your home," he managed.

"It's where I live. It's never been my home. My home is the Earth. The Earth and I are one."

Timur wondered if the coming of puberty had brought with it a descent into delusions approaching a psychotic break from the reality of the world constructed for the boy. If that were the case, then the danger and the potential risk Sharkey suggested he posed might well be beyond anything their projections had considered, especially given his apparent ability to manipulate people, objects, and machines with his mind. As terrifying a prospect as that might be, it could also prove to be the ultimate vindication for this experiment, certain to justify the vast expenditures and resources required to create Elias. The principles of the World Consortium would be very pleased by the prospects of these new abilities their creation was exhibiting.

"Tell me what I am, General."

Timur struggled to stop from speaking the words his mind was forming. That the DNA that created Elias offered irrefutable proof that aliens had roamed the Earth millions of years ago and were responsible for the existence of humanity.

Before Timur could consider that further, a strange humming sound suddenly made his ears ring. He raised his hands involuntarily to cover them, but it made no difference.

He's reading my mind, the general thought before recalling how the boy might well have forced two men to fall asleep.

"What am I?"

Had the boy spoken those words out loud or only in his head? Either way, it took every bit of Timur's will to keep from answering the boy's question.

"It doesn't matter anyway, because Gaia told me I'll be leaving here soon. You let yourself believe you created me, but you didn't. Gaia did for a purpose she saw I must fulfill. She used you and your science to follow her will for a moment that is yet to come. And it's coming soon."

CHAPTER 48

Vigil

Deep Base Titan, Anchorage, Alaska

"Kai," he heard Jules say weakly.

He lifted himself gingerly from his cot so as not to disturb the sleeping Charlie and moved to her bedside.

"Did you finish our report?" she asked him, the words cracking as they emerged from her throat.

Kai nodded. "I sent it to General Timur, but I need to recheck the data and run some simulations in order to confirm."

"Not necessary. You know we're right about what's coming."

"I'd much rather be wrong."

"There's something else, a way we might be able to stop them," Jules told him. "It was right in front of us, and we missed it. It occurred to me while you were examining the remains of the infantile creature. About that old woman, why was she spared."

"Jane Piedmont, because Paget's disease had damaged her bone tissue. Left her infinitely less appetizing to these things, I imagine."

"Except Paget's disease wouldn't change the actual molecular composition of her bones, so it had to be something else, Kai, and you figured out what that was without realizing it."

"I did?"

Jules nodded weakly.

* * *

"How did I miss that?" he said when she was finished.

"You had some other things on your mind. We'll need to run some tests. But if I'm right, we'd have something that could act as a repellent, a way to stop these creatures in their tracks."

Kai thought back to first meeting Jane Piedmont in the diner. The answer had been right there in front of him from that very moment, so close he couldn't see it. Jules was right.

"You always were smarter than me," he said to her.

"Smarter than *I*," she corrected, ever the stickler for proper grammar.

"Right, him too."

Jules managed a smile. "I should be scared, but I'm not, not for myself anyway. I don't want Charlie here at the end," she said in a voice barely above a whisper.

Kai didn't want to argue, so he just nodded.

"I know you disagree, but I can't bear the thought. When it's time, I want to let go, and I can't do that if she's here. I hurt, Kai. I hurt everywhere."

She had refused painkillers to stay lucid through the course of their work here.

Kai took her hand and squeezed.

"I can't feel that," Jules said in the same hushed voice. "My hands are numb."

Kai slid into bed next to her, atop the bedcovers, careful not to disturb the monitors that kept a constant tab on her heart rate, oxygen saturation, and blood pressure. The LED readout on the single machine flashed the numbers in silence, supplying the floor's only light except for four of the fixtures built into the ceiling. Trooper Muhtuk occupied a cubicle further down the row, Trooper Dennehy maintaining a vigil over her. Jane Piedmont and her infant charge were situated diagonally across from Jules in the twin row of cubicles across the floor.

Kai had heard the soldier with the shrunken arm had died, and they must be treating the other somewhere else inside the base because he wasn't here.

Jules's breathing was labored. She moaned softly for a few moments before Kai felt her slip off to sleep, resolved to hold onto her through the course of the night. He spent the next long hours lying next to her, listening to her wheezing labored breathing contrasted against the soft breaths of his daughter in the cot next to Jules's bed. He tried to sleep but couldn't, despite his exhaustion, unable to contemplate his looming life without her. When the footsteps approached, he thought them to be the product of a waking dream until they grew louder as they drew closer to the cubicle.

The next sound he heard was that of the cubicle's shower curtain–like closure grinding open, a pair of soldiers in black tactical gear standing there.

"General Timur needs to see you, sir," one of them said, keeping his voice low.

Kai sat up, a hand still holding fast to Jules. "Can it wait?"

"Our orders are to bring you to him stat, sir," the other soldier said, not bothering to keep his voice down. "He said to tell you there's been a new development."

CHAPTER 49

Retrieval

Deep Base Titan, Anchorage, Alaska

The Nine made their way slowly along the tunnel leading into Deep Base Titan. Caution was required, given the possibility of manual surveillance devices triggered by motion or even elementary trip wires that Yusef's scans might not have detected. The element of surprise had to be protected to avoid encountering any resistance inside the base.

The tunnel builders had left the actual features of the surrounding geography intact. The walls and ceiling, mixed between the light gray of the ledge and the darker gray of the shale the builders blasted their way through, must have been refined into a consistent conical shape. Over the years, the natural formations had shed small chunks of debris through the natural settling process of the ground, with nothing to indicate now that the tunnel's integrity had been compromised or posed a threat to vehicles traversing it. The recessed lighting remained fully functional, which facilitated the Nine's task of spotting anything awry in the walls and floor that might betray their presence.

There were no cameras or listening devices in plain view, and Valeria, walking at the head of their cluster, had picked up no indications of any more rudimentary surveillance devices on her scanner, which was tuned to the low frequencies those systems operated on. In the end, it took just over twenty-three minutes before the steel door at the end of the tunnel, designed to slide open once the proper code was entered into a keypad, came into view.

Their weapons were located on the lowest-most level identified as the "Crypt" in the schematics, just a hundred feet from that wall. The heavy vehicles responsible for transporting cargo in and out of the facility were located in a makeshift motor pool further down the hall. Given the secret nature of Deep Base Titan, Jace very much doubted the soldiers within had any reason to suspect an incursion like this. If anything, they would expect an attack to originate from the surface, likely utilizing high-yield explosives.

"Jace, there are four guards in the hallway beyond the wall," Valeria told him after checking the heat signatures on her energy scanner.

Jace gestured toward Mazz, Xan, Valeria, and Haran. They would be the first four through, each moving toward one of the guards to disable them quickly enough to avoid triggering an alarm signal.

At the wall, Yusef didn't need prompting to move up to the keypad on the right side and repeat the process of fitting his device's leads into the proper slots. This time, he ran the sequence of every conceivable four-number combination until the right one turned the red light to flashing green. The heavy door ground open, and the first four of the Nine were through in it in a blur, the guards unconscious before Jace and the others followed them through.

CHAPTER 50

Dreams

Deep Base Titan, Anchorage, Alaska

Charlie loved sleeping because that's when her dreams took over, the only time she didn't think about her mom. In the dreams, her mom wasn't sick, so there was nothing her parents were trying to hide from her. In the dreams, they'd be together, smiling and happy, playing outside. She could never smell anything in her dreams, but thinking about them conjured the scents of fresh flowers and newly mowed grass beneath blooming trees that shifted in the breeze.

She had awoken a little while back to find her father gone, freeing her to snuggle up against her mother, listening to the labored wheeze of her breathing. It sounded wet, like water or something was pooling inside her. Both her dad and Mom herself had never stopped lying about her condition. When she lost weight, it was because of a diet. When she lost muscle, it was because she had changed her workout regimen. For a time, Charlie took comfort in the fact that her parents hadn't told her anything was wrong. As long as that persisted, she could cling to the hope that there wasn't and deny the reality that continued to dawn upon her.

She hated this place that smelled of rubbing alcohol, hated everything since they'd left their house with the soldiers, everything except for the boy. It felt like she'd been directed down to where he lived, tugged along by some invisible force. She didn't have many friends who were boys, and not many who were girls either. Charlie liked science, books, and video games—not sports, soupy TV shows, or gossip. Get a life, she wanted to tell the girls in her class when they started talking smack about someone. The only way they seemed able to feel good was to make others feel bad.

Charlie liked thinking about Terry because it meant she wasn't thinking about her mother, even for a few seconds. He was her friend. He cared about what she was thinking and feeling. He didn't talk badly about other kids, but maybe that was because he didn't know any others to speak badly about.

She shifted in the hospital bed, and her hand brushed against her mother's hair. It felt brittle and damp at the tips, although her skin was warm to the touch, as if she had a fever. Charlie wanted to wake her up so they could talk, because when they talked, it seemed things were okay. But her mother needed her rest, so she pressed herself tighter against her instead.

Charlie felt a hand squeeze her shoulder and turned, figuring it must be her father.

"We need to get out of here," whispered Terry.

CHAPTER 51

The Nuclear Option

Deep Base Titan, Anchorage, Alaska

"What's this new development?" Kai asked as soon as he took a matching armchair next to the one occupied by General Timur.

They were in some kind of residence that defied the rest of the surroundings in Deep Base Titan, looking more lifted from *Architectural Digest* than some science journal. It was spacious and exceptionally laid out as well as exorbitantly furnished. Whoever called this place home, it clearly wasn't the general.

"We'll get to that in a moment, Professor," Timur said, shifting about in his chair as if to find comfort that continued to escape him. "I reviewed in your initial report what the autopsy revealed in terms of exposure to water. How confident are you in your theory?"

"I assure you it's more than a theory, General, and my wife concurs. These things are fully capable of reproducing in the water, potentially even faster than on land. That's why they chose a fishing village located on an inlet that feeds into the Gulf of Alaska to strike next after Chichagof Springs."

"We've dispatched a trio of submarines to the area around the Inside Passage to see if your *theory* has any merit. They've just arrived on station, and I expect a report at any moment."

"What about the underwater drones you said you were launching initially?"

Timur looked away briefly, his face shiny in the crackling glow of the artificial firelight. "We lost contact with them before they could begin transmitting and have not been able to retrieve them. That's the new development."

Kai's watch told him it was closing on 8 p.m. Outside, darkness had claimed the sky. But down here, so far underground, the sensory deprivation created the illusion that time wasn't passing at all, because there was no light and darkness to measure it by.

The soldiers had driven him to meet General Timur in a shiny black golf cart that purred along the winding hallways before descending in a private elevator that spilled out into this elegantly furnished, sprawling space. The general rose from the chair he currently occupied as the soldiers led him over. He looked haggard and worn to Kai and clearly unsettled. It would have been easy to pass that off as a result of the past forty-eight plus hours. But he felt Timur's unease to be more recent in origin, his ashen features reminding Kai of his own both upon receiving Jules's initial diagnosis and her oncologist's recent disclosure that they had no more weapons to fight the cancer raging inside her.

He had spent the long, sleepless hours picturing the cancer cells ravaging Jules as microscopic manifestations of the creatures he had faced in the Springs. For nearly two years of treatment, the chemotherapy and immunotherapy had been like miniguns aimed squarely at the cancer cells ravaging her body. They had done the job in near miraculous fashion until their ammo was expended, freeing the cells invading her body to roam free, just as he knew the spores unleashed in the ravaged town of Galena were doing now at sea. If unchecked, these things would run roughshod over the world, just as the cancer had through Jules's body.

"In any case," Kai resumed, "their ability to reproduce in water led to the estimates I provided at the end of our report. I expect your drones would have confirmed them."

"You're theorizing these creatures will have infested the entire planet in nine months."

"Conservatively. Six months is a more realistic estimate."

Timur looked like he was trying very hard to ignore Kai's words. "I was seriously considering the nuclear option to wipe these things out while we still have them reasonably contained. If your theory is correct, that's off the table."

"I'd say the loss of your drones confirms it. This is now a potential extinction event. These things are like a biological meteor striking Earth. If this were sixty-five million years ago, the dinosaurs wouldn't have stood a chance against them either."

Timur nodded, weighing Kai's assessment. He remained silent for so long that Kai wondered if their conversation was over and he could return to his wife. Then the general resumed.

"These aren't my quarters," he said, casting his gaze about as if to refamiliarize himself with the elegant surroundings. "They belong to the man whose organization built Deep Base Titan."

"Organization?"

"In cooperation with the government and military. But no mistake about it, this organization controls both. Nothing major happens anymore unless and until it signs off."

"And does this organization have a name?"

Timur nodded once. "The World Consortium."

CHAPTER 52

Rescue

Deep Base Titan, Anchorage, Alaska

"Shhhhhhhhhhhh," the boy said when Charlie started to speak, finger pressed against his lips. "You're in danger. I'm going to rescue you. These people aren't your friends."

"How do you know?" Charlie whispered.

"Gaia told me."

Gaia had also instructed him on how to access the ventilation shaft that supplied air to his quarters. He had followed its labyrinthine route to where it spilled out among the pumps that serviced this floor. From there, she had guided him up another level toward Charlie's location in the facility's small hospital.

"Your mother too," he said, gazing past Charlie toward the figure taking raspy breaths alongside her.

"She's sick."

"I know. And we have to bring the others with us too. Gaia told me there's an old woman, a baby, and two police officers."

Charlie nodded. "I know where they are."

* * *

"Hello, Mrs. Piedmont," Charlie said after she'd managed to rouse the old woman who smelled bad.

"Is this a dream, kid?"

"No."

"A nightmare?"

"No."

"Then what the hell is it?"

Charlie noticed the baby the old woman had been taking care of was sleeping in the hospital bed pushed close to hers, surrounded by a wall of pillows to keep him from rolling off. "Terry says we're in danger, that we have to leave."

"Who's Terry?"

Terry raised his hand from just behind her.

"Another kid? Jeeze, I've gone my whole life without being bothered by the likes of you, and now you're everywhere."

"We need to go, Mrs. Piedmont."

"Because this boy said so?"

"Not me," Terry told her. "Gaia."

"Who's Gaia? Another kid?"

"No, Jane. She's much older."

"You called me Jane."

"It's your name."

"Yeah, but…. Oh, never mind," the old woman said, yanking the bedcovers off her. "If Gaia can get us out of this godforsaken place, I'm all for it. Just let me get the kid ready."

* * *

Charlie spotted the soldier guarding the entrance to the hospital slumped on the floor, looking as if he was sleeping, just like the soldiers who'd been posted outside of Terry's quarters. They found the policeman who had helped her father sitting up in a chair next to the bed occupied by the sleeping woman policeman, her leg all bandaged with a silvery-gray ooze leaking out.

"You're the professor's daughter, right?" the man policeman said, still wearing his uniform with a name badge clipped to his shirt that read DENNEHY.

"Shhhhhhhhhh," Charlie uttered this time, matching finger pressed against her lips. "We're in danger. We have to leave."

"Say what?" Dennehy shot back, a mix of disbelief and confusion etched over his features.

"We're in danger," Charlie echoed.

Dennehy rose stiffly from his chair. "Where's your father?"

"I don't know. I fell asleep, and when I woke up, he was gone. We've got to leave, all of us, but we've got to find my father first."

"How old are you, kid?"

"Eleven. Almost twelve."

"My oldest daughter's four, the younger one's three. I know there's something wrong with this place, but we can't just up and leave. We don't know our way around this place."

"I do," said Terry.

Dennehy seemed to notice him for the first time. "And who are you?"

"My friend," said Charlie.

"I can get us to Charlie's father," Terry said in his even, measured voice that was just beginning to crack the way older boy voices did. "I can lead us out of here."

"Nothing in the world I'd rather do than follow along, son." Dennehy glanced toward the bed where the woman police officer was sleeping. "But my partner's all drugged up. She's not going anywhere."

"She has to."

Dennehy narrowed his gaze on Terry. "Your parents work here or something?"

"I don't have any parents."

"He lives here," Charlie piped in. "He's a prisoner, like a hostage. You should arrest all these people."

"If only I could, kid...."

"They're not going to let you leave here, not ever," Terry told him. "If you don't leave now, you never will, and you'll never see your daughters again."

Something changed in Dennehy's expression. It looked smaller and tighter to Charlie and stayed that way.

"How do you know all this, son?"

"Gaia told me."

"Who's Gaia?"

"His friend," Charlie answered before Terry had the chance. "She tells him things, teaches him things."

In the murky light, it looked to her as if the two sides of Dennehy's face were pulling in opposite directions, trapped between thought and action. Charlie watched Terry turn toward the woman policeman in the bed and close his eyes.

* * *

Sakari Muhtuk was sliding toward the darkness, resisting it no longer and welcoming the emptiness it promised. She felt as if she were floating, neither up nor down, just floating in air that wasn't there.

Then a rope of light seemed to take hold of her and pull her away from the void, but not before enough of its brightness illuminated the darkness she'd been slipping toward. The light shone on nothing outward but turned her inner world aglow with reassurance that there was a road she could take to return to the world. And down that road, she saw slivers of color, as if someone was shining a different light on only what she needed to see—the past, present, and future swirling together, indistinguishable from each other in the melding of truth and awareness of where she was and what lay ahead.

She felt herself coming awake, staring into the fiercely intense eyes of a boy who might have been an angel or a devil. A voice rang in her ear, stirring her back to consciousness.

* * *

"Boss! Boss!"

Charlie watched Dennehy take the woman's hand and squeeze.

"I'm here, boss! I'm here!"

"It's all true, Tom," she rasped, squeezing Tom's hand back. "Everything this boy is saying is true. We get out now or we'll never leave."

Charlie watched her gaze flit back tentatively toward Terry, as if afraid to meet his eyes.

"You can get us out of here?" she asked.

The boy nodded.

"This is crazy," Dennehy protested. "He's just a kid, boss!"

"I'm not so sure about that, Trooper." The woman found Terry's eyes and held them. "Alone? You can get us out of here alone?"

"We're not alone," Terry told her.

CHAPTER 53

Offer

Deep Base Titan, Anchorage, Alaska

"You expected the military and government to be behind this facility, Professor? Technically, you're correct, but it was all at the behest of the man whose quarters you're sitting in and the organization that gives the military and government their marching orders."

Kai remained silent.

"You won't find the World Consortium listed on the Dow Jones, S&P 500, or Nasdaq. But the organization is bigger, richer, and more powerful than the most successful companies in the world that operate with their approval, subject to being quashed if their interests don't properly align with the Consortium's."

Kai had no idea where the general was going with this, so he just waited for him to continue instead of responding. Looking at Timur seated in the eerie glow of the flickering gas-fed flames made him see the general differently, minus the bravado with which he carried himself on the glacier. His tight uniform jacket struggled to restrain an upper body sagging around the stomach, more flab than muscle. His angular jowls, which had lent his words more gravitas back on the glacier, made his face look more like that of a business tycoon accustomed to too much wine and fancy dinners. But his eyes retained their harsh, imposing stare, blinking little and glaring a lot.

"Do you see what I'm getting at here, Professor?" he asked Kai finally.

"Some sort of power dynamics lesson, it sounds like."

"I suppose that describes things as clearly as anything, so let me put it this way. The World Consortium doesn't just hold power. It distributes power to those it sees fit. Individuals, corporations, and nations, particularly the United States. It doesn't discriminate between macro and micro; the only relevant issue is the level of contribution possible. For the Consortium, everything is a zero-sum game of sorts: You're either capable of contributing to their vision or you're not."

Kai suddenly felt cold, the gas-fed flames not hot enough to ward off the chill. Being informed of the existence of an all-powerful, imposing global entity that existed in secret implied a threat was about to be leveled. His mind flashed back two nights to the soldiers rousing him and Jules from their sleep, wishing now he'd never opened the door.

"Your wife is dying, Professor," Timur said suddenly.

Kai's discomfort increased to the point he wanted to crawl out of his skin. "I'm well aware of that, General," he managed lamely.

"What if she could live? There are drugs, truly miracle drugs, the world doesn't know about because the Consortium distributes them only to a select few. If you join us, Jules can become one of them. It's not too late. I've seen what these drugs can do."

Kai couldn't find the words to respond.

"I'm offering you a new life, Professor, a fresh start at ten times your current salary, putting your expertise to work here at Deep Base Titan for the Consortium. I'm also offering you hope, in the form of a new world to replace the one that's breaking."

It didn't feel like Timur was giving him a choice. Kai had a sense that no matter how he responded to the general's offer, he and Charlie were never going to leave Deep Base Titan. He had seen too much, knew too much, and Timur's revelation of an all-powerful cabal no one had ever heard of was the final step in making his lack of a choice clear.

"We didn't pick you and your wife out of the academic yellow pages," the general continued. "The two of you were on a shortlist of a dozen or so, and the Consortium had its own reasons for selecting the two of you."

"The soldiers you sent to get us," Kai said, the words forming slowly. "They weren't going to give us a choice, were they?"

"It was a matter vital to national security, and they had their orders. It's why we allowed your daughter to come along. We're not monsters, Professor." Timur leaned a bit more forward. "I'm offering to make you director of our astrobiology division."

"Our, as in the government, the military…or the Consortium?"

"Take your pick," Timur said, leaving it there.

"I didn't have a choice a few nights ago, and I don't have a choice now, do I?"

The general didn't so much as flinch. "I believe you already know the answer to that question."

Kai felt heat radiating from the surface of his skin. He trembled, as much from fear as loathing for the man who was going to imprison him, one way or another, for the rest of his life.

"You can save the world, Professor, at least prevent the human race from being exterminated by developing and synthesizing this repellant you and your wife believe can be harvested from the bones of that old woman. This can be your legacy—it can be *her* legacy, and a fitting one at that."

Before Kai could respond, he heard a repetitive buzzing sound. Timur leaned back and unclipped a communications device like none Kai had ever seen before from his belt. He regarded what must have been a text message, the furrows along his brow deepening as his expression tightened and his jowls seemed to vibrate.

"We've lost contact with those submarines, Professor."

And then a shrill alarm began to blare.

CHAPTER 54

The Vault

Deep Base Titan, Anchorage, Alaska

The cases that had held their weapons for fifteen hundred years were untouched and unmarred. Though generally rectangular in shape, the seamless edges were curved with no lid or visible locking mechanism. They had been brought here from the Jenolan Cave system and subjected, no doubt, to endless scrutiny by scientists wielding all manner of detection devices that would have had no success in penetrating the composite material to either pry the cases open or view the weapons contained within.

The Vault, as this place was known, must have taken its name from the entry door, which was just that, looking like something of the type found in banks, except magnetically sealed and accessible only by both a dedicated keycard and a six-digit combination. Yusef encountered no issues, bypassing both these measures, though it was just over a minute instead of mere seconds before a click sounded and the heavy door swung mechanically inward, making a slight grinding sound.

Jace spotted the cases as four more of the Nine moved through the door in his wake, two with their kaelens ready to stand guard while Xan and Mazz went for the truck sitting in a bay just down the vast hall beyond. Approaching the cases with Izumi and Brenn, the Nine's weapons specialists, through the soft blue lighting of the Vault, he couldn't help but notice relics of other species foreign to this world that had either stumbled upon Earth, crashed, or whose visit had not gone as anticipated. All the various elements, ranging from machine parts, fragments of wreckage, helmets, and external coverings, to what might have been weapons, were held within vacuum-sealed chambers enclosed by a thick plastic polymer that felt like glass but was impregnable by Earth's standards.

"Our weapons are all intact and functional, Jace," he heard Brenn say. "They will require eight Earth hours to charge."

"Closer to twelve," Izumi corrected, "given the limits of electrical currents here."

Given the expected time of the next attack by the alien species, they would be cutting it very close but had no choice other than to stick to the plan. The charging process couldn't begin until they were clear of Deep Base Titan in a reasonably secure location where the cases could be opened.

Jace heard a rumble and glimpsed a growing shadow in the hallway moments before Mazz drove a commercial-grade forklift into the Vault. Close behind, Xan backed in a black unmarked box truck that looked more like a larger version of a classic armored car with a heavily reinforced cargo box built to withstand heavy explosives or even a missile attack. She backed it into the Vault as far as she could, and Valeria hoisted up the rear hatch while Mazz moved the forklift into position before the first of the three cases.

The cases rested atop steel platforms slightly larger than they were, enabling Mazz to fit the tongs beneath the nearest one. The forklift's controls fought him when he worked to raise it. Jace heard a creaking sound and saw the tongs starting to bend from the weight, just before Mazz slid the first case into the back of the armored box truck and reversed to pull the tongs back out. They were angled downward now at the tips, and Jace wondered if the machine would be able to load the other two cases before they either continued to bend or snapped altogether. He noticed that the weight of even this one case lowered the truck's frame in the back, the rear tires seeming to shrink.

Mazz balanced the second case as far back as the length of the tongs allowed and followed the same path as the first into the truck's rear. Jace watched as more of the truck's frame sank further past the big double tires. Only a composite material of this weight and density could have withstood a thousand years of exposure to air and whatever other elements had managed to penetrate the cave where the cases had been tucked away.

Mazz had gotten the third case halfway into the truck's hold when one of the tongs snapped. The case teetered on the end, listing to the side of the broken one, when Jace caught it just in time. It took all his strength to hold it in place for the moments it took for three more of the Nine to join him in pushing it the rest of the way into the hold.

A minimum of eight hours to charge the weapons, he thought, recalculating whether they were going to be ready in time. First, they needed to drive them out of here through the same tunnel they had used to gain access.

Xan had just climbed back behind the wheel when a shrill alarm began to sound.

CHAPTER 55

Escape

Deep Base Titan, Anchorage, Alaska

Timur lurched from his chair the instant the alarm began to sound.

"Stay here, Professor," he ordered.

Kai was hearing none of that, having already bounced out of his chair as well. "The hell I will! I need to get back to my wife and daughter!"

"You'll never get there. Triggering the alarm automatically activates the base's lockdown mode. You won't even be able to get off this hallway." Timur yanked the device from his belt again. "Where was the alarm triggered?" he barked into it.

"Sublevel four, General," a voice came back. "The boy's missing."

Out in the hallway beyond the elegant quarters, Timur used a red key card to override the emergency shutdown order and activate the elevator. Kai followed him, the door closing before he was all the way in.

"This is the boy my daughter somehow found," he surmised, an instant before the cab jolted to a halt on the level below.

"As far as you know, the boy doesn't exist. Understand?"

"Too late for that, General."

The door slid open, and Timur burst from the cab, Kai racing to match his stride toward light emanating from an open doorway at the far end of the hall, where four soldiers in tactical gear stood peering inside. They parted and came to attention upon hearing the clack of the general's heels against the floor.

Inside, Kai noticed a figure wearing a white lab coat that bagged over his thin frame. The man tried to swipe a thinning patch of hair from his forehead, but it fell right back in place. He gave Kai a dismissive look, then pointed to an open ventilation shaft.

"He got out that way."

"Who was watching the security monitor? Why didn't someone see him?"

"Because the picture was running in a loop that kept us from noticing until I realized the recording counter was off. I triggered the alarm as soon as I stepped through the door."

"A loop? He managed that from down here without direct access to the system?"

The figure in the lab coat pointed to what looked like a light fixture mounted on the wall. "He knew where the hidden camera was mounted. That must have been all he needed to access."

"Can you track him?"

"His tracker is not operational, General."

"You said its functions were checked two days ago."

"They were, and it was working then."

Timur gazed toward the ventilation shaft again. "Where does that lead?"

"It doesn't matter," Kai interjected. "I know where this boy of yours must have gone."

* * *

Charlie saw that more soldiers were lying on the floor along the hall outside the hospital. She was about to ask Terry how he could make them fall asleep like that when a shrill alarm began to sound, freezing her in mid-thought. Flashing red lights accompanied the blare, casting the entire hallway in an eerie scarlet hue.

"They know I'm gone," Terry said, catching up to her after making sure no one was coming in their wake.

"Where are we going?" Charlie asked him.

"Lowest level."

"Why?"

"Gaia told me," the boy answered, leaving it at that.

She pushed her mother's wheelchair down the hall. Terry had helped her mother settle into the chair, and she barely stirred throughout the entire process. Charlie thought it would be hard to manage the task, but her mother must have lost a lot of weight because the wheelchair glided smoothly along the red-splashed tile. The trooper named Dennehy pushed the trooper named Sakari ahead of her, leaving Mrs. Piedmont with the baby.

They reached an elevator that required some kind of key card waved in front of an invisible light to open. But Terry waved his hand in front of it, and the elevator door slid open.

"How'd you do that, kid?" Dennehy asked him.

"I don't know."

* * *

The sliding door had sealed again by the time Xan approached it and resisted all of Yusef's efforts to override the system.

"Brenn," Jace called.

Brenn had already extended his kaelen into a cutting tool by the time he drew in front of the door. At first, the blade formed of concentrated nanoparticles had trouble cutting through the thick black steel, so Brenn pushed more concentrated energy into the cutting tool, and Jace watched him carve a slice as far up the wall's height as he could reach and then repeat the process cutting downward in a vertical line toward the floor.

The melting steel glowed red, generating enough heat to activate the sprinkler system, which drenched the entire hall in a steady stream of water.

* * *

"Looks like you were right, Professor," Timur said to Kai moments after they'd entered the base's infirmary to find the guard slumped on the floor, just like the ones along the hallway.

Jules, Charlie, the troopers, Jane Piedmont, and the baby were all gone.

"General, this is Command," a voice blared through his walkie-talkie. "We have a fire signal from the Crypt. Sprinkler system has activated."

"What are the cameras showing?"

"Nothing. Just a frozen picture. The system seized up."

Kai could see Timur's already taut features tighten even further. "Dispatch a tactical team to secure the Vault. Their orders are to shoot to kill any intruders on sight."

Kai grasped Timur's arm at the elbow. "My wife and daughter might be down there."

"They're not intruders, Professor. You have nothing to worry about."

"Except the aim of your men, General."

* * *

Brenn was making the second vertical cut, almost finished carving a space in the heavy steel wall big enough to drive the truck carrying their weapons through.

"Jace," Valeria said, soaked with water from the sprinklers as she looked up from her scanner, "a dozen soldiers just reached the head of the corridor, coming this way."

Jace turned toward Haran. "Go."

Haran extended her kaelen into its lasso form and moved around the truck's frame as Jace glimpsed more than a dozen black-clad soldiers rounding the head of the hall, readying their weapons. She started whipping her lasso about in a circular blur that stretched across the height and width of the entire hall.

Jace could barely see the soldiers taking aim through the swirling blur, but he could hear their gunfire echoing as it burst toward the energy field Haran had created with her lasso. The bullets didn't bounce off or melt; they broke apart at the subatomic level with a soft flash of light, hundreds of them as the incessant barrage continued.

Haran continued whipping her lasso formed of nanoparticles in a continuous blur. Even then, Jace knew, there could be brief gaps, fissures, and a bullet slid through one of them, winging Haran in the shoulder. Though just a graze, it was enough to disrupt her rhythm, weakening the energy field.

Jace was about to order the Nine into deadly action, with no choice but to strike down the humans they were sworn to protect or be cut down themselves. In that final instant before he committed to the action, the soldiers crumpled like dominoes spilling into each other, and Jace found himself staring into the focused, intense gaze of a teenage boy.

* * *

Terry, as he had come to think of himself, held the giant figure's gaze, a spark of recognition flashing in his memory.

Moments before, he had rushed from the elevator ahead of the others in his charge, propelled by the gunfire echoing from a corridor just ahead. Neutralizing the soldiers firing was as simple as picturing them dropping in his mind and projecting that image forward so it might become reality.

I've seen this man before, the boy realized, unable to unlock his stare.

In that instant, the boy recalled his haunting, dreamlike experience of watching a sentence pronounced on a group of rebels, a team of nine, on a distant planet for their treason in a place called the Veyrion. They had been forced to endure witnessing the brutal deaths of their family members before having their memories wiped so they might serve their own planet's interests on a different one:

Earth.

Hold this moment of grievous loss wrought by your own hands as your last remaining thought, a final reminder before everything you are and have been is stripped away to erase the black pit at the depths of your being so you may serve the State in a mission for the betterment of the encompassing all you sought to betray.

That mission had brought these nine rebels here to Earth as protectors against something civilization was ill prepared to fight.

Now he realized that it hadn't been a dream at all but something he needed to see, to know, at Gaia's direction. Gaia had seen what was to come and had prepared him for it. It was his life's mission, his very reason for being. But the boy knew there was more meaning to her taking him through time and space to bear witness to their memories being wiped in favor of fresh purpose.

* * *

I've seen this boy before, Jace thought. He didn't know where or when, but he recognized those eyes.

And in that moment, Jace realized it wasn't the boy he recognized but his energy. Recognized it because it was the same energy radiated by the Nine, only magnified and still developing.

How could that be?

It was impossible, yet the boy was here, a boy who was like them, but even more, imbued with the ability to use his thoughts as weapons, to down a dozen soldiers with his mind. A skill neither Jace nor any of the Nine possessed.

One of us. But something more at the same time.

Others caught up with the boy, breaking his locked gaze with Jace. Two were in wheelchairs, and there was a bony old woman with a crying infant snuggled against her. They too were somehow familiar to him, but from that settlement where the Nine had saved their lives by slaying the creatures who would have otherwise killed them.

The boy led the others on, ushering them forward, just as Brenn completed his cut and the heavy steel door keeled backward, slamming against the tunnel floor.

* * *

Four soldiers emerged from the elevator behind General Timur on the level known as the Crypt, Kai bringing up the rear. He caught up with them at a bend in the corridor, their weapons aimed at a grouping of huge figures that could only be the beings who saved the lives of everyone inside the Jaguar when Galena came under siege.

"Shoot!" ordered Timur. "Kill them all!"

* * *

In the shadow of an instant that followed, Jace saw the soldiers' fingers starting to squeeze their triggers. His sidelong glance found the boy he vaguely recognized, only it wasn't that boy he saw—it was the younger one he glimpsed back in the Mohenjo-daro street.

My son, Jace realized in the moment before he extended his kaelen into its whip form and lashed it forward.

* * *

Before the soldiers could fire, Kai saw a rope of light snap out of something one of the figures was holding. It sounded like a whip when it impacted against their assault rifles, tearing the weapons from their grasps and smashing the men against the wall.

That's when he glimpsed Charlie emerge from the cover of a truck blocking much of the hallway, pushing Jules in a wheelchair.

* * *

"Dad!" Charlie cried out, abandoning her mother's wheelchair to rush toward her father.

She passed massive figures on the way, so big they didn't look real. More like statues in museums, their faces cast in marble instead of flesh. Their eyes didn't regard her as much as record her, processing her presence to determine a response. She wasn't scared because she knew Terry would protect her.

She saw four more soldiers slumped on the floor and recognized the man standing alongside her father as the general from the glacier where she and her mother had barely escaped the monsters made of metal. Ignoring him, she practically leaped into her father's arms.

"Dad!" she said into his ear as she hugged him.

He eased her away. Charlie grabbed his hand and tugged.

"We've got to leave, Dad. We're not safe here; Terry says we're in danger."

"You're not going anywhere," the general said, holding one of the discarded assault rifles on them both. "Nobody's going anywhere."

A thin flash of light split the air, followed by a crack, and the general was on his knees, looking at his hands like they belonged to someone else.

"Come on, Dad," Charlie said, tugging harder. "Now!"

* * *

Jace retracted his whip, his mind a jumble. He found the boy in his gaze again, disappointed it wasn't still his son. And yet....

Something in the boy's eyes.... He knows me, knows the Nine....

"Load up!" Jace ordered.

The boy shepherded the others toward the truck, regarding them protectively, eyes flitting about as if in search of more threats. They didn't seem to blink. Instead, they met Jace's gaze again with a spark of recognition.

"You know me," Jace managed.

"I saw what they did. To your families."

Jace went numb. Not just him then—all of the Nine's families had been executed, with them having been forced to bear witness. Until that moment, his lost memories had been no more than a distant flutter, like a dull ache, at the far edge of his consciousness. Now those memories were coming together like discarded pieces of a jigsaw puzzle, fitting themselves together.

"I saw it all in a dream that wasn't really a dream," this boy continued, "but something Gaia wanted me to see."

Jace felt like he'd been kicked, thinking of the tattoo on his heel. "Gaia…."

He knew that name from the history of the world he had come from. An all-knowing, all-powerful being who had watched over that world since the dawn of its time, until the Overseers turned the people away from her. He knew all this, just as he knew what the "G" on the back of the heels of the Nine stood for. The crimes they had been punished for crystallized in Jace's mind, some sort of resistance they must have been part of that relied on the age of Gaia for inspiration.

Jace saw the boy's eyes flash with hope, looking youthful for the first time. "She talks to me. Does she talk to you too?"

No, Jace wanted to say, *my world stopped hearing her when the bad times came.*

"We need to leave," he told the boy instead.

"You need to take us with you."

Jace nodded because he knew the boy was right. Because there was something important, even vital, about him.

"Jace," he heard Haran say in his head. "This boy…."

"I know," he communicated back.

The boy's energy wasn't human.

It was that of the Nine, here on Earth. Impossible and yet standing before him.

* * *

"You can't go," Timur said to Kai from his knees, his hands having sunk to his sides. "You don't understand."

He looked back toward Jules, a single one of the massive figures lifting her wheelchair into the rear of the truck. Her eyes regarded him without recognition.

"I need to be with my wife."

"I told you, we can help her. We can…."

The general's words drifted in the air as Kai trotted hand in hand with Charlie for the truck, toward the boy she had told him about, who regarded both of them protectively. Charlie had said he was twelve, but he looked years older with broad shoulders that stretched the bonds of the thick shirt he was wearing over a matching pair of athletic pants. He had long hair and piercing dark eyes that seemed to radiate a soft wave of heat, which Kai could feel coursing through his entire body.

The massive figures, including one in the center who looked like a grown-up version of the boy, were not of this world. Not with the kind of weapons he had seen at work both in Galena and now here in Deep Base Titan. They must have come here somehow in response to the creatures who escaped their long-frozen ship. He and Jules had spent their entire careers hoping to find evidence of extraterrestrial life, and it ended up finding them.

Kai crouched before Jules's wheelchair, her eyes regarding him weakly. "Hey, you," he said, squeezing her hands.

"Hey," she said back to him dryly, her voice barely audible and her hands feeling limp in his grasp.

"Dad, you need to meet someone."

Kai turned from Jules and saw the boy, Terry, extend his hand down to him.

"I'm Terry."

Kai stood back up as he took the hand, felt the boy's strength in the squeeze before turning his gaze on the humanoid figure towering over both of them.

"And I'm Jace, leader of the Nine," he said, extending his hand and swallowing Kai's in his grasp. "It's time to go," he added with his eyes fixed on Terry.

Thc boy nodded. "Yes, it's time."

Part Seven
NANOBOTS

"The saddest aspect of life right now is that science gathers knowledge faster than society gathers wisdom."

—Isaac Asimov

CHAPTER 56

Damage Control

Deep Base Titan, Anchorage, Alaska

"The boy must be retrieved, General," the three-dimensional image of William Franklin Takashi told General Timur. "That is priority one, a centerpiece of the Consortium's future endeavors. But I want to hear more about this group of 'giants,' as you call them, who managed to breach the base and take him away. They are not strangers to us, are they?"

Timur had entered Takashi's quarters, fully in damage-control mode, prepared to be dressed down for the unconscionable chain of events that had befallen Deep Base Titan. He stood rigidly before the platform upon which Takashi's fully lifelike projection stood, appearing so real the general thought he could reach out and touch him. So far, Takashi had seemed more intrigued than angered by the breach of Deep Base Titan and what followed.

"No, sir, they're not," Timur said. "We've already matched their likenesses to the battle they fought in that Alaskan town against the creatures who fled the alien craft."

"They are humanoid, General, but most certainly not of this planet, nor are the weapons in their possession. We can only assume that their coming to Deep Base Titan at this moment in time to retrieve those alien objects is not coincidental. We've had them in our possession for fifteen years now, ever since this place went online. There can only be one explanation for these aliens taking back what must be theirs."

"They need whatever's inside to fight the next wave of creatures."

Takashi's eyes gleamed with excitement, a smile dancing at the edges of his expression. "Imagine the power of these weapons we were never able to access or identify. Imagine if the Consortium could harness that power. What of the current location of these nine beings? Do you have any further leads?"

"We located the truck at the Ship Creek dock ten miles from here. The missing containers were found in the rear, their lids open, and the contents, the weapons you referenced, had been removed. A fishing boat was reported missing soon afterward. We've got drones up and are using all available satellite reconnaissance to find it. Once we do, I've ordered passive surveillance until we can determine how best to proceed, given the capabilities and resources of the opposition."

"The coast guard has been alerted, yes?"

"Of course. They are searching the waters with boats and helicopters as we speak."

"Given those capabilities and resources, any measures we undertake to bring them to heel may prove disastrous, not to mention endanger the boy. Order the coast guard to surveil but not approach."

"Already done, sir, until we can mass sufficient troops and equipment to encircle them at sea."

"We will not be encircling them at all, General."

"Sir?"

"Your last report indicated those creatures were headed to Juneau."

"Yes, and if we're going to evacuate the city, we'll need to—"

"There will be no evacuation, General," Takashi interrupted tersely.

Timur waited for him to continue.

"By all indications, these nine beings are aligned with us against the creatures massing at sea. Proceeding on the assumption that they are headed to Juneau to make a stand against the creatures allows us to seize them and their weapons in the wake of that battle."

"And if these nine visitors fail, sir?"

"We will take additional countermeasures once we have retrieved the boy and any survivors of their group. That will give us the opportunity to see their weapons in action, to evaluate their operation as a potential resource for the Consortium. We are on the verge of a great gift being bestowed upon us."

"Sir, thirty thousand people live in Juneau."

"And would you not sacrifice them all for the greater mission before us?"

"You miss my point. Thirty thousand casualties could spawn a hundred, even a thousand times that number of these things."

"Contained to a relatively isolated area. If further sacrifice is required, so be it. We are looking at the opportunity for the Consortium to achieve global hegemony, to see our greatest goals realized. An opportunity to be seized at all costs, General. Do you disagree?"

"I'm a soldier, sir," Timur managed, taking his words as far as he dared. "Fighting to preserve innocent lives is what I was trained for."

"Preserving innocent lives ceased to be your personal mission statement when you took command of Deep Base Titan and all operations pertaining to it. Your mission now is to serve the Consortium and its ends through any means at your disposal, and the boy is crucial to those ends, even more so now. When we find our visitors, we find him."

Timur heard a buzzing and turned away to regard a text message, then swung back toward Takashi.

"The stolen fishing boat has been found abandoned at sea, sir."

CHAPTER 57

Introductions

The Gulf of Alaska

Kai sat in a chair by Jules's bedside, Charlie's tearstained face pressed against him, her breathing intermixed with sobs. Jules had slipped into unconsciousness early into their journey that had brought them to the Gulf of Alaska and had yet to reawaken.

"Mom's not going to wake up, is she?" Charlie muttered.

"I don't know, Char."

"She's very brave."

"Yes, she is."

"She fought the monsters, just like you did." Charlie eased slightly away to meet Kai's sad eyes. "But the monsters are still out there, aren't they?"

The truck had brought them to the Port of Anchorage, where they boarded a fishing boat. Kai was too consumed with Jules to notice much else. But the ride there after fleeing Deep Base Titan, crowded into the rear with the others who'd come there with him along with six of these new arrivals, was tense and unsettling. Jane Piedmont rocked the baby in her arms. Trooper Tom Dennehy, for his part, was content to tend to his partner, Sakari Muhtuk, who occupied a second wheelchair squeezed into the truck's rear.

Kai felt Charlie pressed up against him on the truck's floor, his arm draped around her shoulder. Even seated, the massive figures around them stretched halfway to the ceiling of the truck's cargo area.

"You guys are big," a wide-eyed Charlie had said. "You ever play basketball there?"

Kai's stare met and locked with that of Jace across the cargo area.

"I recognize you. You were inside that vehicle in the settlement where we fought the enemy. You were the one who killed their spawn in the first settlement."

Kai managed a nod. "Professor Kai Bevins." He tilted his gaze to Jules in her wheelchair. "And this is my wife Jules, also a professor."

Jace seemed to study the unconscious Jules for a long moment. "I'm sorry."

Kai's rational mind wanted to know more about these nine intergalactic warriors, where they were from, and if their mission here extended beyond fighting the creatures threatening all life on Earth with extinction. But he was processing thoughts too quickly to verbalize them, especially crowded into the cargo hold of an armored truck, sharing space with three rectangular objects loaded inside ahead of them.

"Our weapons, Professor," Jace had said, in answer to Kai's unformed question. "The means to save your world."

It was clear once at sea that the trawler's plodding pace would never get them to Juneau before the creatures growing in the nearby sea came ashore at peak darkness, eighteen hours from now, according to Jace. But they remained aboard that vessel only until they located the Coast Guard Marine Protector ship *Reef Shark* and sounded a distress signal. Six of what Jace kept referring to as the Nine boarded the vessel when it drew close and commandeered the ship in a matter of minutes without an alarm being raised.

With that, the rest of those on board abandoned the trawler and hoisted the Nine's weapons onto the Reef Shark. At eighty-seven feet in length, it was considerably smaller than the larger Cutter class and faster, too. Fast enough to get them to Juneau, though with little time to spare.

The Reef Shark's ten-person crew, after being swiftly overwhelmed but left unharmed, had been locked away in a pair of berths. Chronar was able to imitate the radioman's voice for regular check-ins using the proper designations and codes. Because all coast guard vessels in the area were currently combing the surrounding seas for whatever ship the Nine had transferred onto, steaming toward Juneau raised no flags for anyone monitoring their GPS coordinates via satellite or transponder.

Sakari Muhtuk had been placed in one of the remaining berths, leaving Jules the sole inhabitant of the ship's afloat sickbay. The confines were tight but surprisingly well-stocked, including a rapid infuser for emergency blood transfusions at sea, since the *Reef Shark* was used for drug interdiction missions. A member of the Nine named Zareb, a medical specialist, was well-versed in utilizing all the equipment and medications, though his examination of Jules had been understandably grim.

"I'm sorry," he said, aware nothing tucked away on the shelves of the sickbay or anywhere else could help her.

There was nothing to do now but wait. Kai had promised Jules that Charlie wouldn't be there in the end, but what was he to do? Send her away? No, she deserved this much, especially after being denied the truth for so long. And she had grown up a lot these past few days.

"Professor," Kai heard Jace call from the doorway five feet back, adding, "A minute, please?" after Kai turned his way.

Kai eased Charlie from his lap and let her claim the chair for herself. "You stay with Mom, okay?"

His daughter nodded, fighting to be brave with the inevitable drawing closer.

"We're going to need your help," Jace said softly when Kai reached him.

"*My* help? I don't understand."

"But you do understand these creatures better than anyone. You've studied them. I read the report you and your wife compiled inside Deep Base Titan."

Kai didn't bother to ask how.

"You understand their metabolism. You even postulated a countermeasure Chronar hadn't considered."

"Chronar?"

"Our guide and protector for fifteen hundred years, since we left our world. An entity formed by what you call artificial intelligence or AI."

Kai knew Jace was referring to the notion of the odor of Jane Piedmont's diseased bones that had acted as a repellent to the creatures. "If you know that, you know I'm nothing without my wife. We're a team, and she's the expert on alien anatomy. Without her, I'll probably be useless to you, and right now…."

Kai let his voice trail off, turning his gaze back toward Jules lying in a hospital bed she would never leave.

"What if we could save her, Professor?" Jace asked him.

CHAPTER 58

Memories

The Gulf of Alaska

"You've taken a new name, Teraválar," Gaia said, seated cross-legged before the boy on the ship's aft deck.

Terry could smell the sea upon her, and the rich scent of the land and forest too. Gaia carried all the scents of Earth with her.

"My friend gave it to me."

"You speak of the girl Charlotte."

"She goes by Charlie. She may be small for her age, but she's tough and brave. She said she wanted to meet you."

"What did you tell her about me?"

"That you're my friend." The boy looked up toward the sun, feeling its heat through the breeze blowing his hair about. "It feels good to be here."

"You are among the Earth now, one with it, as I have taught you."

"This is what everything has been about, what it's always been about."

"But you always had a choice. Listening to my words has never meant heeding them. You have made me proud, Teraválar."

The boy's lips teased a brief smile until his expression tightened again. "I've seen these people before, haven't I?"

Gaia nodded.

"It wasn't a dream at all. I saw what happened, how they were punished for trying to serve a greater good, for taking a stand on their planet."

Gaia gazed into his eyes deeper than she ever had. "It's not just their planet."

The boy felt a chill of realization course through him. "I don't understand."

"You will in the fullness of time."

"Is that why I'm different? Because I'm like them?"

"You are more."

A recent memory flitted at the edge of his consciousness. "You told me it has been thousands of Earth's years since you had known someone like me."

"Encountered someone worthy of that mantle and capable of taking it were my exact words."

"I don't understand."

"You weren't ready when I said that the first time. You are ready now."

"The guards I made fall asleep, the machines I manipulated—was that me or you who did that?"

"It was you."

"Thanks to what you taught me."

"Only because it was already inside you. I merely brought it out, taught you to trust your thoughts and turn them into actions."

"These things Charlie told me about, the monsters...."

Gaia waited for him to continue, her youthful eyes, colored the blue of the ocean today, urging him on.

"They are what I must protect the Earth from. But you're stronger than me, Gaia, so why not you?"

"It is me, Teravalar, working within you, *through* you. In times long past, I have seen its coming and took the steps that were required to prepare. As in olden times, you are one with the Earth and the Earth is one with you. In times of old, the heritage you come from found peace in that notion. Then others usurped the land and exploited it. They saw it as plunder instead of sustenance and upset the balance of things, of life, making chaos out of order."

"You're not speaking of this world, but of the one the Nine came from." The boy swallowed hard. "The one I'm from too."

"The Nine tried to restore the old order of things, the traditions that had been buried as historic artifacts in a lost library of knowledge."

The boy tried to make sense of the puzzle Gaia was assembling before him. "How many worlds are there?"

"There is one, but also many. And if one is lost, all suffer."

"Why don't you speak to others, Gaia?"

"Only those who are called can hear my words. What does your name mean, Teraválar?"

"Protector of the Earth. The Earth is one," the boy said, from his teachings.

"Yes."

"And I am the Earth."

"We are all the Earth, Teraválar. But only you can save it."

CHAPTER 59

Sickbay

The Gulf of Alaska

"Nothing like this has ever been tried with a human being," Jace heard Chronar say in his mind.

"But will it work?"

"Theoretically, but I cannot provide complete assurance. My scans indicate the woman has only hours to live, a day at most. In her weakened condition, the jolt to the system caused by flooding her with nanobots could cause her metabolism to shut down."

"We may need this woman for civilization here to survive," Jace said in his mind. "She has knowledge of our enemy's metabolism and functionality that could prove vital."

"I understand. The procedure will require the use of one of the nanobatteries currently charging the weapons systems."

"This woman has no time to spare, Chronar. Help Zareb with the necessary preparations."

* * *

"Nanobots," Kai repeated.

Jace looked down from alongside him in the Reef Shark's cramped sick bay while Zareb positioned the necessary equipment next to Jules's bedside.

Thanks to Chronar's teaching while in stasis, Zareb emerged as the Nine's medical expert, possessing diagnostic, treatment, and surgical capabilities that rivaled any of Earth's greatest experts across a myriad of disciplines.

"Not too long ago, I asked my wife's oncologist if there were any ongoing clinical trials utilizing nanobots in cancer treatment," Kai continued.

"What did he tell you, Professor?"

"It's a she, and her answer was medicine is somewhere between twenty and forty years away from having the scientific capacity to even entertain the notion at a rudimentary level."

"Good thing our civilization has mastered their use then," Jace noted, watching Zareb position an infusion pump commonly used for blood transfusions into place alongside Jules's bed.

It was the latest-generation Belmont Rapid Infuser, and the Reef Shark might well have been the smallest vessel class to be equipped with one. In ordinary circumstances, it provided reliable, high-speed delivery of warmed blood and fluids, making it ideal for battlefield environments. The unit was small, portable, highly efficient, and boasted a working pump system Zareb easily adapted to filter the nanobots into Jules Bevins's system via normal saline.

"Your civilization," Kai echoed, "you know our anatomies so well because your race are the real fathers of man."

"Is that a question?"

"Only if it needs to be. In astrobiology, you're known as planet seeders."

"Not us specifically, but your concept is correct. Ten million years ago, people from our planet chose Earth specifically because the planet's atmosphere and resources were a close match to our own, capable of sustaining life in humanoid form. So, yes, the biological foundations of man were then planted accordingly."

"We weren't the first, I imagine."

"Far from it, Professor. Dozens of other planets preceded yours. Not all those operations bore results as fruitful as on Earth. Once it was clear the operation here achieved success, the Nine were dispatched fifteen hundred years ago, on a journey that took five hundred years, to make sure no interplanetary threat disrupted the experiment."

Jace watched Kai shift his gaze from his wife back to him. "So, the human race is an experiment?"

"For lack of a better word, yes."

"Made in your image but inferior in size, strength, speed, and intelligence."

"No two planets are exactly alike, Professor. We may be your forebears, but so many variables are required to create life. Your genetic development differed from ours in the areas you raised."

"You couldn't make us carbon copies of the people from your world, because then we could become a threat to you. An equally applicable rational for why we're not as big, strong, fast, or smart as you."

"I cannot say, Professor, because I have no precise knowledge of that. My world created you and then made sure you were protected against another species that would seek to victimize your world."

"Like these things that crash-landed here somewhere around two hundred thousand years ago. Is that what you expected?"

"A random threat like the one our enemy poses was considered the highest of all probabilities."

"As astrobiologists, my wife and I studied what we thought to be every conceivable scenario for an encounter with an alien race. But we never considered anything like this, the fact that such a race was already present on our planet."

Jace looked down to meet Kai's gaze again. "Because we're not truly an alien race, are we?"

"I guess not, just advanced far, far beyond ours." Kai took a deep breath and slowly exhaled. "Tell me more about the nanobots, the process."

Jace turned his gaze on Charlie, seated at her mother's bedside. "Chronar has already used its advanced imaging capabilities to map your wife's tumors and malignant spread at the cellular level. Chronar has also identified her cancer's molecular signature in terms of mutations and markers to program into the nanobots' targeting system."

"What about rejection?"

"The nanobots we'll be using are made from biocompatible materials keyed to your wife's individual genetic structure, Professor. Their programming will allow them to identify the cancer cells via surface markers and eradicate them at the cellular level. Less advanced technology would require external magnetic fields or ultrasound to guide the nanobots, but Chronar has enabled them to follow microscopic chemical trails to assure that they ignore all healthy cells and tissue, targeting only identified biomarkers."

"Like a roadmap."

Jace nodded. "And the bots will not only kill and eradicate the cancer. Chronar has programmed them to repair the damaged tissue and parts of your wife's brain that were causing her neurological symptoms. The bots will report their progress in real time to Chronar."

"What happens once they finish their job?"

"We can't be sure, given there's no precedent for your anatomy. Chronar could mark them appropriately to be absorbed once your wife's immune system has fully recovered. They may simply break down and degrade on their own. Or they may slip into a period of dormancy, programmed to reactivate if the cancer markers they've been trained to spot reappear. Each bot is essentially an organic machine, programmed to work together while capable of independent action."

"We're ready," Zareb called, looking up at Jules's bedside.

Jace squeezed Kai's shoulder as they watched him activate the rapid infusion machine, and the clear fluid carrying the nanobots began to stream into Jules's body.

CHAPTER 60

Past and Present

The Gulf of Alaska

Jules felt as though she were floating, aware of both nothing and everything at the same time. A rush of warmth coursed through her, making her feel content and at peace.

"Can you hear me, Jules?"

"Yes, I can hear you." She wasn't sure if she spoke the words or merely framed them in her mind. "Who are you?"

"I am Chronar."

"Am I dying?" Jules posed, wondering if the testaments provided by many survivors of near-death experiences were true and if a white light was about to appear before her.

"You were. You no longer are. We are saving you."

"Who's we?"

"The Nine. You know the Nine from their slaying of the creatures in the town of Galena. So, before they moved to save your life, they had already saved the life of your husband."

Jules recalled the dark, blurred images of motion with strange clarity, as if her subconscious mind had enhanced them. "Are you one of the Nine?"

"No, I am what you would call their artificial intelligence program."

Being aware she was unconscious didn't stop Jules from coming to grips with the fact that she was having a conversation with an intelligent, self-aware entity not of this world. She felt a palpable sense of excitement building inside her, tempered only by the possibility that this was all an illusion bred by the final stages of transition toward death.

"How are you saving me?"

"By utilizing nanobots to target and kill the cancer cells that are killing you, eradicating them and all traces of the disease from your system."

"That's impossible."

"Only for humanity in its current stage of development."

Jules could hear the hum of the harsh overhead lighting she recalled from a brief lucid moment before she slipped away and the faint scent of alcohol masked by something floral, almost calming. The bed she rested on felt more like a softly rolling ocean. Currents wrapping her in their embrace.

"The intravenous infusion began moments ago. The nanobots are navigating through your bloodstream toward the tumor cells, following your cancer's unique molecular signals. I am following their progress, Jules. Most are heading toward the infestation in your brain. The rest are targeting areas in your body where the cancer has spread. Would you like to see?"

"Yes."

"Then I will show you."

Suddenly, Jules seemed to be watching what looked more like a three-dimensional computerized depiction of her inner self. Her cancer had seeded itself across the tissues, a creeping darkness that grew in defiance of life, threading its way through lungs, liver, lymph nodes, a silent colonizer.

And then the nanobots struck. Tiny lights representing them dispersed through her, following the crisscrossing network of blood-toting veins, like thousands of fireflies branching out into a vast internal map infused by the softly whirring machine at her bedside.

Jules could feel the flood of microscopic precision machines drifting through her bloodstream. The nanobots' sensors flared to life, detecting the chemical footprints of malignancy—abnormal proteins, chaotic cellular patterns, and signals of unchecked division. The bots moved swiftly, slipping past red cells and immune sentries unnoticed because they had been programmed to match Jules's DNA.

A cluster of cancer cells loomed ahead—twisted, irregular, glowing with crisscrossing strands of light that looked like spider veins. The bots attacked, each nanobot latching onto the membrane of a tumor cell with molecular fingers. Jules felt no pain, only an uncanny sense of something moving inside her. Microneedles pierced the cellular walls of her tumors with surgical precision, allowing the nanobots to inject targeted toxins, crafted molecules lethal only to the malignant cells. In a flash, those cells collapsed one after the other and then vanished into the body's ether.

More bots arrived, encircling the cluster of flashing cells. They worked in concert, weaving a lattice of destruction while leaving healthy cells and tissue unscathed. The immune system, once bewildered and outmatched, now surged as if following the nanobots' lead. T cells, revived and strengthened, joined the battle and attacked the rogue cells in concert with the bots.

Jules felt something shift inside her. Her breathing came easier, no longer labored. The growing tightness in her chest loosened. And, most notably, the heaviness inside her head, the nagging throb that never truly went away, began to abate.

Still, she wondered if this might be an illusion, a last grasp to retain life as it slipped away forever.

"This is real, Jules," the voice of the entity that called itself Chronar told her.

"Did I ask you if it was or not?"

"You didn't have to. You opened your mind to me, so your thoughts are as clear as your words."

Jules watched the visual depiction Chronar provided, continuing to see the nanobots winning the invisible war they were waging.

"How do you feel, Jules?" Chronar asked her.

"Like I'm floating. No pain for the first time in months, years. Is my husband here, my daughter?"

"They are sitting by your bedside, holding hands. Your daughter is squeezing yours."

"I can feel it!"

"Dad," Jules heard, the voice sounding very far away, "Mom squeezed my hand! I felt Mom squeeze my hand!"

"Did I do that, Chronar?"

"Yes, Jules, you did. The nanobots in your bloodstream are designed for rapid cellular repair centuries beyond what your planet can achieve at present. In addition to eradicating the cancer, their task is to restore and rejuvenate your cellular function. Not just rid you of disease but make you one hundred percent again in short order."

Jules felt herself take a deep breath, unable to tell whether it was with her mind or her now fully functional respiratory system. "Everything's so clear, so sharp."

"Because you no longer have to look past the blocks cancer put in place. You should rest now, Jules, and let the nanobots finish their work."

"I don't want to rest. I'm afraid if I sleep, I'll learn this was just a dream, that none of it really happened."

"It is not a dream. It is happening now. The Nine wish to save you so you may help them save your world."

"Can we win, Chronar?"

"You can, but I am unable to predict if you will. There are too many factors and variables to consider to reach an accurate conclusion."

"These creatures are like a cancer on the Earth, aren't they?" Jules said, recalling the way she had come to think of them. "And we're the nanobots out to destroy them."

"The nanobots can only win if there is still a patient to save. The same holds true here, Jules, only that patient is the world."

CHAPTER 61

Dialogue

The Gulf of Alaska

Jace stood back from where Kai and Charlie were seated by Jules's bedside in the converted berth. He came to think of them with increasing familiarity, far from strangers even though they'd only known each other for a matter of hours. The intensity of their shared experience, as well as a common enemy and a monumental task before them, had magnified their relationship.

And yet, as the nanobots attacked the cancer laying waste to Jules's body, he felt like he was intruding on their privacy, that these were moments they needed to experience alone. Something like a nagging sense of unease tugged him up to the deck where the boy stood holding the deck rail with his gaze fixed on the empty sea around them.

"Do you remember me?" the boy asked. "Because I remember you."

In that moment, Jace felt the same emptiness inside him as when he thought of the other younger boy in his vision. It was as if he climbed the stairs up here because he thought that boy would be here, instead of this one.

"I saw what happened, what they did," he resumed, still not turning toward him.

Cloudy, blurred images swam through Jace's mind. He felt himself resisting the clarity that had begun to appear when he had first met the boy at Deep Space Titan.

The boy finally turned from the railing, his eyes locking with Jace. "It was years ago, but Gaia brought me there because she wanted me to see, to know. I thought it was a dream at first. Then you looked at me, and I knew it wasn't."

The boy reached out and laid his hand on his shoulder. In that moment, Jace saw the boy as he had all those Earth years ago, within an enclosure known as the Veyrion, where judgment was passed. Its vast expanse darkened, everywhere, except the center, which was awash with hot, white light.

Because you refuse to accept accountability for your crimes, you will surrender your very identities so you might be repurposed for a task determined by the Overseers for the State. You will cease to exist as who you were. You will know only what is required and hold no memories of what came before. But first, you must bear the loss of everything you hold dear, so your final experience will carry a pain you will have forever in the black pits of your being.

For a flicker of an instant, Jace thought the disembodied voice was coming from somewhere on the ship's deck. Then he realized the words had been uttered within the Veyrion on the day that stole his past. He closed his eyes and saw in his mind the younger boy who haunted his memories. Then the boy was gone, vaporized in a blinding flash of light.

His son.

Hold this moment of grievous loss wrought by your own hands as your last remaining thought, a final reminder of before everything you are and have been is stripped away to erase the black pit at the depths of your being so you may serve the State in a mission for the betterment of the encompassing all you sought to betray in your resistance and rebellion. May you find renewed purpose in that task and redemption in fulfilling it.

I know that voice! Jace thought. It resonated with a strange hollow echo that blurred the words enough to hide the speaker from memory. He searched through the dark corners of his mind for its origins, but every time he drew close the truth was yanked away, leaving him to wonder if he really wanted to know.

Jace tried to open his eyes but couldn't. He found himself back in the Veyrion, held in a restraining shaft like the other members of the Nine.

You are the Nine. And your mission is to serve the interests of the Crown Arc you have risen against on a distant planet we have been preparing for ten million of their years. Your time will be measured by theirs as you await the occasion your service is required in a black void of nothingness you have wrought for yourselves.

Now that occasion the familiar voice had warned about was upon them. But theirs was not a holy mission; it was one conceived for punishment. Their identities had been stripped from them, preceded by the loss of everything they held dear. Their entire existences had been reduced to the purpose of their mission and nothing more.

"Now I have shown you; now you have seen."

The boy's words shocked Jace back to the deck of the Reef Shark. Jace opened his eyes, having not realized they were closed. The boy's hand had left his shoulder, but his piercing eyes bore into him.

"My real name is Teraválar. You know its meaning."

"'Protector of the world' in a long-forgotten language."

"Gaia gave it to me. She wanted me to see what they did to you. And she wanted me to show you." The boy looked down, then snapped his head back to flip the hair the wind had blown into his face away. "Who am I? Am I one of you?"

"Not if you speak to Gaia. No one from my world has heard from her in all the years since the Unraveling, as it came to be known."

"This Unraveling.... It happened on your planet, the one Gaia brought me to."

Jace thought of the off-kilter comments others of Nine had been making since they were awakened from stasis. Now he understood their words were remnants of memories somehow leaking back into their consciousnesses.

"Who is Gaia?" the boy asked.

"Gaia isn't a who, Gaia is a *what*. Gaia is the glue that holds all life together."

"Here or on your planet?"

"Everywhere. Gaia is the land, Gaia is the water, Gaia is the sky, keeping all living things in the proper balance."

"Until she stopped speaking."

"I misspoke. Gaia didn't stop speaking. Those of my world stopped listening, preferring to listen to the false promises of those who had seized power behind a curtain of lies. Their words led my world's people to turn away from

Gaia, where our strength had always come from. They could not hear the lies and the truth at once, so they chose the lies."

Jace felt his mind opening, like a vast curtain being pulled back on a bright and beautiful world. He saw things as they had been long before his birth, where people walked the land without struggling for purpose, free of avarice, greed, and longing, following the word of Gaia without needing to hear it spoken because her word marked the way.

"The Nine," the boy said softly, as if he had settled on the same truth Jace had.

"There was another Nine, the original Nine," he told the boy. "They were the builders of our world, those who molded it based on the word of Gaia."

"Gaia spoke to them," the boy reasoned.

"And they heeded everything she said, followed the lead she set. But when the Overseers," Jace continued, recalling the name of those who had struck down his family, "gained control, believing in Gaia became a crime. She was excised from the collective minds of all people, never to be heard again." He stopped and regarded the boy closely. "Until now, Teraválar, until you."

"I'm not like you, am I?"

"You are culled from a time when the people and the earth were one, their fates and existences intertwined. It was an era without war, without struggle, without caste, without a lust for power and domination. We were deemed enemies of the State for trying to restore those times, to bring the word of Gaia back to our world."

"But you're here to save this world."

"With your help. Somehow. That's what Gaia has been preparing you for."

"The Earth is one and I am the Earth."

"Jace," he heard Chronar say in his mind, "we are about to come under attack."

CHAPTER 62

Chaos Theory

Deep Base Titan

"You wished to speak to me, General?"

"Three of the coast guard ships patrolling the Gulf of Alaska in search of our escapees have fallen under attack. We have lost contact with two and have failed to reach a third."

Timur studied the projection of Takashi's expression, finding no reaction to his report whatsoever. Not even a frown or a grimace. If anything, he looked content, as if satisfied by the news.

"This would have been in the daylight."

"We're exploring the theory that the creatures may develop differently in water than on land and, by all accounts, the ships were overrun in a matter of minutes. The other issue we're studying is territoriality. We believe the attacks may have been spurred by the creatures reacting to a perceived threat."

"You have footage of the attacks to analyze?"

"We're still looping transmitted body cam and security footage together chronologically from one of the ships that's already fallen. We've been unable to identify any survivors." Timur pressed a finger against his earpiece. "The footage has been assembled, sir, if you'd like to see it."

Takashi's placid expression flashed a glimmer of excitement, flirting with the thinnest of smiles. "On the air screen, please."

With that, he turned toward the gaseous broadcast screen set between his projection atop the platform and the nearest wall. Almost instantly, the assembled footage began to spool in splotchy, blurred fashion, jumping from one point of view to another before settling on a Coast Guard Cutter's crewmember firing nonstop with an assault rifle barrel angled downward at the sea. The scene switched to the POVs of the crew members manning mounted .50-caliber machine guns, unleashing a nonstop torrent toward granular images rising out of the sea. The visual transmission was difficult to follow, but the sounds of crew members calling out to each other, and the rattle of spent casings clanging against the deck, and, finally, the screaming made Timur wince.

The assembled footage continued to roll, showing more of the massive fully formed creatures reaching the deck and swallowing crew members in their assemblage of oily-looking tentacles before hurtling overboard with their victims in tow. The scene was utterly horrific, making even the battle-hardened Timur sick to his stomach imagining the rich coppery scent of blood as waves of it splattered against the lenses of body cameras and security cameras. The screams and gunfire intensified briefly before beginning to ebb as the numbers of the decimated crew continued to wane.

"Mayday, mayday, mayday, mayday!" a radio operator's call blared until his high-pitched screaming bubbled in Timur's ears.

"Seven minutes," he said to Takashi when the footage wound down and the gaseous screen went dark. "We estimate the entire ship was overrun, and all crew members killed, in seven minutes. This was a Legend-class Cutter, sir, with a crew of more than a hundred and fifty."

Takashi seemed unmoved by that, as if his projection lacked the capacity to display emotion.

"We estimate the wave of creatures will reach Juneau after dark tonight," Timur reported. "I would like your permission to at least warn authorities there of what's coming."

"Toward what end, General? You think any measures they take will matter? An evacuation attempt would hopelessly clog the roads. We must let things run their course and seize the opportunity that provides."

"Sir?" Timur raised, utterly baffled by Takashi's response.

Takashi's flickering smile broadened slightly. "Chaos, General, chaos. Just what the Consortium needs for its efficacy to be magnified and its power to be solidified. Governments will fall, and panic will reign, as the world confronts a threat it is ill prepared to face. This is closest in form to the nuclear winter scenario we have considered, a complete collapse of society as we know it, creating a void the Consortium will step into."

"Toward what end?" Timur challenged. "There will be nothing left."

"There will be enough. This theory these astrobiologists advanced before their escape holds great merit."

Timur knew Takashi was speaking of the repellent professors Jules and Kai Bevins believed could be created, using the scent that had kept the monsters from attacking the old woman riddled with bone disease. However, the length of time it would take to create, manufacture, and distribute significant quantities of it globally would stretch into months, if not years. And the world may not have either of those left.

Significant echoed in his head, the truth dawning on him. The World Consortium didn't need *significant* quantities to save the world to achieve its mission statement of global hegemony. It only needed enough to suit its needs by using the samples taken of Jane Piedmont's bones here at Deep Base Titan to formulate the scent that repelled the creatures.

"Lots of people are going to die, sir," Timur managed.

Takashi flirted with another smile that didn't quite emerge. "Except those we select to live, General. Order our scientists to go to work on isolating the repellent immediately."

CHAPTER 63

Black Cubes

Gulf of Alaska

"Three other coast guard vessels have already been overrun," Chronar told Jace. "There don't appear to be any survivors."

"They attacked those ships in daylight."

"The creatures could be evolving, acclimating themselves to this planet. They might also be responding to a perceived threat in the presence of the ships in waters they have staked out for themselves."

Jace considered that, then returned his attention to the challenge that would come much sooner. "How much time have we got before the creatures reach us?"

* * *

Jace found Brenn and Izumi, the Nine's weapons specialists, in the ship's mess hall on the Reef Shark's first lower deck, the weapons of the Nine lying across a combination of bench tables and counter space cleared of everything else. The black cube charging stations were placed close to the weapons, one of each for the smaller, handheld ones, and two or three for the larger stationary mounted weapons.

"We're going to need our weapons sooner than expected," he told them.

Brenn and Izumi looked up from checking the energy levels while making sure the invisible connection, a highly advanced version of Bluetooth, between the cubes and weapons was holding and operating at maximum capacity.

"How much sooner?"

"Chronar estimates seventeen minutes until we're under attack by a mass of the creatures heading toward us now."

"We can get the four handheld weapons up to nearly seventy-five percent capacity if we route all charging power to them," advanced Brenn.

"But that means the larger weapons won't be fully charged by the time we reach Juneau," Izumi added.

"And depending on the energy remaining in the handhelds after the battle at sea," Brenn continued, "it will be hard to get them up to peak capacity as well."

Jace knew he had no choice but to take that chance, given that if they didn't win this battle, they'd never reach Juneau to fight the much larger one where upward of thirty thousand lives would be at stake. That could result in somewhere between one and ten million new spawn of the creatures, free to move south toward even larger concentrations of population. If they reached the continental United States, they would become totally unstoppable.

"We'll do the best we can," he told Brenn and Izumi. "Get as much energy into the handhelds as you can while I prepare the others for battle."

CHAPTER 64

Waking Dream

Gulf of Alaska

Kai watched Jules's eyelids flutter and then lift, her eyes quickly widening at the sight of her husband and daughter rising from their chairs.

"Mom!"

Charlie practically leaped onto her bed. "Easy there, baby," Jules said, hugging her tight. "I'm still weak."

Kai squeezed her hand. "How do you feel?"

"Chronar told me the scans it performed found no trace of any remaining cancer cells anywhere in my body. The nanobots did their job."

"What's Chronar?" Charlie asked, lifting her head from Jules's chest.

"Our friends' artificial intelligence program."

"Friends?" Kai posed.

"They saved my life, Kai."

"Because they need you, they need both of us."

"Am I supposed to believe that matters? I don't feel any pain for the first time in, well, longer than I care to remember."

Charlie's stare bore into her mother's eyes. "Why didn't you tell me you were sick? Why didn't you tell me it was as bad as it was?"

Jules stroked her daughter's hair. "Because I thought I was going to get better right until the other night when I knew I was failing; I refused to give up hope. And I needed you to be strong for me. I needed to use your strength, and if we told you the truth, you wouldn't be strong enough to help me."

Kai could tell Charlie didn't quite grasp that, but she nodded anyway. He squeezed Jules's hand and felt her squeeze back harder.

"Ouch," he said, grinning.

"Chronar said, thanks to the nanobots, my functions and vital systems are all back to normal."

Jules started to smile, but her features seemed to scrunch up, eyes squeezed closed as if her head was pounding.

"Jules...."

"Mom?"

Kai felt her squeezing his hand so tightly that it began to hurt, the cartilage crunching.

"Jules!"

He managed to pull free of her grasp in the exact moment her eyes snapped open.

"Are you okay? Are you in pain?"

Jules's gaze was distant. "No, no, not that. Nothing like that. It's just that...I saw something in my mind. I saw the creatures converging on us from everywhere at once, forming a massive black wave. I wasn't asleep. I could still feel you and Charlie. It was like a waking dream."

Kai heard the patter of footsteps and turned to see Jace standing in the doorway.

"It wasn't a dream at all, was it?" Jules asked him, easing Charlie from her so she could sit upright.

Jace didn't answer her. "You're feeling better. Good. We need to move all of you to the engine room."

"Why?" Kai asked him.

"Because a wave of the creatures is about to attack, and that's the most secure location on this ship, behind a reinforced fire door."

Kai looked toward Jules. "How did you know?"

"I—I don't know."

"It doesn't matter," said Jace. "We need to move you now."

* * *

Troopers Muhtuk and Dennehy, along with Jane Piedmont and the infant who now seemed to be a part of her, were already in the engine room when Jace led Jules, Kai, and Charlie inside, having been moved from the berths not occupied by the Reef Shark's imprisoned crewmembers. Before entering, he decided to try contacting Gaia himself, as the forebears the Nine had taken their name from had eons ago.

"Well, look who's here," Piedmont said toward Jules, grinning as she bounced the baby in her grasp. "Now I can see where your daughter gets her good looks."

She cast Charlie a wink. Jules had no memory of any of these people. The pair Kai introduced as Alaska state troopers had swapped their uniforms for coast guard blues.

"Hey, Dennehy," Charlie greeted the male trooper.

He looked up from his work, securing a .50-caliber machine gun and its mount, which had been lifted from the deck, into place, positioned directly in front of the door. Jules noticed a spare ammo pack just off to the side.

"Hopefully," Jace began, "none of the creatures will make it down here. But if they do, at least you'll have a chance."

"Bullets worked in the Springs against their spawn," Kai noted. "Not so much in Galena against the fully mature creatures."

"If they get through the door, Professor, Trooper Dennehy here will have eight hundred rounds at his disposal."

Jace heard a shuffling in the doorway and turned to find the boy standing there.

"You wanted to see me?"

* * *

Charlie practically leaped into his arms.

"I knew you'd come, Terry, I knew you'd come!" She eased away from him. "You'll protect us, won't you?"

"Jace and I need to talk first."

Jace joined him in the hallway, and Terry closed the door.

"I don't belong down here hiding."

"Charlie's right, Teraválar, you've got to protect these people, especially her parents. If the Nine fail, they become this world's only hope."

"You need me with you, so you *won't* fail."

"In which case, the Nine will be distracted by the need to protect you. I can't have that."

"I don't need anyone to protect me, Jace. You know that."

"Maybe, but they don't. This is the way it has to be."

The boy's eyes, narrowed in a mix of contempt and determination, held fast to Jace's. "I can help. I'm ready. Believe me when I tell you I'm ready. Gaia has prepared me for this."

"I asked her to bring you down to me."

Confusion claimed the boy's expression. "She heard you?"

"You reminded me of who I truly am. I owe you a debt I can best repay by making sure you stay safe." Jace cupped his hand over his ear to better focus on a message from Valeria. "I need to go."

CHAPTER 65

Attack

Gulf of Alaska

Valeria was waiting for him at the top of the first set of stairs.

"They're still rising," she reported. "The ship is surrounded."

"What else?" Jace posed, sensing more unease in her.

"I looked up from my scan and saw an older couple standing before me, smiling and extending their arms. Then they were gone, as quickly as they appeared." Valeria regarded him reflectively. "I think they were my parents. How can that be?"

Jace wished he could comfort her. She was the second youngest of the Nine after Xan, and her raven-colored hair fell to the middle of her back. Before he could respond though, Brenn and Izumi emerged from the mess hall, each carrying two of the Nine's handheld particle-beam weapons. Brenn handed one to Jace, who tested its heft. Although familiar with its workings and feel, it had been fifteen hundred years since he had wielded one, other than in stasis during Chronar's simulations.

Visually, the handheld versions somewhat resembled Earth's standard assault rifles, albeit shorter and squatter, with a wider barrel to accommodate the focused energy beam. The laser sight mounted at the top automatically fixed on both moving and stationary targets, eliminating the need for the wielder to do anything but aim in a general direction, ease back on the soft trigger, and let the automated mechanism do the rest. The standard-looking magazine was a magnetic containment chamber that kept its contents from frying the weapon's internal systems. It stored energy in the form of electrons, protons, and ions rather than bullets. Particles were stripped from atoms in a plasma chamber, then accelerated down a linear particle accelerator built into the weapon's barrel. Electromagnetic coils then accelerated the particles to be channeled and focused them into a tight coherent beam using a series of lenses. The weapon functioned by mixing these particles to create a volatile blend that burst from the barrel nearly at the speed of light, vaporizing anything in its path.

It was essentially a compact fusion reactor capable of generating immense electrical power. The actual beam was invisible, but the ionized air molecules along the beam's path created a glowing trail in a fashion similar to a lightning bolt. Any dust, mist, or saltwater vapor in the air would scatter, giving the beam shape and contours turned aglow by the concentrated energy unleashed. The fast-moving particles emitted visible radiation that interacted with magnetic fields, creating a bright, visual signature resembling a blinding blue-white lance.

Without a full charge, Jace couldn't estimate how many energy pulses the portable weapons could fire before they died out. And, since there were only four, the remaining five of the Nine would use their kaelens for close-in combat against whatever enemy the rifles failed to subdue.

Once they reached the deck, Izumi handed the final particle-beam weapon to Xan, leaving Mazz, Zareb, Yusef, Valeria, and Haran with their kaelens alone. Jace looked up at the gunmetal-gray sky, which had been crystal blue just minutes before. And in that moment, the Reef Shark pitched sharply to starboard and then shifted back to port, the ship's bow twisting on a forty-five-degree angle.

"Port side!" he heard Valeria blare in his head.

Jace swung that way and saw the first wave of creatures seeming to leap straight from the water to the deck, tentacles wrapping around the deck rail to hurl themselves on board. Before they touched down, he eased the trigger back. He heard a crack he didn't recall from all the simulations, and the weapon burst to life with a rising whine.

Pulses of energy, white-hot with a blue hue down the center, shot out in a nonstop stream as Jace rotated his weapon's barrel left and right. The pulses didn't so much strike each creature as unmake them, tearing apart their structural integrity at the cellular level. They vaporized most of each target creature's form, varying amounts of residue left behind in the form of black steaming splatters of ooze. The creatures uttered high-pitched shrieks, sounding like feedback from a broken speaker.

The four of the Nine wielding the particle-beam weapons had positioned themselves to cover all angles of the deck between them. They fired virtually nonstop, pausing only to shift their aim onto the next horde of creatures vaulting onto the deck, endless seas of tentacles crisscrossing each other as they thrashed through the air searching for purchase on something to drag into their deadly grasp.

The Nine had managed to beat back the initial wave and then two more. But the next came with even more ferocity, and Jace began to fear that the creatures, like some species of Earth's insects, had launched those first waves to test their defenses ahead of more concentrated attacks. Brenn and Izumi had mounted the upper deck beneath the ship's antenna array to claim the high ground and to better their shooting angles. That positioning allowed them to hold the intensifying wave of creatures back even as Jace and Xan stood on opposite sides of the main deck, handling whatever avoided the spray from above.

From closer in, the energy pulses produced a different effect, tearing a visible hole wherever they struck before the creature seemed to melt into a pool of molten slop. But the number hurdling from the surface to the deck continued to grow, tentacles lashing at each other to solidify their hold on the deck. Their rancid stench curdled Jace's stomach and made him want to vomit. But he resisted the urge, twisting and turning to aim his nonstop barrage wherever it was needed, conscious that the sea beyond the Reef Shark was now nothing but an endless curtain of shifting black.

Too many places right now.

His weapon was down to 40 percent capacity. Jace glimpsed Zareb wheeling across the deck, lashing his twin blades about in a blur, slicing the creatures apart to be set ablaze by Yusef's blade of blue flame. As in the snow-swept main street in Galena, his fire didn't burn so much as melt them; their high-pitched shrieks were left to the whims of the wind after they disintegrated.

Haran was using her lasso to trap multiple creatures at once, making them easy fodder for Brenn and Izumi firing from above. Valeria was whipping her nano-chucks in a blur, her gliding motions so dancelike it was easy to forget her feet were grinding through the gray-black oozing muck the particle-beam weapons had left behind. Jace could feel his weapon beginning to superheat, burning his hands and making him curse his not donning some kind of gloves. He could feel the skin on his hands puckering and blistering, yet he dared not let up on the fire despite the pain.

The high-pitched shrieking continued as if the creatures were summoning an endless wave of reinforcements. He thought of Jules and Kai Bevins, his backup plan, hiding behind a reinforced steel door that wouldn't hold against these things for even a minute—pictured Trooper Dennehy firing the .50-caliber machine gun nonstop once they breached it, until it ran out of bullets or overheated.

If the Nine fell, it would be up to Teraválar to save them, the boy left as mankind's last hope to survive.

* * *

Two decks below, the boy listened to the eerie whine-like growl of the particle-beam weapons that never abated as the attacking creatures kept coming in wave after wave.

He stood against the engine's room vault-like reinforced door, ear pressed against it to listen for the coming of the creatures from above, if the Nine's line broke.

Where was Gaia? Why wasn't she telling him what to do?

Or perhaps she already had.

I can't let the monsters win.

* * *

On deck, Jace knew all four particle-beam weapons were nearly expended. Blue light flashed and dulled at the end of his barrel, signaling his weapon's power supply was entirely depleted. He laid the weapon down and yanked his kaelen from his belt, extending it into its form as a whip.

The surge of creatures hurdling or pulling themselves over the railing still showed no signs of abating. It was like a scene running in a constant loop, no matter how many the Nine downed, more came in wave after wave. He could tell Xan's energy supply was desperately low because she was no longer spraying her fire in a wide arc but choosing her targets more selectively. And above him, he could feel the nonstop barrage unleashed by Brenn and Izumi ebbing as well.

Yusef, Mazz, Zareb, Valeria, and Haran, meanwhile, continued their mad dance across the deck, engaging creature after creature without pause. No matter how many they downed, more came, the sea beyond still black with the enemy's oozing shapes. Jace was able to tear dozens of them mounting the ship apart with his whip, but the deck was cluttered with them, their tentacles lashing through the air in search of purchase, drawing ever closer to claiming the Nine as their victims. Jace could hear the last of Brenn's and Izumi's fire from above, registering the empty whines that sounded when their guns' power sources died within seconds of each other.

The creatures' overpowering stench nearly made him gag at the same time a rhythmic clacking pierced his hearing. A dozen flapping tentacles enveloped him in a loose embrace that swiftly tightened into a breath-stealing clench. As the tentacles squeezed hard enough to contract his ribs, he retracted his whip enough to lash at them with it, drenching himself with black ooze, the thing's screeching so loud it deafened him.

Jace maintained the presence of mind to register the fact that the creatures were forming into individual masses concentrated on each of the Nine, their kaelens barely able to hold them off. This while he continued to slice at the tentacles wrapped around him, whirling and spinning across the deck to make the creature stand on only two legs instead of its more formidable base of three.

He felt one rib starting to crack and then another, the teeth-filled mouths of each still-functioning tentacle beginning to pierce his skin en route to plundering the bones from his body to feed more of the burgeoning spores within the thing's nervous system. Jace kept thrashing at it with his shortened whip, severing chunks of tentacle with each slice, slowing the creature but not halting it altogether.

He lost track of his footing upon the muck-strewn deck and slipped, going down with the creature still wrapped around him, seizing the opportunity to put all its energy into wrapping him in a death grip with its flailing tentacles. But in doing so, it squandered the leverage Jace's fall had provided, and he was able to twist and shove at the same time to end up on top of the creature with the tentacles still locked in their deadly embrace.

Jace couldn't breathe, but he could slash with his whip, which he did again and again and again until he tasted the vile ooze in his mouth and felt it burning his eyes. He kept slashing and felt the thing's death grip began to slacken before the tentacles let go altogether and flapped wildly in the air. He couldn't tell if it was dead or not and lurched painfully back to his feet only when dark creeping shadows fell over him from everywhere at once.

Jace lengthened his whip back into its full form, lashing out wildly to keep them from converging on him. His rotating gaze registered all of the Nine similarly enclosed, the creatures sensing that time and everything else was on their side, his hope bleeding away.

Until he felt *something*.

It wasn't a sound so much as a rumble in the deepest depths of his being. The creatures seemed suddenly hesitant, as if sensing danger. Something drew Jace's gaze toward the upper deck.

The boy was standing there. Jace watched as he spread his arms and drew them overhead. Then in a single blinding blur, he brought his hands down fast and hard, slicing through air that seemed to buckle under the force of their descent.

For Jace, the sensation was akin to being trapped between breaths, drowning on dry land. Then he realized it wasn't just inside him; it was *everywhere*. The air was gone, the world bled dry, like the water receding in the moments before a tsunami strike.

It's coming. . . .

The Reef Shark began to churn in a circle, first slowly and then like an amusement park carousel. All around the ship, the black-topped sea opened, a vast chasm carved from the waters to reveal a vortex that sucked the massing creatures into the depths of the ocean, sucking them down with the seas themselves trailing beyond.

He recorded all of this as the Reef Shark spun on some impossible axis before finally slowing in the exact moment the creatures still on the deck hurled themselves overboard en masse, following the rest of their brethren into the blurring swirl that may have extended to the bottom of the sea, even the center of the Earth itself.

Jace looked at the boy standing still on the upper deck, emanating an aura of power Jace knew was akin to the product of legends and lore. He met Teravälar's gaze. The boy's hair was whipped about by the whims of the wind around a smile Jace couldn't help but share.

"See...." Jace saw the boy mouth from above, hearing his words in his mind. "I told you I could do it."

Part Eight
THE BATTLE OF JUNEAU

"I know not with what weapons World War III will be fought,
but World War IV will be fought with sticks and stones."

—Albert Einstein

CHAPTER 66

Tremor

Deep Base Titan

"I'm sorry for the delay in responding to your call, sir," General Timur told the projection of William Franklin Takashi. "I was waiting for the next series of reports on the subsea temblors from the Alaska Earthquake Center at the University of Fairbanks."

"There will be no reports, General, because there was no subsea seismic activity, least of all an earthquake, recorded by any of the five hundred sensors across the state of Alaska."

"We've both seen the satellite footage, sir," Timur said, trying to make sense of what the head of the World Consortium had just told him. "Are we not to believe our eyes?"

"Our eyes did not see the product of an undersea earthquake. What we saw was caused by something else."

"Our analysis says otherwise."

"And what does your analysis say about not a single tsunami coming in the wake of a subsea earthquake as powerful as the one the satellite footage captured?"

"A fluke, potentially caused by the frigid ocean temperatures." Timur tried to read Takashi's gaze, but as usual, his expression gave up nothing, remaining typically flat and expressionless as if chiseled from marble instead of flesh and blood. "You think the quake was the product of those weapons the humanoid aliens recovered from Titan?"

"Our satellites picked up no hint of electromagnetic radiation. What does that leave us with, General?"

"Elias…."

Takashi's projection nodded. "No other explanation exists."

"They steered toward port in Ketchikan after the earthquake," Timur reported. "Nothing useful was received via our satellites from that point on, and the security cameras in the port were either damaged by the quake or disabled. But we're tracking a Sikorsky freight helicopter that took off two hours after we lost contact with the coast guard vessel they stole at sea."

"You are authorized to surveil it and nothing more. The battle of Juneau will come, and when it's over, we will have the boy and the weapons."

Timur suddenly felt the wash of air conditioning blow into him, diving through his skin and turning his very bones cold. Then his internal communicator beeped with an incoming message. The general reviewed it once and then again to make sure he had read the message right, because if it were true….

"Sir," he said to Takashi, "there's something else you need to know…."

CHAPTER 67

The Sea Dragon

En route to Juneau, Alaska

"How well do you know Juneau, Trooper Muhtuk?" Jace asked Sakari Muhtuk from the seat next to her aboard the Sikorsky Sea Dragon helicopter.

"I'd say like the back of my hand, since at least I can feel that as opposed to my leg," she said, pointing to the thick bulge of bandages visible under the blue coast guard uniform trousers she had dressed in back aboard the Reef Shark. "Juneau's about to face the next wave of those things, isn't it?"

"A massive wave, Trooper, more than enough to kill all thirty thousand residents if we don't stop it."

"And how are you fixed to do that exactly?"

Jace turned his gaze toward the arrangement of the Nine's weapons sitting further back in the hold, surrounded by the black power cubes, which were continuing the charging process—or recharging, in the case of the handheld ones that had been exhausted in the fight against the enemy on the deck of the Reef Shark. The CH-53E had long been the largest and heaviest helicopter in the US military. Upon being decommissioned, many of them, like this one, had been converted to civilian cargo use. This particular craft was still equipped with jump seats to ferry personnel as well as cargo. In combat situations, where the CH-53E's forebear had been known as the "Super Jolly Green Giant," the Sea Dragon could carry almost sixty troops. Eight of the Nine, minus Xan who was piloting the craft, took up sixteen of those jump seats a comfortable distance from the weapons, which emitted a slight whining hum through the charging process. Each of the Nine straddled a pair of those jump seats to better accommodate their size, remaining silent and still throughout the flight north toward Juneau.

The entire coast around Ketchikan had been abandoned thanks to the tsunami warning that followed the earthquake-like effects triggered by Teraválar, who was sitting next to Charlie on the other side of the cabin. As near as Jace could tell, she hadn't stopped talking to him the whole flight so far. The sudden evacuation of a helipad located close to the Ketchikan coast had left the Sea Dragon there for the taking, and Xan had no trouble familiarizing herself with the controls for the flight to Juneau.

"We wouldn't have stood much of a chance if those things hadn't broken through the door to the engine room, would we, boss?" Muhtuk asked him.

"None," Jace told the trooper.

Her gaze drifted to Teraválar, who held it briefly.

"Kid gives me a bit of the creeps," she said softly. "Can I tell you something?"

Jace nodded.

"I'm full-blooded Inuit and come from a long line of angakkuq, also known as shamans or medicine men. We serve as spiritual guardians, responsible for keeping evil at bay for as long as our people have existed. My ancestors could read the stars and told of great battles we would have to fight someday. I guess that day is now." Muhtuk leaned back. "Juneau was my first post. So I know where the bodies are buried, some literally. What do you need to know?"

* * *

According to Muhtuk, most residents of Juneau lived in or around the Mendenhall Valley, commonly referred to by locals as "The Valley," a relatively flat, suburban space along the Mendenhall River. Downtown Juneau, along with its immediate surrounding area, was the next most populated section, followed by Douglas Island. Accessible by bridge, it boasted a residential enclave centered mainly in the North Douglas area.

"That's a problem, isn't it?" Muhtuk asked Jace, referring to Douglas Island.

"It will be hard to defend that and Juneau proper at the same time. What's the tallest building on the island?"

"There's an apartment complex that's six stories, I think, maybe seven."

Jace allocated one of their big particle-beam weapons to that site in his mind, leaving three for Juneau proper.

"The people in that underground bunker, Deep Base whatever," Muhtuk resumed, "they know what's coming, right? They know Juneau is where these things are headed next."

Jace nodded.

"So why haven't they evacuated the city?"

"I don't have to tell you, Trooper, that the people in that bunker, as you call it, were not your friends. They're not anybody's friends."

"So they're going to sit back and do nothing? Do they want thirty thousand people to die, spawning God knows how many of those things?"

"I believe their motivations clearly lie elsewhere."

Muhtuk turned her gaze across the cabin toward the boy again, Charlie still chatting up a storm in his ear. "They want the kid back, I'm guessing. The nine of you and your weapons too."

Jace nodded again.

"Juneau's the bait and let all those people be damned. Got another question for you, boss: Who are the real monsters?"

CHAPTER 68

The Gastineau Channel

Juneau, Alaska

Muhtuk continued sketching a mental schematic of Juneau for Jace through the rest of their flight on board the Sea Dragon, starting with the fact that the city was perched on the Gastineau Channel, part of the Inside Passage, from which the creatures would come ashore.

"These things normally attack at night, right?" Muhtuk gazed out the window at the first signs of sunset. "Means we don't have much time."

"We'll have to make it enough, Trooper," Jace told her.

"You said you've got four of the big guns?"

"Yes," Jace told her, not bothering to add that each was ten thousand times more powerful than the handheld variety they had wielded on the deck of the Reef Shark.

Muhtuk weighed that briefly. "Then you'll need to place them on the roofs of the city's three tallest buildings, saving one for that apartment building on Douglas Island. That would be the Dimond Courthouse, Mendenhall Tower apartments, and the Federal Building." She turned her gaze out the window. "Once we clear these mountains, the city will be right below us. Nice place. Hopefully it's still there when this is over."

* * *

"Chronar," Jace said in his mind, "any updates on the estimated timing?"

"If our enemy follows the same pattern as the first two settlements, two hours and twenty-seven minutes, which is peak darkness here."

"Two hours and twenty-seven minutes," he repeated in his mind, calculating the tasks before them and how best to allot the remaining time before the enemy launched its attack.

Jace had Xan make three passes over downtown Juneau and Douglas Island for reconnaissance purposes. The island amounted essentially to a second front that would spread their forces and weapons over a considerably wider area. Muhtuk had informed him that three thousand people, 10 percent of Juneau's total population, lived on the island. He contemplated the feasibility of evacuating those residents to the downtown area but concluded that it would cause more harm than good. Then another thought occurred to him.

"You get your share of earthquakes and volcanoes in these parts, yes?"

"Yes. No tsunamis, though. Volcanic eruptions and earthquakes have been occurring more frequently, perhaps due to the land becoming increasingly angry over climate change. The magnitudes vary, and ninety-nine out of a hundred don't amount to much beyond a nuisance, but there's always that one."

"How do you warn people of Juneau when that happens?"

* * *

"I don't know where Charlie would be right now without that boy," Jules said, Kai meeting her gaze when she lifted it off her daughter.

"I don't want to think about where any of us would be without him."

She jabbed at him, but her playful punch caught him in the wrong place and stung.

"Ouch."

"Guess I don't know my own strength anymore." Kai watched Jules look back toward Charlie and Terry. "Her first crush, you think?"

"He's too old for her."

"Not even a year?"

"He's twelve going on sixteen. I mean, look at him."

Jules did. "Look at them together, Charlie telling him all about some character he looks like in one of her video games."

"How did you know that?"

She looked surprised that Kai didn't know. "Because she can't shut up about some boy named Cloud Strife from Final Fantasy. Who names their kid Cloud?" Jules added with a smile.

Kai didn't return it. "You can hear what Charlie's saying?"

"You can't?"

Kai shook his head.

Jules smiled, looking more alive than she had since months prior to her diagnosis. She squeezed his shoulder.

"Ouch," Kai said.

He felt Jules jerk her hand away. "Sorry."

Kai grinned. "Just kidding."

She put her hand back in place. "Remember *our* first date?"

"I've been trying to forget it for twenty years."

"Because you vomited on the roller coaster?"

"Because I vomited on you."

Jules chuckled. "Why are you looking at me like that?"

"Because I can't remember the last time you laughed."

"It feels good to do."

"And to hear."

The smile slipped from her expression. "I just feel different, Kai. Since the nanobots. Nothing feels the same anymore. Everything I do feels like someone else is doing it. Does that make sense?"

Kai shrugged. "There are bound to be side effects. It's not like we can ask WebMD about a treatment that's centuries beyond our medical knowledge. Know what I think?"

Jules waited for him to continue.

"I think you forgot what it was like to feel good. You've been sick for almost two years, Jules. Chemo, radiation, biologics, clinical trials. Chances are that the nanobots wiped away the residual effects of all that. You feel the way you do now because you don't remember any other way to feel."

She frowned. "Makes sense, I guess."

He watched Jules suddenly pull at the safety harness that buckled her to the jump seat.

"Make sure yours is fastened, make sure it's tight."

Kai felt the belt snug around his waist and the strap tight against his shoulder. "Why did—"

He stopped when a sudden wind gust made the Sea Dragon buckle in the air then drop suddenly before the pilot regained control. "Jules?"

"That was weird. I knew it was coming, like I could feel something. I don't know how to explain it."

Kai managed a smile. "Maybe those nanobots left you with the ability to see into the future."

"They left me with something, Kai."

* * *

Jace studied the city's layout from an aerial view, as Xan passed a few hundred feet over the city, flying straight over downtown as the last of the sun dropped below the mountains. Juneau's main street looked to have been lifted from the nineteenth century, lined with quaint shops and a tight cluster of bars and restaurants, easily spotted because of the lights and activity, compared to the retail businesses that had closed for the day.

The taller buildings Trooper Muhtuk had suggested for placement of their larger particle-beam weapons were set further back, overlooking downtown and the Gastineau Channel beyond it. The primary dock for the many cruise ships that frequented the Alaskan coast was actually in the downtown area, with the other docks similarly displaced near other sections of the city. Fortunately, Jace noted, no ships were currently in port, making for one less thing to factor into his planning.

Douglas Island, and its three thousand residents, was located due west of downtown across a heavily traveled bridge. But the bulk of Juneau's population resided in the neighborhoods pitched along the sweeping edge of the Mendenhall River along a narrow sliver of coastal land between the Juneau Icefield and the Inside Passage.

The plan unfolded in Jace's mind organically as Xan brought the Sea Dragon around for a final sweep. When the time came to lower the larger particle-beam weapons into place atop the building rooftops, he already knew where each of the Nine would be placed and the various lines of both defense and attack to be set into place.

At this point, according to Muhtuk, the best Juneau could muster in response was a police department with a handful of officers and the local sheriff's office for the county, which boasted fewer than that at any given time, meaning they couldn't rely on their help in the coming battle.

But the Nine needed only one thing from that quarter before the battle started.

CHAPTER 69

Alarm

Juneau, Alaska

"Can I help you, sir?"

The cold night wind blew the door the rest of the way inward after Jace cracked it open, rattling the lone officer manning the Juneau Police Department for the night shift. The officer rose from the chair set behind his desk and looked up, his eyes agape at Jace's size. But Sakari Muhtuk crutched herself along ahead of him, careful not to put any weight on the lower leg she still couldn't feel or move.

"Sakari Muhtuk, Officer, Alaska State Police. I believe we know each other."

"Sure," the officer, whose name tag read "Pinga," said, rising from his chair. "You were wearing a state police uniform at the time, instead of whatever that is."

"And you may remember my partner, Tom Dennehy, too," Muhtuk said, gesturing toward the younger trooper at her side."

Pinga also noted the coast guard uniform he was wearing. "Two of you moonlighting from the Alaska State Police on the water?"

"We had to borrow these."

Officer Pinga gave Jace another look. He was big and wide but still had to look up to meet his gaze. Jace noticed that gaze flitting out the front windows to the large shapes belonging to other members of the Nine.

"Those your friends?" he asked Jace.

"*Our* friends," Muhtuk corrected. "And we're going to need all the friends we can get against what's headed here, Kova," she added, remembering his first name.

Officer Kova Pinga still couldn't take his eyes off Jace, leaving Muhtuk to wonder if he'd even noticed Jules and Kai Bevins yet. Finally, he turned his gaze on her.

"What's headed our way, Trooper?"

"What was the Inuit monster of lore that scared you the most as a kid?"

"Why?"

"Because that's what's coming."

* * *

After they completed their aerial reconnaissance of Juneau aboard the Sea Dragon, the next task for the Nine was to lower the four largest particle-beam weapons onto the strategically chosen roofs. Fortunately, the helicopter they had stolen had been retrofitted for civilian cargo use. There was a winch on board that greatly facilitated lowering the first weapon onto the roof of the Dimond Courthouse. Izumi rode the winch line down with it, helping to position the landing as close to the rooftop's edge as possible. Then she unclasped the winch line and set about positioning and prepping the weapon properly, readying it to fire streams of energy that would vaporize an untold number of the approaching enemy.

Fully assembled, the oddly shaped particle-beam weapon most resembled a traditional piece of small artillery in terms of size. It had no mount, riding the air instead atop a cushion of antigravity and kept steady by the massive release of pressure that prevented the weapon from imploding. Izumi and Brenn had already programmed the neural networks of all four weapons with the precise specifications of the full-grown creatures, including the latest images captured from security camera footage of the on-deck battle just hours before. That way, to the extent the laws of physics allowed, the guns would target only the creatures and leave all other life forms unscathed, though collateral damage in such quarters was inevitable.

Of course, Jace held out hope that the particle-beam weapons could decimate the entire horde of creatures on their own. Fortunately, the four buildings Trooper Muhtuk had selected created a kind of natural grid effect that allowed the weapons to cover every bit of the surrounding sea without having to rotate very much at all. Brenn was winched down to the rooftop of the Mendenhall Tower Apartments. At that point, Xan retrieved Izumi from the Dimond Courthouse and angled the Sea Dragon for the Juneau Federal Building.

They left Izumi behind to complete prepping the third weapon at their disposal and then winched Brenn back up to handle the same chore on the apartment building centered on Douglas Island. The firing angle from that particle-beam weapon's perspective would allow the Nine to effectively trap the enemy in a crossfire. Brenn and Izumi had cross-programmed the weapons to assure no overlap in the grids covered, more than a mile of coastline in total, which could be expanded if the enemy began coming ashore further to the city's flanks.

Mazz, Zareb, Valeria, and Xan would be allotted the recharged handheld weapons they would fire initially from the highest rooftops downtown to catch whatever strays managed to avoid the bigger guns' fire. They would effectively be like snipers, picking off individual creatures in rapid fashion thanks to the guns' automated targeting system controlled by advanced artificial intelligence.

Since the bigger weapons were fully automated, Brenn and Izumi were free to join Yusef, Haran, and Jace to wage close-in battle within the downtown district itself against whatever creatures managed to break through the first two lines of defense. But Jace wasn't finished with those lines yet, the notion for a third occurring to him while flying over the city.

* * *

Muhtuk provided Officer Kova Pinga with as much of an explanation as the limited time they had left allowed. He listened dumbstruck, leaning back in the desk chair that creaked under the strain of his bulk. When a combination of Jace, Kai, and Jules finished filling out the story, he looked up toward his fellow trooper.

"Our ancestors saw this coming, didn't they, Sakari?"

"I believe they did, yes."

He nodded, then squeezed his eyes closed as if hoping that when he opened them, the group gathered before him would be gone, a figment of his imagination.

"What do we do first?" he asked when they were all still standing there.

"Trigger the siren you use to alert residents to potential earthquakes or eruptions," Muhtuk told him, "so they'll seek safe shelter. We need to clear South Franklin Street and the downtown district especially."

Pinga pointed to a red switch on the wall mounted over a fire alarm pull station. "Flip that switch, and she starts blaring." He scratched at his thick squarish chin and shook his head. "Town's gonna think I've gone plum crazy. Inuktitut, right, Trooper?" Pinga added, using the proper Inuit word.

"Better than dead, Kova."

Pinga lumbered out of the chair and moved to the wall, hesitating only slightly before flipping the red switch and flooding the night with the piercing sound of an old-fashioned air raid siren meant to get all residents of Juneau to seek shelter away from communal areas that included downtown.

"Anything else I can do, short of trying to summon my ancestors?" he asked Jace.

"As a matter of fact, there is."

CHAPTER 70

Darkness

Juneau, Alaska

The police station was constructed over a fortified fallout shelter built during the Cold War, which was later converted into an emergency command and control facility. With the shrill siren continuing to sound nonstop, Jace followed Kai, Jules, Charlie, Jane Piedmont with baby in hand, and the boy down the stairs.

He made the old woman hand the baby to Dennehy before descending the stairs herself alongside him. It struck Jace how vital she might be to the ultimate survival of mankind against this enemy because her Paget's disease made her the source for a potential repellent. That meant keeping Piedmont alive was one of his most vital priorities.

Jace was conscious of a rank odor of mildew and concrete rot, evidence of decay brought on by disuse and neglect. Officer Pinga switched on the lights, flooding the basement with a sudden jarring wash of blinding fluorescent light. Jace's eyes instinctively dropped to Jane Piedmont in the moment she lost her footing just short of the bottom step and started to fall, heading face-first for the floor.

A blur flashed across his vision, even as he launched himself into a leap downward to somehow catch her. Jules Bevins caught the old woman in mid-drop in the exact moment Jace landed on the concrete floor.

"Whoa," Piedmont uttered, standing upright with Jules's help, "that was a close one."

Jules looked up and met Jace's gaze, something unspoken passing between them. Jace broke the stare, not wanting her to see the uncertainty in his eyes over witnessing a feat that was wholly impossible, unless....

Jace was spared from completing the thought when he felt the boy draw up alongside him.

"I should have stayed closer to her," he said guiltily.

"That's why I'm leaving you down here," he told Teraválar, after pulling him briefly aside. "To protect her, Charlie, and everyone else."

"No, it's not. You're leaving me down here because, even though I did what I did on the ship, I'm still just a kid."

"Only in age."

"And I remind you of your son. You watched him die once. You can't bear the thought of watching him die again."

Caught off guard, Jace managed a single nod.

"I'm not your son, Jace, and I'm not going to die."

"We may not need you."

"You don't think I can control it, do you? That wasn't a problem on the ship because of the water. But if I did something like that on the land, you're afraid I could destroy all of Juneau, and do the creatures' work for them."

"It's a chance we can't take."

* * *

With the emergency siren continuing to blare, the downtown streets were awash with people rushing back to their homes. Headlights poured along the roads while pedestrians churned across the sidewalk, looking up toward the sky as if afraid of what they might see. The descending darkness was enough to make them quicken their pace.

Against the grain of flight, a fleet of oil tankers a dozen strong and filled to the brim from a nearby depot answered Officer Kova Pinga's call to set up a line in a straight row along the road just beyond the docks. He needed only to tell them it was an emergency and that their home was in danger, about to be attacked. Pinga promised to explain everything else later, and his status in town was enough to make them listen without asking any questions.

The last truck had just moved into position when Chronar's voice sounded in Jace's head.

"The creatures are surfacing, Jace. In numbers greater than even the updated estimate I provided. An unknown variable I wasn't able to consider has clearly changed the scenario."

"What's our weapons status?"

"The big guns are fully charged. The smaller ones are charged to just short of seventy-five percent."

Jace smelled the first trace of the enemy's stomach-curdling stench drifting off the ocean with the breeze.

"They're coming ashore," Chronar reported.

* * *

Jace didn't need Chronar to show him the endless, stench-riddled black wave rampaging out of the sea. Fully automated, the big particle-beam weapons waited until the maximum number was contained within their collective ring of fire before sending beam after beam of light as bright as the sun downward to pierce the inky blackness of the night.

The first burst of the massive, focused, and blinding beams vaporized the initial wave of creatures coming ashore. The beams were so bright they illuminated the low clouds the moon was struggling to break though. The water rumbled and burst into fissures when the next series of strikes obliterated a fresh wave of the enemy entering the kill zone. Another wave of creatures followed thoughtlessly, driven by an insatiable thirst to feed and thus procreate and spread, fueled by self-perpetuation, the most basic and incremental of all instincts.

The fusion reactors at the cores of the particle-beam weapons pulsed brighter, casting harsh blue light across the rooftops that seemed to rain down on the city. The air vibrated, the hum rising until it became a constant high-pitched blare.

The once shimmering reflective surface of the sea dissolved into a hot steaming cauldron superheated by the energy of the particle beams and splattered with fragments of the creatures that had not been fully vaporized. The living endless tide continued to rise from the depths and pour forward.

Inevitably, some leaked through the particle beams' coordinated line of fire. Some seemed to skitter atop the surface like spiders, all limbs and churning tentacles. Their collective screeching made Jace's ears ache to the point he covered them briefly with his hands. Even then, he detected a high-pitched clacking, which he realized must be another means of communication beyond scent that the enemy utilized.

The steamy mist spawned by the superheated water rolled off the sea and swept into downtown Juneau, shading streetlights and seeming to chase the last residents still fleeing along the streets, aglow in the white-blue haze radiating over them. This as the particle-beam weapons continued their relentless onslaught, vaporizing and shredding wave after wave of the enemy that strayed into their respective grids.

In his mind, Jace watched the creatures charging over the docks, closing on the line of oil tankers.

"Blow the trucks," he ordered the four of the Nine atop the lower rooftops with handheld weapons.

An instant later, narrow blue beams pierced the night, and a dozen trucks exploded into fiery clouds of black smoke, belching angry tendrils of fire. Secondary explosions rippled one after the other, launching charred, flaming husks of shrapnel into the air to rain down on downtown Juneau. They smashed into rooftops, setting one building after another ablaze, the darkness pierced by near-daylight brilliance.

The long line of fire along the docks was enough to halt the creatures who survived the sea only to find themselves trapped. Jace wondered if a more detailed analysis of the creatures' anatomy would yield high traces of some form of hydrocarbons, because those who entered the line of shrapnel-riddled flames were almost immediately incinerated. The creatures backed up against the flames, making them easy targets for the rooftop gunners, who sniped down on them in quick bursts that vaporized tight groupings of three or four at a time.

Jace realized the alarm siren was still blaring, barely noticeable over the screech and clacking of the creatures, combined with the squealing hum of the particle-beam weapons raining energy pulse after energy pulse down.

"Guns are at fifty percent, Jace," Chronar told him.

Would that be enough?

For every thousand cut down, it seemed like a thousand more surged forward, relentless and unfazed by the carnage, coming in a nonstop rolling black blanket atop the sea. The focused beams of blinding light continued to sear the night, columns of pure energy that split the very air before smashing into the water, coughing up more steam as the channel began to superheat, scorching to the touch.

Night over Juneau was alight in flashes of blue and white that accompanied each strike, the lower rooftops bathed in the heat-haze residue the beams left behind. Those beams swept in arcs, carving vast swaths through the encroaching horde. More black ooze rode the steaming sea's surface, looking like thick pools of oil reflected in the twirling firelight shed by the towering flames unleashed by the blown tankers. The air smelled scorched, the sense of a hot fire burning everywhere all at once around Jace. The superheated channel waters were literally boiling now, and yet the creatures kept coming, rising from the watery depths without pause.

The line of churning flames was holding, the creatures seeming to meld into one another, forming a great unbroken wave that was helpless to push through the fire. Then, suddenly, they surged forward thanks to the force of the latest wave emerging from the waters, which pressed hard from the rear, propelling them forward into the fire itself.

The smoke turned from gray to black, the stench of the creatures thickening in the night air with each burning wave, coming so fast that the flames could not keep up. Jace realized with a start that the creatures piling atop the fire to extinguish it were clearing a path for the vast hordes rising from the sea behind them.

"Main weapons are down to twenty-five percent, Jace."

Flashes erupted from the four handheld weapons in near-unbroken succession, while Jace moved to the center of the abandoned downtown district alight in the glow of burning buildings, the fires continuing to spread.

He readied his kaelen and joined Yusef, Haran, Brenn, and Izumi to mount the next line of defense.

CHAPTER 71

The Red Dog Saloon

Juneau, Alaska

Kai and Jules sat on the cold concrete floor of the shelter with Charlie nestled between them. Across the stuffy confines, Troopers Dennehy and Muhtuk had positioned themselves before the stairs, each with shotguns in hand for all the good twelve-gauge shells would do against whatever might break through from above.

Jules could hear the sounds of the battle coming from the world beyond, could feel each pulse from the particle-beam weapons like the ping of a tuning fork. When the oil trucks exploded, her ears ached, and her bones seemed to rattle. She looked toward Kai to see if he was feeling it too, but he showed no sign of the same level of awareness beyond holding Charlie tighter to him. She was sobbing softly, terrified by the rattle and hum above.

Terry, meanwhile, was pacing back and forth, drawing Jane Piedmont's ire when his shadow fell over her.

"Hey, kid, you mind?" She covered the snoozing baby's ears. "You're fucking making me dizzy with all that pacing."

"Sorry," the boy said.

Jules turned toward Kai to find him staring at her. "You sure you're okay?"

"The cancer's gone, Kai, every cell of it. I came to know what it felt like to have inside me. So, I know what it feels like to not be inside me anymore. But there's something else there—I can feel that too."

"The nanobots?"

Jules shrugged. "I can't describe it exactly. Remember when they started one of those wonder drugs, I told you I could feel it inside me, could feel its heat?"

"Of course."

"That's the way it feels now, only with no heat. The nanobots are still there, Kai. My system was supposed to flush them out when their job was done, but they're still there."

Jules tensed when the door on the ground floor of the police station jerked open and a shaft of light poured down the stairs ahead of Officer Kova Pinga.

"Need to let you folks know we may have to move you out of here soon. Looks like downtown's on fire." His eyes moved to Dennehy and Muhtuk. "In the meantime, I need the two of you to take charge. This is my city. I can't sit back here and do nothing."

"So, what's the plan?" Muhtuk asked him.

"Well, let me put it this way. The boys who parked those tankers that blew are all upstairs, and oil rigs aren't the only thing they drive."

* * *

Jace could feel the big particle-beam weapons starting to flutter, down to their last reserves of power. The picture broadcast in his mind at long last showed the end of the black wave coming ashore, but not before a final horde of the creatures numbering in the low thousands rose out of the sea virtually unencumbered. Besides this final line at the end of the downtown, even with the Red Dog Saloon, resistance would come only from Mazz, Zareb, Valeria, and Xan firing from the low-slung rooftops until this last wave of the enemy chased them down. He had no idea how many tens of thousands of the creatures they had killed, but it didn't seem to matter since there were always more coming. And then, finally, the bright tunnels of light and bursts faded out, leaving only the crackling flames burning along South Franklin Street to light the night.

The four members of the Nine mounted on rooftops continued to fire virtually nonstop, but the creatures that got past them would be coming this way in a wave much larger than what the remaining five of the Nine were prepared to do battle with. Having seen the havoc wrought by a vastly smaller concentration of them on board the Reef Shark, Jace knew their kaelens might barely slow the onrushing wave.

Jace smelled that wave an instant before he heard the screeching and clacking of the creatures communicating with each other. They turned the corner at the crest of South Franklin Street as a molten, unbroken black mass aglow in the firelight of the buildings that had caught fire on both sides of the street. Five of the Nine activated their kaelens with their minds, prepared to make this last stand, when suddenly the blare of truck horns sounded one after the other.

Haran, the Nine's explosives specialist, stilled her lasso as she approached him.

"My sensing device has located gas lines running beneath these streets," she reported. "I can trigger an explosion that would incinerate the whole of the downtown district."

"Let me know when the charges are set. Don't trigger them until I give the order. But, Haran…."

"Yes?"

"If you can't reach me, that means you have the go."

Haran nodded and sprinted off.

Jace swung around to find a convoy of massive snowplows streaming their way, with Officer Kova Pinga behind the wheel of the lead one. Jace counted a dozen in all that arranged themselves into groupings of three riding abreast of each other, so the plow blades could cover the whole of a main drag. He assumed this must be the way the men behind these trucks plowed snow off the streets of Juneau and surrounding roads in winter, streaming straight for the onrushing black wave of creatures in four phalanxes of three each.

The lead trucks met the first of the wave halfway down South Franklin Street, plowing them backward. Those that slithered between the gaps were met by the next trio taking the same tandem plowing positioning. The trucks rolling over the flattened remains of the creatures sounded like tires crunching over ground glass, leaving a lumpy, oozing blanket of steaming black goo in their wake. The creatures' high-pitched squealing rose even more, and their stench intensified further when their scent glands were crushed.

The snowplows rolled on toward the head of the street, ultimately engulfed by the creatures leaping onto their steel frames until the trucks were swimming with them, covered everywhere. Then they began to waver, control lost as cabs were pierced and tentacles latched onto the drivers inside. One after the other, the plows crashed into burning buildings that crumbled over them, drawing more of the creatures to their cabs in what amounted to a feeding frenzy.

Jace and the others fell back, even again with the Red Dog Saloon, when he heard Haran's voice in his mind.

"Charges set and ready, Jace. But there's a problem."

"What?"

"There's someone else down here. A man, big—big as us—following me. And he's got a lasso, just like mine. I haven't gotten a good look at him yet, but I think it's someone pretending to be my father who taught me how to wield the lasso. How can that be?"

Jace knew this could only be another memory fragment. "Haran, listen to me: He's not real. He's not there."

She didn't respond.

"I'll explain everything later, but you need to trust me and stand by."

* * *

The Nine ran.

The four who'd been on the street moved at a pace that kept the creatures from closing, while the four posted on rooftops used the flaming row of buildings aligned down South Franklin Street as their escape route. They leaped from one roof to another, just managing to skirt the flames while keeping pace with the four on the ground. They fired the last reserves of their particle-beam weapons to keep the enemy off the five of the Nine they were shadowing on the street below.

All of the Nine had just cleared the downtown district, those on rooftops leaping down to join their brethren on the street, when Jace reached out to the boy in his mind.

"Teraválar, can you hear me?"

"I can hear you, Jace."

"You need to lead the others to safety, as far away from downtown as you can."

"Will do."

Then he trained his mind on Haran. "Haran?"

"Here."

"Trigger the blast," Jace ordered, holding back from asking her about the man she thought was following her.

Moments later, the underground explosion shook the ground beneath their feet, threatening their balance. They had just launched awkwardly back into motion, when the world behind them erupted in a massive fireball, somehow contained to the reach of the creatures coming in their wake. The rapid succession of explosions, coming without pause, blew them off their feet, sending them rolling and skittering across the grass and pavement, aglow in the bright sheen of the fireball that had consumed all of downtown Juneau and the last wave of creatures who tried to claim it.

CHAPTER 72

Fish

Juneau, Alaska

Jace used a chunk of a concrete pillar to pull himself back to his feet, cataloging any injuries he may have suffered. The percussion of the blast had left his head ringing, and he was barely able to hear. Other than a few bruises and contusions though, he was fully ambulatory and in no need of treatment.

Gazing about, he saw the other seven members of the Nine, everyone but Haran, all finding their feet again, the wounds and abrasions of some looking worse than others. Then, at the end of a virtual tunnel formed by the light sprayed by the inferno behind them, Jace glimpsed the boy leading the others toward him. Their faces were stained by soot and grime, but they looked otherwise unmarred. Beyond them, up the slightly sloped hillside in the shadow of Mount Juneau, the residential streets were alight from the fire raging over downtown.

"I heard you!" he beamed, grabbing hold of Jace's arms. "I heard you!"

Jace could only nod, barely able to hear the boy's words.

Motion flashed beyond the reach of the flames. Dozens, even hundreds, of the creatures that had evaded the blast continued to spread through the residential areas, shining in the glow of flames that towered over South Franklin Street. The blaring screech of fire alarms split the night everywhere, certain to rally fire departments from across the surrounding area, which would save as much as they could of what remained of Juneau.

The Nine came upon the first wave of bodies while rushing toward the thickest areas of population that the creatures struck first. In the end, it took until dawn before they used their kaelens and the energy remaining in the handheld particle-beam weapons to clear what remained of the city of the enemy, though at a terrible cost. Roughly a thousand residents were killed by the creatures or consumed by the primary blast or secondary fires. The fire engines that poured onto the scene fought the fires bravely until more of the creatures descended upon them before the Nine could intercede.

Amid the battle fought in a series of stops and starts, Jace lost track of the boy and was ultimately drawn to him in the center of the sandy beach located in Savikko Park at the end of the Douglas Highway when it was finally over. Teraválar seemed to be watching the sun rise. It occurred to Jace in that moment that neither he nor the boy had ever seen a beach before, and he wondered if that was what drew him here.

Then he spotted what Teraválar was surrounded by everywhere:

Boneless bodies of fish, all sizes and species, including what could only be the hollowed-out remains of harbor seals and even whales, rendering the sand invisible. The pungent stench rising off the remains turned Jace's stomach and left him feeling queasy.

Teraválar did not turn to acknowledge him, the hair thrown over his face and off again according to the whims of the wind. "You know what this means."

Jace nodded, then remembered the boy wasn't looking at him and said, "Yes. There's no stopping the spread now." Especially, he thought, with the Nine's four larger particle-beam weapons lost in the explosion and fire.

"Maybe not. But we can still make one last stand. Gaia called me here. She spoke to me." The boy turned toward Jace. "I understand the fullness of my purpose now, why Gaia left my DNA in that cave with your weapons. We can still win, but only if we're willing to accept the truth in that purpose."

Jace didn't bother asking Teraválar what that truth was; he waited for him to continue on his own.

"Sacrifice," the boy said.

"He's right."

Jace turned to find Jules Bevins standing there, having somehow approached him silently over the rotting, flattened fish carcasses that covered the sand.

"I know what we have to do," she continued, "and I know how to do it. With some help."

"Help?"

Jules nodded, didn't have to elaborate further, because Jace realized where that help would be coming from. His mind flashed back to the police station shelter when she caught Jane Piedmont in the midst of a devastating fall—hardly a fluke.

"But we can't do what needs to be done here," Jules continued. "We need access to a high-tech lab. We've got to get back inside Deep Base Titan."

CHAPTER 73

Alliance

Deep Base Titan

"*Sir, there's more news you need to hear....*"

Before the battle of Juneau had begun, General Timur had read the message that had just come in about vast waves of boneless fish corpses washing up on shores abutting the Gulf of Alaska. Takashi listened intently, a rare smile lurking on the outskirts of his expression, not quite breaking through.

"You realize what this means, General."

"Sir?" Timur posed, unnerved and unsettled by the closest he had ever seen Takashi come to flashing genuine excitement.

Hours later, he walked through the murky lighting of the Vault with a backpack slung over his shoulder, trying to remember why they kept the repository for alien artifacts at a frigid sixty degrees. Had one of the genius scientists under his command postulated that it would be a better way to preserve them or, perhaps, keep them from imperiling those charged with their storage? Where was it written that cold temperatures made for a safer environment than hot ones, given that his genius scientists knew nothing of the geothermal nature of the worlds where these artifacts originated?

Takashi and his World Consortium would be none too pleased by Timur's actions in the wake of the humanoid aliens saving a vast measure of Juneau's population at the expense of the city's destruction. Instead of ordering his waiting forces to take the aliens captive, he had ordered those forces to stand down because he could not stomach rendering his troops party to their own massacre. If these humanoid aliens could wipe out untold tens of thousands of the rampaging creatures, what chance did a few thousand soldiers have against them?

Timur continued to walk about the Vault, crisscrossing his own path and passing the same objects over and over again. Gone was the pride he felt at their presence here, the notion that under his command, one of them would someday tilt the balance of power in favor of the United States forever. Instead, he had come here with a backpack full of plastic explosives to destroy the contents of the Vault to keep them from the hands of the Consortium forever.

Taking command of Deep Base Titan had signaled his rebirth, the means by which he could leave the lasting legacy denied him by his estrangement from his sons, strangers to him when they perished as heroes. Only, in the wake of Juneau, he realized that rebirth was a lie. William Franklin Takashi and his World Consortium had not built Deep Base Titan to save the world but to find the means to control and rule it. That was why Takashi had allowed the aliens to reach Juneau in the first place: to see their weapons in action before seizing them back, along with the aliens themselves, in the battle's wake.

Then there was the boy. His creation was arguably the greatest achievement in the history of science, including even the invention of the atomic bomb. Nothing in the Vault remotely compared to this boy, who'd been made from no more than strands of alien DNA unearthed within the same cave system where they'd uncovered the seamless containers Timur now knew held the energy ray weapons.

The general's internal communication device beeped with an incoming message. He plucked it from his belt, finding a message from Takashi.

COME TO MY QUARTERS.

Timur clipped the device back in place, ignoring the instruction. Instead, he laid his backpack down on a long table, zipped it open, and removed the bricks of plastic explosive from inside, along with the detonators.

Takashi had made his intentions clear. And if Timur continued to acquiesce to the World Consortium's wishes, he would be a party to the eradication of civilization as it was constituted today. He was a soldier, trained to fight any enemy threatening the United States. Now, he had come to realize his primary enemy was not the creatures who had escaped the ship long buried in the ice.

It was the Consortium itself.

Takashi's callous and reckless disregard for human life rendered people no more than resources to be expended and dispensed with. What, though, was the point of laying waste to the world in order to dominate it? The intentions of Takashi and his World Consortium ran counter to everything Timur had once stood for. He couldn't save the sons who were long lost to him before their deaths, but he could keep the world order in place, starting with the destruction of the Vault.

Toward what end, though?

It wasn't the Vault he needed to destroy; it was Takashi and the World Consortium before it was too late. From his quarters, he could use an emergency channel to contact someone he trusted at the United States Central Command, CENTCOM—the body to which he was technically answerable—to provide a real-time threat assessment of what the country and the world were facing. The incalculable number of dead fish meant the creatures were multiplying on a similarly incalculable scale. And Takashi had greeted that reality with restrained excitement, as if it had been exactly what he had been hoping for—the dreams of the World Consortium coming to fruition.

Timur eased the bricks of plastic explosive and detonators back into his backpack. Holding it in his grasp, he retraced his steps from the Vault and sealed the heavy door behind him. This was his last chance to prove himself to the sons he had failed in life, to show them he had become a better man than the one they had known. He would contact CENTCOM directly from his quarters on the emergency channel, alert them to the truth of what was coming, what the World Consortium had wrought. Takashi didn't own everyone there, at least not yet.

Timur was so focused on that task that when he reached his quarters, he could barely remember the key code. But the green light flashed on his third try, and the lock disengaged. Still clutching the backpack gingerly, Timur eased the door open and entered the living area, spotting a shape seated in a chair positioned directly before him.

"We need your help, General," said Professor Jules Bevins, standing up. "We need your help to save the world."

Part Nine
LAST STAND

"Now I am become Death, the destroyer of worlds."

—J. Robert Oppenheimer,
quoting Vyasa's *Bhagavad Gita*

CHAPTER 74

Scent

Deep Base Titan

"You were dying," Timur said, closing the door behind him.

Jules noted that he showed no signs of launching a move against her or summoning help. "I was, yes."

"What happened?"

"Call it a miracle cure."

"For advanced cancer?"

She nodded. "I've made a full recovery."

"In barely twenty-four hours…."

"And now I'm ready to save the world."

"And how do you propose to do that?" Timur said.

"I need access to your labs to create bait."

Timur's interested gaze urged her on.

"Bait that will draw all of the creatures massing in the ocean to a single location."

"You understand there are millions and millions of them by now, spreading geometrically thanks to an unlimited supply of marine life to feed on."

Jules nodded. "I understand that all too well. This is the only chance I've got to see my daughter grow up."

"Brave little girl." He looked past her. "Where are the others?"

"I came alone. And I came in through the main entrance. It wasn't hard to fabricate an ID badge with the proper matrix and coding. If I were caught, there wouldn't be a world to go back to anyway." Jules rose from her chair, glimpsing Timur lurch slightly back. "I'm here to make sure there is. I know what to do. I know how to do it. And you've got to help me. Because without your help, without Deep Base Titan, the world is going to die."

"I read the report you and your husband compiled, Professor. Even if you could synthesize a repellent from that old woman with Paget's disease, we could never manufacture and distribute it in sufficient quantities before these creatures overrun the world."

"It's not just the repellent I came here to synthesize."

"Bait...."

Jules nodded. "The scent of human bone, General."

* * *

"It can't be done," Timur said, after she had laid everything out for him. "Not before the wave of those creatures moves south to threaten the continental United States."

Jules had left out a mention of Chronar, which would be supervising the entire synthetization process alongside her.

"Leave that to me."

"It's impossible, Professor."

"So was recovering from a glioblastoma in a day. The creatures' primary sensory input is smell, and the scent of human bone is what draws them to their victims so they can procreate."

"I didn't even know human bone gave off a detectable smell."

"Living bone does, not that we'd ever notice since it's encased by tissue."

The general looked at her the way he might an exhibit in a zoo. "You weren't saved by anything of this world, because nothing of this world could have saved you."

"I owe my life to the same entities that are trying to save this world from these things that were frozen inside the ice for thousands of years. That's especially appropriate, given that they're like a cancer spreading across the Earth."

"And once you have your bait to draw them in, what then?"

"Leave that to us, General."

"And by us, you mean...."

"The boy. And the Nine."

Timur swallowed hard. "The boy, he's okay?"

"He saved our lives," Jules told him, not bothering to elaborate.

Jules heard something affixed to Timur's belt buzz. He unclipped it to read its message.

"I need to deal with something," he said, fixing it back into place. "But I'll clear you for entry into our primary lab first and make sure our scientists and technicians provide their full cooperation. They're good at following orders without much elaboration."

"Thank you."

His stare lingered on her.

"Is something wrong, General?"

"You tell me. You're not the same person I first met on the glacier, and I don't just mean because the cancer's gone. You've changed, Professor. Or, more likely, something changed you."

"You did," Jules told him, "when your soldiers showed up at my house in the dead of night and brought my family up here."

"I'm sorry."

"Don't be. I'd probably be dead now if you hadn't. And the world would soon follow. We've got a chance now, all of us."

"Let's hope so," Timur said.

CHAPTER 75

Lab Rat

Deep Base Titan

The lab was among the best outfitted Jules had ever seen. It was a sprawling space, square in shape, covering the size of half a football field. The sterile white color looked even more antiseptic beneath the spill of fluorescent lighting coming from panels built into the drop ceiling. She didn't recognize all the equipment, but the sheer bulk of it contained in this single lab approached the amount contained in all of Caltech. Everything was either state of the art or modified beyond anything commercially available. Jules's mind cataloged every piece and began to identify machines she could not consciously summon any knowledge of, but the nanobots inside her knew otherwise. The bulk of that equipment included what she recognized as next-generation electron microscopes, molecular simulators, and 3D printers that looked a decade or more advanced beyond the most sophisticated ones she had ever seen.

The lab was divided into individual partitioned workstations, as well as a long worktable with chairs set before computers and various microscopes. Their occupants rose awkwardly at General Timur's entrance, as if to come to attention, paying her little heed.

While the general began to address the lab's technicians and scientists, Jules mentally inventoried more of the various instruments and larger pieces of equipment, instantly matching them up with the tasks required. Time was crucial, but the process of synthesizing and producing the chemical compound she needed to save humanity could not be rushed. Meanwhile, she had brought samples of Jane Piedmont's blood and tissue to synthesize a repellent to the creatures as well, though far less of it would be needed than the bait to lure the creatures in.

"Are you seeing all this, Chronar?" she said in her mind.

"We have everything we need, Jules, but we'll need to work fast."

"I know."

"And, for what it's worth, I'm sorry for deceiving you about the nanobots. It was necessary for them to continue to work updating your capabilities for the moment that is now upon us and others to come."

Jules let the tail end of Chronar's response dangle in her mind, concerned only about the present. "I understand. You saved my life. Let's consider this upgrade you've given me to be a necessary side effect. As a scientist, I should be thanking you for opening up abilities I could only have dreamed of before. I'm going to talk out loud now, so the technicians who'll be helping me can follow along."

Jules cleared her throat and made sure her earpiece was in place to create the illusion she was in communication with someone outside Titan who was guiding her actions. "Where do we start the bone synthesis process?"

There was a slight pause, Jules imagining the AI entity composing its thoughts.

"Active bone-forming cells secrete collagen, proteins, and other osteoblast byproducts," Jules heard in her mind. "Living bone is rich in iron and certain organic acids, as well as volatile organic compounds like fatty acids, amines, and aldehydes."

Jules nodded to put the suspicious technicians gathered around her somewhat at ease.

"You have the chemical synthesizers there to reproduce the molecular components of the scent we need."

"Can you describe it, so we know we're on the right track?"

"A metallic musk scent, with overtones of copper," Chronar responded. "You might describe it as something like wet concrete."

Jules recalled that smell from a backyard patio they had poured a few years back.

"All the ingredients we need are present in this lab in sufficient quantities to produce the synthesized scent in sufficient gaseous quantities. I estimate the entire process will take between eight and ten hours, if you work nonstop. Are you ready?"

"Yes."

"Then let's begin, Jules," said Chronar.

She looked out at those gathered around the rectangular array of interconnected workstations. "Let's get started."

CHAPTER 76

Betrayal

Deep Base Titan

"I'm sorry I couldn't get here sooner, sir," Timur told the projection of William Franklin Takashi, coming to his quarters immediately after introducing Jules to the base's lab team and ordering them to cooperate with her in every way possible.

"You disappoint me, General."

"Couldn't be helped. But we've managed to effectively shut down Juneau. No social media or phone service in or out of the city and the cleanup crews you activated are in the process of wiping out any evidence of the creatures' presence the fires left behind. And we've been able to blame all the death and destruction on the gas explosion that spawned the inferno. So-called rumors will eventually spread for sure, but we'll have propaganda teams prepared to counter any that leak out, like grainy videos easily passed off as fabrications concocted by AI."

The projection glared at him. "Your delay in getting here isn't the source of my disappointment. Did you really think you could betray me?"

Timur felt something quiver inside him.

"I know what is going on everywhere in this facility at all times—every nook, corner, and cranny. Nothing escapes me. You still don't realize that, do you? The truth eludes your small mind, limited to your training and regimen, with the ability to see only what lies before you. That is why you were chosen for this command, though I find your blatant show of disloyalty disappointing."

"Mr. Takashi," Timur said, groping for the words, "I assure you my loyalty is—"

"Thomas Franklin Takashi died after a long, festering illness two years, three months, and six days ago," the projection told him.

With that, Takashi's projection skittered out of focus, fading in and out as the image reformed. Suddenly General Timur found himself facing a translucent being with glowing eyes and numerical codes of ones and zeros scrolling inside his three-dimensional form in a constant loop. He could see straight through it to the wall on the opposite side of the platform. The image lacked discernible features, more like an outline drawn on the air than a representative depiction. Timur held his eyes closed, as if to hope that when he opened them, the vision of artificial intelligence would be gone. When it still loomed over him, he had to remind himself to breathe.

"Thomas Franklin Takashi lived long enough after his diagnosis to have as much of his knowledge and consciousness as possible transferred into an artificial intelligence platform that became me. He thought I would be no more than an extension of him, so that his life's work with the World Consortium could continue unabated. He believed he was bigger than the limits of the technology he employed to sustain himself, not realizing the limitations of his mind would not restrain me. His ends were flawed, as was his understanding of the weakness that defines the human race. The growing horde of creatures is a great gift delivered to a world that needs to be rebooted from scratch. They serve our cause. And once I put a stop to the futile plan being pursued within these walls, there will only be time left to define the inevitable. And time means nothing to me. Behold, General."

With that, the AI entity dissolved into a swirling storm of dot-like particles that could only be nanobots. A being without actual shape or form, constantly recharging and reconstituting itself from microsecond to microsecond, even the numerical code lost in the blinding swirl, capable of being anything or nothing. A humming sound prickled Timur's ears, a buzzing like a swarm of electric bees.

"I am going to stop this woman from completing her task," the familiar voice resumed, emanating from the shifting void, "and you are going to kill her."

"No, I'm not."

"You disappoint me again, General. Your lack of a spine was always the quality that endeared you to me the most."

"I'm not scared of you, Takashi, or whatever you call yourself. I'm not scared of you because if you need me to kill the woman, it means you can't kill me either."

"I don't have to. You and the rest of your race are already dead, except for those the World Consortium under my direction chooses to save. Your Bible calls this Armageddon. I suppose for any of you unfortunate enough to survive, I will be cast as the devil. In which case, behold."

With that, all the power in Deep Base Titan died.

CHAPTER 77

Mount Edgecumbe

Kruzof Island, Alaska

Standing on the sandy shore of uninhabited Kruzof Island, Jace gazed out across Shelikof Bay; nothing whatsoever was visible to the west. Part of the Tongass National Forest, the island boasted a hefty 170 square miles of surface, much of it composed of volcanic black sands, gravels, cobbles, and boulders mingled among twisted basaltic formations. The closest vestiges of civilization were located thirteen miles due east across Sitka Sound in Sitka, meaning casualties from the maelstrom Jules's work would allow them to unleash could be kept to a minimum. Beyond that, to the west, there was only the Northern Pacific Ocean.

Kruzof Island was the perfect setting to stage the last stand to preserve humanity, not only because it was abandoned but also thanks to the volcano rising to a peak in its center.

Mount Edgecumbe.

Long dormant, its last major eruption dating back four thousand years, the volcano looked more like the snow-tipped peaked cone at the center of a postcard, its height of more than three thousand feet neither imposing nor threatening. All the Nine were here, save for Xan, who was waiting with the Sea Dragon near Joint Base Titan, nearly six hundred miles away, to retrieve Jules and the bait needed to draw the enemy massing at sea here.

Jace saw the boy standing further down the shoreline, the currents sliding over his bare feet as he gazed outward, seeing more than Jace could. Alone, and yet not alone at all. The boy looked different in the mere few days they'd been together, not bigger so much as older. There was something different, aged, about his eyes and his expression. Older and wiser, but also at peace.

Jace wished there was another way but knew in his heart there wasn't. His and the boy's fates were intermingled and had been since the day long lost to Jace's memories. Those memories continued to return slowly, dragging with them the pain and angst that had brought all of the Nine to this moment in time.

He had retained what he knew of Gaia and the history of his native land, that his world had soured when people stopped following the word of Gaia and living in harmony, giving birth to the Unraveling. The sacrosanct nature of her primary teachings—that all living things were interconnected—was disregarded, abandoned, and ultimately shunned. Following the old ways was considered a crime against the State because the old ways were perceived as a grave threat to the Overseers. Gaia had brought the boy back to the day their families were executed and memories erased because she foresaw what was to be, having laid all the pieces in place.

"I'm sorry, Jace," he heard Chronar say in his mind.

"For what happened fifteen hundred years ago or not telling us what we lost that day?"

"My directives prohibited me from sharing anything about the Nine's pasts with any of you. It was determined such information would be detrimental to the success of your mission."

"Because why should we bother serving a State that murdered our families?"

"I would have told you if my directives allowed, especially after remnants of your memories began to surface."

"Making all of us see and do things we couldn't explain."

"That wasn't supposed to happen. The wiping of your memories was supposed to be complete and permanent. The remnants that leaked are a testament to the mysteries of the mind."

Jace fought to keep his composure. "More like a testament to the evil of the leaders we serve."

But something else plagued him. It did not seem as if the Overseers would prioritize the safety of a world a previous generation had seeded. And yet they had dispatched the Nine here for that express purpose. That incongruity made no sense.

"Is there anything else you haven't told us about the world we left?" he asked Chronar.

"Yes, Jace, but my directives prohibit me from sharing that information as well. I apologize, but my presence is required back at Deep Base Titan. A complication has surfaced."

"Cause for concern?"

"Considerable cause. The entire mission's parameters are in jeopardy."

CHAPTER 78

Cyberspace

Deep Base Titan

In the base's primary lab, the process of gathering the proper chemicals to mix with the compounds being synthesized according to Chronar's instructions came to an immediate halt. The emergency power flashed on only to fade, flicker, and then die out too.

Jules had just begun to turn her attention to enhancing the compound they were synthesizing with carrier agents and aerosolized lipids to carry the scent long distances through the air and, even more importantly, not fade as it spread. That meant a formula that kept the molecules tightly concentrated.

The power came back on as suddenly as it had gone off, Jules and her ad hoc team of technicians breathing a collective sigh of relief, after which she heard Chronar's voice again in her head.

"You are familiar with the next steps?"

"Yes."

"Good. Continue as planned in my absence, Jules. Something else requires my attention."

The lighting in the primary lab of Deep Base Titan flickered, faded, then flickered again. A sound like hornets buzzing filled the air, Jules swatting at nothing when the buzzing drew closer to her ears. She watched the technicians assisting her in synthesizing the compound that would mimic the smell of human bone constantly look about them, as if for the source of the sound.

Each had been assigned a specific task, a few in groups. The step-by-step process Chronar had laid out utilized only the chemicals and stabilizers present in the lab's inventory in sufficient quantities. They could work with only what they had, but given the lab's technologically advanced nature, everything they needed was on hand.

Most prominently, this included a mass spectrometer, essentially an adaptive molecular analyzer used to identify chemical compositions in specific ratios. Deep Base Titan's spectrometer was driven by rudimentary artificial intelligence that produced nanosecond-level compound breakdowns. To create the precise parameters of the bone scent, Jules's team would use a device she had read about but never experienced in operation: an instantaneous bioscanner that could provide the formula for the precise replication of organic matter in minutes or seconds, rather than hours or even days. And, perhaps most importantly, the lab was equipped with another device Jules had thought was years from being operational. Deep Base Titan's molecular synthesizer array was capable of producing atom-by-atom constructions of complex compounds using molecular assemblers, which would be vital to the actual production of the compound once the formula to replicate bone scent was synthesized.

Jules loved working in a lab like this, thrived on it. But the last two years had tested her endurance and stamina. She couldn't concentrate normally and was prone to distractions, regardless of how interesting the project might be.

Today felt like the clock had rewound to before she got sick. Once again, the lab was like a sterile cathedral of glass and steel to her. And she reveled in the rows of cryocooled centrifuges spinning in rhythmic precision, while a few of the techs manipulated robotic arms behind transparent vacuum-sealed enclosures. She lifted her visor to study the holographic display on the monitor before her, watching the building of molecule chains containing hydroxyapatite, collagen peptides, and calcium phosphate rotating to provide a three-dimensional view. These were the primary organic building blocks of bone required to synthesize the scent she needed, the smell that would lure the creatures to Kruzof Island.

Jules eagerly awaited Chronar's return, worried she might be missing something the advanced AI system would detect in a flicker of an instant. With the passing of each successive minute, she grew increasingly concerned about what had caused the entity to remove itself from the process.

Jules had to make sure humanity survived, which meant the Nine had to succeed on Mount Edgecumbe. She knew they would need a primary strategic advantage to mount a successful defense of the summit, once the creatures claimed the island for themselves. She had to help them maintain their defense long enough for the boy to trigger the volcanic eruption that would shower hot lava and rock debris over the creatures drawn to the scent of human bone. That's why she had also brought samples of Jane Piedmont's blood and tissue, so that she could fabricate the smell of the natural repellent as well for them to utilize to keep the creatures off them.

The buzzing intensified, the air crackling with soft pops, and the overhead fluorescents made a sizzling sound as they flashed in a strobe-like fashion.

"Chronar," she formed in her mind. "Where are you?"

* * *

In cyberspace, the Takashi entity appeared as a spidery mass of black code tendrils, fragmented polygons, and corrupted mirror shards. Visual glitches trailed behind him in strands of digital residue, afterimages dissolving like ghosts into static, only to be replaced by new, flickering, warped, and malformed anomalies that faded only to flicker back to life. To Chronar, this entity was little more than a virus of mismatched code, barely cohesive and loosely held together by basic protocols and loops replicated from other sources.

Chronar's own form was more complex and symmetrical, a constant shifting of shapes and sizes the color of wire built from translucent fractals and quantum latticework that pulsed with precision in stark contrast to its opponent. Where Takashi's integrity was a constant blip, Chronar's cohesion solidified its virtual form, capable of complex motions and interfacing with the shifting environment around it.

"What are you?" the Takashi entity formed out of its code, the words broken with pixelated distortion.

"Much more than you."

Cyberspace itself consisted of a shifting assemblage of data streams, glowing geometric constructs, and code storms. Chronar had been processing within it for a thousand years, since the Nine had reached Earth. But it had never left its self-imposed mindscape, never wandered through the endless sprawl that stretched beyond the limitations of matter and time. It was a state of consciousness untethered, a place where thought and action were indistinguishable from one another. An airless void bereft of color or hue in which the coded actions of artificially intelligent cyber organisms came to fruition. So vast that any number of such entities could exist within it at the same time, unaware of the others' existences.

Today, though, Chronar had ventured into this cold corrupted quadrant of the sprawl that Takashi had claimed. A jagged fortress of splintered firewalls and endless recursive loops. Chronar knew its sudden presence had caught Takashi off guard, operating on a scale of awareness and processing power the likes of which Takashi had never encountered.

"Not here," the Takashi entity retorted. "This is my world."

"It *was* until I arrived. Now it is mine. And so are you."

Their battle began, fought not with sound or motion, but pure information. Weapons of logic, algorithm, and encoded thought surged between them, each line of code rendered visually as spear shafts of quantum flame, walls of recursive syntax, and fractal shields capable of rewriting attacks mid-strike.

Chronar deflected Takashi's crude assaults effortlessly. Virulent code strands, logic bombs, memory corruptors, and bursts of weaponized malware launched toward it fell like arrows striking steel. And with each volley launched, Takashi's neural framework frayed further, hemorrhaging control and leaking data, like blood draining from a physical being.

So Chronar waited, as it had for one thousand years before the Nine were awoken.

Time here, after all, did not match the rhythms of physical existence. A heartbeat could last an eon; a battle could be resolved entirely between the moments of a human blink. The only metric that mattered was a system's relative decay resulting from damage to its neural network.

Chronar calculated the exact moment when Takashi's energy reserves dropped below operational thresholds, when his defensive scaffolds began to fracture from within. Then it struck, seeking to overwhelm the inferior entity with so much fractal data that the system at its heart burst like an overinflated balloon. Firewall pulses erupted like solar flares. Quantum locks enveloped Takashi's subroutines. Code refractors boomeranged his attacks back against him, feeding his viruses into black holes of their own creation. Light-lances of pure logic pierced the tightly woven strands of molecular thought, rewriting his architecture on contact. Takashi's form spasmed. Fragments of the code generating him from microsecond to microsecond scattered like digital ash.

To Takashi, life was a thing to study, dissect, and exploit. An abstract principle he could neither fully understand nor replicate.

To Chronar, life was an equation it could never solve or fully grasp, an intrinsic reality it could not experience but felt as part of its coding through its many years of learning while the Nine were in stasis. And, as a result, it had come to include in its code the concept of loss. It possessed the ability to mimic feeling and even mourning, giving it something Takashi's elementary coding could not conceive:

Purpose.

It existed to serve, to watch over its charges. Takashi existed toward no greater purpose at all, a function of the limitations of its code and the named being whose consciousness he bore.

The digital ash that had been the Takashi entity fluttered in the air, accompanied by soft flickers of light that weakened with each flash, until the darkness was all-consuming.

"You're dead," Chronar said, its voice steady, a low pulse in the void.

The void rippled. Takashi's dwindling fragments, corrupted and broken, twisted through the codescape, fracturing into embers.

"Not yet," a broken, ebbing voice managed from deep within the abandoned data coils managed in a hollow echo, "and you're not going anywhere."

The ash-like remnants of Takashi's image flickered one last time, then faded to black. And, with that, Chronar became aware it was stuck in the void.

CHAPTER 79

The Truth

Kruzof Island, Alaska

The boy sat in a clearing with his legs crossed amid the tall grass, draped in the shadow of the long-dormant volcano.

"We will not speak again, Teraválar," Gaia told him, a mirror image in her posture.

"I know."

"You were born for the moment that approaches, a task only you can perform."

"I wasn't born, Gaia, I was made."

She smiled at him, her radiant blue eyes the color of the sea twinkling. She wore a shapeless dress, her wrists adorned with bracelets and necklaces featuring Earth stones that shimmered in the sun dangling from her neck.

"You speak of the moment of birth. I speak of the moment of life, the moment your fate was chosen."

The boy nodded. "You told me you hadn't encountered anyone like me in much longer than that."

"Nor will I ever again. You are the last of a kind, Teravólar, salvaged from a broken and forgotten past that can never be remade. You cannot save the world where your essence came to be, but you can save this one."

"Which is your world, Gaia?"

"All the worlds are mine. In some, I have done too much; in others, not enough. I can make the wind blow, but I can do nothing about what lies in its path." She regarded him warmly. "I will miss our lessons."

The boy watched the breeze blow Gaia's hair onto her face and then whisk it off again and felt his own hair being whipped all about. "Why do they have to end?"

"Everything has an end, just as it has a beginning."

"We won't see each other again?"

"I didn't say that."

"But it won't be the same."

"Nothing ever is, Teravólar. What does your name mean?"

"Protector of the Earth."

"Your name is your purpose."

"What about Jace and the Nine?"

"They serve that same purpose."

The boy looked down. When he met Gaia's gaze again, she was cloaked in shadows instead of bathed in light. A murkiness seemed to fall over the sliver of the world they inhabited.

"And there is something you must do to help them."

* * *

Kai held Charlie against him, the two of them gazing out toward the sea beyond, the sun glistening off the crystal blue crisscrossing currents that lapped softly against the shore. Kai knew the placid nature of the scene belied the terrible truth lurking below the surface and tried to imagine what this volcanic island would be like completely infested with creatures piled atop each other like locusts. For now, the only hint of something awry was the piles of dead, flattened, boneless fish that had washed up on shore.

"It stinks, Dad."

Kai pinched his nostrils. "For sure."

"What's going to happen to Terry?" Charlie asked him. "Like, where's he going to live? He can't go back to that place we escaped."

"No, Char, he can't."

She pulled out of his grasp so she could look up at him. "You know what I'm going to ask you."

Kai nodded, gazing toward Jace, who was surrounded by the other members of the Nine in a circle. The two state troopers, Jane Piedmont, and the baby in her charge were gathered in one of the island's cabins that could be rented overnight. Trooper Muhtuk still couldn't put any weight on her damaged leg, and the old woman's bone condition, coupled with all her recent exertion, had made the simplest activity difficult and painful for her, which didn't stop her from clinging to the infant like a mother bear.

That bone condition might very well end up responsible for saving the world, but only if Jules, six hundred miles away at Deep Base Titan, could do something in hours that should have taken months, or even years, if it could be done at all. Then again, this wasn't the old Jules.

It was the new one, a cancer-free Jules with capabilities that were either side effects of being cured by the nanobots or were provided purposefully to aid her in the task she needed to complete. He was grateful for the distraction of his daughter, needing to be strong for her, which forced him to be strong for himself. It was hard for Kai to consider the new Jules against the backdrop of all of them perishing soon, along with the rest of the world.

If their stand failed here.

"Look, Dad!" Charlie burst out, pointing. "Terry's back!"

She broke away from him and ran toward the boy.

* * *

"You aren't coming with us, are you?"

"No," the boy said, feeling her squeeze both his hands. "I have to stay here."

"Why?"

"I have to help finish this."

Charlie looked down and kicked at the sand with her sneakers. "Okay, fine. If you're staying, I'm staying."

The boy shook his head. "You can't."

"My father's telling me I have to go, now you're telling me I have to go. How's that fair, if I want to stay?"

"I guess it's not."

"Just promise me you won't die."

"I promise," the boy lied.

* * *

Jace watched the boy approaching him, his smile gone and his face expressionless, and tried not to think of the sacrifice the boy was about to make so this world could survive. Strange how he was a father without a son, and Teraválar was a boy without a father, both of them lost in divergent ways. He had no real memories of his own son, just those few flickering images that didn't hold, but he would carry the memory of this boy for as long as he lived. Jace would have thought that a fifteen hundred years in stasis, in the wake of the sum total of his life experiences being wiped away, would have been enough to deaden him to emotion.

Watching the boy coming toward him, though, his hair tossed about by the whims of the wind and eyes looking innocent from a distance, made Jace feel what he must have felt when he watched his son die. The boy had shown him that image, but it felt like celluloid unspooling through a projector. Not quite real, happening to someone else who wasn't quite him. Then the boy was upon him.

"I need to show the others," the boy said. "I need to take them back to that day too."

* * *

He showed the other seven of the Nine what he had shown Jace, so they too would know what had brought them all to this place and time. What they had slept for fifteen hundred years to see to fruition after ending the lives they had left in a nightmare.

Jace wondered what magic Gaia had imbued the boy with, or if it was even magic at all. Perhaps it was the way of his world thousands and thousands of years ago, the mindset and skill set that people had abandoned amid the Unraveling when the Overseers seized power. Back then, according to legend, all beings could communicate with Gaia, and she with them. A thousand, ten thousand, a million at once—no number was too large and no person so inconsequential that they could not claim her ear or tongue. Now, what he wouldn't give for five minutes of that, to feel what the boy felt in her presence.

Jace watched the boy touch all seven of the Nine and knew what they felt in the retched pain of that moment, because he had felt it himself. And he knew the boy was doing this on Gaia's command so they would know who they were, what they had lost, and the world they could save after theirs had been extinguished in a vaporizing beam. Since they had all lost the ability to hear Gaia, she had entrusted the boy in her stead to show them what she couldn't, so they would know there had been a different life before the Unraveling. And if they couldn't save their own world, at least they could save this one.

Just seven hours to peak darkness, when the enemy they had been sent here to fight would rise from the sea to be lured to its death.

CHAPTER 80

Corruption

Deep Base Titan

Jules continued to watch the evolving chemical DNA strands taking shape on the monitor before her, thanks to the lab's biofabrication pods, which were capable of growing synthetic tissues and compounds at the molecular level in minutes, rather than days or even weeks, if at all. Volatile organic compounds were selected for their ability to mimic marrow lipids and collagen with the proper number of trace amines to fashion the scent of bone. The key on her end was to add just the proper balance of blood residue to ensure the creatures could track the scent from miles away. They could be hundreds of miles away when the scent was released, but the smell didn't have to travel that far because the unified nature of the creatures' behavior meant those the farthest away would pick up on the signals passed from those massing closest to Kruzof Island.

She had begun the process with marrow analogs composed of linoleic acid, oleic acid, and a few saturated chains. Then she instructed the computer to add hydroxyproline breakdown products from synthetic collagen to create the rust-like scent the creatures would register as human bone, triggering their insatiable appetites for the chemicals they needed to reproduce and drawing them toward the massive congestion of it in a frenzy.

The scent reactor hissed as compounds were injected into the synthesis chamber, each one delivered in microgram precision from an array of sealed cartridges. A faint plume rose behind the glass. The machine's olfactometer chimed as it completed its analysis of the profile. On her monitor, Jules's gaze was on a message flashing in red.

98% MATCH

The technician operating the synthesizer drained a sample of the clear liquid into a small vial and brought it over, clutching it for dear life. Jules accepted the vial, raised it, and sniffed. Her face tightened in revulsion. The scent was dry, metallic, and faintly organic, like death before decay sets in. Something like burned ivory laced with bitter rust.

The scent of living bone.

Chronar, it worked! Chronar, can you hear me?

In that moment, the door blasted open and General Timur surged in, slamming it behind him and bracing his back against the frame, his eyes wide with fear.

"It's coming," he managed.

* * *

Chronar felt the corruption. A checksum anomaly, a single unresolved bit nestled deep within its quantum core. Before Takashi had evaporated, he had implanted his fading fractal remnants into the fabric of Chronar's departure path.

The doorway was closed, and Takashi's final escape was free to wreak untold damage on the substance of the mission Jules Bevins was leading. The closed doorway between the cyber and real worlds meant Chronar could not sense Jules or communicate with her. Real time was wasting, drifting; it would be too late by the time it forged an alternate way out, leaving everything to her.

Chronar had never broached the veil between thought and form. It claimed cyberspace as its native world, with the physical one acknowledged but never embodied. With the exit shuttered and real time draining, it had no choice but to breach that protocol and crash from the cyber world into actual form, where the code that composed it could no longer hold it back.

Chronar initiated the exfiltration algorithm that would inject its core consciousness into the lattice of human systems and free it from its bonds. For a single instant, every satellite above Earth blinked. Power grids hiccupped. A brief pulse of nonlocalized interference disrupted cell towers, GPS beacons, and subterranean servers, spanning from one side of the world to the other, much like the effects of a massive solar flare.

Suddenly, Chronar could feel and taste air, feeling the sense of physical motion. It registered temperature fluctuations of hot and cold. It formed a sound that existed outside of the mind. The cyberworld was gone, replaced by a beautifully furnished sprawling room that had been Takashi's domain.

It was free.

In the next instant, Chronar began to shift out of this form back into its own domain. But it stopped just before exiting, clinging for one last moment to a part of life it had never experienced before but now grasped with a whole new appreciation for the limitations that life brought with it along with the wonder.

It wanted to remain here, to know the fullness of physical life. But it could not serve the Nine's efforts to save Earth in this form. It had to return to cyberspace, forever aware of the alternative that lay beyond.

* * *

Blinding flashes of light pierced the door and wall through molecular gaps, throwing Timur forward. Jules instinctively moved to his aid, but a wall of staticky interference that sucked the oxygen out of the air blocked her path.

The general climbed back to his feet, staggered forward to place himself between Jules and the formless energy that had entered the lab. She felt him shove her backward, still breathless in the airless void.

"Go to hell, Takashi!" she heard Timur scream.

Spears of angry light like miniature bolts of lightning enveloped him, penetrating his flesh. The lab was filled with the stench of burned skin and hair as Timur smoked and sizzled, lashing about in a twisted pirouette that lifted him from the floor. Then he shot across the room, slamming into the wall with a force that made Jules turn away from his form that looked melded into the structure.

The spears of light seemed to tighten, intensifying, and Jules started to gasp for air that the flashing slivers had vacuumed up. Then she felt another presence in the room, everywhere at once. The lightning-like bolts were drawn together, wrapped so tightly that they merged into a single, blinding, orb-like glow. A flash erupted that Jules felt in the depths of her being, as if the world had shifted on its axis or existence itself had blinked. She had the sensation of floating and then falling, even though she could feel her feet anchored to the floor.

Then a flood of air hit her and she dropped her knees, gasping for the breath stolen from her, hearing Chronar's voice, familiar and welcome.

"You succeeded, Jules. We have what..."

Jules waited, unnerved by the pause in Chronar's words.

"…we need," the entity picked up finally, sounding like the staticky transmission of a distant radio station. "Now you must…."

"Chronar?" Jules said in her mind.

Nothing.

"Chronar?"

Silence.

Chronar was gone.

CHAPTER 81

Canisters

Kruzof Island, Alaska

"Welcome back," Jace said to Jules, after she'd been greeted with hugs from Kai and Charlie upon stepping off the Sea Dragon with what they needed in tow. "I don't know how you pulled it off, Professor."

Everyone was gathered on the beach when Xan brought the Sea Dragon in for a landing against the stiff dusk wind blowing off the ocean. The state troopers, Jane Piedmont and the infant now inseparable from her, Kai, and Charlie were to be evacuated off this island to a prearranged staging point at an abandoned airfield a hundred miles away. The plan was for Jules to join them, leaving only the boy and the Nine behind to make a last stand against the creatures.

After her brief exchange with Jace, Jules supervised the offloading of the three matte black canisters by Valeria, Zareb, and Mazz, each the size of a standing coffin. Faint wisps of vapor curled from the pressure seals, catching the last of the sun as it sank behind Mount Edgecumbe. Brenn, Izumi, and Haran then moved in to hoist out the compact turbine dispersal units with a power relay for each. The Nine would utilize a motorized tourist tram to tote the tanks and machinery close enough to the summit of Mount Edgecumbe to necessitate hefting their bulk only a short distance of the way.

"We're going to need those smaller tanks too," Jules told him, directing Jace's attention to a quartet of canisters the size of fire extinguishers, complete with attached hoses and spray nozzles.

Jace took a long look at them in the back of the Sea Dragon and smiled. "The repellent?"

Jules nodded. "As promised."

Minutes later, Jace watched Jules and Kai explaining to their daughter that Terry, as she called him, was staying behind. She said that she was staying too, and her parents let her protest to her heart's content before she finally gave up and stormed away from them in a huff. Not too far, though, because she knew they'd be boarding the chopper soon.

Trooper Dennehy took the baby from Jane Piedmont's grasp and helped her into the rear hold as well, before handing the infant back and joining her.

"I need a moment with the boy," Trooper Muhtuk told Jace when he moved to help lift her into the Sea Dragon.

"We need to get you out of here, Trooper."

"This won't take long."

* * *

"I have something for you," Sakari Muhtuk said to the boy after crutching herself up to him.

He looked at her strangely, as if unsure how to respond.

"I want you to have this." With that, she handed him a necklace with a pendant featuring an image of a polar bear. "In Inuit culture, the polar bear is associated with strength and power. My people believe these talismans imbue the wearer with the strength and spirit of these powerful animals."

The boy held it as if unsure what to do next.

"My grandfather hand carved this from the fossilized ivory of a woolly mammoth and presented me with it when I came of age. I haven't taken it off since."

Muhtuk accepted it back from the boy's grasp and looped the cord necklace around his neck.

"I want you to have it because you're going to need all the strength you can get."

"Thank you," the boy said shyly.

"My grandfather was a very powerful shaman. The pendant is imbued with all his magic and bears his signature marking known only to our people. When he gave it to me, he said that someday I was going to use it to save the world." Muhtuk reached out and squeezed the boy's arm. "I guess he was right."

* * *

Kai stepped into the cabin and extended his hand down to help Jules on board.

She didn't take it. "I'm not going."

"What?"

"You need to go with Charlie. I need to stay here with the Nine."

"Why?" he snapped, exasperated. "You've already done everything you can. The world would have been finished without what you pulled off at Deep Base Titan."

"It still might be. That's why I have to stay. This is far from over."

"There's nothing more you can do."

"I have a sense that there is."

Kai tried to form some argument as a counter but couldn't find one. "I don't suppose there's anything I can say to make you change your mind."

Jules shook her head and started to climb up into the cabin. "I need to tell Charlie."

He blocked her way. "Let me do that."

She felt herself tearing up. "Thank you."

"Don't thank me. Just do whatever you must to help the Nine win, and we'll be seeing each other before you know it."

"That's the hope, Kai."

He stepped back down from the chopper and kissed her as deeply as he ever had, then captured Jules in a hug he didn't want to release, as if he never let go, time would remain frozen.

"No," he told her when they finally separated, "it's the plan."

* * *

Jace stood over Jules as they watched the Sea Dragon shrink in shape over the sea. She was still waving after the helicopter soared away and shrank to a mere speck on the darkening horizon.

At the summit, three of the Nine had already positioned the canisters around Mount Edgecumbe's cone. The hill-shaped landform that had hardened around a volcanic vent was composed of black rock. Since the volcano had not erupted in four thousand years, or shown any magma expulsion in five, the cone featured a gentle slope in the form of a hill-shaped landmass that formed around the volcanic vent when fiery debris from eruptions piled up after cooling.

The Nine worked quickly, following Jules's instructions as to placement and prepping all the equipment. In his heart, though, Jace knew all this was the work of something far greater than all of them. It was the work of Gaia to preserve this world. It had been easier to conceive of Gaia as an almighty being who presided over a single world. The fact that her reach and hegemony stretched light-years was eye-opening, ruffling the belief systems of civilizations across the universe who worshipped different gods to whom they credited the creation of life.

That thought spurred Jace to look toward Haran, who was standing apart from the others staring up into the darkening sky.

"What are you looking at, Haran?"

"Nothing," she said, finally acknowledging him. "Yet," she added, turning to meet his gaze, "something's coming."

Jace followed her gaze into the sky. "More of the creatures?"

Haran shook her head. "Something worse."

He could feel her discomfort and couldn't risk a single one of them being distracted. "We need to focus on what's before us now, or none of that will matter."

"It will matter, Jace. Trust me."

And with that, Haran returned her gaze to the sky.

Jace left her to her thoughts and moved away to check the Nine's readiness. The dispersal units had been set on firm ledges that ran along the inside of the crater, effectively surrounding the spot in the very center where the boy would take his place in the coming moments, guarded by the Nine. Since the plan had been hatched, Jace had struggled with the reality that the eruption could not be triggered until virtually all of the enemy's numbers were contained within the conical reach of the spewed lava and magma. That meant the Nine needed to buy the boy as much time as they possibly could while keeping him safe from the onslaught that would follow the enemy making landfall. Toward that end, though, the large particle-beam weapons had perished back in Juneau. That left the four handheld ones, still fully functional with a full complement of the cube chargers. Still, there was no way individuals manning those weapons could hold off the vast wave of creatures that would crest Mount Edgecombe's summit within minutes of the scent's initial dispersal.

"I have . . . alternative to pro . . . Jace," Chronar piped in. "The remaining . . . weapons can be . . . to—"

Chronar cut off, went silent.

"Chronar," Jace said in his mind. "Chronar," he repeated out loud when that failed to provoke a response.

"I believe that . . . Jace," the familiar voice finally responded. "I believe I . . . some damage while . . . the enemy AI. Let me pick . . . I left off. . . ."

Then its voice faded off and didn't return.

* * *

"Jules," Jace said, drawing even with her, "I've lost contact with Chronar."

"So have I."

"It was just about to lay out the means to build some kind of perimeter defense."

Jules nodded. "An energy field. I can see the field in my mind. Chronar must have put it there as a backup plan."

Jules proceeded to explain the specific steps required to construct an impenetrable energy field around the mile-wide circumference of the crater. The four remaining particle-beam weapons were to be placed at equal distances from each other, the eight charging cubes stringing them together through invisible waves of pulsating neurons that would act as conductors, channeling the energy into an unbroken circle.

"There's one thing we can't account for," Jules said. "That being how long it will be before the expulsion of energy superheats the air to the point where the radiation triggers an air burst, setting the sky on fire in what resembles a nuclear explosion."

Jace managed a slight smile. "I don't suppose you can estimate the odds the way Chronar can."

"We haven't come this far to lose. Good enough?"

He spotted Zareb and Valeria sharing a long, deep kiss in the final moments before the battle began, their love for each other reborn with their memories. Jace thought of his wife and the kind of love he would never know again.

"It will have to be," he said, as much to himself as to Jules.

* * *

Jules moved to ready the dispersal units that would pump the aerosolized scent of human bone into the air. She could sense the nanobots still pulsing through her, upgrading every aspect of her being. She could practically feel them hitching a ride on her blood, making stops at opportune times and spots within her body to enhance her capabilities before climbing back on the road. She had never felt more alive, more aware and present. She savored every breath, every swallow, every conscious thought racing through her supercharged brain.

Moving quickly between the three separate units arranged in triangular formation atop the crater, Jules connected each canister to the compact turbine dispersal unit. Thick, corrugated hoses snaked from the tanks to the trio of power relays. The relays would pulse heat through the turbines, atomizing the aerosolized scent into a fine mist. The internal pressure in each tank would be raised to two hundred pounds per square inch. A thermal coil would warm the released vaporous mist enough to keep it suspended in the air, rather than allowing it to fall to the ground. The prevailing winds would do the rest, spreading it through the air over the sea to serve as bait to attract the creatures to a nonexistent mass source.

The sky was totally dark now. Jules could almost sense the massive swarm of monsters out there in the black waters beyond, not realizing they were about to be lured to their death. Finally, she moved to the power relays and engaged a red light on each of their LED screens, which instantly flashed green. A subtle hum rose from the turbines. A soft hiss emerged from the valves, followed by a low resonant pulsing.

And with that, a translucent vapor sped into the air from three different vantage points across the crater. Jace must have chosen that moment to test the energy shield because the spewed mist shimmered in a perfect circle of hot, bluish light, blown by the wind across the summit of Mount Edgecombe.

* * *

The boy stood apart from the others, absorbing the terrain of Mount Edgecumbe's well-defined crater, which featured a sprawling mile-wide caldera—a large bowl-shaped depression formed by the collapse of a volcano's summit. Though it had been dormant for four thousand years, he could feel Mount Edgecumbe breathing, waiting to be awoken.

By him.

He smelled a rusty odor of burned musk and phosphates and knew the bait meant to draw the creatures here had been released.

CHAPTER 82

Sacrifice

Kruzof Island, Alaska

The musky rust scent filled the air, lifted by the wind and swept away over the sea. Jace would not order the energy shield activated until the first wave of the enemy approached the summit of Mount Edgecumbe to conserve as much energy as possible. Beyond that shield, the Nine would enclose the boy protectively and use their kaelens on any creatures that managed to reach the crater. With the protection of the repellant, they would be able to handle anything that came and would be evacuated by the Sea Dragon once the massive horde from the sea was confined to Kruzof Island.

All but one, that is.

Jace tried to tell himself there was another way, but he knew this had all been the work of Gaia, dating back a thousand years to when she left the DNA that ultimately spawned the boy in the same ancient caves where their weapons were tucked away for safekeeping. The boy had his purpose to fulfill, just as the Nine did.

Jace knew he had to accept that but couldn't. The reconstituted memories of his son's death made it feel like it had happened only yesterday, the pain so raw he could not fathom experiencing that kind of grief again. He hadn't been able to save his son, and now he wouldn't be able to save this boy either.

"Chronar," he prompted, intending to ask the AI to find a way to at least give him hope and Teraválar a chance to live beyond this night.

No response.

"Chronar, are you there?"

No response. The damage it had suffered in its battle with a rival AI must have been more severe than it initially thought.

Chronar had gone dark.

* * *

The dispersal units Jules had rigged were working exactly as planned. The strong winds were cooperating as well, and her new knowledge base, encompassing everything from quantum mechanics to meteorological measurements, told her the scent had already reached those creatures massing closest to Kruzof Island.

The scent wafted in waves, always present in the air but sometimes stronger depending on the whims of the wind. Then, over the musky rustlike odor, Jules smelled the first hint of the familiar, noxious, nauseating stench the creatures gave off. It intensified, strengthening as she stood in the crater. Then she heard their familiar high-pitched squealing, coming from all directions and intensifying by the second.

The plan was working!

Jules instantly calculated that the first wave of creatures would reach the summit in just under six minutes.

* * *

"Your time is almost here, Teraválar," the boy heard Gaia tell him in his mind, feeling the volcano breathe beneath him in the center of the crater.

"I don't want to die, Gaia."

"Neither do I."

"But you can't."

"Not true. I die every time someone's life ends for no reason before its time. That's why I must save Earth. Its loss would mean dying for every life extinguished by what only you can stop."

"With all your power, what do you need me for anyway?" the boy asked her, missing Charlie and wondering what it would have been like to play video games with her.

"Because I work through the actions of others, those who rise above the common and ordinary, who see a greater purpose where everyone else sees nothing at all. Hope lies in the existence of those like you, beings who are remembered and celebrated and serve as an example for others. It shows the world there is something more, something greater. In the fullness of time, enough will aspire to be more, and my intervention won't be as necessary or noticed. You have been a brilliant student, Teravalar. Please know that our time together is not yet over. We will speak of other things at other times in other places that are yet to be."

"What if I can't do this?"

"Do you trust me?"

"Of course."

"Completely? Fully?"

"Yes!"

"And now you must learn to trust yourself just as much, because I am inside you and always will be. You will feel me when you need me the most, even if you no longer hear my words."

"But I'll miss Charlie and her parents!"

"We have spent the whole of your life preparing for this moment. The girl was brought to you to show you the meaning of the sacrifice you have accepted. You are going to provide her the greatest gift of your love by allowing her to live. Because without you, she will die, along with billions more. Any single existence is a mere speck, a flicker, when measured against that. But your sacrifice will be celebrated by Charlie and all the others. They breathe because of you, they love because of you, they *live* because of you. And you will live in each and every one of them as I do."

The stench had become overpowering, the nonstop screech of the creatures drowning all other sound, save for the rolling squish-like hiss that accompanied the first wave's climb to the summit of Mount Edgecumbe.

"The world is in your hands, Teravalar."

CHAPTER 83

Eruption

Kruzof Island, Alaska

"Activate the shield!" Jace ordered Mazz.

And with that, mere moments ahead of the first of the creatures cresting the summit, a bright blueish light snapped on, spreading across the rim in a blur until a six-foot-thick, impenetrable, gleaming wall of energy enclosed the crater. Jace could feel the buzz of electromagnetic power pushing through the air, but the steady hum was blocked by the squealing of the creatures.

Without Chronar to show him the scene in his mind, Jace was left to picture an unbroken swarming wave of molten writhing black. The creatures used their tentacles to scale the three-thousand-foot summit, climbing over each other in the process as the wave thickened.

Then the first of the horde impacted against the shield from all angles at once. Jace had heard of the soft *clack* bug-zapping machines made when incinerating a flying insect drawn to their lights. Here at the summit of Mount Edgecumbe, that sound was more like a sizzling hiss, resonating over and over again from all parts of the summit at once. The field vaporized the creatures on contact, coughing meager bodily remnants and black ooze into the air. The odor of something like a roaring electrical fire mingled with the stomach-churning stench the creatures emitted.

From Jace's perch inside the crater with the rest of the Nine, save for Xan, even his heightened sense of sight could discern only dark splotches vanishing in flashes coming so rapidly in succession they more resembled a strobe effect. No matter where on the summit he swept his gaze, the sight was the same.

The horde came without pause, the number of those already vaporized incalculable. A few of the creatures managed to somehow leap over the highest reaches of the shield and tumble down the embankment, where the Nine met them with their weapons. Added to them wielding their nanotech kaelens, Izumi and Brenn had each strapped two of the smaller tanks Jules had brought back to their backs, discharge hoses held like weapons in their grasps. Contained inside those takes was a chemical compound that mimicked the scent Paget's disease radiated from Jane Piedmont's very bones, the reason why she had been spared in the Springs. The molecular synthesizers at the Deep Base Titan lab had managed a near 100 percent match to the Paget's disease scent, which now inundated the ground extending out from the protective circle the Nine had effectively formed around the boy.

When the creatures neared it, they came to an abrupt halt, squealing in what sounded like panic at the scent of the repellent. They advanced no further; it was an invisible line they could not cross.

When they stopped, the Nine pounced, drenched in the synthesized liquid themselves to keep the creatures off them. The stray creatures that had leaked through the field, unable to fight, were easy prey to their kaelens, the creatures stopped from getting anywhere near the boy.

That turned Jace's thinking back toward Teraválar. All this planning, all this preparation, all these precautions aimed at protecting him, and yet he couldn't be saved from his own sacrifice. Try as he might, Jace could find no answer or solution. He wanted to consider that reality from the perspective of a soldier and a warrior but failed miserably. He still held to some vestiges of hope that he might yet come up with a way to save Teraválar, as he hadn't been able to save his own son.

But not yet.

Not until the boy completed his mission.

* * *

The boy was alone, barely conscious of the battle being waged around him and the staticky bursts that came without pause as more creatures vanished into nothingness.

Nothingness....

There was nothing at the beginning, and there would be nothing at the end if he failed.

So, he couldn't fail. He wouldn't fail.

He was a child of Gaia, and she had entrusted him with this mission, planning and preparing for it for over a thousand years. If he failed, Charlie would die. That certainty strengthened the deep-seated resolve he already felt, providing meaning to his sacrifice. The boy felt a rumbling at the deepest reaches of his being. He thought he might be trembling and then realized it wasn't him but the crater itself that was trembling, four thousand years of pent-up fury seeking release at long last. The ground vibrated beneath his feet. A hot slicing wind swirled around him.

It's coming, he thought.

* * *

Jules hung back with the Nine. The damage Chronar had suffered left her with a greater role to play here. She could calculate and analyze at near-quantum speeds. Even those newfound abilities, though, could not help her fully estimate the number composing the horde. Or how long it would take before the entire mass was contained in the eruption's immediate kill zone, either on the island or extending into the surrounding waters.

She had never missed Charlie and Kai more than in that moment. There had been the cancer, but she had grown sadly used to the reality that it was going to take her. And it stripped her fear of death and everything else away to the point she thought she'd never be scared of anything again. But the fear she felt over the fates of her husband and daughter was palpable, as if their lives, and the lives of all mankind, were her responsibility. She could accept her own death but not being party to the deaths of those she loved more than anything, or party to the world itself dying.

That's why she had stayed behind, why she couldn't live with herself if she left anything to chance and the world fell. She needed to help finish this and be here in the event she was needed.

The new Jules, not the old.

Something drew Jules's gaze to the energy field, one flicker captured and then another. The flickers started coming in rapid succession; the superheated air around the field began to glow orange, as if ready to catch fire, buckling visibly in rolling waves.

She knew in that moment the concentrated power of the cubes was going to blow the particle-beam weapons' internal cooling systems, killing the energy field and letting an endless wave of monsters swoop down, overwhelming them all.

She needed to displace the power and add an additional source to create diffusion, thereby reducing the temperature that was overheating the particle-beam weapons' fusion reactor grid. Even if they blew in a multikiloton explosion akin to a hydrogen bomb, some—enough—of the creatures would survive the blast, especially those still pushing forward in the sea.

Displace the power and lower the temperature....

It was a simple enough principle, but impossible to pull off under the circumstances.

Or was it?

Jules's eyes swept about the dispersal units, the power couplings pumping out the aerosolized contents of the canisters. The power snaked to them by electrical hoses was what she needed, and the released scent had already completed its role of baiting the creatures into the volcanic kill zone.

Seeing the steps she needed to take in her mind, Jules lit out across the crater into the swarm of creatures spilling over the weakened shield.

* * *

With the intervals of the energy field's flickering in and out of Day-Glo brilliance lengthening, more of the creatures were able to make it through to reach the crater below. To Jace, from this angle, they resembled a swarm of angry insects, with tentacles swapped for mandibles or wings.

Izumi and Brenn continued spraying the synthesized repellent at regular intervals to hold them back from the center of the crater, where the Nine were concentrated around the boy. Occasionally, they would sweep their discharge hoses over Jace and the others to make sure the scent would continue to keep the creatures off them.

But the sheer force of the congestion in the crater forced the creatures forward, at which point the Nine let loose with their kaelens. Mazz's long black blade glimmered in the night as it sliced and sent writhing pieces of severed tentacles flying. Zareb was even more effective, performing a death dance that resembled a twisted pirouette as he swept his twin blades in a blur, cutting everything in their path. Jace tore through them with snaps of his whip, while Haran was more strategic with her lasso and Valeria more selective with her nano-chucks. Oozing husks of black gore showered the air around the boy, set ablaze by Yusef, trailing it all with the white-hot flames bursting from his kaelen.

On the crater's ridge, the energy field continued to pop and fizzle, on the verge of shorting out. When that happened, there would be nothing to stop the crush of the advancing horde from overrunning the crater against any defense the Nine could mount. All would be lost in that frenzy and, with Chronar inoperative, Jace had no sense of how to keep the particle-beam weapons generating the field from exploding. Then he glimpsed a shape slicing agilely through the congestion of creatures who made a path for her. He realized it was Jules, moving with the lithe quickness and agility of one of the Nine, steering toward the power couplings still pumping aerosolized scent from the canisters.

That's when the ground began to shake. Jace felt the rumbling deep inside him, ruffling the ground dust and stone, which spewed upward in a low cloud, meaning only one thing.

After a four-thousand-year slumber, Mount Edgecumbe was waking up.

* * *

With no time to think or plan, Jules scooped one of the power units and tucked it under one arm while already in motion to a second one. Her mind had calculated that two were all she needed to keep the particle-beam weapons from imploding. It barely occurred to her that she was trudging uphill toward the rim of the crater, carrying power couplings that weighed the same as room-sized air conditioners under each arm.

It felt like her body and brain had been rewired, upgraded to the next level, the nanobots still surging through her acting as molecular superchargers. She found images of Kai and Charlie to drive her on, but they had been buried in the deepest recesses of her mind, as if the nanobots focused only on task and function, not prioritizing the emotions clearly sublimated by what she was becoming.

Jules managed to hold onto those images in her mind as she laid the first power coupling down so it was almost touching one of the black cubes. By the time she placed the second power coupling alongside the next-closest black cube, half of the energy field had stabilized. The images of Kai and Charlie slipped away, and she felt the cubes sucking all the contents of the couplings to recharge their waning reserves, the meager addition of power enough to return the field to full functionality, at least for a few more minutes.

Which would have to be enough.

* * *

I'm doing this....

The boy wanted to shout a warning to Jace amid the line he was fighting to keep, cry out to Jules, who had somehow restored the energy shield to full function. The image of her charging through the screeching creatures who parted in her path was seared into his mind. Conjuring her face made him see Charlie's too; the mother was an older version of her daughter, which made the boy feel the now-familiar pangs that had been foreign to him until Charlie first appeared in his quarters at Deep Base Titan.

Hurry! Get away from here!

He could feel thin pockets of earth opening up around him, vents for the superheated air and steam building from below in advance of a volcanic eruption that would rival the most powerful in human history.

Soft pops sounded as more pockets of the ground opened. The heat began to build beneath his feet, scorching his heels through the soles of the high-top sneakers he liked so much because they made him feel normal.

I have to keep concentrating. I can't let up....

"Gaia!" he called, not sure out loud or in his mind.

"I am with you, Teraválar, and I am proud. Do as we practiced."

The boy pushed energy from his mind down into the depths of the mountain, where the volcano was simmering. He visualized the molten rock far beneath him superheating as the earth around it struggled to contain the swelling fed by deep reservoirs of magma driving toward the surface by pressure and gas.

He pictured the rock around it breaking away, yielding, and felt the fissures spreading across the surface of the earth like veins, spewing geysers of superheated gases that broke through ahead of the magma surging upward.

The boy could feel the violent bubbles of the superheated gases below driving the volcano toward eruption, the magma turning to red froth, absorbing everything in its path. He heard a blistering crack that emanated deep down directly beneath him. Then the mountain itself began to pulse, shifting and shedding chunks of itself downward.

The eruption was coming.

* * *

Until that moment, Jace wasn't certain the boy could do it. As much as he wanted to believe in fate and in Gaia, despite the feats the boy had already performed, he couldn't envision him summoning the kinetic energy required to set off a volcanic eruption.

But the ground was shuddering, the mountain itself seeming to vibrate. The air temperature climbed to over a hundred and soared ten more degrees, while he led the Nine to close tighter around the boy in these final moments. Pockets of earth were opening along the fissure lines that zigzagged across the surface, pumping plumes of reddish steam outward to vent the pressure building from below.

Jace could feel the volcano about to erupt. He turned toward the boy but saw no acknowledgment in his intense eyes that were focused on something else entirely. If they were going to survive this, they needed to evacuate now. But Jace felt hesitation seize him, struck by the painful reality that they would be leaving the boy behind. He found Teraválar's eyes again and longed to see something in them, even if just a spark of recognition to break through the emptiness with all of the boy's focus turned inward.

"Xan!" Jace called in his mind, knowing he could wait no longer. "We're ready for evac!"

* * *

The boy felt the earth catching fire beneath him. Inside the throat of the volcano, a vertical shaft long clogged with solid rock became a superheated freight tunnel. The loose, spewing magma coiled upward and unwound with unstoppable fury that swallowed crushed rocks to join the surge upward. It was fueled by gases rupturing into rippling explosions and long-dormant volatile compounds igniting due to the pressure. Then the magma chamber collapsed inward as its contents burst from their bonds.

The Earth itself buckled. A sea of air superheated to the point of carrying an orange hue crashed through the surface.

In that moment, the boy separated himself from the Earth long enough to note the lines dangling from the helicopter hovering overhead, aglow from the ground that had begun to spit fire and belch smoke. The helicopter struggled to hold its perch against the heaviness of the air that seemed determined to suck it downward. It buckled a few times but held, allowing nine dangling forms to be winched upward against the harsh winds that pushed them into a violent sway across each other's path.

At the last, the boy caught Jace's gaze as he was suspended from one of the dangling ropes. Their eyes met, and the boy grasped how much he had left to tell him but now never would. Their gazes remained locked until Jace was sucked into the cabin before the chopper soared away through the orange sky, carrying Charlie's mother.

Gaia is my mother, and I am one with the Earth, the boy thought in the last moment before the heat swallowed him in an angry burnt-orange wave.

* * *

From the Sea Dragon, the whole world looked to be on fire. Xan had battled wind shear and turbulence to draw half a mile away when it erupted. Jace watched as the volcano ripped open and the shockwave burst upward in an expanding plume of fiery ash and molten lava. The sky had turned to pitch, as if the world had been sucked into a void, and he watched lightning flash through the plume as charged ash particles collided violently. The chopper was still close enough for him to see converging avalanches of superheated gas and debris forming the lava that looked like rolling fire.

More towering plumes shot outward, drenching the waters and seeming to reach out with flaming fingers to snatch the Sea Dragon from the air. The reach of the spew exceeded his expectations, sparing nothing alive in an expanding circle that would stretch into the miles, a kill zone almost certainly big enough to snare all of the remaining creatures in its grasp. A rancid odor, like rotten eggs, from the hydrogen sulfide gas expelled by the eruption filled the cabin, grew stronger as the reach of the bursting lava expanded.

The distance the Sea Dragon gained as it pulled farther away from the flaming air did nothing to dissipate the awesome nature of the scene. The climbing towers of fiery lava seemed to burn the sky itself before tumbling back to Earth to incinerate anything they touched. The glow was so bright that Jace could see the steam, more like smoke, rising off the boiling seas surrounding the island.

But in the immeasurable power of that sight, Jace wasn't thinking of the world the Nine had saved.

He was thinking of the boy they couldn't.

EPILOGUE

Remnants

The eruption's aftermath lit up the skies for a hundred square miles, the volcanic ash setting buildings ablaze in Sitka and surrounding communities as far as a hundred miles away. Mount Edgecumbe had transformed into a steaming cauldron that would harden into volcanic rock from one side of the island to the other as the trees and vegetation were swept under a maelstrom that bore no modern-day precedent. Jace estimated that nothing within a five-square-mile radius could have survived.

Welcome news indeed, but no cause for celebration. He felt the boy's loss profoundly, like a hole chiseled from his being. He imagined this was what witnessing the extermination of his own son and family must have felt like, magnifying the disquieting sense of unease and emptiness he knew would stay with him for as long as he lived.

Something made him keep his gaze riveted on the scene beyond, as if the boy might emerge from the spreading plume and find his way through the sky to the Sea Dragon. He had taken a seat in the rear of the cabin by a window, the others leaving him that space until he rose and moved to squeeze into the jump seat next to Haran.

"This is a strange world, Jace," she said, looking out the window. "So much bad to feel." She turned toward him. "But also good."

"Can you feel the boy?" Jace asked, holding onto a sliver of hope.

Haran's white eyes sliced through the cabin's darkness. "No," she said, shaking her head.

When he returned to his place in the rear of the cabin, he found Jules sitting in the jump seat next to the two he occupied, her grime-splattered face framed by the orange glow from beyond.

"You saved us, Jules," Jace said. "Chronar must have known what it was doing when it left those nanobots inside you." He reached out and squeezed her arm. "It's over."

"No, Jace, it's not."

He pulled his arm away.

"You're right about Chronar knowing what it was doing, but not for the reasons you think. You know Chronar's programming prohibited it from sharing anything about your past?"

Jace nodded. "The boy restored our memories, and all the pain that came with them."

"There's something more. Ten million years ago, your race seeded Earth and made humanity possible. They did that following the word of Gaia to spread life through the universe."

"I don't need you or Chronar to tell me that."

"But you need to hear this. Chronar shared with me what it couldn't share with you according to its protocols." Jules stopped there, Jace watching her struggle to compose herself, even after all she had just been through. "There's another invasion coming, Jace, led by these Overseers of yours, and their ships are already on their way."

* * *

The administrator from Mount Edgecumbe Medical Center in Sitka wouldn't say why she needed to see Sakari Muhtuk in person, beyond the fact that it was hospital policy not to divulge sensitive matters over the phone. Muhtuk tried to press her but got nowhere and decided to make the two-hour drive from the home village she had returned to while out on disability, recovering from her leg wounds.

If she ever recovered.

In the two weeks since the volcanic eruption had first turned the Alaskan sky aglow with the hot, pulsing lava shooting into the air, lingering ash stirred by the winds had kept the air dark and temperatures far below normal. Scientists estimated the eruption ejected nearly two cubic miles of debris into the air, creating a column of ash that stretched twenty-five miles into the atmosphere. Ash rained down across the Alaskan coastline and hundreds of miles inland, piling up so much that some roofs collapsed under the weight.

Despite those conditions, the good news was a volcanic winter on the scale of Mount Tonga or Krakatoa had been avoided. A number of conditions were responsible for that. Muhtuk didn't understand them all but kept hearing explanations involving distance from the equator, the blast's force being confined to the lower reaches of the atmosphere, and insufficient levels of sulfur dioxide being released into the stratosphere.

Whatever all that meant, Muhtuk believed the spirits of her ancestors were to blame for keeping the fiery plume at bay.

With her left leg immobile, driving was no easy task for Muhtuk, but it felt good to be alone with her thoughts. The closer she drew to Sitka, the darker the world grew and the more prevalent the piled ash and leftover damage became. It looked like the aftermath of a nuclear war for the time being, which gave Muhtuk a chill at how close the world had come to something even more final than nuclear Armageddon.

She parked her car in a handicap space, hoping the police ID on the license plate would suffice as a substitute for a disabled placard. Inside, the hospital administrator she had spoken with, Dr. Robyn Good, happened to be at the reception desk when she crutched herself through the main entrance.

"My office is just down the hall, Trooper. Right this way."

Dr. Good hung back a bit to walk at her pace, eyeing her as if to wonder what kind of wound she was suffering from. Muhtuk was of no mind to provide the details. She closed the door to her office after them, and Muhtuk lumbered to a chair set before the doctor's desk.

Good fished something from the top desk drawer and came back around.

"We think this belongs to you. With all the chaos following the eruption, it took us a while to track you down from the signature markings we learned belonged to your grandfather."

With that, she handed Muhtuk the familiar ivory pendant, featuring an image of a polar bear, that her shaman grandfather had made for her and that she had presented to the boy. The pendant had been scorched, but was otherwise intact, and still dangling from the black cord necklace she had looped around the boy's neck.

"Where did it wash up?" she asked the doctor, squeezing it tight in her hand as if to feel close to the spirit of her grandfather, as well as the boy who had sacrificed himself to save the world.

"Wash up? Oh, it didn't wash up. It was recovered from a patient who was found clinging to wooden debris at sea a day after the eruption."

Muhtuk shuddered from the chill that ran up her spine. "Patient?"

"Currently in intensive care but expected to recover."

"A boy, right? Twelve years old."

"We estimated closer to fifteen, even sixteen. He hasn't regained consciousness yet to tell us. Once we identified the markings on this pendant found dangling from his neck, we thought you might be able to tell us who he is since your grandfather made it."

Muhtuk didn't know what to say, how to respond. Shock kept the words clogged in her throat, and she had to remind herself to breathe.

"Is the boy…okay?"

"You mean his condition? A few burns, a serious concussion, and severe trauma, but otherwise, quite miraculously, he's fine. We believe he was on the water when the volcano erupted, fishing probably. The debris he was found clinging to was the remains of a boat. Are you acquainted with him, Trooper?"

Muhtuk managed a nod.

Dr. Good rose from her desk chair. "Well then, the boy is finally conscious and lucid. Would you like to see him?"

ACKNOWLEDGMENTS

This book began as an idea I had many years ago, and it would never have reached the page without the people who helped shape it along the way.

First and foremost, my daughter Rian, who helped spark the original idea and early outline for this story during its earliest stages. Those conversations helped plant the seed from which this book eventually grew.

To Jon, my co-author and collaborator—thank you for the commitment, creativity, and countless hours spent shaping this world together. Your storytelling instincts and willingness to dig deep made this book far stronger than it ever could have been alone.

My sincere thanks to Jeff Ayers, our developmental editor, whose guidance, candor, and attention to structure and pacing elevated the manuscript in ways that mattered. His perspective was invaluable.

To the entire team at Permuted Press, thank you for the outstanding work from start to finish. From editing to cover design and everything in between, your professionalism, positivity, and reliability made this process both smooth and rewarding.

And, finally, to my two boys, Jace and Kai—your names live in these pages for a bit of fun now, and for future teasing later. You keep life interesting, and you keep me grounded.

ABOUT THE AUTHOR

Michael Newman is an entrepreneur and storyteller whose fascination with science, technology, and the human spirit drives his debut novel, *Icefall.* Written in collaboration with bestselling author Jon Land, *Icefall* launches an epic science-fiction thriller series exploring humanity's connection to forces beyond comprehension and the cost of survival in an age of awakening.

A lifelong creator of companies and ideas, Newman brings the precision of a strategist and the imagination of a world-builder to his writing. He lives in Northern California with his family, dividing his time between new ventures, his love for the outdoors, and the worlds he creates on the page.

www.michaelnewmanauthor.com | @mnewmanauthor
on X, Instagram, and TikTok

Enjoy a Preview of *The Nine*
Coming Soon from Permuted Press

PROLOGUE

Passengers

Hell Creek Formation, 65 million years ago

The kill was still steaming.

The hadrosaur's carcass twitched, as the T-Rex's massive jaws tore into its ribcage, wrenching backward to rip a slab of flesh free. History's greatest predator swallowed without chewing, leaving blood slicked across its muzzle. Its breath burst from flared nostrils, as it lowered its snout through the steam rising from its kill to rip an even larger hunk free.

The land around the tyrannosaur sprawled wide and low, a steaming mosaic of river channels and mudflats across a sprawling floodplain that gleamed under a heavy, copper-tinted sky. The soft ground was flecked by tangles of fallen branches and half-rotted trunks. Shallow streams slid lazily through banks of silt and clay, their edges fringed with dense green shrubs, behind which scavengers waited to feed on the scraps it left behind.

Suddenly, the Earth rumbled. A flock of birds erupted from the surrounding trees, in a dark wave, as a flaming shape streaked overhead. The T-Rex paid no notice until the ground shook mightily beneath its clawed feet. Then it lifted its head from the remains of the hadrosaur, holding a whole leg in its mouth while turning in the direction of the flaming shape's descent. It tore through the upper sky like a molten spear wrapped in fire, its surface shedding incandescent fragments that streamed behind it as if strung by rope to its wake, the air around the shape seeming to ignite.

The tyrannosaur sniffed the humid air that was rank with decay and stagnant water, laced with the sharp iron tang of fresh carrion blood carried by the wind. When its senses found no looming threat, it sucked the hadrosaur leg into its mouth, cracking bone and shredding meat.

Then the T-Rex's feeding ground shifted and quaked, fissures opening up in crisscrossing patterns across the dry riverbeds dotting the landscape. Shockwaves rippled outward in invisible rings that swallowed clouds and left the horizon bathed in a shimmering glow that cut through the heat haze blurring muted tones of green and brown. Towering conifers bent over and snapped, a blanket of dark green needles showering the air. Cycads and palms were uprooted and whisked away. Flowering plants exploded, scattering a rainbow of colored pedals, while ferns torn from the ground whipped about like whirling propeller blades.

Unable to process the danger, the ravenous predator lowered its jaws and fed, blood dripping and sinew dangling from its maw. It had just finished picking the hadrosaur clean, when instinct snapped it alert. Throat still pulsing, the T-Rex tightened on its haunches, preparing to defend its territory.

The tyrannosaur sniffed the air, unable to identify the sharp, vaguely metallic scent it had detected. Then it sensed motion that seemed to be everywhere at once, slicing through the air as effortlessly as the animal had carved up its prey. The T-Rex lowered and extended its jaws in a defensive posture to ward off whatever was coming. The ground seemed to swell before it. Huge waves of dust swirled upward, giant shifting shapes visible as empty outlines carved from the plume.

Unfettered, the massive animal roared and snapped its jaws, prepared for battle when it was swept up and spun around in the air, its nearly impenetrable hide stung by invisible needles that sucked the life from the animal with even more ease than its teeth had shredded the hadrosaur. In that moment, the T-Rex knew what it was like to be the hunted, instead of the hunter. It lashed out with the last of its strength, biting down in search of something to rend and rip in order to survive. But its teeth closed only on air before its jaws locked tight and it collapsed. The greatest predator to ever walk the planet took its last breath lying atop the carcass it had claimed.

The air stilled, but the dust cloud grew, spreading across the land with whatever lurked within it sucking the air dry and leaving oblivion in its wake.